A Bitter Harvest

Peter Yeldham's extensive writing career began with short stories and radio scripts. He spent twenty years in England, becoming a leading screenwriter for films and television, and also wrote plays for the theatre, including the highly successful comedies *Birds on the Wing* and *Fringe Benefits*, which ran for two years in Paris. Returning to Australia he won numerous awards for his television screenplays, among them *1915*, *Captain James Cook*, *The Alien Years*, *All the Rivers Run*, *The Timeless Land* and *The Heroes*. His adaptation of Bryce Courtenay's novel *Jessica* won a Logie Award for best mini-series. He is the author of nine novels, including *Barbed Wire and Roses, The Murrumbidgee Kid, The Currency Lads*, *Against the Tide* and *Land of Dreams*.

For more information please visit
www.peteryeldham.com

PETER YELDHAM

A Bitter Harvest

Penguin Books

PENGUIN BOOKS

Published by the Penguin Group
Penguin Group (Australia)
250 Camberwell Road, Camberwell, Victoria 3124, Australia
(a division of Pearson Australia Group Pty Ltd)
Penguin Group (USA) Inc.
375 Hudson Street, New York, New York 10014, USA
Penguin Group (Canada)
90 Eglinton Avenue East, Suite 700, Toronto, Canada ON M4P 2Y3
(a division of Pearson Penguin Canada Inc.)
Penguin Books Ltd
80 Strand, London WC2R 0RL England
Penguin Ireland
25 St Stephen's Green, Dublin 2, Ireland
(a division of Penguin Books Ltd)
Penguin Books India Pvt Ltd
11 Community Centre, Panchsheel Park, New Delhi - 110 017, India
Penguin Group (NZ)
67 Apollo Drive, Rosedale, North Shore 0632, New Zealand
(a division of Pearson New Zealand Ltd)
Penguin Books (South Africa) (Pty) Ltd
24 Sturdee Avenue, Rosebank, Johannesburg 2196, South Africa

Penguin Books Ltd, Registered Offices: 80 Strand, London, WC2R 0RL, England

First published 1997 in Pan by Pan Macmillan Australia Pty Ltd
This edition published by Penguin Group (Australia), 2009

1 3 5 7 9 10 8 6 4 2

Design by Cameron Midson © Penguin Group (Australia)
Cover image: Leaves © iStockphoto.com / Landscape © Australian Scenics
Typeset in 10.5/15.5pt ITC Legacy Serif by Post Pre-press Group, Brisbane, Queensland
Printed and bound in Australia by McPherson's Printing Group, Maryborough, Victoria

National Library of Australia Cataloguing-in-Publication data:
Yeldham, Peter.
A bitter harvest / Peter Yeldham
Rev. ed.
9780143010388 (pbk.)
A823.3

penguin.com.au

In memory of Marjorie,
whose idea it was to go to the Barossa Valley
in search of a story

Prologue

BROKEN HILL, NSW, 1886

The man stood listening in the dark as the sounds of anger grew and disturbed the night. They became wilder, spreading from the canvas saloon bar of Connolly's Hotel and beyond it, down Argent Street where miners lived in their shanty dwellings, past Stuart Lane and the lanterns held by the girls parading and plying for hire, reaching the edge of town and the stables behind the blacksmith's shop, where he knew he had only a few minutes to save his life.

He refused to panic. Taking precious moments to calm the horse as he fitted the saddle and tightened the girth, he then fastened the bulging saddlebags securely to the pommel. With infinite care he led the animal out of the shadows. He could hear the growing fury of the mob of men baying for blood - his blood - he could imagine them brandishing knives and rifles along with their share certificates, the worthless scrip he had sold them so successfully. The promoters he had used as a front were bound to lose their nerve and betray him to save themselves; it was all he could do to restrain himself from mounting the horse and galloping headlong into the night. But he had to remain composed, stick to the plan. It would be madness to try to outride those men, or to give the police time to receive a telegraph message and be waiting for him. It was vital no-one witness his departure, but far more importantly, that nobody even suspect the direction he had taken.

As the distant crowd's wrath became a growing tumult, the man carefully tied hessian around each of the horse's hooves, and only then, keeping to the shadows and avoiding campfires, knowing there would be no tracks to follow, did he ride the horse quietly through the dusty streets named after the rich ores on which this barren place had grown and flourished. From Argent Street he turned into Chloride Row, down Zinc Street, Mercury, then Cobalt Road, until the gaunt skyline of the Silver City was behind him.

In the bar of Connolly's Hotel, passions flared and lamps flickered on the flimsy canvas walls, as one of the promoters tried to pacify the crowd.

'Listen to me,' he shouted, and for an instant they did. 'Your investments are safe. All stock securities are certified by the company and personally guaranteed by the manager himself.'

There was a moment of silent disbelief, more threatening than the shouts and hostility.

'So where is he?' someone asked. 'Where is the bastard?'

If the frightened promoters had been able to answer this, what followed might have been avoided. But they hesitated, and the men who had been swindled out of their hard won scraps of silver knew in that instant their savings were lost. They had been cleverly robbed, and while the missing manager was the prime object of their rage, these two men had most certainly played a role. If the Silver City Trust Company, as it had been so extravagantly advertised, was a sham, then this pair posing as its trustees had contributed to the fraud.

Someone in the crowd threw a brick. It cut the forehead of one promoter. Blood streamed into his eyes. Another missile aimed at his colleague smashed an oil lantern. Moments later flames were licking at the canvas walls. Violence exploded inside the tent, as the crowd panicked and tried to fight their way towards the exits. In the suffocating smoke, men were trampled on and women were pushed aside amid screams as the flames spread. Within ten minutes, Patrick Connolly's hotel was burnt to charred scraps, and more than a dozen miners were suffering from burns and serious injuries.

A mile to the south, the rider looked back to see the flames against the night sky, and wondered what had happened. He felt a trace of fear. He knew by dawn he must put at least thirty miles between himself and the town – after that they would never find him.

It was on the third day he faced the fact that he might die. That morning the relentless sun had seemed fiercer than ever, the arid land more hostile, the circling crows increasing, their raucous cries more threatening. The barren, dry route he had chosen seemed to stretch on through succeeding heat hazes into a parched infinity.

He had planned it so carefully, knowing they would mount searches for him along the roads that led east, and telegraph messages would be sent to every police station with his description. But apart from revealing he was a tall man, and young, not yet thirty years old, there was little to distinguish him. He knew this would not concern the authorities; they would be confident of intercepting his flight, for there was only one direction in which to flee – eastward, to the coast. All coaches would be stopped and searched, strangers questioned, and the name JEFFREY McINTOSH would be tacked up on Wanted notices in every town. They would never for a moment anticipate their quarry might head inland and then south - across a thousand miles of mulga and waterless desert. They would dismiss this as sheer insanity. To travel this way led only to dehydration and death.

He had thought he could beat the desert. Worked it out with such care. Apart from the heavy bars of silver, he had brought all the water bags his horse could carry. Food was less important: he had provisioned lightly, for he had heard nourishment could be found in the roots of the mallee - enough to sustain life - and that the human body could function for a long time provided it had sufficient water.

By the third day he knew this to be untrue. By then there was not enough water in the whole world to slake his thirst. He was also desperately hungry. His horse was nearly lame and might not last the day. Worst of all, he was beginning to hallucinate. Four times throughout the blazing afternoon, the haze on the dusty plain turned into water. Once it was the deep blue of the harbour. Another time a wide, placid river, and when finally it became a stream cascading over rocks through a rainforest, he knew he was close to madness.

They trudged on side by side, horse and rider, both limping now as he kept the sweltering sun to the west. He hoped it was the west. He found himself unable to deduce direction or distance. All time seemed to have stopped until the sun ceased to torment him, and had sunk below the rim of the earth. After this would come the frozen night. He had not known until now the desert cold could be so bitter.

During the fourth afternoon he lost the feel of his limbs. He also began to consider the saddlebags of silver, aware of their weight, conscious they were a savage burden for the horse. Too late, he realised this was an impossible journey without a second animal. He found himself considering the idea of abandoning the silver, and once, to his horror, became aware of his hands unbuckling the straps. He started to wonder how to prevent himself – once his mind went – from leaving the precious saddlebags behind.

Later on, he had no conception of how much later, he found himself talking to his wife. Their conversation, as so often happened, ended in a quarrel in which Edith blamed him for leaving her alone for so many months. She complained that she and the child were almost starving in their shabby, rented city slum, and she expressed her opinion that he was a fool not to have brought a packhorse. It was with a feeling of relief that he turned to his daughter, Elizabeth. She ran to him. He heard her voice and her enchanting laughter. It was a celebration – there was a birthday cake, although his vision blurred and he was unsure whether there were six or seven candles on it. He reached out to lift her in his arms, and felt her silky blonde hair brush against his face – grateful that this was reality, and the lame horse, the burning heat and relentless thirst were all a product of his wild imagination.

It was after Elizabeth vanished, after she just smiled at him and then disappeared, that he finally accepted he was insane. In his madness he saw, emerging from the same heat haze into which she had evaporated, a bearded Afghan and his team of camels.

That night, after the Afghan had killed the exhausted horse and they had cooked and eaten all they could manage, that night as the flames of the fire became embers and they huddled close to it against the chill desert air, the man bartered for his life. The Afghan spoke no English, but language was not necessary. Silver was the commodity understood by both men. They were each aware, that if the Afghan wished, he could kill the other man and take the heavy saddlebags – but only the Afghan himself knew that such an act was repugnant to him and outside his code of behaviour.

In the end they settled it amicably enough; one saddlebag of silver in return for two camels, another bar of silver for a supply of food and water, plus a map scratched on the ground to show him the site of a soak forty miles south-east, and directions on how to find a river another two days' ride beyond that.

At dawn they parted, and before long the Afghan and his team became absorbed into the shimmering haze of landscape, like a mirage that had never existed.

It was almost another four months, and by then the camels had long since been traded for other horses, that the rider finally turned eastward towards the coast. In a few more weeks he would be safely home. The police notices seeking the arrest of a man calling himself McIntosh had been shredded by wind, and faded in the sun. There were new notices, more recent crimes to be solved. The violence at Connolly's Hotel, in a town inured to violence, was soon forgotten. Most people supposed the man had perished somewhere along his escape route. Following his presumed death, the Silver City Trust Company with its fraudulent scrip and non-existent shares became part of the folklore, another burst bubble, one more scandal in a boom that had left so many broken dreams.

But it was not only in the Silver City, now officially named Broken Hill, that fortunes were being made and lost. Greed was rampant everywhere. The banks boomed then crashed in Melbourne and Sydney. Land prices soared, and fell as rapidly. It was a time of tremendous financial turmoil, of collapsing values both economic and moral, an era ripe for opportunists.

Astute speculators benefited from the chaos. They bought fine townhouses and set about the business of advancing themselves. Shady street-wise profiteers became rich enough to buy their place in the world. It was called 'social change', and people soon learned it was better not to enquire too closely into the sources of their neighbour's new-found wealth.

SYDNEY, 1889

William Patterson sat in an open carriage with his wife, Edith, and his adored daughter, Elizabeth, being driven towards their new home opposite the fashionable and prestigious Centennial Park. He was confident he had nothing to fear. His innate caution had delayed this day. It had taken over three years, since his return from nobody-knew-where, to remove his family from the tiny slum terrace in Glebe to this imposing Victorian residence with its extensive grounds, its summerhouse, tennis court and waiting servants.

He had been - unlike some contemporaries - fastidiously careful. Not for him the outward show of sudden wealth. He had hidden the remaining saddlebags, and with great patience had begun to cash small amounts of silver. He never did so twice in the same district. Already he was guarding himself against future speculation, for he had deep ambitions, and was intelligent enough to realise the questions that might someday be asked, even in innocence.

Where did he come from? How did he make his money? It was essential to have, not only the right answers, but the credentials to withstand any scrutiny.

The money slowly accrued, and with it he had bought land. His timing, more by luck than judgement, was impeccable. Once £30 an acre, prime land close to the city rose to the dizzy and phenomenal heights of £300 a *foot*, and the pundits all declared it must soon double that. The rush to buy became a stampede. The pundits - most of whom had already acquired large tracts, and like William had an instinct for what was to come - sold out at vast profits before the crash. It made them enormously rich. More importantly, for William, it clearly established the source of his wealth for all to see. It created what he craved as much as the money itself, an aura of respectability. He was meticulous in other ways, finding a teacher to discreetly improve his speech, and an instructor to teach him the art of simple social graces.

He gazed about him as the servants hurried to greet his wife and daughter: he observed the ritual of them being assisted from the carriage with immense satisfaction. Few men with his paltry start in life had reached such a position by their early thirties. It had all been worthwhile; the frightened months in the mining town, the fear of arrest, the desperate journey which would have seen him perish but for an itinerant camel driver. He used to wonder about the Afghan: what he had done with his bars of silver, whether he had prospered, or drunk it all in some trading post, or lost it at cards. Lately he thought of him less and less, and of the Silver City Trust Company, hardly at all. Like the name McIntosh he had used there, it was essential such details should fade from his mind. What mattered was the future. He must think and act as if this grand house was the style of living to which he had always been accustomed; as if money and position belonged to him by right of birth; it was imperative he be accepted by the social leaders of the city if he was to do the many things he had planned.

'What do you think of it?' he asked his wife, as they studied the house and the sweeping lawns.

Edith looked daunted, and as often happened, her answer disappointed him.

'It's very large, William. Bigger than I thought.'

She had seen it only once, driving past, the day he told her he had bought it.

'You'll have servants,' he said, taking care none of them overheard him. 'All the staff you require.'

'Yes,' she answered, and he sensed that already she was half afraid of the people who would wait on her and do her bidding. Why must she be so timid, so unable to adapt.

He turned away, the pleasure and expectation of the day spoiled. He saw his daughter looking eagerly about her.

'Do you like it, Lizzie?' he asked her.

'It's wonderful.' Nine-year-old Elizabeth's eyes were bright with excitement. 'Just like a palace. Is it all ours, Papa?'

'All ours, my love,' he replied, feeling an immense affection for her. 'And one day it'll be all yours.'

He took her by the hand, and like a pair of children in search of adventure they went into the house together.

PART ONE

Chapter 1

William stood at the window as the carriage with the crested emblem of the State Premier entered the gates and stopped in front of the house. Behind him in the large formal room a fire crackled in the grate. Above the carved mantelpiece hung a painting of Elizabeth on her sixteenth birthday. It was a luminous and striking portrait by the noted Melbourne artist Tom Roberts.

'The Right Honourable Mr Reid and Mr James North, sir,' his housekeeper Mrs Forbes said, showing in the two men.

'Mr Premier.' William smiled, as they shook hands. It was their first meeting. James North, a neighbour and recent friend, as well as being a prominent member of Reid's party, had arranged it.

'A whisky, gentlemen?'

George Reid hesitated, like a man about to refuse.

'Bit early in the day. Perhaps a wee one though,' he said in his Scots accent.

'Malt?'

'Splendid.'

'James?'

'Thank you.'

William poured the drinks, one discreetly more generous than the others. He handed this to the Premier, and they raised their glasses to each other.

'Handsome house,' Reid said.

He tasted his drink, and nodded his approval. It was not everyone who served whisky of this quality. He looked up at the painting that dominated and enlivened the room.

'Damned pretty girl.'

'My daughter.'

'Magnificent picture.'

'By Tom Roberts - of the Heidelberg school. One of his rare portraits,' North said, slyly aware that the Premier had never heard of Roberts, or the Heidelberg school.

'A great compliment to Elizabeth.' William looked fondly at the brush work which captured her beauty, and was so admired by everyone who visited here. 'I miss her very much.'

'Where is she?' Reid asked.

'Travelling in England and central Europe. Completing her Grand Tour, accompanied by her mother.'

Reid finished his drink. He thought there had been enough polite small talk, and when William obligingly took his glass to refill it, he said, 'North tells me you're interested in politics.'

William nodded, and waited for the Premier to continue.

'James said we might have things to talk about. Matters best not discussed at Parliament House. Which is why I'm here.'

'It's a privilege to have you in my home, Mr Reid.'

'Aye, but let's cut the bullshit, shall we, and get down to cases. What matters could we possibly have to talk about, you and me?'

'I want a seat in the Legislative Assembly,' William said.

'Do you, by Christ?'

The Premier swallowed enough of his drink to suggest it might soon be time to leave. The bluntness of the request had clearly shocked him. In his world things were done more delicately than this.

'Marcus Sway is resigning. It's a safe seat.'

'I'm well aware of that. And being safe, a great many loyal supporters have their eyes on it.'

'No one supports you more strongly than I do,' William said. 'I'm for Free Trade, as you are. I also want to make a donation to party funds.'

'Very kind.' Reid was about to put down his empty glass, and signal his departure. 'But donations are made through normal channels. I'm sure James would have told you that.'

'This donation,' William said, carefully watching the flushed face of the Premier, 'is for ten thousand pounds.'

George Reid was startled. William sensed that even North was surprised. The amount was double what he had intended.

'Ten thousand . . . that's extraordinarily generous.'

'The money is to be put to whatever use you think fit.'

The silence was eloquent.

William allowed it to continue, until he felt sure of his man.

'It will be paid in two stages. Half now – today, before you leave here – in cash.' Reid moistened his lips. 'The balance,' William continued, 'the day after I take my seat in the House.'

'You devious bastard.'

The Premier was staring at him, and William had a moment of alarm and uncertainty. Had he misjudged his man?

'Several people warned me you were a conniving prick – and they were right. "Don't shake his hand," they told me. "You don't know where it's been."' He chortled at his own wit.

I'd like to shake you firmly by the throat, William thought. *Silly, pompous old bugger.*

But Reid smiled and held out his glass to be replenished.

'On the other hand, I never listen to gossip. And we need new blood. An infusion of energy - young men with ideas and public spirit - that's what will make this country great.'

'Hear, hear,' North said, as William refilled the Premier's glass.

They stood on the front steps, hands raised in a farewell as the carriage drove away. North had elected to remain, as he lived only a block away, while Reid had urgent matters awaiting his attention in his office. Before leaving he had accepted custody of the money - a large envelope bulging with cash - strictly as a donation on behalf of the party, as he was at great pains to point out.

'You handled the old goat perfectly,' James complimented him as they went inside.

'How long do I have to wait?'

'Marcus will step down tomorrow. You can count on being nominated, as long as you convince the party hierarchy you support our policy to oppose Federation. After that it's a mere formality.'

William offered him another malt whisky, but James said he would rather have a beer. They took a chilled bottle of Resch's to the side garden, to where there were chairs on a terrace that overlooked the tennis court. Last year it had been filled with his daughter's circle of friends, the sound of their play and frequent laughter.

'The place feels empty without Elizabeth,' William said.

'When does she arrive back?' North asked.

'Three months. Via Suez, then India and Singapore.'

'You'll be an Honourable Member by the time she's home. You can write and tell her – and Edith, too,' he remembered tactfully, 'that you're on your way.'

'On my way?'

'Come on, William,' North said smiling, 'you don't expect me to believe the back bench of the Legislative Assembly is your ultimate goal. You're after something a lot bigger than that.'

When North had gone, William strolled in the grounds. The shrubs had matured greatly in the eight years they had lived here, and the lawns were always kept immaculate. It was a prize garden, an elegant estate and the envy of the neighbourhood.

So James North guessed he was after a larger prize. James thought he knew William, but he did not know the half of it.

It had taken time. He had forced himself to be patient, despite his ambition, delaying this move into public gaze until he felt fully secure. Now, at last, it was time to take the next step in his life.

He had a brief discussion with the head gardener about pruning the roses and putting in the spring bedding plants, then told Mrs Forbes he would be dining out, and did not require the carriage. He had to share his news, and there was only one person in whom he could confide.

He knew she would be expecting him.

The parliamentary chamber was rowdy with abuse. It was not without good reason that it had become widely known as the bearpit.

'Mr Speaker,' James North shouted, his voice almost drowned out by jeers from the Opposition benches. 'Mr Speaker, it gives me great pleasure to introduce the new Member for the electorate of Curtis, the Right Honourable William Foster Patterson.'

William rose to rousing cheers from his own side of the house, and a robust booing from the coalition of forces opposite. He stood tall and composed, allowing the noise to slowly die down, while he glanced carefully up towards the public gallery. He knew she would be there; they had previously arranged it, but he still felt reassurance when he saw her. He was also aware of how discerningly she had dressed, the trimmed lace gown and bonnet were in subdued tones. Bright colours enhanced Hannah Lockwood's looks and made her a figure of admiration in any company. Today she had chosen to blend discreetly into the background, to sit passively in the back row away from any chance of public notice, and for this he was grateful.

'Mr Speaker,' he began, when the House was finally quiet, 'I thank my colleagues for their support. And I certainly wish to thank the Honourable rabble opposite for booing me. Had they chosen to greet me with applause, I would have felt most uneasy.'

Hannah joined in the laughter in the public arena.

He looks so assured, she thought. *As if he belongs. It means so much to him.*

'The Members on my side of the House already know many of the causes for which I stand. I am unashamedly for such objectives as Free Trade, for private enterprise, the protection of property, and the upholding of Law and Order . . .'

'Just another filthy-rich Tory,' an Opposition stalwart shouted to general acclaim around him. 'Bloody bloated capitalists.'

He was joined by other cries of derision.

'Look at 'em. Arrogant bastards. Think they're born to rule.'

'I was about to say,' William's resonant voice managed to slice through the invective and silence them. 'I was about to tell you bunch of ratbags across there, as well as the gentlemen over here, that I am also for progress, which means I am for change. I do not mean minor changes to gratify public opinion. I mean significant change. Real change. This collection of colonies ruled from London has been smothered by overseas self-interest for too long. It is time to demand a new way – and take our destiny in our own hands.'

Hannah watched him, aware the entirely male membership of the Assembly had gone very quiet, and were now listening intently. Among the Opposition were some surprised faces; on his own side there were puzzled glances and startled frowns.

'I wish to make it clear, despite any opinions against it in my own party, that I am completely *for* Federation.' There was a roar of surprise from around the chamber. William raised his voice, forcing them to listen, as the House went quiet: 'I am for a Constitution to form the six colonies into one nation, a Commonwealth of Australia. I am also in favour of votes for women – whether my colleagues support me or not – and those two issues are the reforms for which I will fight, and the reason why I stood for election and am here today.'

George Reid was red-faced and open-mouthed. He wrote a hasty note, and passed it along his front bench to James North. North nodded his agreement, glaring at William. It was clear both felt they had been taken in by this upstart opportunist.

There was a stony silence among his Conservative colleagues as William resumed his seat. On the other side of the Legislature, some surprised Opposition members began to applaud. Upstairs in the public seats, people around Hannah joined in, while the only two journalists in the press gallery who had bothered to attend were scribbling details of the speech as quickly as they could manage.

'I didn't go on too long, did I?' he asked.

'Certainly not,' she said and slid her hand between his legs. He laughed, but was already stirring and responding to her touch.

'I meant the speech.'

'I know what you meant,' Hannah said. 'The speech was not too long.' Her fingers caressed him. 'The speech was lovely.'

'Truly?'

'Stop fishing for compliments. I was proud of you, darling.'

'The gallery seemed to enjoy it.'

'So did the Opposition,' Hannah said. 'I'm not sure about your own side.'

'Jimmy North was upset.'

'Upset? He looked absolutely furious.'

'He refused to talk to me afterwards. And George Reid called me a bloody traitor.'

'I think they're going to find out about you.'

'What about me?'

'That you're nobody's tame poodle.'

'Dead right,' William said.

They were both aware they were going to make love again. Hannah felt elated; like William she was still highly stimulated by the day and its impact. She parted her legs, guiding him into her. She began to probe his ear with her tongue because she had discovered how this aroused him, and she felt her own senses surge as his hands fondled her breasts, then played with her buttocks. They had both learned how to excite each other, but today was unusual and special. He was euphoric at his success, and by the reports in the afternoon newspapers already casting him as a new political figure of substance. She was thrilled for him, and their shared elation had generated this desire from the moment they reached the privacy of the bijou house. She felt out of control. She matched his thrusts with her own movements, and cried aloud with delight as they climaxed.

Later, they bathed and dressed, opened a bottle of wine and touched glasses in an intimate salute to his debut. Hannah knew she had shared one of the important days of his life. But she was no fool. She realised it was only possible because of the absence of his wife and his daughter Elizabeth, who were on their way home from their world tour. When they returned, many things would change. She would have to grow accustomed to that again, even though she felt despondent at the thought of it.

Chapter 2

Stille Nacht, Heilige Nacht, sang the voices of the carol singers in the candlelit square, so nostalgic in his mind. Stefan Muller tried to shut out the persistent cry of the scavenging gulls that trailed the ship, and to cling to a memory which, with every passing day, was becoming more difficult to recall. He was unhappy and homesick for the cobbled streets and spires of his native Augsburg.

Already on this foreign ship, he missed the noisy *Gemütlichkeit*, the fellowship that was so much a part of life in the Bavarian university town. His own student days had been abruptly terminated by the death of his parents in an influenza epidemic, and he had been reluctantly taken in by his Uncle Uhlrich and Aunt Cordula in the small apartment over the *Apotheke*, where Uncle Uhlrich dispensed prescriptions and every Thursday played the cello in a string quartet. They had three children of their own, and Stefan felt like an intruder, although he earned his keep by making deliveries and sweeping the shop each day.

It was a dull unrewarding existence, without prospects, and it was this more than anything else which made him interested when Aunt Cordula first spoke of her brother Johann. Uncle Johann, it transpired, was a sailor who had walked off his ship on the other side of the world, in a place called Australia. There he had met and married a Westphalian girl from Coblenz, and was now settled and growing grapes on a farm in the hills above Adelaide, a city named for a German Queen born in Saxony. It was a *wirklich Deutsch* community, Aunt Cordula explained, managing to make it sound romantic and adventurous, and Uncle Johann Ritter like a blend of poet and pirate, a seafaring man who wooed a Rhine maiden and now ran his prosperous vineyard in the New World. He was looking for someone to help share in the venture, Aunt Cordula said, and Stefan, then an ingenuous nineteen year old, began to dream of lush pastures and barefoot girls with sunlight in their hair singing *Leidenschaft* songs as they trod the grapes.

Communications were slow and Uncle Johann a somewhat tardy correspondent, so it took almost three years before arrangements were completed. By this time, at close to twenty-two years of age, Stefan was no longer certain if his destiny lay across the world. Especially since by then he had met Christina.

He smiled at the memory of their first meeting. The smile transformed his thin, unhappy features, and surprised the girl who had been watching him from the upper deck. He looked up and noticed her, and they gazed at each other for what seemed to be an inordinately long time. She was very pretty. He was not sure what her open appraisal meant, but she was boat deck and he was steerage, so he merely gave a polite nod that was almost a bow. He was aware she stayed there, looking down and watching him as he turned away.

His thoughts returned to Christina. He had collided with her, literally, on a windswept corner of the *Keplerstrasse*, in a tangle of arms and legs and bicycle wheels, and after a heated exchange during which her dark eyes snapped indignantly and her attractive mouth pronounced her opinion of idiots who rode their bicycles so carelessly, they suddenly realised they had known each other most of their lives. She was fat Christina Gressmann, the teacher's pet from *Kindergarten:* he was shy, skinny Stefan Muller, whom the girls at high school declared they would be safest with, if locked in a closet. She was no longer fat and he no longer shy, and moments later they were in the nearest coffee shop. He learned Christina had been a music student in Leipzig, and was now teaching pianoforte. He was uncomfortably aware of his own lack of position, and that, in his early twenties, he was little more than an errand boy with no vocation.

He was, however, about to embark on a journey no one else in Augsburg had attempted. Most families knew someone who had migrated to America, and indeed there was a town in Pennsylvania called Pittsburgh said to contain many Germans, but nobody Christina knew had settled in Hahndorf, in far-off Australia.

It invested Stefan with a certain distinction. He was an adventurer setting off to cross the world, where in time he would become a vigneron. Never did he mention what his Uncle Johann's one smudged letter had conveyed to him: that the hours would be long, the work hard, and he would travel steerage because Johann Ritter did not believe in wasting money on relatives. Nor did he say what was constantly in his mind – that now they had met again, the last thing he wanted was to leave her and migrate to some distant, foreign place.

He could not tell her this. He realised, all too well, the effect it would have. Christina, with her good looks, had many admirers and was constantly sought out by students and young army officers. In her eyes, Hahndorf was Stefan's special cachet, the singular distinction which gave him a place in her orbit. Without it, his status would rapidly decline to that of a nobody, a messenger boy who swept up in his uncle's shop. If he decided not to go – assuming such a decision was possible – he and Christina would no longer have an interest in common. Hahndorf was what linked them, and what would separate them soon enough, and if he chose not to go to Hahndorf, separation would be equally certain but far less glamorous. It had an irony that was not entirely lost on him, although it could hardly be said he found it amusing.

He was roused from his reverie by the cries of the seagulls, fighting over scraps of garbage tipped from the ship's galley. He looked back towards the boat deck. The girl was still there, still watching him – her blonde hair gently blown by the sea breeze.

He did something then, that he would remember for the rest of his life. He raised his hand, in a token of admiration to her. It was completely instinctive, an accolade bestowed, a recognition of her youth and beauty – and as if understanding this, the girl accepted it naturally. She smiled, waved in reply, then vanished into one of the staterooms.

It was almost a week before he saw her again.

By then he had managed to find out more about her. Her name was Elizabeth Patterson, and she was travelling home to Sydney with her mother. The German-speaking sailor who told him this warned him not to waste his time. Miss Patterson, he said, was every officer's choice as a dance partner. She was popular, the best-looking girl on board. He advised Stefan to forget her.

Elizabeth wrote to her father.

Dearest Papa,

The Egyptian traders came aboard at Port Said, and it was

like a bazaar, with them trying to sell us veils and cloth, and even postcards which lots of the men seemed interested in, but Mama would not allow me to look at. The canal is amazing, about one hundred miles long, and you can stand on deck and see both shores, and sometimes see tribes of Bedouins making camp. From a distance they look quite romantic, but the ship's officers tell me that's only from a distance!

I think the officers only like English people, because they didn't have a good word to say about the Italians when we called at Naples. Tomorrow we reach Suez, and turn left (that's port!) across the Indian Ocean. Looking forward to Singapore and Raffles.

Much love as always, Lizzie.

She paused thoughtfully and added: *P.S. Mama sends her love.*

It was more a note than a real letter, but she wrote to him each day, no matter how briefly, and had done so all the time they had been away. At each new port of call or city, she made up a package addressed to her father, and sent them home. It was like a diary, and he had written to say how he would keep them in a folder for her, so she would always have them, to remember her first world trip when she was seventeen.

She rose from the desk in their stateroom. The door to her mother's cabin was shut, and she did not disturb her. She felt sorry for Mama. Elizabeth knew this long tour had not been easy for her. So many cities, the constant travel, the numerous hotels. There was the heat wave in Rome, and the exuberant Italian youths following her, ignoring Mama's indignation as they blew kisses and called out cheeky invitations. She smiled as she recalled her mother's astonished face the day when she – her Mama – had had her bottom pinched on the Via Veneto. From that day on she had carried a parasol ready to strike back, but no one had pinched her again.

Elizabeth went outside and found some people playing deck quoits. She shook her head when a young man asked her to join them. The Second Officer saw her from the bridge, saluting with a confident smile. She nodded politely and turned away. The Second Officer was extremely handsome; and no one knew it better than he did. Elizabeth found him dull and self-opinionated. She walked towards the bow, where she could be alone. It was nice at times to be on her own.

That was when she looked down and saw the boy again.

Stefan's cramped six-berth cabin was stifling and noisy, because of its proximity to the engines. He spent every moment possible on the small deck available to third-class passengers. The area was restricted, with barriers and notices warning that it was prohibited to pass beyond this point. But the tiny deck space was better than the hot cabin, where he would lie awake wondering why he had decided to come, trying to recall Christina and her soft dark hair, the gentle curve of her breast, remembering his last night with her and the voices of the carol singers. And how, after the carols, he had escorted her home, taken her hand for the last time and chastely kissed her.

It had been Christina who responded. Her lips had grown warm, and then they were straining together, his groin bursting with an erection. Stefan knew that she was aware of it as he felt her heartbeat quicken, and she thrust herself against him. He was dizzy with sudden excitement and a passion about to be fulfilled. And then the moment was gone.

Christina stepped back, the start of tears in his eyes as she swore she would miss him desperately, and if only they could – but they mustn't – they couldn't. She had been swept away by her fondness for him. His senses numb and reeling with thwarted lust, an embarrassing testimony to it between his legs, he dimly remembered agreeing it would be wrong. He swore he would write, declared he would be home again within a few years, his fortune made; she promised to remember him every night; while these and other lovers' lies were exchanged, he stood there, the tell-tale bulge in his trousers refusing to go down. He wanted to kiss her hand, to say something clever, to leave with style – but it was hopeless.

In fact it was worse than that. He fought, tried to control it, but as she wistfully kissed his cheek he felt the first spasm, the involuntary ejaculation, the inside of his trousers now moist and –

'Hello there,' a voice beside him said, shocking him out of his memory. He found himself gazing into astonishingly blue eyes framed by light blonde hair. She laughed at his surprise.

'Goodness, you jumped. Did I give you a fright?'

Stefan gaped at her, unable to answer.

'You seemed awfully deep in thought, or else dreaming. Was it a dream? Did I interrupt?'

Her words ran into each other; his English, although improving, was not yet able to cope with this deluge.

'*Guten Morgen, gnädiges Fraulein*,' he said clumsily.

'Sorry,' the girl said. 'I don't speak German. Is it German?'

'*Ja*. Yes,' he hastily corrected himself.

She waited, as if it was now up to him to continue, rather than gaze blankly at her. He wondered what he could say. She was poised to leave, to move to the stairs that would take her out of his orbit, as if regretting whatever impulse had brought her here. He felt inadequate, her sudden appearance having frozen his mind; and he could think of nothing he might do or say to delay her.

He dearly wished he could. He liked her smile, and the brilliant eyes, and he wanted to listen to the English she spoke, with its flattened vowels and sometimes rising inflection. It was an accent new to him, and from her delicate mouth, enchanting.

'You're staring at me,' she said. 'Did you know that? Do you always stare at people?'

'I beg pardon,' he was conscious of his guttural intonation, and anxious to eliminate this. 'I am, how do you say, without too much of English speaking.'

She laughed, but not unkindly. It was soft, like music. He did not mind that the laughter was because of his fractured syntax. It was suddenly important to keep her there, to hear the laughter again, to see the way her face animated like a mischievous child's.

'Elizabeth?' The voice came from somewhere above. The girl made a face.

'It's my mother,' she said hurriedly. 'She's not seasick today, so she's worrying where I am and if I'm behaving myself properly. It really is so dreary up there in first class. Lots of snobby English people getting off at Singapore, only they call it *orf*.' She smiled at his bewildered expression, and when he failed to reply, she continued, 'Even worse, snobby Australians all telling each other how much money they have, and who they met on the Grand Tour. You can't believe how dull and awful they are.'

'Pardon,' he managed finally to say, and she laughed again.

It was entrancing. He wished he could go on making inane remarks and keep her there, laughing, forever.

'Elizabeth . . . ?'

The voice was more plaintive than peremptory. It was also considerably closer.

'I must go,' the girl said. 'Poor Mama hasn't had much fun, and I don't want to upset her.'

She opened the gate, passing through the barrier that prevented him from accompanying her. He watched in despair as she began to leave, climbing the metal stairs of the companionway. Then she paused and looked back at him.

'Tomorrow,' she suggested. 'This time tomorrow?'

He did not fully understand, but clearly a question had been asked and she was awaiting an answer.

'*Ja*,' he said. 'Yes.'

'Fine,' the girl said, smiling. '*Ja*. I'll look forward to it.'

He watched her the rest of the way, then after she had gone he went in search of the same sailor to ask him what the phrase 'this time tomorrow' meant. The sailor clearly thought he was crazy, when, after being told, Stefan threw back his head and let out a shout of joy.

Chapter 3

It was quite different this time; quite different from his relationship with Christina. In its way, it was far more innocent. Their meetings on the third-class deck, the following day and every day after that, were animated by their attempts to communicate. She told him to call her Elizabeth, and taught him to pronounce it the way she did. He learned that her family home was opposite a park in Sydney, and they had servants: in particular a coachman named Forbes, and his wife who served as the housekeeper. Her father was a well-known businessman, and had sent her on a world trip as a present for her seventeenth birthday, with her mother as chaperone.

She had loved it, every minute, but her poor Mama suffered from seasickness, and had little interest in foreign places. Also, her mother was not good with strangers, so the months they had been away, with the necessity to communicate with others and the tribulations of travel - it had all been rather an ordeal for her.

It took time to absorb all this. They used his German dictionary a great deal, and she laughed frequently at his jumbled phrases. The sound of her laughter never failed to enthral him.

There was no lust in his feeling towards her, nothing sensual. He was too busy trying to interpret her sentences, too tired at night, his mind engaged with remembering new words and the complexities of English tenses, to have amorous or romantic dreams. Their meetings became the focal point of each day, and time flew because they were engrossed, she the teacher, he the pupil. He felt more able to converse and knew he was learning; thus he looked forward eagerly to every meeting, rehearsing words, planning things to try to tell her.

They became - before anything else - friends.

The ship docked at Singapore, and for a desolate forty-eight hours he did not see her. She and her mother had gone ashore, she later told him, and spent the night at Raffles Hotel. Her father had arranged for her to see this historic landmark. She described the famous bar with its string orchestra, the pink gins favoured by English planters and administrators with their pampered wives, the notices forbidding entry to Malays and Chinese, and how the bathrooms were the largest she had ever seen, vast marble retreats even more luxurious than Claridges in London.

As for Stefan, he hated Singapore and the Raffles Hotel, and the entire forty-eight hours. He had spent it trudging in monsoonal heat around the dockyards of the Tanjong Company, and the crowded beggars' bazaar at Lo Pan. With some of his cabin companions, he had dutifully toured the few public buildings of note: Sir Stamford Raffles' first Government House, the law courts, a cathedral, the gaol and the lunatic asylum.

He missed her more than he could have believed possible.

It was after they left the Malay Archipelago, that their feelings began to change. There was less laughter. They found they were no longer at ease with each other. They were conscious of pauses in their conversations, sudden silences. They framed things they wanted to say, thought about them, and said something else.

Their meetings became uncomfortable.

The ship steamed south-west, staying a day at Batavia, through the Strait of Madura and Surabaya, and on to Timor where Elizabeth and her mother went ashore as guests of the British Resident at Kupang. It was there she received a letter from her father with the news he was now an elected politician in the New South Wales Parliament. She told Stefan about it, and expressed her pleasure. It was what he had always hoped to be, and she looked forward eagerly to seeing him in action.

Stefan said little. He was becoming afraid of the passing days. At night in the cramped cabin he would lie awake, calculating the ship's speed, the few stops still to be made, the distance left to Sydney where Elizabeth's voyage would end. He would be continuing on to the port of Melbourne, and then overland by train to the Victorian border where he would change to the South Australian rail system, travel to the town of Murray Bridge, and then by bullock cart to Hahndorf. It had all been painstakingly written down in Uncle Johann's solitary letter.

Each day he read the ship's progress report, and with sinking heart saw the number of nautical miles diminish. By the time the vessel was in the Torres Strait, with a call to be made at Cairns and a brief stay at Brisbane, he calculated there were only ten days left. He grew morose and despondent, knowing that once she left the ship the chance of ever seeing her again was negligible. He had moments when he felt it might have been better if they had never met. He could still be dreaming his silly distant dreams of Christina, whose features by now he could hardly recall.

And then they were off the port of Newcastle, a mere twelve hours out of Sydney, and there was no time left at all.

Stefan could hear the strains of the orchestra from the upper-deck salon. The first-class passengers were attending the Captain's Farewell Ball. The sound of gaiety, of raised voices and laughter, came clearly to him, as he stood at the stern of the ship, the wash fanned out on the surface of the sea behind him. He could make out the dark shoreline to the west, the occasional fringes of sand and silver gleam of surf in the moonlight. It seemed forbidding and very alien.

He had been waiting for some time. She was late, but he would wait all night if necessary. He hoped there would be no patrol, no purser or steward to challenge his presence. He had climbed the companionway and stepped over the notice which forbad him to trespass further. If she had asked, he would have intruded into the salon itself, except that it would have embarrassed her and upset her mother, whose voice he had so often heard calling Elizabeth, but whom he had never met.

There was a sound of light footsteps on the rungs of the metal stairway, as she ran down towards him. He could hardly believe how she looked, in a white ballgown, her hair flowing and framing her face, her eyes alive and sparkling as she gave him a mock curtsy, then pirouetted for his inspection. He wanted to tell her that he loved her, and couldn't live without her; that she looked like some princess in every child's favourite fairytale.

But he said none of this. He stammered that she looked 'goot'. He hoped it had not been difficult or inconvenient to leave the ballroom. He was most grateful for her company on the voyage, and hoped he had not been a nuisance. Then he stood, feeling miserable, hopelessly tongue-tied and inadequate.

She took his hand.

'You goose,' she said softly, 'stop it.'

'Stop what?'

'Being so polite.'

'You don't wish me to be polite?'

'I wish,' she said mocking his formality, 'that you ask me to dance.'

'Here, on the deck?'

'Please,' she said, and held out her arms to him.

They began to dance. Above, in the lantern-lit salon, the ship's orchestra was playing the lively strains of a polka. They did not dance to this music. They moved to their own beat, to a slow romantic rhythm that only they could hear. Their bodies swayed in perfect step. And then Stefan stopped dancing, and held her close to him.

'I love you,' he said.

'Yes,' she whispered. 'Yes, my darling Stefan.'

She leant forward and kissed him on the mouth. They clung together. They were oblivious to anything else, until above them, from the salon, the figure of a ship's officer and an anxious woman appeared and looked down at the embracing couple.

'Elizabeth!' Edith Patterson said, in shocked disbelief.

'I'll take care of it,' the officer said. He clattered down the metal companionway.

'Are you travelling first class?' he asked Stefan aggressively.

'I think you know I'm not.'

'Then get down to the dregs where you belong.'

'Please don't speak to him like that,' Elizabeth said.

The Second Officer, whose advances she had rebuffed at least twice, had his moment of retaliation.

'You've upset your mother, Miss, and you ought to apologise to her. You've behaved most improperly.' He turned to Stefan. 'And you get off this deck at once.'

'When I have said goodbye,' Stefan said, and paying no further attention to the officer, he took Elizabeth's hand.

'I'm sorry, *Liebchen*.'

She gazed at him, as if the ship's officer did not exist.

'There's only one thing I'm sorry about,' she said, 'I'm sorry it's over. I love you.' She gently kissed him on the lips again, then turned and started reluctantly up the steps.

'Little slut.'

The remark was deliberately loud enough for them both to hear. For the first time in his life Stefan lashed out and hit someone with intent to do him serious bodily harm. The officer staggered and fell backwards, clutching his nose as blood started to flow from it.

Elizabeth turned and saw this and then watched Stefan make his way down towards the lower deck. She wanted to follow and beg him not to go to his family in faraway Adelaide; she wanted to hold him and feel his arms tight around her. Instead, she walked up to the boat deck, to meet the gaze of her mother's outrage.

It was later, in their luxury stateroom with its adjoining cabins that the recriminations flew.

'You've been seeing him the entire voyage. Deceiving me.'

'I did nothing I'm ashamed of, Mama.'

There was no question of their returning to the Captain's farewell dance, nor did either of them wish to do so.

'He's a nobody – a penniless foreigner.'

'That's not true,' Elizabeth declared, close to angry tears. 'His family have a property in South Australia. A vineyard. His relatives in Bavaria told him that they're quite wealthy.'

'Nonsense. People like him make up fanciful stories for silly girls like you. If they're well off, why is he travelling steerage?'

'Because his uncle only sent him a cheap fare. He wrote to say that was how he came to Australia, and that Stefan had to do the same. And I don't in the least care how he's travelling,' she said passionately. 'I love him.'

'Don't talk rubbish.'

Edith Patterson was not going to admit it, but she did feel some sympathy for her daughter. She had little liking for the ship's officers who clearly made a practice of pursuing any available young women on every voyage. Nor she did care particularly for the other first-class passengers, some of whom had patronised her. The young man had at least seemed pleasant looking and decent. But quite unsuitable, she thought with a sigh, and expressed the real source of her concern.

'Your father will blame me.'

'No,' Elizabeth said, 'Papa will understand.'

'Oh, no he won't.' Edith's voice was suddenly certain. 'He may dote on you, but he won't tolerate this. Better for you, and for me, if he never hears about it.'

William found out almost as soon as they had docked. He came aboard, while Forbes waited on the quay with the new landau. William was fastidiously dressed, a tall and handsome man not yet forty years old, and many a feminine eye assessed him as he made his way up onto the boat deck, wondering who he might be meeting. Elizabeth saw him with grateful relief. She and her father had always shared secrets; it would make such a difference to be able to talk to someone understanding and sympathetic.

'Papa!'

She ran towards him, and his face lit with delight and pride as he enclosed her in a possessive hug. Neither of them saw Stefan in the background among the first-class passengers. No one else had time to notice a lone intruder from steerage. For most people the voyage was over. Time to collect their luggage, tip stewards, greet friends and relatives. No one noticed him but Edith.

'Edith, dear.' William kissed her on the cheek, and made a suitable comment about being glad to see her home.

It was her mother's glance backwards that made Elizabeth realise Stefan was there. She detached herself from her father's arm, and moved towards him. Before Stefan could do more than take her hand, her father had joined them. Elizabeth, composed and determinedly matter-of-fact, introduced them.

'Father, this is Stefan Muller.'

Stefan gave a formal bow. William stared at him.

'Muller? German?'

'Yes, sir,' Stefan said. 'From Augsburg.'

'It's in Bavaria,' Elizabeth said.

For almost the first time in her life, her father ignored her.

'Have you met this person, Edith? Is he travelling first class?' he asked his wife, as if Stefan was not there, did not exist. 'Are you acquainted? He and our daughter seem to know each other. Did you know about that?'

'Not until last night.' Edith shook her head, and then turned rather ineffectually to Elizabeth. 'I'm sorry.'

Elizabeth said nothing. Before either of them realised what she intended, she stepped forward and kissed Stefan.

'*Auf Wiedersehen*,' she said. And then she uttered a few whispered words that only he could hear, which ended abruptly when her father firmly took her arm.

It should have been a cheerful drive home. Lots of excited talk about the trip, and Elizabeth's impressions of London and Paris and Rome. William had been so looking forward to it, counting days, eager to see his beloved Lizzie and hear what she thought of the rest of the world. He had even bought the expensive new landau, specially imported, the latest and most fashionable horse-drawn conveyance in the city. There were few others; not many people could afford them.

William Patterson had wanted to bring his daughter home in style. Instead the journey was endured in an unhappy silence.

'It's over and done with,' he said, as they drove through the gates of the house. 'Don't let's spoil a happy day.'

Nobody replied. Elizabeth seemed close to tears. Edith appeared not to hear him.

'We'll say no more about it. For everybody's sake, let's try to act as if it never happened.'

But dinner was even worse. Pretence was impossible.

'Now that you're home,' William kept trying his best, 'you must come and see me perform in "the bearpit". It's what they call the House of Parliament – and with good reason.'

After the first course, which she hardly touched, Elizabeth rose and asked to be excused. She did not wait for their response; she was already on her way out of the large, austere dining room.

William shook his head with disappointment as he watched her go. Edith remained mute, but already seemed to sense that by tomorrow it would be considered her fault. As though in confirmation of this, he said, 'You should have kept a closer watch.'

She felt the unfairness of the comment. He realised he had offended her and tried to make amends.

'I'm sorry – we mustn't quarrel. I've missed you.' She looked at him, her disbelief clearly showing. 'Anyway, this damned German is on his way to Adelaide. She'll soon be over it.'

'She's in love with him.'

'Rubbish. She's not old enough to know what love is. He's gone, Edith. He's out of her life. He no longer exists.'

On the other side of the open door, Elizabeth was halted by these words. She had returned to apologise, to try to salvage what remained of their homecoming dinner. Instead, she heard the finality of her father's words.

He's gone. He's out of her life. He no longer exists.

This was the man she had grown up adoring. He was glad, relishing the thought Stefan had sailed with the ship, relieved she would never see him again. She went slowly upstairs to her room, the large bedroom that overlooked the tennis court, filled with so much of her life; a once-loved teddy bear, school photographs, a Certificate of Merit from Miss Arthur's Academy for Young Ladies, her desk where she had done her homework, the bed she had slept in since she was nine years old. She sat by the window and wept, and went on weeping as if she would never stop.

Chapter 4

A rat scuttled along an open drain where unsewered effluent ran down Ferry Lane to the terrace houses of Windmill Street. Below them lay the imposing wool storage buildings of Pitt, Son and Badgery. Nearby, two women in ankle-length dresses gossiped and watched a thin, pale child skipping.

The houses huddled against each other. At intersections it was possible to glimpse the ships at anchor in Floods Wharf, and the company dockyards in Darling Harbour, but the view was spoiled by the stench from the backyard privies, the tiny brick and iron 'dunnies' that stood like primitive sentry boxes all the way down the hill. It was an ugly land-sweated area - haphazard and sub-standard. No building regulations had ever been enforced here; there were rooms without windows, and entire streets had no water or conveniences of any kind.

A billy-cart clattered down the lane, and Stefan had to hastily step back or the shrieking small boys in it would have collided with him. He walked past the Lord Nelson Hotel in Argyle Place, shook his head at the hopeful prostitute outside the Miller's Point Post Office, and made his way into Clyde Street. The squalid locality appalled him. Washing was strung across narrow streets. The tiny backyards were littered with hovels. They were made of rusty iron and hessian, and were let as 'rooms'. The lack of sanitation and disinterest of the authorities had contributed to the wretchedness of the area as much as the venal landlords. Bounded on three sides by water, what might have been a desirable neighbourhood had deteriorated into a sordid slum.

The house in Clyde Street was no worse than any other. The door hung open. A half-naked child played in the passageway. There was the smell of offal and cabbage being cooked in one of the rooms, and a client of the girl on the first floor passed him on the narrow stairs. He made his way to the top-floor back room, little more than a cramped attic, which he shared with an elderly man who had been a dock labourer. The room, tiny as it was, had been divided into two by an improvised partition. Grain bags, sewn together, hung on a length of wire: the old man lived on one side, and Stefan on the other. His share of the windowless space measured two paces in width and three in length. The sloping iron roof, descending steeply at one end of the attic, made it difficult to stand upright. For this Stefan paid a shilling a week, and had been told to think himself fortunate.

He sat on the sagging, makeshift bed, which occupied most of his section of the room, and counted his money. He had almost three pounds remaining, and calculated he could manage for a few months.

He realised he had been insanely rash. After they had danced, after her mother's intervention and Elizabeth had kissed him and left, Stefan had stayed on deck all night, his mind in a turmoil. He had seen the sun rise across the sea, and illuminate a series of beaches and coves. Sometime in those predawn hours, he had made his decision. He would disembark when the ship docked, remain in Sydney, and write to his uncle. He would stay in the city where Elizabeth lived. Anything else, now he knew how she felt, was unthinkable.

When the vessel turned through the twin heads to the harbour, his spirits soared. The shore was no longer so distant and forbidding. The arms of land that enclosed the massive harbour were sprinkled with houses. There were waterfront jetties, small vessels plying their way between them, and crowded ferry boats with people on board them waving to the ship. Stefan waved back. He saw a series of bays and tiny sandy beaches all the way down the harbour until they reached the warehouses and the maritime wharves. It was a city, the like of which he had never imagined. Already he could make out people crowding onto the quay, and see cable trams on the curved and hilly streets. There was a sense of excitement as he gazed about him, seeing settlements on both shores of the harbour, the grand homes that seemed to straddle the best promontories; feeling the light breeze, the gentle rock of the ship, the crystal water, the bustle in the streets as they slowly came into view.

It made Stefan light-headed. Here, in such a place, with a girl like Elizabeth in love with him, anything was possible. He had pushed his way towards the upper deck, ignoring the notices and disregarding an objection from the Assistant Purser. By the time he managed to locate her, the hawsers had been secured and the stampede to disembark had begun. He saw her father, a well-dressed man, make his way assertively through the crowd. And then, her mother's glimpse of him, her father's anger, and Elizabeth's sudden movement that took them all by surprise. Her warm lips against his.

Only he heard what she whispered then.

Auf Wiedersehen. I wish it could be different. How I wish we could see each other again.

Her father was speaking sharply to them. Stefan could sense his anger, and then they were gone. The last thing he heard was William Patterson rebuking his wife for not being a proper chaperone, and failing to keep the riff-raff and foreign fortune-hunters at bay.

The house was absurdly grand. This was his first dismayed reaction, as he crossed the road from the park and stood outside the ornamental gates. There were two gardeners at work in the spacious grounds, clipping shrubs and edging the lawns. They gave him a curious glance as he stood there in his shabby suit, hot and tired after the long walk across the city from Clyde Street. He looked again at the scrap of paper in his hand, the address she had written down for him on board the ship. He thought perhaps he had come to the wrong place.

'Want somethin'?'

The younger of the two gardeners had strolled across, watchful and suspicious. His eyes had already assessed Stefan, and decided he belonged at the back gate, not here at the visitors' entrance.

'Miss Elizabeth,' Stefan said haltingly.

'What about 'er?'

'Is she home, please?'

'Dunno.' The gardener, not yet nineteen, was enjoying a rare moment of authority over this stranger. 'Have ter see, won't I? Give us yer name.' The words, strung together in a nasal monotone, confused Stefan. He looked blank and shook his head.

'Your name, matey – 'ave you got a name?' the gardener said, now slowly and rather loudly, as if dealing with a half-wit.

Stefan told him.

'Wait there.'

He strolled unhurriedly towards the house. Stefan felt the curious gaze of the other gardener watching him. In the distance was the sound of a piano being played. He felt sure it was Elizabeth. Perhaps he was only moments away from seeing her. Then he saw the gardener return, motioning to the other, so that they both moved off as William Patterson emerged from the house and crossed the immaculate lawn towards him. Finally only the iron gates stood between them.

'Jumped ship, eh?' Her father's voice was quiet, but his eyes were like flint.

'Yes, sir. I wrote to my uncle that I remain in Sydney.'

'Did you now?' There was no heat in his voice, no hint of the torrent of rage to follow. 'Well, if you don't get out of here and stop pestering my daughter, I'm going to call the police and have you chucked in a cell. Do you understand that, you fucking German bastard?'

If he did not know the words, there was no mistaking the tone. Or the anger with which Patterson stared at him.

'Please,' Stefan said, 'I wish nobody harm. May I see her?'

'No, you can't see her.'

'Can you please tell me why?'

'Because I say so. And because she thinks you're a thousand miles away in Adelaide, where you should be.'

'But I wrote to her. I told her I was here.'

'She didn't get the letter,' William said, as Stefan realised with a shock what he meant. 'And if you try to write again, I'll rip that letter up, too. I didn't send her to the best schools, give her all the advantages, to have some dirty fortune-hunting bloody foreigner get his lousy hands on her.'

Again he did not have time to translate all the words, but they remained in his mind, so unmistakable was their venom.

'So clear out or I'll send for the police. You don't want that. Neither of us want that.'

Stefan looked at him helplessly. He heard and registered the word 'police', and knew that he was being threatened.

'Look, son,' her father's tone became a shade more conciliatory, 'you see the way she lives. You know you don't belong here. She's not for you. She's a romantic and inexperienced girl who's got some stupid idea she's fond of you.'

Fond? We love each other, Stefan wanted to tell him, but knew it would be useless.

'Come on, be sensible. In a few weeks she'll have forgotten all this, and so will you.' He brought out his wallet and selected a five pound note. 'Here. Bet you can use this. Get yourself on a train to South Australia. Don't come here and bother us again.'

'I don't want your money,' Stefan said. 'I must see her.'

'You try and you'll end up in gaol. Now go to buggery,' her father said, and walked away.

That had been three weeks ago. Since then he had tried to find work, but the recent series of bank collapses were cutting deep, and most employers were paying men off.

'You got Buckley's,' a foreman at the shipyard alongside Mort's Dock told him, and although Stefan did not know who

Buckley was, he understood the message. A newcomer with a limited knowledge of the language and an accent that advertised his recent arrival had little hope of finding a job with the economic recession worsening daily. It was clear that the colony was in deep financial trouble. Starving families were scavenging in the streets for food. People were begging. Factory owners took advantage, exploiting the labour surplus to make profits. A rope manufacturer, so the story circulated, dismissed most of his adult employees and hired children as apprentices. As they were aged only ten, he was not required to pay them wages for three months, and after that their earnings were a prescribed two pence an hour for a twelve-hour day. The growing trade union movement condemned him, while the local business community seemed to admire him for his acumen.

Stefan spent every day in his vain pursuit of employment, and began to despair of his prospects. He had made several more attempts to see Elizabeth, all of which ended in failure. Once he had glimpsed her in the distance, walking beside the tennis court with her mother, but by the time he had made up his mind to climb the ornamental railings, they had gone inside. Stefan wondered if her mother had seen him. He felt the younger of the two gardeners had. That seemed confirmed the next time, when he had stood in the park and watched a policeman patrol past the house and back again. William Patterson was making good his threat. Each night Stefan wrote, and spent a precious penny on the stamp, but knew with bleak certainty the letters never reached her. He began to admit to himself that his decision to leave the ship here had been a terrible mistake.

~

Elizabeth finished the letter and addressed the envelope in her neat handwriting. *Mr Stefan Muller, c/o Johann Ritter Esq, Kavel Farm, Hahndorf, South Australia.*

Edith came into the room as she was doing this.

'Do you want to read it, Mama?' she asked, her mother's appearance creating an instant hostility.

Edith shook her head and sat to resume crocheting. She felt sad. She was fond of her daughter – love was not a word she used easily – and she felt it a terrible injustice she was being blamed for what had happened on the voyage home.

'I'll go and post it. You will trust me as far as the post box?'

'Please, Elizabeth,' Edith said. 'Don't do this to me.'

'Do what, Mother?'

'You're angry. You feel life's unfair.'

'Isn't it?'

'I never meant to harm you, or make you unhappy. I was upset that you deceived me, but I never wanted it to be like this. I wish you'd believe that.'

Elizabeth didn't answer. She took her coat and hat. There was a storm threatening and as she looked out the window towards the park, she frowned as she saw a distant figure on his steady patrol.

'Why is there a policeman out there?'

'Out where?'

'In front of our house. He was there yesterday.'

Edith joined her and looked out the window.

'I don't know,' she said truthfully. 'Perhaps it's something to do with your father.'

~

'A few ratbags,' was William's explanation when Edith asked him. It was later in the day, and he was leaving for a late sitting of the Parliament. 'A couple of loonies made threats. As a public figure I'm entitled to protection.' He smiled for both their benefit.

He's lying, Edith thought. *I wonder why.*

Forbes was waiting outside the front door, with the landau. As William went out he hugged Elizabeth, dutifully brushed his lips against Edith's cheek, and climbed into the carriage. Before they drove off, he said there was some extra committee work and a meeting that would keep him in town until late. He told her not to keep dinner – he would have it in the Dining Room with one of his parliamentary colleagues.

Edith knew he was lying about that, too.

Stefan walked in the park. Leaves were falling, and misted rain was making the ground slippery. He turned up his collar, but tried to otherwise ignore the weather. It would soon be dark, and already lamps were lit in the house on the other side of the road. The policeman must surely be recalled from duty soon. When he left, Stefan had decided to climb the railings, and make his way to the house. The front door? Or the back? He thought on reflection he might have more success at the back. But *somehow* he would see Elizabeth. He knew that she might ask him to leave, might tell him it was just a shipboard romance, but at least he must make her aware he had remained in Sydney, tell her his feelings, and find out the truth of how she felt about him.

The policeman, however, showed no sign of leaving.

Stefan sighed. It was futile and hopeless to loiter here under the dripping trees, in the summer rain, like a furtive lover. The word 'lover' was a hopeful and optimistic overstatement, but he knew he did look furtive; a solitary figure who had been watching the house far too long. If the bored policeman had been more alert, by now he would have been spotted, labelled suspicious, and been asked to provide some reasonable explanation for his presence, or else move on.

He heard the clatter of hooves, and the sound of a carriage approaching. For a moment, because the landau was hooded against the weather, and the coachman wore a sou'wester and a mackintosh, he did not recognise the vehicle. When he did, he gambled with courage born out of desperation, and ran to block its way. The driver pulled the horse to a halt just short of him, then, raising his whip threateningly, he ordered Stefan to stand aside.

'Crazy idiot. Mighta been killed. G'on, out of the way.'

Stefan ignored him. He moved to the door of the landau and opened it. There was nobody inside. He came back to confront the coachman, regardless of the raised whip or his own personal safety.

'Please,' he said, and gave the man - who he suddenly remembered from Elizabeth's stories was called Forbes - gave Forbes a note with a few words scribbled on it, 'please give this to Miss Elizabeth.'

'Not me, mate,' the coachman said, trying to hand it back.

'It's only my address, Mr Forbes. To say I am here in Sydney.'

'It may be,' Forbes was surprised this troublesome young foreigner knew his name, 'but I can't go passing any of your messages to Miss Lizzie. Ain't possible, sonny. Be worth my job, that would.'

Stefan felt in his pockets and found a precious florin. He gave it to the coachman, who shrugged. He found another, almost half a week's living gambled now, and handed that to Forbes as well.

'Please,' he said, 'help me.' Then without waiting for an answer, he swiftly walked away.

But there had been no help. Nothing that night, or the next day. The man had simply taken his money, and torn up his note. The duty policeman still patrolled, the house remained a fortress which he would never be allowed to enter.

It was too late for regrets, but he had been a fool. He should have remained on board the ship, proceeded to Melbourne and then to Hahndorf. By now he would be there, safe with his own people. Instead, Uncle Johann would receive his letter, and no doubt resent his impulsive behaviour and ingratitude. In the letter he promised to repay the cost of the steamship fare when he was able, but already that seemed an improbable and futile hope.

Again he counted his money, attempting to estimate how much time he had left. In money terms, less than two pounds. No matter how he tried, even reducing himself to one meal a day, a few more weeks was the most time he could last. If there was no work by then, it meant begging for scraps of food at a soup kitchen. It was too late to write a contrite second letter to Uncle Johann, admitting his stupidity and asking for assistance to reach Hahndorf. He doubted if his uncle would be very forgiving.

Obsessed with his difficulties, he paid no attention to the sound of a horse cab stopping outside. Nor did he hear the hurried footsteps on the stairs. He looked up when the door opened, and with a feeling of amazed disbelief, saw Elizabeth standing there.

Chapter 5

After they had made love, and reached a blissful climax, Hannah rested her head on his chest until they both regained their breath. It had been one of their most ardent encounters. He had felt a real need of her today, sitting through the morning in the parliament, while his leader droned on about the few advantages and many disadvantages of a link with the other states in a Federation, declaring that New South Wales would be in the position of a sober man trying to share a house with five drunkards. William had dubbed him 'Yes-No Reid', the press had taken up the name, and William and the corpulent Premier now disliked each other intensely.

He had left after the debate, and had Forbes drive him to Glenmore Road in Paddington, where he asked to be put down. He said he had a meeting, and would walk home. He wondered if Forbes knew about Hannah. The coachman and his wife had worked for them ever since the move to Centennial Park, and whatever Forbes might have guessed, he knew he could trust him. Yet today, the man seemed uneasy, and strangely on edge. He appeared glad to be dismissed and to drive away.

'Penny for them,' Hannah murmured, and stroked his cheek.

He smiled and shook his head. It would hardly do, at a time like this, to say he was wondering why his coachman had seemed nervous. She kissed him, then slipped out of bed, and he watched her slim dancer's body as she walked naked to the bathroom. He lay there and reflected on how empty his life had been before they met.

He had married Edith when they were ridiculously young, both barely twenty years old. She had been a pretty but nervous slip of a girl, working as a loom operator in the bookbinding section of the government printer, where he had been a storeman. He had seen the pretty face, but not the diffidence, the nervous and shy manner that made her so often afraid of people. William was brash, afraid of no one. Thus ill-suited, their marriage had been an unfolding disaster, a sad and polite masquerade, enriched only by the birth of one daughter who had become the centre of his life, and in fact, the *raison d'être* for the risks he had taken, the illegalities, the fraud in Broken Hill and his determination since then to succeed and become respectable.

The physical bond between him and Edith had been increasingly tenuous. Even before they had left on the world trip, she had barely been able to conceal her aversion on the few occasions when they were intimate, managing to convey a feeling it was a marital obligation that had to be endured. Because she suffered from insomnia, they had agreed some years ago on separate bedrooms. After one loveless visit there since her return, he had not troubled her again.

Inevitably he spent more of his time at this secluded house in Paddington. A 'bijou house' the property agent had called it, extolling its virtues as a fine example of 1860s architecture, eminently rentable, and a perfect time to buy with prices rising and the area becoming fashionable. William promptly corrected him, pointing out there was deep pessimism about the housing market; apart from which Paddington was a working-class area and likely to remain so, even though this 'bijou house' – he invested the agent's words with a mild scorn, as if disparaging them – did have a reasonable position at the end of a quiet cul-de-sac, and therefore had no noisy traffic or nosey neighbours.

In fact he was delighted; it was exactly the kind of place he had been looking for, though he had no intention of admitting that. He secured the freehold at a favourable price. The agent was right and its value had already increased sharply, and would continue to do so. But he had not bought it for profit or resale. He had, quite simply, bought it for Hannah.

The day was still vividly clear to him. He had collected her by cab from her lodgings, a third-floor room in Phillip Street, which was all she could afford on her irregular salary as a dancer. They had driven here, and he had produced keys and opened the door of the sandstone cottage, pointing out the best features like an eager salesman: the secluded front courtyard, stained-glass sidelights; the central hall with dining room on one side and elegant sitting room on the other; the main upstairs bedroom and adjacent bathroom. After their tour of inspection, they went out to see the walled back garden.

'It's charming,' Hannah had looked around admiringly.

'I'm glad you like it,' William had said. 'I've bought it.'

By this time she was hardly surprised, but said nothing.

'Useful investment. Freehold. I got it at a good price – I'm a hard bargainer.' He hesitated, then blurted out the truth, 'Actually I bought it because – I hoped you'd like it. Enough to live here, I mean.'

'And leave Phillip Street?' Hannah could be ingenuous when required. She had already sensed what this was about.

'If you like the idea, that is.' Usually articulate, he felt anxious and unsure of himself. It was so important to him that she agreed. 'You could - er - furnish the place. And do it up - decorate it to your own taste.'

There was a garden seat under the shade of a jacaranda tree in the garden. They sat there and he held her hands. He cleared his throat nervously. Those who had heard him lash the Opposition with his eloquence would have been astonished.

'I don't mean just leave your lodgings,' he told her. 'I mean I'm asking you to change your life. Give up the dance troupe.'

'But William —'

'There'd be - a reasonable financial arrangement.'

'William . . .'

He felt somehow he'd made a blunder.

'I don't mean . . . er . . . payment in that sense. I mean money to run the house. An allowance for clothes - and for yourself. I can't ask you to give up a career and live on nothing.'

'Willie, please . . .' she tried once again, but he was too intent on pressing his case, and aware he was not making much of a job of it.

'I realise you've been with the ballet for a long time. You'll miss all that. But perhaps you could think it over. I don't expect an answer straight away. I just want you to live here, and be happy. Be my mistress - I suppose people would call it. Although I wouldn't call it that.'

'What *would* you call it,' she asked him.

'My . . . companion. My other life.'

There was a brief silence, while she considered this.

'Don't say anything now,' he begged. 'At least, don't say no. Think about it, please. I need you, Hannah.'

At thirty years of age, Hannah Lockwood knew how to recognise her blessings, and how to count them. She had been a dancer since she was fifteen, and had begun to realise, soon afterwards, that she would never be quite good enough to become a soloist. For ten years she had been with Madame Ranasky's touring *corps de ballet*, but when this brave and struggling enterprise ran out of money and had to be disbanded, those who had been merely the swans and not prima ballerinas found it difficult to survive. She tried not to remember the series of dubious engagements, the dancing troupes in bars and tent shows where local dignitaries or officials had to be placated, and where the dancers, to retain their jobs, were expected to grant such favours. She was not a particularly moral person, but the idea of being pinioned by a sweating Shire Clerk on a lumpy mattress in a country hotel or pursued by some lascivious licensing sergeant-of-police made her feel a sense of outrage at what her life had become. She was also acutely aware, even for this sort of existence, that time was not on her side.

She had met William one evening, when a party of political men without their wives had come to the basement music hall where she and the rest of the girls in the chorus (most of them younger than her) were baring their legs and dancing the notorious new French dance, *Le Can Can*. Sir Henry had been there, of course, the grand old gargantuan with his fierce eyes and whiskered jowls, who could thunder speeches about the forthcoming federation of Australia, but could not pronounce his H's, and so to the girls in the troupe who loved his ribald ways and fund of risqué stories, he was Sir 'Enery Parkes forever.

Henry had introduced William as a young man with political ambitions who might amount to something. They had shared a bottle of champagne and William asked if he could take her home. Before they left, Emile, the owner of the music hall, whispered that Mr Patterson was chairman of the property company who owned the lease on the premises, and to treat him with care. Hannah knew what that meant; she had been there, in that situation, before.

He suggested a cab, but she had asked if they could walk. It was not far to her lodgings. On the way he talked of his daughter, of her schooling and the trip abroad he planned as a finish to her education the following year. When they reached the narrow doorway of the rooming house in Phillip Street, she invited him in, but to her initial surprise he declined. He did, however, ask if they could meet again. It was not until they had dined several times, and one evening been to the theatre and had supper afterwards, that he accepted her invitation to have coffee in her room, and they had slept together.

By then, Hannah had begun to sense this was no transitory affair. She realised the rich, successful and still young William Patterson was lonely; clearly his marriage was lacking, and all his attention was vested in his daughter. He was shy with women, and found it difficult to form other relationships. Hannah saw this; she perceived a need in him, and resolved to fill it. She dropped former liaisons; previous lovers were no longer welcome. She found out his interests, and read copiously about politics. When they first made love, she feigned an ecstasy that so stimulated and aroused him, that she in her turn lost control and they reached a vigorous and erotic climax. For someone whose main diet had been his wife's passive endurance, it was like a sexual fantasy.

She knew then she was determined to attract and hold him by whatever means she could. The result had been more than a little surprising. William kept returning, as she intended he should. It became a regular arrangement. He bought the Paddington cottage, and she was persuaded to live there. He proposed an allowance and when she refused, accepting only half of what he offered, he insisted on her having an account to buy her clothes at David Jones, the drapery emporium. None of this was a particular surprise. It was, she knew, what she had subconsciously hoped for, and set out to achieve. The surprise was in her own feelings towards William.

Hannah had never considered that she would fall in love with him. She *liked* him, and had from their first meeting. He was generous and kind; he confided in her and talked to her as a friend and an equal, and he was fastidiously clean. She grew to care for him. She came to look forward to and enjoy their afternoons together, and to miss him when business or politics kept him away. It developed into love so gradually that she was hardly aware it had happened; but it had, and one day she realised with quiet incredulity that she did indeed love him, and could not name the day or the month when it had occurred. Now, all this time later, and respectably installed in the house in Paddington, she could hardly imagine a life without him.

After they had dressed, she served tea in the living room which looked out onto the walled garden. The furnishings in the room appeared expensive, but he knew most had been acquired at bargain prices. Hannah had revealed a talent for scouring the city salerooms, where she bought with care, exhibiting a flair and taste that had transformed the house.

He felt so much at home here. He watched her trim figure as she poured the tea, and reflected on the fortunate day when he met her. She filled a huge void in his life. Without her, he was acutely aware of how empty his whole existence could be. Especially lately.

'How is Elizabeth settling down?' Hannah asked, as if reading his thoughts.

He sighed and frowned. Elizabeth was not settling down. His daughter was behaving like a deprived and petulant child, ever since he had sent that German fortune-hunter packing.

'She'll get over it,' Hannah said, doing her best to console him, after he voiced his concerns.

'I hope so. I've been wishing to God I never sent her on that damned trip. If Edith had been awake to what was going on . . .'

Hannah never said so, but sometimes she felt sorry for his wife. They finished their tea. Often afterwards, they sat in the garden surrounded by tulips and climbing roses and he talked of his business successes, or his political ambitions. But today he was restless, strangely uneasy, and half an hour earlier than usual she saw him to the front door, kissed him fondly, and watched him walk up the slope of the hill in the direction of Oxford Street.

William generally enjoyed the walk, which was a brisk ten minutes, up Liverpool Street, past the Victoria Barracks and the new Paddington Town Hall. Today he strode more quickly than usual, as he left Oxford Street and headed back towards the park and his house which faced it. He could not have said why he felt uneasy, but as he turned the corner and saw a distraught Edith outside the front gates, he began to run.

Chapter 6

She lay awake in the darkness of the squalid room, listening to the two men breathing. Her arms were around Stefan, the weight of his sleeping body pressing on her left arm which lay beneath him. It was beginning to ache, as she tried to move it without waking him. The lumps and sharp protrusions in the straw mattress made sleep impossible for her. On the other side of the hessian bags which divided the room, the old man who shared the room grumbled in his sleep, a harsh sound deep in his throat like a death rattle.

Due to the proximity of the other man, they had not been able to make love. She had not even been able to remove her clothes. The attic beneath the iron roof was fiercely hot, and she was aware of a constant rivulet of sweat trickling down between her breasts. The night seemed endless, and filled with alien sounds. Below in the street a bottle smashed, and a drunken voice shouted obscenities. A child woke in the room opposite, and began to cry.

Elizabeth felt desolate and afraid.

After Forbes had handed her the letter and she discovered Stefan was here in the same city, she had agonised over what to do. She had hurriedly sought out the nervous Forbes, insisting he tell her, and for the first time learned of the deception and the way her father had lied to her. While she had been writing daily to Hahndorf, Stefan had been here to the house trying to see her. He had even written her letters, which had been intercepted and burnt.

Under her questioning, Forbes admitted all of this. He had been instructed not to tell her mother. It was her father who had done it all. Deceived and lied to her. He had never, as far as she knew, lied to her before. It was that, above all else, which prompted her swift decision to run away.

She realised she had to be careful. She had thought it out; had packed almost nothing, just an extra dress and a pair of shoes, and made them into a parcel. She had worn two additional sets of undergarments beneath her dress, taken the small amount of money she kept in cash from her dressing table drawer, together with her few pieces of jewellery including a silver locket she had been given for her twelfth birthday, and strolled out of the house, unnoticed. In the garden she waved to Mrs Forbes, who was cutting flowers for the dining room, and indicating the brown paper parcel, told the housekeeper she was going to post it. In Oxford Street she hailed a horse cab, and asked to be taken to the central Post Office in the heart of the city. After the cabbie had set her down and driven off, she walked a city block and hailed another cab to whom she had given the address of the house in Clyde Street.

It was a simple but necessary precaution, for she did not underestimate her father's anger or his influence. She was prepared to defy him, and to cover her tracks until she was safe with Stefan and able to plan their future. What she was not prepared for was the squalor of the neighbourhood, the garbage, the smell of the open drains, and above all the hostile glances that assessed her, priced her clothes and categorised her as someone to resent, or if the opportunity presented itself, to rob.

She lay awake beside Stefan, her arm imprisoned beneath his body. She was unable to avoid thinking of the joyful and passionate night she had envisaged, comparing it to the grim reality. She knew that they must move from here, or else she would soon return in defeat and humiliation to her parents. Tomorrow they must try to start a new existence together.

But not here. Nothing could begin here.

In the darkness, while the men slept, she tried hard to curb the feeling that her emotions had played some terrible trick on her, as she counted off the hours, waited for the daylight, and endured the longest and unhappiest night of her young life.

Edith stared out of the living-room window. The rain that had begun before dawn fell relentlessly, and ran down the pane like tears. Neither of them had slept. Her head throbbed from the shock and the same repetitive argument.

'You must go to the police,' she said yet again, and when he failed to answer she realised with astonishment that he was crying. 'William,' she said, touched by this rare show of weakness, and ready to comfort him, but he merely blew his nose angrily and wiped at his eyes as if they had betrayed him.

Pretending not to notice, she fixed her gaze on a puddle outside the window, and watched the huge raindrops splashing into it. *I wonder*, she thought, *if he would cry for anyone else*? Not for her, she knew. Probably not even for the woman he visited at the house in Paddington, whose existence she had only learned about by accident.

'Please,' she begged, 'ask the police to start a search.'

After some moments he spoke. 'You know perfectly well,' he said at length, 'we can't do that.' Then he left her alone in the gaunt living room.

She was in a mood, for once, not to be dismissed. She pursued him through the house, past hushed and nervous servants. When the study door slammed shut in her face, she flung it open and confronted him.

'You're frightened of a scandal,' she accused him. 'You won't report it because you're afraid of it getting into the newspapers.'

'They'd love to get some dirt on me. It's taken me years to be accepted, socially and politically. I won't be humiliated, lampooned as someone who can't control his own child.'

She felt rage, but with an effort kept her voice composed.

'She's not *your* child. She's *our* daughter. For God's sake, don't you care?'

'Of course I care, Edith. But there'll be no police. And no talk outside this house.'

'She's not even eighteen yet. It's infatuation. If we don't get her back, she could spend her life regretting it.' *As I have*, she wanted to add. Instead she said, 'You can't abandon her just because of the gutter press.'

'I haven't abandoned her.' His voice was colder than she could ever remember it. 'She made a choice. I loved her and I gave her everything. She never lacked for a single thing in her life.'

'Perhaps that was a mistake.'

He continued as if she had not spoken. 'In return she chose to reject us for a penniless immigrant. Well, if he hopes for a handout from me, I'll see him in hell first.'

'Is that what you think? He'll come for money?'

'Eventually.'

She could no longer constrain her anger. 'You call it a choice,' she said, 'but we made her choose. We wouldn't let him visit. We don't know what he was like, because we wouldn't allow ourselves to find out. Perhaps he was nice –'

'What?' He stared at her, as if she was possessed.

Edith was aware of the words pouring out, unchecked. She, who so rarely had a word to say, could not stop herself talking. 'There must have been some quality about him that made Elizabeth feel this way. Some attraction.'

'Are you serious?'

'There were so many other young men competing for her attention. If she picked him he can't have been entirely unlikeable.'

'Don't talk like a fool,' he said.

Whenever I talk to him sincerely, she thought sadly, *I'm told I'm talking like a fool.*

'Is it foolish to want her found?'

'I'll find her,' William insisted. 'But no police. I'll find her my own way.'

'What way is that?' she asked.

Ignoring her question, he said, 'Warn the staff. If anyone gossips, they're out. Sacked.'

He shut the study door on her again, and this time she made no attempt to stop him. There seemed no point in further pleas. She guessed why a public police search with its chance of publicity so concerned him. It was nothing to do with politics, she knew. He had lied about that, as he had about so many things.

Though Edith knew no details, she nursed a secret belief that the source of their wealth had been dishonest. She could not say why she felt this. A great many other men had vanished for months to the gold or silver fields and returned triumphant, but William had not done that. He had arrived back almost stealthily, evasive about where he had been, secretive about the bars of silver which he cashed from time to time, and anxious always to have it known he had made his money from land deals. Even now, in political life, he disliked being photographed, and she believed this fear of his past prevented him initiating a full search for their only child.

Edith wanted to hate him. But, instead, she was possessed of such a feeling of loss and desolation, she thought her heart would break.

'Ten shillings,' he suggested cautiously, eyeing the locket, while trying to gauge how desperate the young couple might be.

'Sorry.' Elizabeth put out her hand to retrieve it.

The jeweller smiled. 'It's just a trinket, lovey. A toy.'

'It's silver,' she said, 'and I want five pounds - or I'd rather keep it.'

'Two pounds,' the jeweller offered.

Stefan had been standing by, watching. 'The lady has changed her mind,' he said.

'What do you mean - changed her mind?'

'She now wants *six* pounds.'

Elizabeth tried to hide a smile, but the man saw it and was indignant.

'Five was what she said. Four I might think about. Not a penny more.'

'Sorry,' Stefan said. 'It is now *seven* pounds.'

'All right – five,' the jeweller snapped, confused by this alien and unusual method of bargaining.

'Done.' Elizabeth nodded.

He paid her, counting out the money with bad grace. She produced several other items, among them a necklace, a brooch and a ring. The jeweller made a pretence of studying them, and gave his best impression of an off-handed shrug.

'What can I say? They're just baubles.'

'You say what you like, but I want another five pounds.'

The jeweller decided not to argue. He opened his cash drawer with an audible sigh. He paid out the five single notes, as if each one caused him acute physical pain.

'Five. And may you never come back to cheat me again.'

They walked out of his tiny shop, as pleased with themselves as the jeweller was with his day's work. Ten pounds was a great deal more than they had hoped for; the jeweller, on the other hand, knew he could resell this little lot for four times that sum.

The sign on the door said: HORACE PERKINS, PRIVATE ENQUIRIES. CONFIDENTIALITY GUARANTEED. William made up his mind and entered. Mr Perkins was a large man, who had formerly served in the police force, and came well recommended. His modest office was sour with the smell of cheap cigars, but he seemed to know his business.

William refused a cigar, and produced a recent photograph of Elizabeth. He explained the situation, or as much of it as he felt Perkins needed to know. Mrs Forbes had supplied him with a description of the missing dresses, and the enquiry agent wrote these down. William also gave him details of the jewellery. Mr

Perkins said he would begin with the pawnshops and loan offices. His fees, he said, were four pounds daily plus all expenses, and he knew he had assessed his man accurately when the client accepted the price without protest. Mr Perkins wrote out a receipt for his first payment, a ten-pound commissioning fee, and assured William he would give it his immediate priority.

He expressed his hope for a quick and successful outcome.

The room was in lower George Street, above a bootmaker's shop. They followed the stout landlady up narrow, uncarpeted stairs. It was small and contained a double bed, a tiny wardrobe, and a dresser with a wash basin and jug. There were flimsy curtains, and beyond them the sound of horse traffic from the street below.

'It's clean, dears,' the landlady promised, 'it's quiet, and it's four bob a week. The dunny's in the backyard. A chip heater for the bath downstairs - tuppence a time.'

She watched them trying to make up their minds, while wondering about this good-looking young girl, and her foreigner. She hoped they weren't in trouble, but times were bad in the bootmaking trade, her husband was ill, and she needed to let the room.

To her relief they nodded, paying her four shillings, the first week's rent in advance.

'I like it,' the girl said. 'We can be happy here.'

It was a surprise; someone like her saying this about the tiny, unprepossessing box room. She had thought the girl was from a good family, but appearances might be deceptive. Perhaps she was unused to anything better?

The stout landlady went down to tell her husband they had

tenants, unmarried and very young, but beggars couldn't be choosers. For some reason she kept hearing the words. *We can be happy here.* She found herself hoping, certainly for the girl's sake, it might be true.

There was little traffic as they approached Oxford Square, and for that Forbes was grateful. His mind could not focus on other vehicles today. He was still stunned by the past twenty-four hours, the enormity of what had happened and the part he had unwittingly played in it. Unwittingly? It would not be deemed so if his employer found out. The old man, always in his mind he called him that, though William was not yet forty and younger than him, the old man would blame him and boot him out in an instant.

He could not even tell his wife. She was close to Mrs Patterson, who was distraught, and neither would ever forgive him. He could not forgive himself. This family had always been kind to them, and he would not willingly have done anything to hurt them.

Yet he had done this.

In his own defence he could only have said the young foreign man had seemed so vulnerable, quite decent really, so hurt and desperate. And Elizabeth - Miss Lizzie - had been so unhappy. Ever since the day they had come to work for Mr Patterson he had had a soft spot for her. With all the family wealth and advantages, she had been a nice girl, kind, natural, always considerate. If he and Mrs Forbes had been able to have a child, which sadly had not been possible, he would have wanted a daughter like her.

He wished he had burnt the piece of paper with the address on it. He almost had. But he had felt sorry for the boy, and uncertain of what was best, so he had left it in his pocket. Then the following day, when he was marking and rolling the grass court, he had heard this sound from the tennis hut. It had shocked him, for he had never heard such grief. He had found Miss Lizzie sobbing her heart out. And because he could not bear the thought of her being so unhappy, he had taken the scrap of paper from his jacket and placed it in her hand.

Two hours later she was gone, but not before she had sought him out, found details of the letters which had not been delivered, and the young man's visit when her father had kept them apart. He had not wanted to tell her these things. He had an obligation to William Patterson, as well as great respect, quite apart from the spacious quarters and well-paid employment. But Elizabeth was special. She always had been, both to his wife and himself.

So he had told her everything. And ever since, Forbes had been in torment, and felt like a Judas. He barely heard the call to stop as they reached lower George Street, and he saw the jeweller's shop.

'He claims he gave her thirty quid for the lot,' Mr Perkins said, while the jeweller managed to look upset and offended at this insult to his veracity.

'I did - honest. Thirty quid.'

'Liar. I know him, sir, and his kind. He's a robbing bastard.'

'Never mind that.' William looked down at the delicate silver locket he had given Elizabeth on her twelfth birthday. 'Where did they go?'

'No idea,' the jeweller said, relieved to be able to give an honest answer at last. 'Just took the money and left. The young foreign man had a suitcase. If you ask me, they went to find a room.'

'In this neighbourhood?' Perkins persisted.

'Not the faintest,' the jeweller said.

He looked carefully at William Patterson. He was used to assessing people's worth, and this was clearly a rich man, if a distressed one. He asked him if he would like to buy back his daughter's locket, saying he was prepared to forgo any profit if it was of sentimental value. He would be pleased to accept only the eighteen pounds he'd paid for it.

William put the money on the counter, took the locket and left without a word. He waited for Perkins to join him.

'Should've let me bargain, sir. I'll start a search. Put on extra men. More than likely they're not far away. Lot of rooms to let in this part of town.'

William shrugged. He felt sick and despondent.

'Do whatever you think necessary, Mr Perkins,' he said.

He would pay the bills. Go through the formality, although he knew it was pointless. Even if they found her now, he had lost her. He climbed into the landau and was driven away.

The letter came a day later. It was left in their mailbox early, before anyone was awake. It was in her neat and upright handwriting.

Dearest Mama and Papa,

Please try to find it in your hearts to forgive me. I wish I could ask you to our wedding, but I know you would try to stop us. When we hear from his relatives in South Australia, Stefan and I will go there. Meanwhile, he has found a part-time job, and we will manage. I do truly wish there had been some other way,

but you wouldn't even let us meet or give us a chance. You should have done that, Papa. I will write when we are in Hahndorf, and remain, please believe me, your loving daughter.
Elizabeth

He read it in silence, and returned it to Edith. He was aware of her reproach. For a moment he felt tempted to give this letter to Perkins, order him to hire an army of observers to watch every church and registry office, and prevent the marriage. But it was already too late. She had turned her backs on them, chosen this stranger.

They went to find a room, the jeweller had said.

By now she would have been ravished - his mind shied from the word, but there was no other for it - ravished by this bastard. The trusting child, so often his companion on walks, her small hand in his; the schoolgirl in her long skirts at Miss Arthur's Academy; the images went through his mind and returned yet again to the image he could not bear but also could not obliterate; Elizabeth naked and . . .

He experienced such a rush of fury towards the youth, that he saw the room and his wife's face in a red mist. There was a weight in his chest. His hands clenched so tightly that the nails drew blood, and bile rose in his mouth.

It was the last time he showed such emotion. He wrote to Mr Perkins, terminated their arrangements, and requested his final account. From that day on, for more than a year, William Patterson devoted his time to business and politics, and consoled himself with daily visits to Hannah. He and Edith lived in their austere, oversized house in a state of unforgiving politeness, and he did his utmost to forget he'd ever had a daughter.

Although it could not, even for a moment, be said that he succeeded.

They did not hear from Johann Ritter in Hahndorf until July. By then Elizabeth was four months pregnant. The money raised by selling her jewellery and the locket was diminishing. Stefan had found a part-time job with a clothing factory in Redfern, but it was a two-mile walk each way. He had no choice but to walk; the pay of four shillings per day was little enough without the expense of fares. It helped safeguard their dwindling resources, while waiting to hear from his family. There were times, as weeks went by, when she thought it might have been wiser to set out for Hahndorf and arrive unexpectedly, rather than wait for an invitation which took so long to come. But Stefan insisted this way was more tactful. He had written to his relatives with a full explanation. There would be a reply. His uncle was no doubt busy with the grapes, and was not a man who put pen to paper swiftly.

Despite this delay, and the growing anxiety over money, she was content. The first awful night was now a dim memory, and had she not felt so guilty about her parents, Elizabeth would have proclaimed herself happy. There were times, indeed, when she was deliriously so. After the first uncertainty, their lovemaking had taken her by surprise; the pleasure she experienced startled her. Her enjoyment of their bodies, her longing each night, the wild climaxes that came in waves were so impassioned they almost frightened her. She had no knowledge before this of her intense sexuality. At times she wondered uneasily, never having been able to discuss it with anyone, least of all her mother, whether it was a sin to so enjoy an act never spoken of in polite society.

When they could afford it they took a ferry across to the north side of the harbour. At Milson's Point, the cable tram took travellers into the countryside of St Leonards, and although this was beyond their limited means, they once took the tram to Crows Nest, formerly a rural area, and now rapidly burgeoning into streets of workmen's cottages. They picnicked on a grassy slope that overlooked the harbour then, quietly happy, walked hand in hand down the hill to the ferry.

They still lived in the room over the shoemaker's shop and sometimes, on days when Stefan's shift finished early, they walked to Hyde Park. Once, when they were alone there, he gathered her a posy of flowers, and they walked homeward with their arms around each other. In less than a city block, the tenderness they felt for each other became a quickening desire, and the moment they reached home they went to bed, barely able to contain themselves. That night their hunger for each other was insatiable, until they fell into an exhausted sleep.

But there were other days - days when the small room oppressed her, times when the walls seemed as if they were closing in to smother her. There was hardly, in her childhood home, one room as tiny as this one in which their lives were spent. There were days when she missed that house and her parents dreadfully, when she wanted to write to them again, or even catch a tram, alight where Oxford Street joined the corner of Centennial Park, and walk in there and greet them as if nothing had happened.

There was the first day when she was sick, when she had run shudderingly to the backyard privy, and heaved what little breakfast she had eaten into the rancid pit. And another day later, when the landlady told her what this meant.

'But it can't be,' Elizabeth said, and the stout woman, who had become a friend, laughed.

'It is, lovey. And no wonder, the way you two children enjoy yourselves at night.'

Stefan was filled with pride and joy. He kissed her, held her lovingly, and spoke of what was in both their thoughts.

'Do you want to tell them?' he asked.

'I should. They have a right to know.'

'Yes.'

'Will you come with me?'

He shook his head. They both knew her father would never accept him, and a confrontation with him would be humiliating for Stefan, and disagreeable for them both.

'He hates me. But you should write. Or visit, if you wish.' His English, though fluent now, still had an accent, and in moments of stress could be markedly formal. She sensed a tension in him, and knew he did not want her to visit her parents, as if he still feared their influence.

She decided to think about it, and had still not made up her mind, when the long-awaited letter arrived.

Stefan had not expected forgiveness, but the cold hostility of the reply stunned him. *You are*, his uncle wrote in local Deutsch, in pencil and in indignation, *undankbarer*. The smudged page, the gross misspellings accused and castigated him. *If you still wish to come, you must pay the fare*, the letter concluded, *though your aunt is most unhappy that you have married a foreigner.*

A foreigner, Stefan thought. *What kind of place do they live in, when an Australian girl like Elizabeth is a foreigner? And how can I tell her, after we have waited all this time and built our hopes so high, that after reading this letter I am not certain if we should go there.*

'What does it say?' Elizabeth asked. She had been watching him while he read the letter, but his face remained impassive. Which made her wonder.

'Here,' he said, and offered it to her. She made a face at him.

'Fool,' she said fondly, 'you know I can't read German.'

'This we must change.' He smiled at her. 'It is not right that Mrs Stefan Muller, soon to be the mother of Heinrich Muller, cannot read German.' He was playing for time, trying to decide what to tell her, and for once deceived her.

'Perhaps it won't be Heinrich,' she gave him back the crudely printed letter. It did not look promising to her, but then the man was a farmer, not a scholar. 'Perhaps it will be Hilde. And anyway, in this country he shouldn't be called Heinrich, he should be Henry. So there.'

She waited for him to tell her what the letter contained.

He knew they must go. It was their only chance. Each week, no matter how many hours he worked, they were falling slowly behind - each week a few shillings, slowly whittling away the pitifully small nest egg her locket and jewellery had brought them. In another six months or less it would all be gone. By then they would have a child. He would have no alternative but to go abjectly to William Patterson and ask for help. Or else subject Elizabeth to even deeper squalor and deprivation.

She watched his face. 'Is he angry?' she asked.

'A little. He says I have been a *dummkopf*.'

'Stefan, if he doesn't want us there, we have an alternative.'

He knew it; he didn't need to ask.

'Soon I have to tell my parents about the baby. My father would help us. He'd almost insist on it.'

'I know,' Stefan said.

'If he offered, would you accept his help?'

'You know what it would do, don't you?'

'What would it do?'

'Confirm his opinion, that I am a dirty fortune-hunting bloody foreigner.'

Elizabeth felt shock. She had not known her father had used those words, but could almost hear him saying it.

Stefan saw her distress and took her hand. He was aware that the rift with her father had caused her pain, and the last thing he wished to do was hurt her further. He loved this girl, loved her with his entire being, and wanted to be able to give her a proper place in the world. But that could not come from the charity of her father, surrounded, as it would be, by conditions. William Patterson's help would be for one purpose only; to drive Stefan away and regain his daughter. He doubted if any kind of life was really possible for them here in this city, where every day must remind her of the ease and comfort of her former life.

No, it had to be far-off Hahndorf; that was the only place that offered them a chance. Uncle Johann's surly hostility or not, there they would begin their real life. There was nowhere else.

He picked up the letter.

'It says,' he was determined not to lie more than necessary, 'I am an ungrateful fool, and caused much concern. But it seems I have come to my senses, and married a nice girl. They will make us welcome.'

She smiled with relief, and he hugged her gently, grateful that she could not see the troubled uncertainty in his eyes.

~

Elizabeth thought about it long and hard, and finally decided not to see her parents. Nor did she write to them, giving news of the expected birth, before leaving Sydney. She was now committed to this journey halfway across the continent; she had sensed something of Stefan's feelings, his need to begin their real life together far away from the city and the scenes of her childhood. She was aware that if she saw her father and told him the news, he would do all he could to stop her leaving the east, and would certainly offer the kind of financial aid they would find difficult to refuse. For Stefan's sake, for their only chance of a future together, that situation must not be allowed to arise.

In early August, Elizabeth Muller, by then nearly five months pregnant, travelled with her husband by third-class carriage to Albury. They sat up all night, and huddled together for warmth, as the train laboured its way through the wheat belt on the far side of the Dividing Range, and reached the border town on the Murray River the following day. There, passengers crossed the platform to climb aboard another train, this one on Victoria's wider gauge rail system. They passed through the customs posts of both colonies. Neither Elizabeth nor Stefan had anything to declare.

When they reached Melbourne there was a mishap that had a disturbing affect on their perilously low savings. They missed, by less than an hour, their westbound train to Ballarat and the South Australian border. It meant an overnight stop in Melbourne. The miscalculation almost dealt a mortal blow to their slender budget and planned schedule. They settled on the cheapest lodgings they could find, in Little Lonsdale Street, and were kept awake most of the night by drunks and fights and a furious row across the pavement between the girls of rival brothels.

In the morning they paid out most of their remaining money on third-class tickets, and risked fourpence in the railway refreshment room to buy cups of tea and two buns. The buns were hard and stale, but they wolfed them ravenously and barely noticed.

They were excited and confident, without fear of the future, no matter what it might hold.

When they crossed over into South Australia, through another customs post and onto a new rail system, they did not have enough money to go much further. The clerk in the ticket office of the border town of Pinnaroo looked at the few shillings they were able to offer him, and shook his head.

'Not enough for two tickets,' he said. 'Enough for one.'

'Then my wife will go,' Stefan said. 'I'll walk.'

'No,' Elizabeth said. 'We'll go as far as that money will take us, then we'll both walk.'

Out of Yumali, on a long stretch of line halfway to Coomandock, the small train stopped to unload mail at a cattle station siding. The guard looked regretfully at Elizabeth and Stefan.

'I've given you an extra fifty miles,' he said. 'If the Inspector gets on at the next town, I'll cop it.'

They thanked him, and waved as the train left them on the tiny and empty siding. They were still nearly sixty miles from the Adelaide Hills and their destination. They had no money left, and had not eaten all that day. But their hearts were high with expectation, and they never, even for a moment, contemplated failure.

~

The earliest Adelaide Hills settlers lived in the Mount Lofty forests, but in 1830 there was a new wave of immigration. Silesian Germans, fleeing from the religious intolerance of King Friedrich Wilhelm of Prussia, took ship to the infant colony and founded a community on the eastern slopes of the Hills. They were Lutherans, peasant farmers, and the ship on which they travelled was commanded by a Danish seaman, Captain Dirk Hahn.

It was Hahn who realised, during the long voyage, that these people had no future unless they could find land to farm. It was he who helped them discover and lease an area several days' travel from the port, and he even walked with them while they carried their meagre possessions to their new hillside home. In grateful tribute of this rare kindness to them, they named the place Hahndorf.

The first years were bitter. Crops were difficult to raise. They had no money to buy farm implements, and dug the soil with jagged scraps of wood. Their homes were shacks. The winters were cold, and many died. But they were zealots, these pilgrims; their faith helped them survive. For six days each week they worked themselves to exhaustion; on the seventh they held church services in an open field, where their Pastor thanked the Almighty for giving them a new home where they could worship Him and not the King of Prussia.

As the years passed many of the settlers began to flourish. They built new homes, churches and Lutheran schools to educate the children, instil religion, and prevent them from forgetting the old ways.

By the time Johann Ritter left his ship to begin a new life here, Hahndorf had become an established township with wide streets of handsome stone houses. Ritter took lodgings and attended church with the dominant purpose of looking for a wife, finding among the congregation a girl from Westphalia named Anna, from whose family he borrowed sufficient money to purchase four acres of hillside land.

They planted vines and had four children, who attended the local village school where the lessons were in German. None was yet old enough to work when a letter came from his sister Cordula in Augsburg. She told him of their orphaned nephew Stefan, and his wish to find employment in the New World. She spoke in such glowing terms of Stefan, so invaluable to her husband in his shop, that Johann, who could never be called an impetuous man, spent the next year wondering why his sister wanted to be rid of this paragon. Finally, it occurred to him his sister's eldest son was now of an age to replace Stefan, and after a further six months of deliberation, he wrote offering a third-class fare in return for work on the farm.

When Stefan failed to arrive, Johann and Anna merely assumed the boat had been delayed. Time was of little relevance to them. The weeks were divided by the sabbath, the seasons by the planting and harvesting of the grapes, the years by their own religious festivals. They were barely aware that three years had passed since their nephew had first expressed a youthful wish to join them.

The first letter they received after Stefan left the ship angered Johann greatly. He had never been a generous man, and the original outlay of the passage money had caused him considerable misgiving. To be told by this ungrateful upstart that he had fallen in love, and intended to remain in the city of Sydney, a den of iniquity so far away, infuriated him. Even the pledge to repay the cost of the voyage did not placate Johann; he had little trust in the empty promises of profligate relatives.

The second letter with news of his marriage divided the household deeply. Johann himself was slightly consoled, seeing an opportunity to recoup his investment. Anna was resentful. It was *geschmacklos*, boorish and tactless of him to marry an *Ausländerin*, a foreigner, when there were many eligible German girls in their district. At least four women from church, all with daughters of marriageable age, had already made discreet enquiries about Stefan's arrival.

The discord in the family resulted in the dispatch of the crude reproach, which Stefan had so carefully paraphrased to make it palatable for Elizabeth. The letter he had destroyed, but the tone of it, the anger, he remembered only too clearly, the more so the closer they came to Hahndorf, and the end of their arduous odyssey across half the continent.

From the rail siding they walked steadily across the open flat land near Coomandock. They passed a wheat field, and later an orchard, the apples reminding them of their hunger. In mid-afternoon, when Elizabeth was desperately weary, fortune smiled on them. A farmer in a dray stopped alongside.

'Going to Long Flat, near Murray Bridge,' he offered, and they gratefully climbed aboard. In a few minutes, despite the rutted road and the jolting of the dray, Elizabeth was asleep against a bale of hay. Stefan watched her with great affection.

Are we mad? he wondered. *So few clothes, not a penny to our names, on the way to a place we have never seen, dependent upon people we do not know*. But before he could answer his own question, he, too, had fallen asleep.

Before dark they reached the farmer's small-holding, where

he insisted they spend the night. He brought them cups of hot, sweet tea, and bread and cheese. The next morning, following his directions, they walked the remaining twenty miles to Hahndorf. They saw the spire of the church a long way off, then soon afterwards there were buildings and Stefan began to notice Bavarian architecture, and to see familiar German names on the road signs and outside the shops. Despite the chill of his uncle's letter, this sense of familiarity cheered him. His spirits began to rise. A passing woman greeted them.

'*Grüss Gott,*' she nodded.

'*Grüss Gott,*' Stefan answered.

All at once it was difficult to believe he was twelve thousand miles away from Bavaria. He took Elizabeth's hand. Despite his own excitement, he knew she was close to exhaustion. He led her to rest in the shade of the German Arms Hotel verandah. The proprietor emerged, exclaimed at her swollen stomach and the fatigue that showed on her face, and in German invited her to come inside. Stefan nodded his thanks, and translated for her. Elizabeth smiled her gratitude. It was a good omen, an act of kindness from their first encounter here.

'*Danke,*' she said, and asked Stefan, 'is that correct?'

'That's correct,' he said tenderly, and leaving her resting in the hotel, he went to ask how to find his relatives.

Chapter 7

The baby kicked inside her, and she felt a moment of alarm. Inside the shed, Heinrich began to cry. She knew it was too hot for him in there; also the old woman, *Grossmutter*, would soon complain. Sure enough, as she turned the wheel of the churn to separate the milk, there rose a querulous voice from the direction of the rocking chair on the verandah.

Grossmutter was Aunt Anna's mother, a formidable old lady forever attired in black, as if in mourning for her life and its approaching end, here in this foreign place. *Grossmutter* did not like Hahndorf. She had obeyed her husband when he chose to emigrate from Westphalia, but had remained mutely disapproving all the years of her long exile. She had seen her daughter marry Johann Ritter, who in her opinion was an unimaginative, tight-fisted *hoffnungslos*, and had watched him try to sweat a living out of this infertile land. When her husband died, she had come to live with them; no other choice was open to her.

Grossmutter had not welcomed Stefan and Elizabeth. She had bitterly frowned upon their arrival, as if fearing she might be dispossessed of her tiny room. Her objections were silenced only when she found out this new great-nephew and his *Ausländerin* wife would not be dwelling in the house.

Elizabeth still graphically remembered that day. Stefan had found directions while she rested in the hotel, and after the publican had given her a drink of milk and some food, they set off towards the farm. They had come down the dirt track to a rusty wire fence and a broken gate. A box beside the gate was painted in faded creosote with the name RITTER. She knew at once it was an impoverished place. A lone cow searched for grazing. A tethered goat bleated. There were rows of vines, stunted and stripped of their grapes. The wind was soft, but bringing a breath of heat from the desert to the north, like a whispered warning.

As they approached, several children appeared from the field to peer at them. A woman came out of the small wooden house, joined a moment later by a man in work clothes. Both seemed to be in their forties. There was no trace of welcome in their faces, only a careful appraisal and a guarded hostility. And soon afterwards came the realisation that none of them spoke English. She had stood by helplessly, while Stefan and his uncle had a long and heated exchange in their native tongue. It became an argument, in which Stefan seemed to be protesting, and Uncle Johann began to shout. Then he abruptly hurried away.

'What is it?' Elizabeth was very weary. She could not recall ever feeling so discouraged. 'What's wrong?'

'Everything,' Stefan said. 'It seems he never wrote and said he had a prosperous farm. My aunt lied. He's always been poor here. Always struggling. It was a struggle to send me thirty-seven pounds for the boat fare – and he wants it back.'

In her state of mind she did not understand what he meant. 'Wants it back?'

'Or else I work here and pay it off.'

'And live where?' she asked.

'In there.'

He pointed at a shed, the kind where cattle might be kept, or else farm equipment. The walls and roof were unpainted sheets of corrugated iron. She walked across to it and went inside. There were no cattle, but chickens had roosted here. Pellets of their faeces lay on the dirt floor. She felt, more than anything else, more than her incredulity or disgust, a sense of exhaustion and defeat. She was aware of Stefan beside her.

'He said there's no room in the house. I told him this is not fit for habitation, and that we'd leave.'

'How can we leave?' Elizabeth said. 'I'm tired - and we have no money. None at all. At least until the baby is born, we have to stay here.'

She was disturbed from her reverie by the creak of the rocking chair on the verandah, and the old woman's complaints. She realised Heinrich was still crying. Leaving the milk, and covering the pail to protect it from flies, Elizabeth went into the shed to pick up her son.

It was still a primitive coop, and she and Stefan had done little to make it a home. To them it was a temporary shelter, and one they would not live in for a moment longer than necessary. Or so they reassured each other, almost every night after he came in exhausted from work, cultivating and pruning the vines, often too tired to make love to her although she wanted him, needed this comfort desperately - and later when he was lean and toughened by the physical work, and eager for her, then it was too close to the birth - even then they would lie in each other's arms and plan that once the child was born and Elizabeth recovered, they would leave here, tell Uncle Johann the debt was repaid, find other work and somewhere better to live, far from this awful place and these unforgiving people.

But it had not turned out that way.

She was deeply unhappy, and had been from the first day, after the lack of welcome, the appalled realisation of where they were to sleep, and the ordeal of their first meal with the Ritters. She had been aware, as Uncle Johann said a long incomprehensible grace, and afterwards when the greasy *Dicke suppe* was served, of the entire family watching her with a steady speculative stare. It was alien to her way of behaviour, and disturbed her. There was not only *Grossmutter* and Aunt Anna's critical gaze, but all the four children, from fifteen-year-old Clara to seven-year-old Kurt, watched her with a scrutiny that made her feel exposed and uncomfortable. Only Uncle Johann, head down and spoon shovelling, showed no interest, as if his prime concern had been solved by the appearance of Stefan, and he could now begin to recoup the investment of the passage money. Which he had assuredly done. Stefan worked from sunrise until dark, with barely time to wash and sit at the table before the food was blessed with the same interminable Lutheran grace.

Many times Elizabeth felt she must write and tell her parents the truth; ask for help, confess it had all been a dreadful mistake. Yet she had not done so. A fierce pride, although she was loath to acknowledge it, held her back from this final admission of failure.

She picked up the crying child, his small face mottled with rage, kissed him and smiled as his tantrum turned into a gurgle of recognition.

'Little beast,' she said fondly. 'Think you've won. Well, you have.' She cuddled him, found a damp rag to cool his tiny brow, then wiped and changed him, and carried him from the heat of the iron shed into the shade of the flowering red gum, one of the few trees that had been spared on the property.

Heinrich was a fair-haired, healthy infant with his mother's intense blue eyes. He had been born on a wild night, when a violent summer storm and driving rain had delayed Doctor Boettcher, and instead the midwife from the local village had delivered him. The Ritter family approved of the chosen name of Heinrich. Elizabeth's murmurs of dissent were only fleeting; Stefan was so thrilled with the baby and so proud, so hopeful he should be named after his dead father that she did not have the heart to voice her concern at her child being given such an alien name.

Heinrich Muller, squalling lustily, was baptised in the oldest of Hahndorf's Lutheran churches. The ceremony was entirely in German, and she had not understood a word of it. She had felt like a stranger watching a curious ritual in which her husband and son took part while she was a bystander.

The baby moved inside her swollen body again, and she sat carefully on the ground, placing Heinrich in the shade of the red gum. She had not intended to become pregnant again, certainly not so soon. There would be little more than a year's difference in the children's ages.

'It'll be company for Heinrich,' Stefan said, trying to console her, the day they first knew of her condition. The family gave one of their rare smiles of approval at this foreign girl their nephew had brought among them, while shaking Stefan's hand in congratulation. To Elizabeth it seemed to imply she was now performing the function for which she was fitted, allowing her body to be the incubator in which offspring would be bred. At nineteen years of age, she was not enthralled by their biblical concept of multiplying mightily. She felt there had to be more to life than having her womb occupied annually to produce future farm workers.

She had tried to explain this to Stefan. The night the doctor had confirmed it – she had insisted on this, although Aunt Anna had shaken her head at the expense – that night they sat on fruit boxes outside the shed. It was peaceful, with only the murmured rise and fall of Uncle Johann's voice from inside the farmhouse, where an oil lamp glowed.

'They are saying prayers for the health of the new baby,' he told her. She made no response. The tension between them was tangible. He felt a deep guilt for bringing her here, aware of the stresses that were dividing them. Often he wanted to tell her to give in and write to her father, but knew if she did it would almost certainly mean the end of their marriage. Yet much more of this bleak life and that might happen, anyway.

He looked towards the house, as the prayer continued. 'I know they are hard, difficult people.'

'They are.'

'I am not excusing them, but all they have is their land – and their God. They've come to realise the land is poor. It won't produce good crops. They wonder, sometimes, if God looks the other way.'

She wanted to ask if their God was as harsh and forbidding as they were, but instead she said, 'I'm tired, Stefan. I'm going to bed.'

He took her hand. 'You don't want this child, do you?'

She hesitated. The truthful answer was no.

'I want us to have a chance. We've been saying for months we'll get away from here. What hope have we, with another baby?'

Despite the shade of the red gum, the air was searingly hot and Heinrich began to cry again. She heard the rocking chair squeak on the verandah, as the old woman, *Grossmutter*, gazed out towards her. The dislike, the malevolence was unmistakable.

Why do you hate us? Elizabeth thought despairingly. *We came here with such hopes, wanting to give so much affection to you. All we asked was to be a part of your family. And what did you give us in return? No welcome and this silent hostility. You spoilt it, old woman, you and your daughter and Uncle Johann. We came here wanting to be happy – we hadn't any money and we were hungry, but we loved each other and life was fun. And then you frowned and spurned us and ruined it. Why ? Why do you sit there hating me?*

The thought of writing to her parents kept recurring and she kept rejecting it.

Lately, William often stayed for dinner. He now cared little for what Edith thought, and she asked no questions. They rarely communicated, except at breakfast or when he had to entertain political associates at home. Apart from these occasions, they lived their own lives, little more than silent acquaintances in a house much too large for them.

It was so different here. He still marvelled at how warm and decorative Hannah had made the bijou house. He grew to realise and appreciate her intellect and social graces. She could discuss politics, knew the arguments for and against the federation of the states, and that the forthcoming referendum would mean political in-fighting and crossing of party lines. It could be a time of opportunity for William. She had begun to subtly interest him in the theatre. On her advice he made donations to a new ballet company, and invested in the theatrical venture started by the American actor, James Cassius Williamson. She pointed out that local interest in drama had been kindled by the visit of the great Sarah Bernhardt, and to be a modest patron of the arts would do no harm to his political ambitions or his public image.

In this way Hannah contributed to his life. He was immensely proud of her. He wanted, above all else, to be seen openly with her, but this seemed to entail a risk to his position. He felt he didn't care. In the name of love he was prepared to give up all he had striven for.

'I sometimes think Edith would be relieved if I moved out.'

'You can't.'

'I used to be fond of that house. Now it's not much more than an empty shell.' She watched him, knowing of his loneliness since Elizabeth's elopement. 'I really wonder if a political career is worth it. Sometimes I want to say, "To hell with it all," and come and live with you.'

'You know what I think, William?'

'What do you think?'

'I think you should stop talking, and take me to bed.'

Later, lying entwined and tranquil, he raised the matter again. It was Hannah who convinced him it would be foolish.

'You'd lose everything.'

'People do get divorced these days,' he argued.

'Not if they want a public career, and high office. You surely don't intend to stay on the back benches once Federation comes.' She smiled at him. They were both aware of his ambitions. 'So, no divorce, no scandal, my darling. I'm content, William. I'm very happy, believe me.'

'I hope so. I lost Elizabeth,' he said. 'I couldn't bear to lose you.'

It was simply spoken, not a declaration of any kind, yet it moved her deeply. She felt its truth. Those who knew his past reputation would have been amazed at this absolute sincerity.

Around midnight Hannah saw him out. An oil lamp lit the front courtyard. She adjusted his tie, then kissed him gently on the lips. There was something she wanted to say, and she wasn't quite sure how to go about it.

'Write to her,' she said.

'To who?'

'Elizabeth. Write and say no matter what, you love her.'

'I can't,' William said. 'I think of her every day. I try not to, yet I do. But writing is like . . . like forgiving. I can't do it.'

Heinrich was asleep in the shed. Elizabeth found a pad and pencil and sat beneath the red gum. She moved slowly, clumsily, her body more swollen, and felt fatigued by the summer heat. She carefully headed the letter: *Hahndorf, December 12th, 1898.*

Dear Papa, I feel I must now tell you the terrible situation in which we find ourselves, and to ask for your help . . . It would be so easy, she thought, then regretfully tore up the page and began again: *Dear Mama and Papa, I am sorry I have not written for so long, but we have all been busy. We work hard here, but we enjoy it.* She looked down the paddock at Stefan in the distance, stripped to the waist as he vigorously swung a pick, and resumed her letter. *Stefan is well, and so is Heinrich, who will soon have a brother or a sister (I hope), as I am expecting again in March. I will write and give you more news then. I send you both my greetings for Christmas and the New Year. Your loving daughter, Elizabeth.*

She had never written the truth to her parents, and knew now, despite moments of temptation and the knowledge that any plea would bring an instant response, that she never would. Her first letter, on their arrival, had avoided any details of their reception, and had dealt mainly with the journey. It had elicited a quick and agitated reply from her mother, who demanded to know if she was well. Was she happy? Were these people kind to her? Wouldn't she reconsider and come home when the child was born?

Elizabeth had replied, touched by her mother's concern, but confident she and Stefan could manage to find their own way, so to stem the emotional flow, she had lied a number of times about their welfare and their living conditions. Now, nothing in the world would allow her to confess the bitter truth: that not since her first night with Stefan in the Clyde Street house, had she faced the future with such a sense of despair.

Chapter 8

Edith Patterson was not prepared for how deeply she would miss her daughter. By nature rather reticent, she and Elizabeth had little in common, and from infancy she had accepted the fact that the child had always shown a preference for her father. When Elizabeth ran away she felt devastated; she felt in some way to blame, and often wished she could reverse time and change her attitude that night on board the ship – when she had looked down and seen her daughter dancing with the boy, slowly and sensually, as if, in some way, they were standing there making love.

Now Elizabeth was gone and the house that had always been too large for her, was even bigger, and emptier. Edith felt bereft. She knew her husband had his politics, his business interests and his liaison in Paddington, but she had nothing. Not until the first letter. She had immediately replied to it, but had been perhaps too anxious or too intrusive, for there had been no reply for many weeks, and then a polite response giving no real answers to the many questions that troubled her.

Now, at long last, there was another letter.

William gave it to Mrs Forbes to hand to her. They were at

breakfast sitting, like distant but polite strangers, at each end of the long baronial table that had never known dinner parties.

'Heinrich is well,' she read from her daughter's careful hand. 'What kind of a name is that?'

'It was his father's,' William replied. 'Read the rest of it.'

She read on, and felt her heart stop. 'Another child?'

'In March, she says.'

'How could she be having another child? She's hardly more than that herself.'

'Do you find anything at all strange about the letter?' he asked.

Edith had a moment of bitter anger. 'I find everything strange about it. I find it strange that our daughter is called Mrs Muller – and lives so far away with German people – and has babies we've never seen.'

It was not the answer he hoped for. Though, to be fair, he didn't know what answer that should be. He finished his cup of tea, and rose from the table, telling her not to expect him for dinner. The House was sitting late, and he would not be home before midnight.

It had troubled him, and William was unsure why. He had left the letter with Edith, and felt constrained about discussing it with her again, or asking her for its return. One night, unable to sleep, he had gone downstairs to her private sitting room, found the letter in her writing desk, and read it again. There was nothing to concern him. So little news, really. It was like one of her daily snippets she had sent him while abroad, and yet . . . somehow it was not the same. Not like that at all.

Hannah had been aware all week something was worrying him, and knew that he would tell her when he was ready. She made a jug of cold lemon drink, and they took their glasses outside to the garden. In the ornamental pots and window boxes, trailing petunias and dianthus created a profusion of colour. It was late in the afternoon, but the heat persisted. Humidity lay heavily over the city and the day was likely to end with a violent southerly buster.

William sipped his drink, and felt in his pocket for the letter. He gave it to her to read.

'Elizabeth,' she said, recognising the writing from some of the correspondence she had been shown from their trip abroad.

'Came a week ago. Dated well before Christmas, but it didn't arrive until well after New Year. Makes you wonder what the damned postal service is coming to.'

'Or else she didn't get to town to post it.'

'Perhaps,' William said. 'Who knows if they're near a town? Probably out in the sticks. At any rate,' he hesitated, 'I don't know why, but it worries me. Has for days. All morning, while we had that debate on whether to build a bridge across the harbour, all I could think about was - Lizzie. What kind of life she's leading. What the child looks like. Dammit - she's going to have another one. Read it.'

She bent her head and read the lines written under the red gum almost a month ago. William watched her as she frowned and read it carefully a second time.

'Well?' He felt unusually tense, and didn't know why.

'She's unhappy,' Hannah said finally.

It was not the answer he expected. 'How can you tell that?'

'You felt concerned yourself, William. Otherwise you wouldn't have spent all this time worrying about it.'

'But she doesn't *say* anything.'

'It's what this letter *doesn't* say that's important.'

'What do you mean?'

'It doesn't say she's happy. It doesn't say she's in love, or thrilled about the baby. It says,' she read aloud from the letter: '*we work hard but enjoy it*. I'd hardly call that boundless enthusiasm. It doesn't sound like the girl you used to tell me about.'

She returned it, and he folded the letter away, troubled by her comments, but uncertain of his own opinion.

'Still, she doesn't say she's miserable.'

'Willie, I've read those little notes she used to dash off to you, and I'll tell you one thing about this letter – there's no happiness in it. She's nineteen years old, my darling – wilful, impulsive.' She held up a hand to prevent his dissent. 'She ran away because she loved the boy, and that's a fact of life, whether you wish to hear it or not. The letter should be bubbling with news, but it isn't. It's just dull – and dutiful.'

That's it, he thought. *That's what I felt*. Like someone obliged to write, but only a grudging minimum. *Dull and dutiful*. That described it exactly.

'Then why bother to write at all,' he wondered.

Hannah had a moment of rare insight. 'I think,' she said, 'it's a cry for help.'

It was harvest time again, and the line of women and children bent over the wooden churns as they stripped the vines. The grapes were small and disappointing, and Johann Ritter had already decided they would have to be sold as fruit, for they could not make wine. It was a bitter blow, and his mood was sombre as he and his eldest son Franz, now a tall fifteen-year-old, carried the oak buckets from one end of the field, while Stefan collected them from the other, and they loaded them into boxes on the dray. Later, they would fetch the mule loaned by a neighbour, and drive the produce into town to the co-operative.

All the family, except for *Grossmutter*, picked the grapes. Stefan had protested at Elizabeth's being asked to help. Listless and wanting to avoid a confrontation, she had not supported him, and now, too heavy with child to kneel like the others, she sat on a churn beside Aunt Anna and felt the noon heat sapping her strength.

Stefan came past, and this time he insisted. 'Enough,' he said.

'In a moment. I'll just finish this vine.'

Very soon now, Heinrich would wake from his midday sleep, and she would have to feed and wash him.

'Please, Elizabeth.' Stefan took her arm and raised her. 'You're tired and you shouldn't be doing this. Go and lie down. Get some rest before Heinrich wakes.' He looked towards his uncle. 'I don't care what they say. To hell with them.'

'All right,' she said, grateful for his concern. It was not the first time of late he had defied the Ritter family. It seemed as if, ever since the night when he had realised she did not want this child, he had become positive and more assertive.

'Go and rest,' he said. 'Please, *liebchen*.'

She nodded. She was, after all, more than a month off her expected time. So the sudden knife-thrust of pain, when it happened, frightened her.

'What is it?' he asked her. 'Elizabeth?'

She shook her head. It had gone as swiftly as it came, but left her feeling breathless.

'Is it the baby?'

'No, of course not. It can't be.'

Clara, the eldest of the Ritter children, came along the furrow between the vines. She was now a strapping sixteen-year-old, who had caused the family some concern with more than one local youth at the recent *Schutzenfest*. She had long blonde hair plaited around her head, and pendulous breasts beneath her thin cotton dress. She paused and looked curiously at Stefan still supporting Elizabeth.

'*Was ist das?*'

Elizabeth screamed as a new shaft of agony seemed to dissect her, and she felt her clothes and legs flood with fluid. She dimly heard Stefan shouting something; he was telling them to get the *doktor,* she heard and recognised that word. Then the pain stabbed at her again, like a punishment tearing and ripping her body. Once more she screamed, but this time it was with fear. She felt Stefan lifting her, and yelling at the others, and Clara's voice and then Uncle Johann's, and after that it became a confused hubbub. Then a strange silence settled upon her that gave way to a dark and empty space.

PART TWO

Chapter 9

'Where in God's name are we?' William demanded of the driver, who had come with the carriage when he hired it in Adelaide.

The road was little more than a track in places, and the landau bounced uncomfortably over the ruts and corrugations. It was a spacious vehicle, but more suited for the cobbles of city streets.

'Glen Osmond,' the driver said. 'Used to be silver mines. Big battle here once.'

'A battle?'

'Miners. Rounded up a mob of Chinese and killed 'em. 'Bout forty years ago, thereabouts it was. Bad blood between 'em. Still is.'

The driver had been quiet until then, but now began to acquaint his passenger with local history.

'Lots of small communities. Strathalbyn, down south's where the Scots settled. Duke of Edinburgh, Prince Albert he was, come to visit in '67. Then there's the Germans. Went to Clare and Mount Pleasant. And Hahndorf. Hardly anyone lives in Hahndorf, 'cept Germans.'

William nodded. He was alert and refreshed by a night at the Wellington Hotel in North Terrace. Despite the comfort of a first-class sleeper, he had found the rail journey tedious, the customs posts at each state border an anachronism, reinforcing his belief that this absurd colonial divisiveness must end soon.

He wondered in what section of the train, and under what circumstances Elizabeth had travelled, and doubted if it had been a particularly pleasant experience. He felt a growing impatience, an eagerness to see her.

'What time will we reach there?' he asked.

'Late afternoon, I reckon. Depends what sort of stop you want for lunch.'

'Just a beer and a sandwich.'

'Goodo,' the driver said, pleased at this evidence of his passenger's informality. He had been told Mr Patterson was a wealthy Right Honourable from New South Wales, an important man, and he had expected some old stuffed shirt, but Patterson was quite young, and seemed all right. Good clothes, a gold watch with chain, smart polished boots; the bloke obviously had money, but wasn't a la-di-da like some.

'It's a funny place - Hahndorf,' he said, after a spell.

'In what way?' William asked.

'Dunno really. Just sort of funny.' He reflected for a moment. 'Houses are different. The people - hardly any of 'em speak English. They got great big churches where they yabber in their own language, and the cemeteries are full of dead Germans. You kin tell by the tombstones.'

They stopped for their beer and a sandwich at a roadside inn outside Crafters in the Mount Lofty ranges.

'Some of the Germans went up north,' the driver told him, 'to the Barossa Valley. Ever hear of it?'

William shook his head.

'Tanunda way. Good country for grapes. Better than here. I met a fella called Joe Henschke, once. Come from Prussia, brought vines, years back. Now I hear he's got a great big vineyard, big as Johann Gramp at Jacob's Creek.'

William sipped his beer and listened. The fellow was agreeable, and a fund of information.

They reached Hahndorf two hours later. While the driver went to seek directions, William waited in the carriage. He found himself reluctantly impressed by the graceful town. The Boarding Academy and the Old Mill were substantial stone buildings, and the rows of cottages were tidy and well kept. There was a sense of order about the place. A bell clanged further down the street, and a group of children emerged from the timbered Lutheran school, and sedately dispersed for home. There was no boisterous or unruly behaviour; he doubted if larrikinism, the current scourge of the Sydney streets with their gangs and 'pushes', was known here.

The driver came back.

'Only a mile or so on the north road.' He flicked the reins and the horse began to trot, the landau travelling more comfortably on the graded town street.

Just a few minutes more, William thought, and the expectation of his first glimpse of her after so long made his heart quicken.

He had decided on this journey the same day that Hannah had read Elizabeth's letter, but it had taken longer than he expected to arrange his absence. A vital debate on Federation in the House had required his presence, and he had made one of his best speeches, asserting the time had come for those who continued to equivocate to step aside, and let people vote on their own destiny. Ever since inveigling his way into politics

William had maintained his crusade on Federation, and was now identified in the public mind as one of the leading proponents of its cause. If people sometimes wondered what had inspired this radical stance, often against the leaders of his own party, he was not about to enlighten them. It went back further than any of his contemporaries would ever know.

As a boy, growing up in poverty, forced to take employment for a near-starvation pittance when he was twelve, he knew his only escape from this kind of life was to educate himself. This he did determinedly. The factory floor became his place of learning. His older workmates unknowingly became his tutors. He listened to them, heard and noted everything. Their invective, as they railed against the bosses and 'the system'. Their slender hopes and aspirations. The paucity of their lives. He realised their existence was intolerable, as his would be, unless he could find a way out. He had no idea how this might happen, but late at night, by the stub of a candle, he fought fatigue to concentrate on improving his reading, while he continued asking questions, learning to judge and store what was of value, while rejecting the inconsequential.

In rare moments he heard them talk of politics. They envied or despised their leaders, but seemed to admire an up-and-coming politician named Henry Parkes. He was, they told their young and avid listener, a man after their own hearts with the gift of the gab. Not only was he no toff, but he'd gone bankrupt, which made him fallible and human. It was well known he liked women, and they certainly seemed to like him - his randy exploits were making him famous, and if he could get his hands beneath so many petticoats he couldn't be too bad an old bastard.

And he had this idea all the states should be one country, and it sounded like a fair sort of a notion. Might even be better. Couldn't be worse than the way things were, they all said.

The boy had listened. Curious. It had begun as simply as that. When Henry Parkes campaigned for the next election, fourteen-year-old William had gone to see him, and had stayed, entranced. In one unforgettable afternoon, he had become a convert. Despite the fact that later on Parkes had begun to vacillate, was at times erratic, and was even scorned by opponents as a demagogue, William never veered from his first youthful homage. He accepted the concept – and the man. Barely sixteen years later, not long after his escape from Broken Hill, newly rich and politically ambitious, William had been proud to meet Sir Henry, then conceded by most to be the father of the gathering push towards Federation. They had become firm friends until the grand old man's death. In fact, William reflected, he and Henry had been dining together the first time he met Hannah Lockwood.

Hannah, he thought. *Dear Hannah*. She was so often there, a discreet spectator in the public gallery, as she had been the day of that speech. It was why, after attacking his own party for apathy on Federation, he then denounced the indifference of both sides of the chamber towards the vital matter of votes for women. For it was his relationship with Hannah which had made him so aware women of discernment and intelligence could not vote, while any dull-witted or drunken man was assumed to be more worthy of political wisdom – and had the right to exercise it. He found it truly unjust, and lost no chance to say so. On this particular day, mindful not only of Hannah but of the press gallery busily taking notes, he had made much of the fact that New Zealand was the first country in the world to grant universal suffrage.

Why should we across the Tasman remain blinkered and aloof from progress? he had demanded. His own staid party were demonstrably outraged: William had, in effect, crossed the floor, and was now a major figure in a centralist group. By doing so, he had established a small but solid power base.

It had been a fruitful time in other ways. He had finalised the purchase of a cluster of tenement houses in Wexford Street, near the Belmore Markets. He knew, from a Parliamentary Commissioners report, that the district was soon to be demolished. The Commission, on which William had served, had investigated the quarter, a crowded Chinese ghetto comprising cheap food stores, factories, slum houses, brothels and gambling dens, and had found much of the housing lacking in basic sanitary conditions and unfit for human habitation. The owners of the properties were to be compensated and also given a grant for rebuilding. This was not yet public knowledge, and using the protective umbrella of one of his companies, William had purchased a row of the derelict buildings at a price far below the figure set for compensation. He stood to make a handsome profit, as well as retaining ownership of the rebuilt houses.

It had been an excellent period, given zest by the knowledge he was going to make his peace with Elizabeth. He told Edith about his travel plans a few days before his departure. Although he felt she was pleased, to his relief she did not ask to accompany him.

The landau came along a narrow road, past a field of stunted vines already stripped of their grapes. There were two cows grazing listlessly in a barren stretch of land, fenced by sagging wire. Ahead of him was a squat wooden house, with several tin sheds attached to it, as if the original building had spawned these rusty extensions. The place had a forlorn look, and though city born and bred, William could tell this was a failed piece of farmland. There was nothing of substance, no beauty anywhere, except for a flowering red gum tree near the house. As the driver pulled up, he stared at the place with a sinking heart.

'This?' he said, bewildered. 'Is this it?'

'So they said in town.' The driver himself was surprised. William told him to wait, and pushed open the leaning gate. A thick-set man stood by the vines, watching him carefully. He saw no family resemblance, but he assumed this was the boy's uncle.

'Good day,' he greeted him. There was no response. 'My name is Patterson,' William said.

'*Grüss Gott*,' Johann Ritter replied, and although William had no concept of what this meant, it was clearly some kind of greeting, so he nodded and held out his hand. They eyed each other warily, and shook hands, then wondered what next to say and how to say it. He guessed the farmer had no real idea of his identity.

'Elizabeth,' he spoke slowly, enunciating with care. 'I am her father. Her papa. Where is she?'

He repeated her name, investing it with an accent he thought might register, as the other seemed to be gazing at him with a curious expression. 'Eliza-bet.'

Johann Ritter began to speak rapidly in German, trying to explain something, gesturing agitatedly with his hands, ignoring William's confusion. A middle-aged woman appeared from the house, and behind her several children of varying sizes and ages, who all gathered around, staring openly at him. In a rocking chair on the verandah, a very old lady sat watching

'For Christ's sake,' he said impatiently, 'doesn't anyone here speak English?'

'Stefan?'

The man had stopped his incomprehensible babble. He pointed, and with almost a feeling of relief, William turned to see the young German approaching. He looked different. Tanned by the sun, and tougher somehow. Then William watched him stop, eyes widen in shocked recognition.

'Mr Patterson!'

'Will you tell him,' William said, 'that I can't understand a single word he's said. And tell my daughter I'm here to see her.'

It was only then, judging from the way they both gazed at him, that he began to realise something was wrong.

Chapter 10

The telegraph boy rang the front doorbell, and when the young housemaid opened it, she scolded him for not taking it to the side door where the post was usually delivered. The boy, who was sixteen and had just joined the new Workers' Union, told her he was not post, he was telegraph, which was different because they carried urgent messages, and did she wish to accept delivery or not? He also said that in her frilly uniform she looked like a capitalist's lackey, but would she walk in the park with him on Sunday? The maid told him to ask her again when he was grown up. She shut the door in his face and, smiling to herself, took the message in search of her mistress.

On the way through the house she looked at the strange envelope with interest. It was the first one she had seen, and she doubted if such things brought good tidings. She found Edith sewing in the morning room, placed the strange envelope on a silver salver and handed it to her.

Edith seemed equally ill-at-ease with the telegram. She hesitated, then tore it open. When the maid went back to the kitchen, she announced to Mrs Forbes and the other staff that one of them telegraph things had arrived, and by the look on the mistress's face, it was bad news.

Later that day the same telegraph boy crossed Glenmore Road, and went into a secluded cul-de-sac. At the end house with wisteria growing around the front door, he rang the bell, and a nice-looking woman answered. He gave her the envelope, received a threepenny piece together with a smile that made her look really pretty, and departed whistling.

Hannah took the telegram inside and also opened it with some trepidation. It read: ELIZABETH DANGEROUSLY ILL. DELAYING MY RETURN UNTIL I CAN BRING HER BACK WITH ME. ALL MY LOVE, WILLIAM.

He had never been so enraged and filled with fury in his life. When they led him awkwardly towards the house, then skirted it to enter one of the galvanised iron sheds at the side, he had been puzzled, but in his concern and urgent desire to see her it hardly registered. For Stefan had stumblingly told him the news of the premature birth, and that in the ten days since then she had not been well. It had been painful and difficult, he was told, so he was prepared for the shock of finding her ill, but not for everything else.

When he felt the gust of heat from the iron walls and roof, saw the bleak interior, the dirt floor, the makeshift bed with Elizabeth dozing in it, he had one moment of incredulity, of disbelief, then he experienced such a surge of ungovernable anger that he wanted to kill someone. He wanted to strike out and hit Stefan and his uncle, and go on hitting them until his rage was quenched. Though it never would or could be.

Stefan recognised the turmoil in his face. Beside him, Johann Ritter began to speak, pausing for Stefan to translate. Before he could do so, William snapped at him to shut up, and go away. He ignored them and knelt beside his daughter. He didn't trust himself to look at either of them. To think that for more than a year she had lived in this *barn*, like some bonded farm servant. Why hadn't she told him? How could they have allowed it? This *pigsty. How dare they*?

He gently stroked the sleeping Elizabeth's brow, and felt it clammy and far too hot. He tried to calm himself. There were decisions to be made, things to be done. He got to his feet, pushed past them and went out to the landau. The driver was waiting there, the same cluster of children gathered around, staring at the vehicle.

'Inquisitive mob,' he said. 'Everything all right, sir?'

'No,' William Patterson said. 'Drive into Hahndorf. Fetch a doctor, and we'll need an ambulance.' He gave him money, watched the carriage speed off, then he returned to the shed.

Elizabeth was still asleep. Ritter and Stefan had not moved. The farmer was again speaking, a low urgent guttural stream, and seeing William he directed it towards him, and waited for Stefan to interpret. Stefan shook his head, reluctant to do so. Ritter gestured, insisting.

'My uncle,' Stefan said, plainly loath to translate, 'is sorry. He asks if you will please accept a glass of schnapps, while he tries to explain.'

William simply gazed at them as if they were both insane.

Stefan shrugged. 'I said you would not agree. He wishes to try to make you understand why we live in here. His house is tiny, and there is no room. His own children sleep in sheds like this.'

'You tell the fucking bastard,' William spaced his words like stab wounds, 'I don't care what conditions his children live in.

How dare he allow my daughter to live like this? *How dare you?* Tell him to take his filthy bloody schnapps and go to hell. Now get the bastard out of here, and you go with him.'

He turned away, as if the sight of them was an offence he could no longer tolerate, and saw Elizabeth stirring. He knelt and took her hand. Her eyes opened, and she blinked at him in wonder.

'Papa? When did you come? How long have you been here?' She tried to sit up.

'Rest, darling,' he said gently. 'I'm getting a doctor.'

'But the doctor's been. He came a week ago. Stefan insisted, and he walked into town to bring him. I'm really much better.'

'We'll see about that. I'm going to bring a proper doctor from Adelaide.' He was shocked by how thin and pale she looked. He did not want her to sense it, but he was afraid. She seemed so fragile.

'Have you seen the baby?' she asked.

He had almost forgotten there was a baby. She indicated an improvised crib on the far side of the bed. It looked like a fruit box, with blankets inside. He realised, with a fresh rush of anger, that it *was* a fruit box. He gazed down at the tiny crinkled face of the sleeping child, less than two weeks old.

'Boy or girl?' he asked.

'Another boy,' she said, and he remembered from her letter she had wanted a girl.

There was a sound that made him turn. In the dark corner of the shed there was an actual cot, and in it a child sitting up, sleepily rubbing his eyes.

'That's Heinrich,' his daughter's voice said, and William saw a tiny replica of himself, who gazed at him and began to cry.

~

It was a busy twenty-four hours, but by the following day Elizabeth was installed in an upstairs bedroom of the German Arms Hotel, with a trained nurse brought from Adelaide in attendance. The children were in cots in the adjoining room, with an English-speaking village girl engaged to care for them. William himself occupied a room at the end of the hall, after having been driven back to Adelaide, where he engaged the services of a leading physician. He kept the hired landau and its driver, and billeted him at one of the smaller Hahndorf inns. It was costing him a considerable amount, and he sent a telegram to his bank for more money.

The Adelaide doctor had charged an exorbitant fee, and after a long and careful examination had diagnosed anaemia and fatigue, but found no evidence of septicaemia.

'She's simply exhausted,' he told William. 'She had her second child far too soon after the first. No rest at all, and as for working picking grapes . . .' He shook his head at the thought. 'It's all very well for these peasant women. They could drop one, and go on chopping wood,' he said, although there were no peasant women and little wood chopping in his exclusive Goodwood practice. He prescribed a tonic and complete rest, recommending the local practitioner, Doctor Boettcher, as perfectly capable of handling the case.

With some reluctance, William accepted this, and the mild, middle-aged German doctor visited daily. As he explained to William, he should have been called to see Elizabeth in the weeks prior to her birth, but many of the farming community were so poor, that the doctor was only called as a last resort.

'Are the Ritters very poor?' William enquired, for while their farm appeared almost destitute, he had no way of measuring their means by local standards. He meant to find out, and this medico appeared well informed and obliging.

'They're careful, frugal people,' Boettcher said. 'But this year they're poor. His grapes were too stressed to make wine, and his vintage last year was also disappointing.'

'I thought this was not a good wine-growing area,' William said. Boettcher gave him a speculative glance, and nodded. He realised he was being used by this wealthy visitor from the east to gather some information he required.

'It's not. He's a stubborn man - Johann. He'd be better pulling out the vines and planting turnips and cabbage.' He did not add that he had not been paid for delivering the child, or for his subsequent visit, and felt unable to ask for payment from Stefan, who had nothing, or from Ritter who was, as an Australian friend had once expressed, as tight as a fish's arsehole. As if suspecting this, William took out his wallet and extracted three five-pound notes, which was more money than the doctor had seen all month.

'How soon can my daughter travel?' He asked it while still holding the notes in his hand.

'To where?'

William hesitated. He had discussed his plan with no one, least of all Elizabeth herself. He needed more time to formulate the proposal.

'To Adelaide,' he said. 'I thought the change may be good for her. Or even perhaps a trip to Sydney, to visit her mother.'

'I would not recommend the longer trip just at present.'

'When? She'd have a sleeping compartment, and there'd be a nurse for the children.'

The doctor could sense his eagerness.

'In that case, within a month,' he said, expressing his thanks as he was handed the fifteen pounds.

'You'll give me your full account in due course,' William said, after arranging for him to continue to call. 'And I'd be obliged if you'd keep the matter of any travel to yourself. I've not yet raised the matter with my daughter - or her husband,' he remembered to add.

The doctor took his leave. He wondered if he was being paid so liberally for his medical opinion or his silence, and contemplated the cheering thought of several more weeks of daily visits. He could soon afford to think about that new buggy he needed.

Stefan came late each afternoon. On the first occasion, William had been in her room, talking with her. By chance he moved to shut the window, and saw him approaching along the street. He told Elizabeth it was time he left her to rest, and went downstairs. There was a guarded moment, as they met at the hotel entrance.

'How is she?'

'Sleeping,' William told him.

'I'll sit with her until she wakes up.'

'There are to be no visitors,' William said. 'Doctor's orders.'

Stefan gazed at him. *He is different*, William realised. He was nothing like the apprehensive boy he remembered from Sydney.

'You have every right to be angry,' Stefan said, 'but no right to keep me from seeing my wife.' He did not even wait for a reply, but moved past William, into the hotel and up the stairs.

William had no choice but to tolerate it. He dared not run the risk of alienating her, nor yet put her into a position where she would have to make a choice.

The days passed slowly for him. While he felt hopeful that what he planned would come to fruition, he had to curb his impatience. Meanwhile he took several journeys in the landau, with the informative driver, and talked to land agents and vignerons. It was a way of passing the time, and natural for him to show an interest in property values. He soon had a thorough knowledge of the prices and the worth of land in the Mount Lofty area and the valleys beyond. He composed a careful letter to Edith giving details of Elizabeth's progress, and wrote to Hannah every day.

He saw little of his two grandchildren. The baby slept a lot. Heinrich showed some signs of affection, and would smile and take tottering steps towards him whenever William was near, and once or twice he picked him up and felt a stir of fondness. But it was difficult for him to accept a grandchild of his own blood with the name of Heinrich Muller, so he kept his reserve, bided his time, and waited for his daughter to recover. Then they could discuss the future.

Elizabeth was improving daily, and Boettcher was well pleased. She began to take her meals downstairs. The small hotel dining room was immaculate, but it smelt of *Sauerkraut* and furniture polish, and he became heartily sick of the limited menu, the main items of which were *Wurst* and *Schnitzel.* One day he suggested they take the landau to the nearby town of Balhannah, where he bought her a pair of new shoes and a shawl, and they strolled together then enjoyed a lunch of salad and cheese in the garden of a local inn.

It was a picturesque spot, their table shaded by flowering vines, with a view across a valley to distant windmills. William knew the time had come to broach the subject.

'I'll have to go home at the end of next week, Lizzie,' he said almost casually, 'although I could wait a little longer if you'd like to come east with me.'

Elizabeth had suspected for some time that such an offer would be made. She had had many hours, recuperating in the hotel bedroom, to contemplate her father's course of action. That there would be one, she had no doubt. She had understood the angry disbelief with which he had seen their living quarters. She knew herself that she could not go back to that awful shed, or to the surly insensibility of the Ritter family.

'Did you hear what I said?' He looked at her. 'I'd like you to come home with me. You and the children.'

'For a visit?' she asked, although she knew the answer.

'For good,' William said.

'And my husband?' There was a distinct pause. Elizabeth would not allow it to continue. 'What about Stefan?'

'Any man who lets his wife live like that doesn't deserve her,' William answered. 'Why in the name of God didn't you write and tell me how bad things were?'

'Papa, does your offer include Stefan?' she persisted.

'No,' he said firmly, 'it doesn't.'

'Then let's not discuss it any further,' she answered, and although he had intended to remain calm, her attitude so infuriated him that he lost his temper.

'He's not worth bloody tuppence,' William snapped. 'He can't provide for you and the children. He's a useless no-hoper, and the sooner you're rid of him, the better.'

It was not how he had planned to discuss this, but he was too incensed to stop now.

'What has he ever done for you? He persuaded you to run

away, dragged you halfway across the country to slave on a farm and live in a tin humpy. As well as giving you two kids in double-quick time, and not having the sense or decency to know you were sick.'

They were the only people in the garden, but a maid from the kitchen heard his raised voice and looked out.

'Don't shout, Papa,' she said. There were so many half truths, so much distortion in the tirade, that she hardly knew how to begin to answer him. She knew she must remain composed.

'He didn't persuade me to run away,' she continued quietly. 'And he had no way of knowing his uncle was poor and mean. He did know I was sick; he was desperately worried and brought the doctor. I was the one who said we had no money to pay for more visits.'

'All you had to do was write to me. You'd have had money.'

'And a reply saying I told you so.'

'Well, I *did* tell you so.' He felt resentment again affecting his judgement. 'You could have married any bloke in Sydney. Anyone at all. But you had to go and choose this foreigner.'

It was true, he thought. She could have married into one of the leading local families, given herself status and position and provided him with a son-in-law to respect, and grandchildren of whom to be proud, instead of tying him to a bunch of peasants who could not even speak the language. He knew he was being unwise, but he could not help himself.

'You ran away,' he said bitterly, 'after all I did for you. How could you have done that, Lizzie? Hurt your mother and me, and run off like some lovesick kid?'

'How could you have lied to me, Father? Torn up his letters, hired a policeman to keep him away, as if he were a delinquent?

Deceived me and let me be unhappy, because *you* decided he wasn't suitable.'

'Well, by Christ he wasn't.' His voice rose again, and he paused to regain control. 'He couldn't provide. But you were too damn proud to write and ask for help. And now I want you to come home and start again. I want to give you and your children a decent life, and you still want to hang on to this bludger.'

Elizabeth put down her knife and fork, and stood up from the table. She looked down at her father.

'Stop calling him a bludger,' she said, her voice still quiet but sharper than he had ever heard it. 'I won't have it. I'm not going to leave him, no matter what you say.'

'You'd go back and live in that shed?' he asked.

'If I have to.' But her heart sank at the thought of it.

'Rather that, than come back to Sydney without him?'

She forced herself to nod. He shook his head in bewilderment.

'What in God's name do you see in him?'

I can't tell you, she thought. *How do I explain the way my blood runs hot and my body craves him when we're naked together. The joy I feel with his body inside mine, and the way we can make each other so happy. Perhaps that's just lust, but it's something I've never felt for anyone else, and there've been lots who've tried, Father, many more than you know. All those spoiled, rich young men – the ones you invited to my birthday parties, to tennis and dinners. But it's not only lust. We can talk without having to speak, just by looking at each other. In a room full of people, we can tell what the other is thinking. You wouldn't understand how he is sometimes discouraged and needs me, and I can feel despair and unhappiness and need him, and how we've never really had much of a chance to do more than struggle, and the one thing in my life I want is for us to have some sort of hope. No silver spoons, Father. No big gestures. No rich handouts. That would make us your hostages.*

Just a chance to make our own way – to find out if we can survive. I care about him, and I don't want to see him hurt, and that's not lust. That's love, but I can't tell you that, because you and Mama have never known love – I've realised it for a long time. I could use the word, but I don't think you know what it means.

She suddenly felt a great sadness for him. She put her hand on his, and said instead, 'Finish your lunch, Papa. I'll go for a walk. I'm sorry we had to quarrel.' She forced a smile. 'It was such a nice day.'

He watched her walk away, a slim, fair-haired girl in a rather shabby dress, and he knew that he'd lost her. He would have to make the alternate offer. She would not be coming home to enliven the gaunt Centennial Park house. If they went on living on the Ritter farm in that primitive shed, virtually as bonded servants, the marriage might ultimately collapse out of sheer misery.

On the other hand, he knew he could never allow it. In all conscience there was only one thing he could do for her now. But he fully intended to do it in his own way.

Chapter 11

'Segne, was Du uns bescheret hast.' Uncle Johann's voice solemnly carried across the dinner table and his wife and children dutifully chorused, 'Amen.' William sat midway along the scrubbed table, listening to the guttural grace, observing them all, the bare kitchen, the sparse helpings of dumplings on plates in front of them, the sudden movement to pick up spoons as soon as the blessing finished.

'Just a moment,' he said with quiet authority, and though they did not understand his words, the command in his voice demanded their attention. They had hardly recovered from their astonishment at his arrival a short time earlier, with a recuperated and radiant Elizabeth, who was wearing a new dress. Or the fact that he seemed to have recovered from his anger, and was sitting among them at the table, although he had refused the offer of a glass of schnapps.

William gazed at them, until they put down their spoons. They watched as he bowed his head, and they followed suit. Across the table, Stefan began to understand what his father-in-law intended.

'Merciful and bounteous God,' William began, 'we thank Thee for Thy food, which you have placed on this table to sustain us.

We, your servants, thank you for all manner of things.' William, who had not been inside a church for years, struggled to remember phrases to make it as interminable as the other had been, while beside him Elizabeth fought a desire to giggle. 'So for what we are about to receive, may we be truly grateful to God the father, God the son, and to the Holy Ghost and the Holy Spirit. Amen.'

'Amen,' said Elizabeth. The Ritter family all chorused the familiar word and prepared to eat.

'Wait,' William Patterson added in his most authoritative voice, and was again the focus of all their eyes. 'Stefan, I want you to translate to your uncle exactly what I am going to say. Do you understand me?'

'Yes,' Stefan said, realising it was the first time this man had ever addressed him by name.

William knew he had their attention; the meal was ignored.

'Tell him that my daughter is leaving this house, and you and the children are going with her. Tell him any debt you owed for your passage has been repaid, with interest.' Stefan hesitated. 'Tell him.'

He translated. There was a frigid silence, then Johann Ritter began to speak sharply in German.

'Tell him to shut up,' William's voice was like a whiplash, 'tell him to keep quiet and not interrupt.'

He waited until Stefan had spoken, and knew his words had been accurately interpreted by the indignation in Ritter's face. It was what he had planned, a calculated retaliation for their treatment of Elizabeth, to sit here and insult the man in his own house. Nor had he finished yet.

'Yesterday I purchased a piece of land. Twenty acres, with a house, and I am having a firm of lawyers prepare title of ownership in my daughter's name, with myself as trustee.' He was aware of Stefan's astonished gaze. 'The farm is not in this district. It is in a place called the Barossa Valley, some fifty miles to the north, an area which, I am reliably informed, is far better suited to grape growing and winemaking than here. Here, the soil is fit only for turnips.' Elizabeth smiled to herself. William looked around the table, relishing the effect he was creating. 'I chose there, not only because the earth is more fertile and the climate more agreeable, but because it is far enough away for my daughter to have nothing more to do with any of you.'

He turned from Johann Ritter, to Aunt Anna and *Grossmutter*, and there was no mistaking the animosity in his gaze.

'I want it understood that none of you, not one person in this family, will ever be welcome there.'

While Stefan was still translating this, William left the table and strode out, without having touched his meal.

Elizabeth rose from her seat. She saw their offended faces, the hostile stares that had always disconcerted her. They had disliked her from the start, for no reason. Well, now they had something to be resentful about. She felt free of them at last, felt a tremendous relief and great affection for her father.

'*Auf Wiedersehen*,' she said – to no one in particular – and walked out of the farmhouse for the last time.

'There are several conditions,' William said. At the German Arms Hotel an hour later they were discussing his plan. 'First of all, the property always remains in Elizabeth's name. Hers alone. If anything should ever happen to her, it reverts to me. Do you accept that?'

Stefan nodded. He knew he had no choice in the matter.

'Second – that Elizabeth visit us with the children. Not yet,' he anticipated her protest, 'but as soon as you're established and on your feet. I'll send the fares, and arrange for a nurse to travel with you to mind the children. Let's say – in a year. I don't think that's unreasonable. I'd like to go home able to tell your mother to expect you.'

'That is fair,' Stefan said, while Elizabeth was still hesitating.

'Very well, Papa,' she said eventually. 'A brief visit as soon as we're properly settled.'

'Not too brief,' he smiled, and she knew he had not given up hope of getting her back; he had just changed his tactics.

'My third condition is that I want your son – my grandson – called Henry, not Heinrich.'

There was a silence.

'Heinrich was my father's name,' Stefan answered. 'Our son has been christened to carry on that name.'

'Your father lived in Bavaria. My grandson will grow up here. I want him called Henry – is that clear?'

Stefan did not reply.

'Lizzie?' He appealed to her.

'It's not something you can insist on, Father. I'll discuss it with Stefan, and we'll make a decision.' She came to stand beside her husband, and for one of the rare times in his life, William Patterson felt ineffectual.

'I promise we'll consider your wishes in the matter,' she added, and he understood he would have to be content with that.

'Lastly,' he said, 'I'll give you enough money to stock the land, to buy vines or cattle or whatever you decide. Not a lot of money, but enough. I want you to have someone to help look after the children. I've talked to this German girl who likes them, and would be prepared to move with you. If you agree, Elizabeth, I'll offer her the job and make arrangements to pay her each month.'

Within a week it was settled. The girl, Sigrid, accompanied them. William hired an extra carriage, and they drove to Adelaide, where the legal documents were drawn up and witnessed, and the following day they headed north-west to Angaston and Tanunda, and the cluster of small towns enclosed by the hills that comprised the Barossa Valley.

People working in the vineyards looked up as the two vehicles passed. Elizabeth smiled and waved, and they waved back to her. Stefan saw spired churches and fertile fields with their orderly rows of vines. It was as if the old traditions of the Rhine Valley had been handed down from the first viticulturalists who had fled here half a century earlier. He felt a sense of excitement, and an affinity with this place he had never seen before.

When they crossed a wooden bridge over a creek, they saw the gently sloping land that led to the farmhouse. The pasture was pitted with weeds, and the vines unkempt. The house was small, needing paint. But to them it was a dream come true. While Elizabeth and Sigrid took the children inside to explore the house, Stefan tried to express his gratitude with stammered thanks, but was cut off abruptly.

'I don't want your thanks,' William said bluntly, 'because none of this was done for you. I want you to work this land, and make a living so you can give my daughter some kind of a decent life.'

'You'll be repaid for this - in time. Every penny.'

'I don't require that.'

'But I do,' Stefan said. '*I* require it, Mr Patterson. I insist on not accepting your charity.'

'The hell with you,' William looked at him angrily. 'Since when was a gift to a man's own daughter considered charity? You repay me by treating her properly, you hear – or by Christ you'll answer to me.'

With this as his farewell to Stefan, he walked across the land to the small three-bedroom house, and listened to Elizabeth's exclamations of pleasure as they inspected it. It was difficult to recognise as she enthused about the rather primitive and cramped farmhouse, that she had grown up in style and luxury, and then he thought of his austere house opposite the park, and how little he cared for it in comparison to the cottage he shared with Hannah. In that brief moment he almost understood his daughter.

The driver was waiting for him with the landau. The baby was asleep inside, with Sigrid minding him. Elizabeth held her first born, who smiled and reached out his arms towards William.

'He's fond of you, Papa. Kiss Heinrich.'

'Damn silly name. Promise to think about changing it.'

'Kiss him.'

William carefully kissed the child, who wanted to hug him.

'I'm always scared they'll break in half.'

'Not this one. He's tough. Takes after you.'

'Hmph,' he said, trying hard not to show his pleasure.

'He even looks a bit like you, I think.'

'Poor little bugger.'

Elizabeth laughed.

'You write,' William said, and blew his nose noisily. He kissed her and got into the landau, before he made a fool of himself.

'Goodbye, Papa.'

'Take care, Lizzie.'

He nodded abruptly to the driver, and the landau drove away.

As they crossed over the creek, he could see her there, still waving to him. He waved back, feeling an unbearable sense of loss, and saw her hand flutter a last time, then the trees hid her from his sight.

The following morning he left Adelaide to begin the long train journey home. For almost a month, his days had been spent with her, and he felt overwhelmed by loneliness. He was disappointed to be returning without her, but still nursed a secret hope that it would not be for long.

Chapter 12

Elizabeth could see Stefan down near the creek, his arms rising and falling, the sunlight glinting on the blade of the pick-axe as he tilled the new piece of land. Above him, in neat rows, their older vines were already heavy with grapes. In less than a month they would have their first precious harvest. She watched him for a time. He had removed his shirt, and his muscular, tanned body moved rhythmically, and even from this distance she felt a pleasant stirring at the sight.

He was almost unrecognisable from the boy on the ship whom she had pursued, initially out of boredom with other passengers and the advances of the preening officers – she could admit that to herself now. There was not only a physical difference; he had developed that on the Ritters' farm during their time at Hahndorf. It was a new and different Stefan, confident and assured, who felt at home here, was popular and friendly with their neighbours, and loved this vineyard with a possessive pride and a fierce determination to succeed.

In the first months, he had dug and cleared six of the weed-infested acres and planted new vines. He constructed a chicken coop, and they now had eggs, the manure as fertiliser, and a flourishing vegetable garden. He began work at daylight, and she usually took him a sandwich in the fields at lunchtime, and sat a while with him, knowing Heinrich and the new baby, whom they had christened Carl, were being well looked after by Sigrid. He worked all afternoon, rarely finishing until after twilight, and then they ate together by lantern light at the kitchen table.

These were the best hours of the day, when the children were in bed and Sigrid had gone to her own quarters, when they sat and talked and sometimes calculated their flimsy finances, and he helped her dry the dishes - a most unusual thing for a local husband to do. Then they washed at the tank stand behind the house and went eagerly to bed, their glowing flesh hungry for each other, their lovemaking once again uninhibited and delirious.

Elizabeth had never been so content. It seemed that her life now had a purpose. She had been indulged as the only child of a wealthy and fond father, pampered and waited on by servants in their large home, sent to Sydney's leading college for young ladies, and then on her Grand Tour. She had spent her seventeenth birthday at the Antico Martini in Venice. Her eighteenth would have been the occasion for a lavish ball at the new Hotel Australia, where her father planned to launch her socially by hiring the Wintergarden with its Palm Court orchestra, but by then she had fled and was living with Stefan over the shoemaker's shop, in the crowded and unpalatable end of town. Such a short time ago, yet it was part of another life.

She sometimes found it hard to believe she was barely twenty years old, the mother of two growing children whose piping voices could be heard as they played near the chicken enclosure. She walked to the corner of the verandah that Stefan had built on to the house, and watched them at play. Heinrich was now two years old, while Carl had recently had his first birthday. He was a plump and contented child, who, since his birth, had never given her a moment's trouble. He spent most of his time idolising and trying to follow his older brother. The children saw her, and ran to her, Heinrich scampering ahead, Carl tottering behind, managing not to fall over, as he reached her and clung to her skirt with his happy smile. She scooped them both up, and felt a great wave of love as she hugged them.

They had chosen not to comply with her father's request to change Heinrich's name. Stefan refused to contemplate calling him Henry, and she now felt indifferent about it. In the harsh Ritter household, where she rarely heard an English word, the constant use of a foreign name for her son had depressed and disturbed her. Here it no longer had that effect. She did not mind the times when Sigrid lapsed into German, or when friends from Bethany or their close neighbours Gerhardt and Eva-Maria Lippert came to visit and occasionally conversed in their native tongue. Stefan discouraged it; he always replied in English, making it clear Elizabeth must not be excluded.

She felt, in addition to her happiness, very secure. It seemed as if nothing could disturb the serenity of their life together.

One afternoon, Gerhardt and Eva-Maria delivered a crate of young hens for their new chicken yard, and stayed to supper afterwards. They ate on the verandah, by lantern light. It was a typical meal of the kind they often shared; soup, then *Wurst*, cheese, their own home-grown tomatoes, and wine. They had brought a copy of the German language newspaper, the *Australische Zeitung*, and Stefan was frowning over it.

'What does it say?' she asked.

'The war in South Africa.' It was Gerhardt who answered. 'The British fare badly. Their troops are surrounded by the Boers at a place called Ladysmith.'

'It's far away,' Eva-Maria said. 'Nothing to do with us.'

'Nothing? The stupid German government has declared they support the Boers.'

'So?' Their friends enjoyed nothing more than a lively spat. 'We belong here. We're not ruled by the German government.'

'I agree with Eva-Maria.' Stefan put the paper aside. 'It's all on the other side of the world, Gerhardt. Stop worrying.'

'He likes to worry,' his wife chided. 'If there is nothing to worry about, and everything is fine, he worries it might not last.'

They all laughed, even Gerhardt. A companionable laughter.

'So . . . I am wrong,' he said. 'It is a little war, a long way off.'

'Good. Now drink your wine.'

'But remember one thing – the newspaper says German shops in Adelaide had their windows smashed last week. Australia has sent troops to South Africa, and some people think we Germans secretly want the Boers to win. They don't like it.'

Eva-Maria picked up his glass and handed it to him. 'How long have you been in this country?'

'You know how long. When we were first married.'

'How long is that? Or have you forgotten?'

'How can I forget, when you always remind me of the anniversary day? Twelve years.'

'And what nationality are we?'

'Australian now. Naturalised.'

'Goodo,' she said, producing a broad Australian accent that made Elizabeth giggle, 'in that case, mate, drink up. And shut up.'

Elizabeth liked Eva-Maria better than anyone in the district. Though she was older, at thirty-five a full fifteen years Elizabeth's senior, they had formed an immediate friendship from the day twelve months ago when Gerhardt and Eva-Maria had walked across from their farm bringing a basket of food to share with their new neighbours.

Twelve months. Carl's recent first birthday had been an uneasy reminder of her promise to take the children on a visit to Sydney. *Within a year*, her father had said, and she had agreed. She had written to her mother and confirmed the promise, without arranging an exact date. There had been one of her mother's rapid replies, suggesting Christmas would be perfect, or if not, then early in the New Year. Elizabeth had written back to explain this was the worst time for them, their busiest period. The vines were harvested in February, and afterwards there would be a great deal of work to be done, crushing and bottling. She promised the visit would be soon, but she could not say exactly when.

The truth was, she did not want to leave this place and Stefan, even for a brief time. Life was so good here. So simple and satisfying. Though she had missed her father deeply when he left, and was grateful for all he had done for them, the animosity between him and Stefan remained a divisive factor that troubled her. If she went home to visit, however briefly, this would be rekindled; she knew that. It would always be there, an undercurrent between them. Which was why she had delayed until now, reluctant to set a date that would commit her.

Now she knew she would have to write and tell them it was no longer possible. Certainly not in the foreseeable future.

~

'Another child.' Edith handed him the letter, and he read it in silence. 'You wouldn't think after the last trouble that she'd want another.'

William shared her dismay. If she had only just discovered she was pregnant, as the letter suggested, it would be late in the year before the baby was born. Then a time to recover, and after that the blasted harvest again. Another year or more before she could make the journey to Sydney.

'I had her room redecorated,' Edith said, and he looked at her with sudden compassion. He did not know this. 'And the large one at the end of the hall picked out as a nursery.'

'I'm sorry. Perhaps she'll be able to come, once this child's born. After a brief convalescence.' It was a shock to have this rare insight into the extent of her loneliness, and he did not want to mention the harvest. But he did not need to.

'No,' Edith shook her head. 'Then there'll be the harvest.'

'Well, after that.'

'I doubt it, William. After that there'll be something else. I have a strange feeling there'll always be something more important.'

'Would you like to go there? Visit her?'

'She hasn't asked me.'

'I'll write and suggest it.'

'No, please don't,' Edith said. 'Then they'd feel obliged to agree, and we'd all be most uncomfortable. Besides, from what you've told me of the house, there'd be no room. It would mean people having to share. I'd be a nuisance. And anyway, I've never liked travel.'

He could sense her bitter disappointment, but knew of no way to console her. He wished he could, but they had grown too far apart.

~

Chapter 13

Elizabeth screamed. Frau Fischer, the midwife, nodded encouragingly, and said in *Barossa Deutsch* to push down more, push hard, and Eva-Maria held her hands and translated the instruction.

'Tell her I *am* pushing hard,' Elizabeth gasped. 'It's worse than the other times. Who said it gets easier with each baby?'

'Some man,' Eva-Maria said, which made her laugh, until the next contraction gripped her. This was the worst agony of all; she felt as if she would die.

Outside, Stefan could hear the screams. He had been chased from the house by Frau Fischer, after protesting that he wanted to help. He'd been tartly told that he'd given all the help necessary nine months ago, and to get out, because there was nothing more useless in the act of childbirth than an anxious father worried by a few screams. He paced outside the new fermenting shed he had built, sharing her anguish with frightened and helpless frustration.

Gerhardt Lippert came from the back of the house, carrying a lantern and a cup of coffee.

'Drink it.'

'Who's looking after Heinrich and Carl?' Stefan asked him.

'Sigrid's looking after them. Who else would be looking after them?'

'But where are they?'

'I took them all to our house. Now drink the coffee and relax. Stop making everybody so nervous.'

Stefan tried to drink the scalding sweet liquid. 'What do you think?' he asked Gerhardt.

'What do I think about what?'

'A boy or a girl?'

'I think it's sure to be one or the other. Now drink.'

They gradually became aware of the total silence from the house. It was far more unnerving than the screams. Then there was the faint cry of a new-born child.

'Ohh Christ,' Stefan whispered, and dropped the cup. The hot liquid splashed on his boots, but he didn't notice. He ran to the window of the bedroom and rapped urgently on it. The window was pushed up. Eva-Maria looked out, exhausted and terse.

'Stefan, we're busy.' Then she relented and kissed him. 'It's a little girl.'

'Elizabeth?'

'Elizabeth's worn out. She's had a hard time.'

'But she's all right? Please say she's all right.'

'She's all right. Truly.'

'Thank God.'

He felt weak with relief. He had barely realised, until now, how afraid he had been. Through the last months of the pregnancy he had been possessed by fear. He turned to relay the news, and realised Gerhardt was already there beside him.

'A girl.'

'I heard. *Ich gratuliere.*'

They gripped hands, then hugged each other. Stefan looked up at the crescent moon, and the sky full of stars above. He threw wide his arms and shouted with joy.

'*Ein Mädchen.*' He flung his arms around Gerhardt again. 'A girl. It's wonderful. She's to be called Maria. If she was a boy we thought we'd call her Gerhardt.'

'I'm glad she's a girl. Much better a girl is called Maria than she is called Gerhardt. Now I think I am going to pour you a great big brandy – because I need one.'

'Maria. It's a nice name,' Hannah said, reading the letter, and smiling. 'She sounds so happy. A different girl.'

William moodily sipped his aperitif. She glanced at him.

'Aren't you pleased? She always wanted a girl.'

'Yes, of course. It's just – it means another six months before we see her. Edith's upset.'

'I'm sorry. But it's nice she's happy – isn't it?'

There was another silence.

'If she is happy, I can't understand it,' he said. 'The place is a primitive farm, an ordinary little house and a few wretched acres. In her letters she makes it sound like the bloody Garden of Eden.'

'But my darling, she's in love. That's exactly what it is.'

'They work their guts out for a few tons of grapes. Ninety bottles of wine last harvest. Is that what you'd call a raging success?'

'Only their second harvest. Give them time.'

'Dammit,' William said abruptly, 'whose side are you on?'

Hannah considered her reply, before she answered. 'Theirs, I think.'

'I see,' he said coldly, showing a rare anger towards her.

She knew she was on delicate ground, but was not prepared to be intimidated. 'You know me, William. I speak my mind.'

'I've always been aware of that. But I didn't bring her up to live so far away, with a bunch of foreigners.'

'Do you have a choice?'

'She's only twenty-one. A child.'

'Hardly. She has three of her own.'

'Don't keep reminding me. I'm too young to be a grandfather, Hannah, even once – let alone three times.'

'You haven't really given up trying to get her back.'

'What do you mean by that?'

'If you could break up that marriage, you would.'

He put down his drink, unfinished. She watched him collect his hat and coat.

'I can see you'd rather I didn't speak my mind.'

'When did that ever stop you?' William muttered.

'Then accept the situation you've created.'

'What do you mean, I've created?'

'It's thanks to you – however unpalatable that may be – that they're happy. Write and tell her you're pleased – about the new baby and the harvest. Ninety bottles of wine. Tell her you're proud of her and you congratulate Stefan.'

'Don't be bloody ridiculous.'

'That's what I'd do.'

'I daresay.'

He went towards the front door.

'I'm sorry you're so angry with me,' Hannah said.

'I'm not angry,' William insisted.

'You sound it. You look it,' she replied.

'Dammit,' he shouted furiously, '*I am not the slightest bit angry.*'

'That's good.' Hannah smiled.

He took his hat and coat. 'And if I am angry, it won't last. You know perfectly well it won't – and you know why.'

'Why?'

'Because I'm in love with you,' he almost snapped, and walked out of the house, slamming the door behind him.

He had never said it before, and Hannah was astonished at how deeply she was moved by this stormy, unromantic declaration.

A week later he told her he had written to Elizabeth.

'I said I was happy to hear about the baby girl. And that Maria was a nice name.'

'And Stefan? Any message to him?'

'I just said that ninety bottles of wine was a fair harvest.'

'It's a start. She'll be pleased. Well done, my darling.'

'There's a concert at St James' Hall tomorrow night. Will you come with me?'

'That wouldn't be very discreet.'

'Damn discretion,' William said. 'You were the one who told me a politician should be seen to patronise the arts.'

'But not in the wrong company.'

'Please, Hannah?'

She was about to agree, when they heard the doorbell ring.

'Are you expecting anyone?' he asked.

'Certainly not.'

Hannah put on a negligee and a discreet housecoat, and went downstairs. She opened the front door, and there was a man waiting there, already framing apologies for disturbing her. She recognised him, and knew at once that something terrible had happened.

The baby was asleep. Carl was being minded by Sigrid, who had become a part of the family, and Heinrich was out among the vines where Stefan was doing the autumn pruning. He had built Heinrich a tiny wooden handcart, a replica of his own into which all the cuttings were thrown. In an hour she would collect him, and put both boys down for their afternoon rest, although Heinrich had reached the age when daytime rests were strenuously resisted as being only for babies. He was an active, bright boy, with an engaging smile. He was going to be tall. And there was something else.

She had first noticed it when he was much younger, and wondered if it was her imagination, but now with each passing month, she could see the growing resemblance to her father. On his third birthday they had taken him to town, to the photographic studio, and had his portrait taken. She had sent it to her parents, but as yet had no reply. Her mother had written far less since the postponement of her visit. She decided she must write again, and agree on a date to soon bring the children. Though the days passed with such enjoyment, she kept delaying the commitment.

Heinrich came running towards the house, pointing to the road across the creek. She saw Gerhardt in his pony and trap on his way home from Nuriootpa. He called to her, waving a letter he had collected for them at the post office.

'Can I see Uncle Gerhardt?' Heinrich asked, and Carl who had heard came running around the verandah.

'Me too, Mama.'

'All right,' she told Heinrich, 'but don't leave Carl behind.' He immediately raced off, leaving Carl to totter in his wake.

'Don't leave me behind,' Carl wailed, then tripped over, turned back to look at her as if to burst into tears, but thought better of it. He then ran towards Gerhardt, who was already opening a bag of boiled lollies he kept under the seat, a fact which both children knew well. Gerhardt distributed one to each of them, and gave them a hug. He called to Elizabeth.

'Don't forget, you all come to our house for dinner on Sunday.'

'We'll be there.'

They exchanged waves. She watched as he pretended to put the bag away, then surreptitiously handed each of them another lolly before he drove off. He and Eva-Maria had no children of their own; one of the many things that bound both couples so closely was the Lipperts' genuine love for the boys, and now for the new baby who had been christened Maria in the Bethany church, and who was their goddaughter.

The letter was from her father. She could tell at once by the bold handwriting, and after Sigrid had collected the children for their rest, she sat on the verandah step to read it.

My dear Elizabeth,

I don't know how to phrase this, but please prepare yourself for dreadful news. Your mother has had a very serious accident, and for some days was not expected to live. She suffered a dizzy spell, and fell from the upstairs balcony, causing severe injuries. I know it will come as a terrible shock, but there was little point in telegraphing you until we had more information, and now I feel it is better expressed in a letter than alarming you with a telegram.

Doctor Fairfax says she will recover, but it is certain she will never walk again. He suggested that I took a second opinion, which I have done, but unfortunately the diagnosis is unchanged.

Please keep your promise and visit us. I know the baby made that difficult, but I miss you deeply, and I am sure it would cheer your mother, and aid her recovery to know that she would see you soon.

With love, Papa.

'I can't cry,' she said to Stefan that evening, 'that's the awful part. I wish I could. But it feels as if it happened to someone I once knew. Someone I didn't know well enough.'

Stefan kept his arms around her, trying to comfort her. The moonlight filtered through the window, and lay across the flimsy sheet which covered their bodies; the night was strangely still and oppressive for autumn.

'Poor Mama. She was always rather afraid of Papa, and often unhappy, and I'm sure I made her unhappy, too.'

She suddenly realised she was talking of her mother in the past tense, as if she were dead, not merely crippled for life. She started to sob at last, the sound of it a shock to Stefan; it was so harsh and melancholic, as if her confessed lack of love for this stranger who was her mother made her suffering unendurable.

It was arranged that she should go the following month, as soon as her mother was home. Elizabeth wrote to her father to this effect, and received his reply enclosing first-class tickets. But there was an additional delay, when he telegraphed to advise that Edith was not yet well enough to leave hospital, and thus it was two months later, July 1900, when she finally took a coach to Adelaide and, accompanied by Sigrid and the children, began the long train journey across three states. They spent a night in Melbourne, staying at the Windsor Hotel, Elizabeth acutely aware of the luxurious contrast to her last visit. The next day another train took them as far as the border town of Albury, where they passed through customs and changed onto a New South Wales express.

It was four days in all before the train clattered through the crowded inner suburbs of Sydney, past the backs of terraces and endless tiny fenced yards and rows of outdoor privies, the untidy and squalid landscape that welcomed the traveller to the continent's first city.

The children were exhausted by the immensity of the distance. Sigrid was full of wonder as she gazed out of the window at the cluttered houses. Elizabeth, despite her fatigue, felt a growing excitement. It was three and a half years since she had last passed these same shabby tenements that backed onto the railway line, but then she was running away from the scene of her childhood, pregnant, frightened and almost penniless.

Now, despite her reluctance to leave Stefan, there was a sense of anticipation as the train steamed into the cavernous Central Station. She saw William on the platform, scanning the carriages, spotting her with a wide smile, opening the carriage door and enveloping her in his arms. Then the introductions, the children shy, her father organising a porter and making their way out to the waiting carriage. Forbes, the same dear old Forbes, welcoming her and making much of the children and how growed-up-they-were, and she suddenly remembered they shared a secret; it had been Forbes who had given her the note from Stefan with his address in Clyde Street, and that act had altered her life, and as if Forbes realised this he gave her a smile as though to say he was glad it had worked out well, after all.

Then the familiar streets; lower George and Castlereagh, with their dingy shops and dwellings above them, like the one she lived in over the bootmaker's shop; Hyde Park where she could still vividly recall the bunch of flowers Stefan had gathered for her, and the rush home to make love afterwards; Oxford Street with its grander terraced homes; the fine stone building of the Victoria Barracks; the overblown and slightly grandiose Paddington Town Hall.

Strange but familiar sights; a few years had brought little change. She pointed out landmarks to Sigrid and the children, while her father watched them all and Heinrich sat on his knee and didn't, after a puzzled first moment, voice any objection to being called Henry.

In a moment they were at the edge of Centennial Park, then the carriage turned in through the familiar iron gates, past the garden, colourful with dahlias and hibiscus, and the last tinted leaves of the liquidambars - only the tennis court was unmarked and looking forlorn, as if the players had long since gone away. The servants were waiting for them on the front steps - Mrs Forbes and the household staff, all fussing and exclaiming over the children, who loved it, and began to show off outrageously.

Her mother was sitting in the gaunt living room, a rug across her knees. Elizabeth knelt and kissed her, and realised tears were trickling down, wetting her own cheeks, as Edith tried to speak. And then the two older children were brought forward to be introduced, and she held Heinrich up to be kissed. He smiled and clutched his grandmother.

'Grandma,' he said in his small clear voice, 'are you crying?'

'Yes, darling,' she said, blowing her nose.

'Are you sad, Grandma?'

'No, Heinrich. I'm happy.'

His face looked puzzled as he contemplated this. Then he gazed at her. 'If you cry when you're happy, Grandma, what do you do when you're sad?'

They all smiled indulgently, at such youthful observation, except for Edith, who cried even harder. She reached out and captured him, tears cascading, her face transformed and alive with joy.

Later, in her room, Elizabeth no longer felt tired. It was exciting to be home. It was pleasant to hear her children being praised, to look at her father and see his pride and love, even to observe her stricken mother and be aware of her happiness that they were there at last. It was nice to undress in a room that she did not have to clean, to sit at table and eat off dishes that she did not have to wash, to walk on the soft lawns and along the remembered paths of her childhood.

Chapter 14

'Look at them, the Right Honourable Ratbags opposite,' the Opposition spokesman Hubert Mountjoy thundered. 'Humbugs and hypocrites.' Jeers and cheers interrupted him. 'Look at all the oily, odious, over-privileged opportunists, the objectionable, overbearing old farts . . .'

William rose to his feet. 'Mr Speaker, I object to the word *old*,' he said, amid laughter that became applause. William quelled it with a gesture. 'The flatulent Mr Mountjoy, who, despite his claim of convict ancestry has absolutely no courage of his convictions, fulminates against those of us in this house who support Federation. I assure this chamber, and all the doubting Thomases, all the mice and the minnows and even the Mountjoys –' he had to pause for renewed laughter '– that the people are ready. They have made their choice. It took two referendums, but the mandate is now clear. They want – no – they *demand* an end to colonialism, they demand our promises be kept, and that in a few months from now, on the first day of the new century, we become one people, one nation.'

It was a speech like many others he had made before, but today it had an added verve. Elizabeth was in the parliamentary chamber, the first time she had ever seen him here. Not since the day when he had openly attacked his former leader, George Reid, pillorying him as 'Yes-No Reid', a fraud who opposed Federation while claiming to support it, had he shown such zest and energy. On that occasion William had demolished the paunchy Premier and severed his links with the Free Trade group. Reid had lost office soon afterwards, and there were many who claimed the speech had accelerated his downfall. Mountjoy was a far easier target.

'If the Gentleman – and I use the word with extreme caution – chooses to align himself with the Honourable Mr "Yes-No" Reid and other dullards and dinosaurs who would like to emulate King Canute and hold back the tide, I suggest this House repair to the nearest beach and let the waves of history wash them into obscurity.' He looked at the furious face of James North; they were now on opposite sides and no longer associated. 'I invite you others, timid or dominated, who would have us remain an imperial realm of Mother England, to join them. Command the flood of public opinion to subside. Order it to ebb, to recede, to stop,' he taunted. 'But beware. This is a surging current, a stream of belief in favour of change for the future. Ignore it and it may drown you.'

He resumed his seat. In the public gallery, Elizabeth looked down and caught her father's eye. She smiled, enormously proud of him, impressed by his wit and his passionate support for Federation. She noticed a well-dressed, attractive woman opposite who was also smiling in approval. Their glances met.

Hannah looked away, to avoid drawing attention to herself. It was the first time she had actually seen Elizabeth. A photograph William had shown her of a sixteen-year-old in school uniform had barely done her justice. *What a truly beautiful girl she is*, Hannah thought. *I never realised quite how lovely.*

'I really enjoyed it,' Elizabeth said the following morning. 'So did everyone else.'

She and her father were having morning tea in the study. The children were outside, playing near Edith in her wheelchair.

'You must come and watch again,' William said.

'If there's time, Papa,' Elizabeth reminded him.

His heart sank as she said it. It was the third mention of her return to South Australia in as many days.

'You've only been here two months,' he said carefully. 'Your mother really loves those children. It's made such a difference to her.'

Elizabeth nodded. She knew Edith's entire day was devoted to them, in particular to Heinrich, displaying an affection for him she had never been able to show her own daughter. It was a wry thought.

'I've never seen her so happy,' William continued, as if he had guessed what was in her mind.

'Nor have I, Papa.'

'Then you can't be thinking of leaving us just yet.'

The prospect of it filled him with dismay. He had not realised how a house could be transformed, the way this gothic Victorian relic had been transformed by the presence of his daughter and the two boys. The baby, Maria, he discounted; she was a pretty little thing, but it was the boys who made the difference. Their childish laughter and the clatter of their feet up and down the stairs had caused concerned frowns among the staff, but when Mrs Forbes had scolded them for their high spirits, Edith had promptly rebuked her, and made it clear they were to have free rein without restrictions. It was an extraordinary *volte-face* for Edith, and because of it the house was filled with happy juvenile voices, and was alive the way it had never been in the past, not even when Elizabeth herself was growing up here, and certainly not in the cold unforgiving years since her departure.

William watched his daughter sipping her tea, her long skirt and white linen shirt-waisted blouse, with her fair hair tied back, making her look absurdly young. Elizabeth could have been home from school; it was scarcely credible she was the mother of the two boisterous young rascals turning somersaults outside in the garden, and the third child asleep in the pram. He would give anything to keep them all here. It was one of the reasons why he had not felt able to tell her the truth about Edith.

For the fall that crippled her had not been an accident. Edith had tried to kill herself.

It had been Forbes at the door of the house in Paddington, who had stumbled an apology to Hannah, and managed to convey that he was looking for Mr Patterson, because there had been a dreadful accident.

He did his best to be circumspect by saying that he may have come to the wrong house, but if she should know – or had any means of conveying the news – would she please do so. Hannah simply ran upstairs and called him, and ten minutes later he was at home, watching the attendants bringing Edith's crumpled body on a stretcher and carefully placing it in the back of the horse-drawn ambulance.

Doctor Fairfax was already there. Mrs Forbes had summoned him. Charles Fairfax was a prominent physician, and a business colleague. They had mutual dealings in property, but on this occasion he had been coldly clinical and brusque.

'They'll take her to Sydney General. I'll let you know when there's any news.'

'What chance has she got?'

'Not much. Half the bones in her body are broken.'

William had shuddered, as he looked up towards the balcony of her room, then at the spot where she had landed. It was a pile of stones the gardeners had left there to construct a rockery.

'How could she have fallen?'

'Who said she fell?' Fairfax replied quietly. They were alone, out of earshot of the servants.

'But Forbes said it was an accident.'

'Let's talk about this later, William. In the meantime, I hope your staff are loyal. I told them what I'll tell the hospital, and the press if necessary, that in my opinion Edith suffered a dizzy spell and lost her balance. She consulted me recently, to complain of attacks of dizziness.'

'Did she?' William had asked, grasping at this straw.

'No,' was the doctor's curt answer.

That night, in the privacy of his rooms, Charles Fairfax was uncompromisingly blunt.

'We've done all we can. She may recover consciousness, but at this stage no one can say.'

'Do everything possible, Charles. No expense spared.'

'That's hardly the point. If she has no will to live, then she'll certainly die. It's not the first time she's tried to kill herself.'

William stared at him blankly.

'Not the first time?'

'She tried to take an overdose of laudanum some months ago.'

'Where did she get the laudanum?'

'I prescribed it for her. She had a kidney complaint. When I found out what she'd done, fortunately in time to take measures, I then replaced it with a less dangerous drug.'

'I didn't even know she had a kidney complaint,' William said, feeling shocked and bewildered.

'Of course you didn't.'

'Why the hell didn't you tell me about this attempt?'

'She begged me not to.'

'But, Charles, surely I had a right to know.'

'Edith was my patient,' Fairfax said. 'I had to take her wishes into account.'

'Why wouldn't she allow me to be told?'

'She's afraid of you, William.' Fairfax was blunt, choosing his words without discretion. 'She's always been afraid. She was frightened you might use the information to get her committed.'

'Good God. Jesus Christ Almighty!'

He was aghast. The idea made him want to be physically ill. No matter how joyless their marriage had become, she surely couldn't have imagined him capable of such an act.

'If she could believe that, she must think I'm a monster.'

Fairfax could see his distress, and became more sensitive.

'She's been very disturbed. Losing Elizabeth. Your marriage, well, I don't have to tell you. She hasn't been entirely rational.'

'Jesus Christ,' was all he could mutter.

He was terribly shaken. Lying close to death in hospital, Edith had a far greater impact on him than ever in their life together. He felt an overwhelming sense of guilt. And an impending concern.

'It'll get out,' William said with certainty. 'These things always do.'

The House had been sympathetic about the accident.

'We express our deep sympathy to this most gracious lady,' said the Speaker of the Assembly, who had never met her.

'A tragic blow,' the new Premier Sir William Lyne was reported saying in the *Sydney Morning Herald*. He took the opportunity to commend his Honourable friend Mr Patterson as a man of courage and principle, which was to be expected, since his Honourable friend's ambush of George Reid had helped him gain the leadership.

In other quarters there were different murmurs. Some said it was known William had been consistently unfaithful to his wife for years, and had a mistress; there was even, in certain circles, a whisper that the fall had not been accidental. Some in Parliament who had felt the lash of his tongue subscribed to this rumour. He was aware of gossip and speculative glances.

Through all this, Dr Fairfax remained stalwart.

'A dizzy spell,' he told all and sundry, and persisted with it when Edith returned home in a wheelchair.

William often wondered when he would pay for the favour the doctor had done him. In his world, no such considerations were granted without expectations in return. But in this he was apparently mistaken. Fairfax had not raised the matter since, and apart from William offering him occasional stock market tips, and asking him to make one visit to the house in Paddington when Hannah was indisposed with a chill, they rarely met now.

Hannah was the only other person who knew the truth. He had not intended to confide in anyone, but found it impossible to bear the burden alone. He was racked with guilt and torment at causing Edith such acute unhappiness. The senseless violence of her act had brought a deep remorse. Often at night, unable to sleep, he bedevilled himself with her state of mind, her fear of him, unable to shut out the vivid images of her climbing over the iron rail of the balcony to hurl herself into oblivion.

Telling Hannah had been a necessary relief, but it had been a mistake. It had only transferred the guilt.

'I feel sick about it,' Hannah had said. 'I'm to blame.'

'Don't say that,' William insisted. 'Stop it. I won't have you say that.' He came and put his arms around her. 'I'm to blame, not you. Never say that again.'

'But – what if she knew about us?'

'She didn't know. She has no idea. And our marriage was over long ago, before you and I ever met. Don't you ever say or think that again, do you hear me?'

For a time he could not allay her feeling of responsibility; her own remorse was like a barrier between them, and he began to fear he might lose her. He spent every possible moment he could with her; it became imperative to make her realise she was blameless. She was the one real constant in his life. The thought of being without her was not something he could contemplate.

Since Elizabeth's arrival he had seen her less, reverting to his former arrangement of afternoon visits. Hannah had insisted on this. He needed time with his daughter and grandchildren, and the visit should not be marred by any hint of another woman in his life.

'Papa?'

'Mmm,' he said, disturbed from his reverie.

'Mrs Forbes said there's a telephone call for you.'

He rose reluctantly, and went into the hall to answer it. He had been persuaded to install the instrument, now so many business people in the city were subscribers, but did not like it. He never felt comfortable speaking to someone, without being able to see their face.

'It's Dr Fairfax,' Mrs Forbes said.

He picked up the pedestal.

'Charles,' he said loudly into the mouthpiece, and in the living room Elizabeth looked up from her newspaper, amused by his well-known antipathy towards the invention. She went back to reading the disturbing news about Australian casualties in the Boer War, and on the opposite page the alarming resurgence of bubonic plague in many inner areas of Sydney.

'What is it?'

William was guarded, concerned the doctor should choose to telephone him. He had not been entirely at ease with him, ever since Edith's fall.

'I think we should meet.'

'When?'

'Today. As soon as possible.'

'I'm due at the House later,' William said, and began to have an anxious feeling when he heard the other's reply.

'I wouldn't go there. Not today. Most certainly not until we've met.'

'Do you mind telling me why?'

'I'd rather not,' the doctor answered. 'Not on this machine. I'll talk to you in person.'

'Very well. I'll expect you here.'

'No. Not your home or mine.'

'Then where?' He was certainly apprehensive now. Fairfax was not the kind of man to behave like this. 'Where shall we meet?'

'Somewhere discreet. I recall a house in Paddington, where I attended a person of your acquaintance. Could we meet there?'

'I daresay,' William replied. 'How soon?'

'An hour,' the doctor said, and hung up.

The rats had been multiplying and running amok all summer. They proliferated in the steep sandstone streets between the western quay and the wharves of Darling Harbour; they bred in the primitive and unsanitary backyard toilets; they feasted on food in open butchers' yards and ran unchecked in the fish and fruit markets. They prospered in the filth and garbage of the city hovels, formed colonies in the burgeoning warehouses of Sussex Street, and spread southward into the haphazard chaos of Campbell and Wexford Streets, and the crowded slum neighbourhoods huddled around the Belmore markets.

A ship docked – it could have been from South China or a Pacific island – and the rats that came ashore brought with them an epidemic that fed on the stench of summer drains, creating terror and contaminating the city.

Bubonic plague was first identified in China in 1893. It was reported in Mauritius and Noumea in 1899, and reached Sydney early in 1900. The first victim, an inhabitant of Ferry Street, died in January. His immediate neighbours were quarantined, but the disease spread and rampaged along the waterfront, and there was panic. Within months over three hundred people caught the disease; more than a hundred died. Many residents fled their homes, and took trains to the remote but safer Blue Mountains. The government, accused of apathy and bungling, set up barricaded areas where the plague was rife, and began lime-washing the festering streets. In the worst affected localities, buildings were burnt or demolished. A committee charged with the administration of Public Health appointed George McCredie, an engineer, and the Chief Medical Officer, J. Ashburton Thompson, to stamp out the epidemic.

Rat catchers were hired, and hundreds of unemployed men clamoured for the jobs. Rats by the thousand were caught and burnt, the daily newspapers recording the numbers. Fearing the main enemy was sewage and silt, this was dredged from dock areas, while a massive amount of garbage was collected and dumped far out to sea. Despite these measures bubonic plague remained, and although the first wave of hysteria subsided with the onset of winter, public panic was never more than a headline away.

William had reluctantly contemplated writing to Elizabeth to suggest she delay her visit, but a lull in the outbreak made him gratefully reconsider. By then, all infected areas had been identified and isolated, and when she arrived in Sydney it seemed the plague was virtually over. Nevertheless, there were still occasional reported cases, and McCredie's rat catchers continued to patrol like vigilantes. For this reason, William made certain Elizabeth and the children went nowhere near the danger spots, the fetid and barricaded streets of the Rocks and the inner regions of the city. Their outings were strictly confined to the open spaces of Centennial Park or the shores of the harbour.

It had been barely a week ago that the picture had radically changed. With unseasonably warm, almost heat-wave conditions, there was a sudden massive increase of admissions to hospitals. Each day the number of reported victims rose steeply; the death toll climbed causing renewed alarm. This apprehension increased as the infected area widened to the suburbs. There were cases reported in Waterloo and Glebe; more ominously, some in Paddington and Waverley. With the approach of a new summer, speculation grew that the plague might rage unchecked for months to come, and many more areas would have to be evacuated.

BUBONIC PLAGUE. FURTHER OUTBREAKS FEARED was the major morning headline in the *Sydney Morning Herald*, which sounded an alarm in a newspaper otherwise noted for its small story headings and its sobriety. This oldest and most respected of the state's dailies chose to print a bizarre advertisement, by which time the public mood verged on a consternation that was akin to hysteria.

GRIM BUBONIC PLAGUE
The Scourge of the East

Grim bubonic plague has marched with stealthy strides to these shores. The foe is at the door.

Public sanitary vigilance is imperative. Let the sewers be flushed, and every form of impurity swept away. Let the health of the community be maintained to the highest degree; but in addition let every individual be on the alert. The human body has the most perfect system of sewerage, defying the utmost art of man to rival.

A wise Creator has provided means for the eradication of all impure materials from the human body. DR MORSE's INDIAN ROOT PILLS have such a perfect combination of the best and most energetic remedies provided by a beneficent Providence for the true purpose of cleansing the whole system, 'flushing the sewers', rousing up the liver, kidneys, and the whole intestinal tract to their proper functions, that it is with the utmost confidence we recommend them to the public as a preventative of the fearful ravages of that dread disease – BUBONIC PLAGUE.

DR MORSE'S INDIAN ROOT PILLS

They stand alone as the Perfect Blood Purifier!

~

Hannah was awaiting William's arrival, and looked concerned. The doctor was already there.

'He's in the living room,' she said.

He kissed her and went to join Fairfax. William could see he was pale and upset.

'I cancelled all my appointments,' Fairfax said. 'I trust we can talk here without being overheard, or interrupted?'

'What the devil is it, Charles?' William was feeling more and more uneasy.

'McCredie. I knew the bloody man was going to be trouble.'

William looked at him, confused. Neither had welcomed the choice of the abrasive Scot, George McCredie to take charge of the plague campaign, and William had lobbied against the appointment. But that was months ago. He had to admit McCredie had tackled the job with enthusiasm, and until this new outbreak, with some success.

'What's he done?'

'You mean you don't know? It was announced by the Premier in the House late last night.'

'I wasn't there last night. I took Elizabeth to the theatre and we dined afterwards. For God's sake, Charles, what's this about?'

'McCredie –' Fairfax had an irritatingly ponderous manner at times, '– McCredie has persuaded the government to issue a register of owners of all quarantined property. Sub-standard housing areas in particular. The Rocks, Wexford Street, the whole Chinatown district.'

William felt a sudden stirring of alarm. 'He can't do that.'

'He can. He's convinced Lyne, who sees votes in it. Blame the landlords, not their tenants, for the filthy conditions that spread plague. There's a deal of panic since this resurgence, and they need scapegoats. Already some quite respectable people have been named, and the lists have gone to the newspapers to be published tomorrow.'

'How did you find out?'

'Ashburton Thompson.' The city's Chief Medical Officer had his consulting rooms in the same building as Fairfax. 'He said names are already being bandied about.'

'What names?'

'Hardie and Gorman, the real estate people. Sir Philip Lacon, Anderson, Raine and Horne, they're all listed. And the Regal Property Trust has been identified as the owner of half the houses in Wexford Street.'

William began to feel very cold. The Regal Property Trust was himself, with three minor nominees, of whom Fairfax was one. If these lists were to be published, no journalist worth his salt would fail to look into the public register, to find the directors of a company that held the freehold of so much property in the affected district. It would not be difficult to establish he owned ninety per cent of the Trust, and had bought the Wexford Street tenements at bargain prices two years ago. It would be an easy matter from there to discover he had done so after serving on a Parliamentary Commission which had recommended demolition of the area, with a high figure for compensation as well as a grant for rebuilding. Before the report had been made public, William had formed his Trust Company, appointed Fairfax and two others as nominees, and purchased forty of the derelict houses.

At the time he had considered it a brilliant piece of business opportunism. Although there had been a delay in acting upon the report, he had not at first minded. The longer the period between purchase and eventual compensation, the less likely his link with the Commission or the Regal Trust would be apparent. Meanwhile the houses paid a dividend, rented to Chinese tenants. *Rather too many tenants*, William reflected uncomfortably, for those more prominent Chinese to whom he had offered the head leases had sub-let to as many of their compatriots as they could cram in. That was out of his control, but there were several occupants to a room, at least a dozen to each squalid house, with no facilities other than a backyard cesspit and an outside water tap. It would not make pleasant newspaper reading.

'What are we going to do?' Fairfax asked, and William had no answer. The condition of the houses, he knew, was appalling, and in the past year he had begun to hope for implementation of the report without further delay. If it had been done, and Wexford Street demolished, he could have taken his handsome profit and dissolved the Trust. Instead, the bubonic plague had made this impossible. All funds and resources had been diverted to McCredie's quarantine plan. Now McCredie, to stave off criticism of this new lack of success, had used his persuasive tongue to convince the Premier that a register of owners would allow them both to deflect the blame.

'What can we do?' Fairfax repeated.

'For Christ's sake, shut up and let me think.'

He ignored the doctor's resentful look. It was inconceivable this could happen. He had been so careful, taken every precaution. If he had campaigned actively in Parliament, Wexford Street might be history by now. But he had been cautious not to take too public a stance, in case his personal interest became known. And now it was to be published in tomorrow's newspapers!

'It'll be a scandal,' Fairfax said. 'For the others it may mean a slight embarrassment, but the Regal Trust is different. Once the papers get hold of this, you're gone. Finished. And I don't intend my career to be ruined with you.'

William did not bother to reply. He tried to repress his sudden dislike of the man. Anger would achieve nothing. He had to solve this. He walked to the window and looked out at the vines and profusion of colour Hannah had planted there. *It could all go*, he thought, *everything I own. This could destroy me.*

Outwardly calm, he said, 'I'm glad you were able to warn me.'

'I didn't do it for you,' Fairfax said. 'Let's get one thing clear. I cannot be involved. Not in a shady company exploiting the Chinese, never mind the fraudulent use of your position for financial gain.'

'What do you propose doing?'

'Making a statement that I'm innocent. You took advantage of our friendship, persuading me to lend my name to what I believed was an honest venture. I've talked to the others. They'll support me.'

'I'll bet they will.' William did not disguise his bitterness.

'I'm sorry, it's nothing personal. A matter of survival.'

'There's no need for any statement. I'll make it quite clear that you were just an innocent dupe.'

Fairfax frowned.

'Dupe? I'm not sure I like that. Dupe makes me sound –' he fumbled for the right word '– unintelligent.'

Which you are, William thought with cold contempt, but merely said, 'I'll make it clear you were not a party to any fraud. You had no knowledge of the inside information I possessed. You were nothing more than a nominal director, a name on the notepaper, who stood to make no profits. Satisfied?'

'Thank you.' The other smiled. 'After all, it's virtually the truth. You were ninety per cent of the company.'

'Because my cash bought the houses. You stood to receive ten per cent once we made any money, just for the use of your name.'

'I don't believe that is in writing,' Fairfax said.

'No, we decided on mutual trust. A handshake.'

'Then I'd be careful about saying I'd receive a payment. It could not be proved, and could only bring you further trouble.' There was a brief silence. 'Let's both agree we don't want your political foes to know about certain personal matters. You do take my point?'

William nodded. The favour he owed Fairfax for Edith had just been paid off.

Chapter 15

Stefan felt lost. First the days, now the slowly passing weeks had become interminable. Some of the time he was alone he spent improvising an irrigating system. It was a clumsy but effective way of watering the growing young vines, essential now that such hot spring weather had come after a late and chilly start. He was yoked to this strange device, a wooden bar with drums on either side, the bottoms of them punctured to create a spray. He had seen a market gardener use something like it, in a closely cultivated few acres. This was a great deal more exhausting, the land to be irrigated much larger and terraced all the way down the sloping hillside. Trudging along the vines, he felt the weight lessening as the water diminished. In another two rows, he would return to the well, refill both drums, and resume the tedious process.

In the distance he saw the pony and trap crossing the wooden bridge over the creek, and tried to wave to Gerhardt and Eva-Maria, although the yoke made it difficult. He walked down the trench between the vines towards them hoping that, since they were coming from the direction of the town, they might have brought another letter from Elizabeth. The last one had promised she would arrange her return journey, and expected to be home in late

October, or early November. Stefan had written back to say early November would be fine, but late October would be even finer. Not wanting to spoil her visit, he tried to say it carefully – that he missed her and the children desperately, and their home was empty without her.

'My new invention,' he called to his friends, as Gerhardt pulled on the reins. 'The Stefan Muller watering system.'

There was no response.

'Come and have coffee.' When there was again no reply, he suddenly realised that Eva-Maria's face was covered with blood. Stefan dropped the wooden yoke and the drums, and ran to them as Gerhardt was helping her down.

'What happened?'

'Someone in town throws a stone.'

Gerhardt was cradling her, agitated, as he tried to stem the flow of blood.

'Why?'

'He was drunk,' Eva-Maria said.

'The others weren't drunk. The ones who call us German bastards, and say that Kaiser Wilhelm sends guns to help the Boers kill Australians in South Africa.'

'It's nothing,' she insisted. 'Don't let him make a fuss.'

'Nothing!' Gerhardt shouted. Stefan had never seen him so enraged. 'Some lunatic throws a stone, and you call it nothing? And other people watch and laugh, but we mustn't make a fuss.'

'Gerd, please . . .' she said, but could not calm him.

Stefan helped her inside. He cleaned her face, found liniment in a first-aid tin, and put a dressing over the cut. Then he made them both sit and rest while he poured coffee.

'It was just a drunk,' she repeated.

'You should have called the police,' Stefan told them.

'The police?' Gerhardt erupted again with anger. 'The police were standing there – watching.'

'Is that true?' Stefan looked at Eva-Maria, hoping she would deny it.

'Yes.' She nodded reluctantly. 'I'm sorry, but it is. They saw it, and they did nothing.'

'But why?' he asked.

'I'll tell you why,' Gerhardt said. 'I told you once before, but you wouldn't listen. It was a warning, Stefan. I'm sorry – but this is no longer a little war, a long way off.'

He looked at Eva-Maria, and read the same concern in her eyes. They both watched him, knowing something was on his mind. Stefan was silent for a long time.

'Will you do me a favour, both of you? When Elizabeth comes home, don't tell her.'

Elizabeth and her father sat late over their coffee in the living room. The nights were still cool, and the remains of a fire flickered in the grate.

'Please, Lizzie, stay and see me through this.'

'But, Papa . . .'

'I need help. The place will be full of vultures, and it could last for weeks.'

Over dinner he had told her a sanitised version of the trouble confronting him, suddenly realising it could be a means to prolong her stay.

'Don't go back until I have this straightened out. I need your help,' he added, and seeing her quizzical glance, said truthfully: 'I also can't bear this house without you and the children.'

'Papa, I can't stay here indefinitely.' She was touched by his admission, but knew her father. She could not allow him to dominate her. 'I have a husband and a home.'

'I'm not talking about *indefinitely*,' William said. 'Just while this is hanging over me.'

'Will there be a fuss in the newspapers?'

'Bound to be. It's filthy luck it had to happen like this, to spoil your visit –' He stopped as she rose abruptly, interrupting him.

'I may be able to stay until the end of November,' she said, taking their coffee cups and kissing him as she wished him goodnight.

He remained there a long time after she had gone to bed, gazing into the embers of the fire. *The end of November.* It was a reprieve. In that time a lot could happen. But first of all, he had to survive the week ahead.

The four of them were in the parliamentary bar, waiting for him. George Roland was drinking his usual whisky; the other three men had schooners of beer. They were puzzled by his summons, and rather wary, for they had heard the rumours. There had been a story in the morning newspapers listing owners of the city's slum properties, and talk had been circulating in the parliamentary building for much of the day. The list was not specific. While it named the Regal Trust, no one had yet named William Patterson. But these men knew; and they believed he was done for, his political career finished. Within days he would have to resign. Why then, they wondered, did they feel uneasy?

'Anyone care for another?' he asked them, but no one did. The four were not his type; they had little use for him, nor he for them. But today he was fighting for his life, and whether they knew it or not, they were going to help him. From outside there came the sound of carriages driving towards Hyde Park, where a new statue of Queen Victoria had been unveiled outside the Supreme Court. It was a sight familiar to the four, and they were all indifferent to it, absorbed in watching William as he began to speak.

'I've seen Lyne. I told him I have no intention of resigning.'

'You'll have to – or he'll be forced to sack you.'

'I'm staying put. I've done nothing wrong.'

'You've done a few things wrong, Patterson,' George Roland said with more than a hint of malice. 'For a start you made the cardinal mistake, and got caught.'

'Politically you're dead,' one of the others said.

'So why wait to be kicked out? If you had any decency, you'd resign like a gentleman.'

'But I'm not a gentleman,' William said, 'never have been. So let's have no fucking bullshit about that.' He laughed at the expressions on their faces, and his laughter disturbed them, as he intended it should.

They gazed uneasily around, to see who might be in the bar to witness the meeting. Roland was a wealthy bookmaker. Of the others, Edgar Shrewsbury and Harold Cartwright were property agents. Leslie Ross had come from Lancashire to inherit a relative's thriving lumber business. All four were influential party members. William intended to convince them he spoke from a position of strength.

'Got caught, did I? Do you really think so?'

He watched their cautious faces, as they tried to assess his tactics. These were men who understood the abuse of power.

'I bought houses in Wexford Street. So what? Yes, I was on the Committee that recommended the area be demolished. *If* that had happened – the houses pulled down and the owners compensated – it could be fairly said I'd profited. That I'd used my position to make an illegal gain. Did it happen? You know bloody well it didn't. I'm stuck with forty lousy tenement cottages, falling to pieces, and damn all profit. So tell me what I've done wrong.'

There was a pause while they thought about it.

'You've got the place full of chinks,' Ross said.

Roland was swift to agree. 'Crammed with Asiatics.'

'I rent the houses,' William shrugged. 'Nothing I can do if they fill the places by sub-letting to their friends and relatives.'

The property agents both said they could not see much wrong with this, uncomfortably aware their own firms did likewise.

'I'm no prude,' George Roland said sententiously, 'but the Chinese gamble, smoke opium, and fuck white women.'

William thought there was little point in reminding him he was a bookmaker, one whose fortune had been made from gambling. He would be antagonising Roland soon enough.

'Let's get back to the point,' he said. 'I'm not resigning. If it comes to a censure motion, I have enough personal votes to win.'

'Rubbish,' Ross said. 'Reid and North and the Free Traders would give their balls to get rid of you, since you crossed the floor.'

'I'd say you're history.' Roland's malice was unmistakable.

'And I'd say you can't count, George. I have the numbers.'

'Impossible.'

'On the contrary,' he smiled. 'I have more than enough votes, with you four backing me.'

'*Us* back *you*. Don't be stupid.'

'Why do you think you'd get support or sympathy from us?'

'Because if I don't, you'll all go to prison.'

They stared at him. They glanced at each other. He enjoyed prolonging the moment, certain that he had them now.

'What the hell are you talking about?' Roland asked.

'It's simple,' William said. 'The tramway contract.'

There was an intake of breath, then a shocked silence.

'You fine, upstanding citizens were the transport committee that awarded the new cable tram extension to Ferris Bros. Ferris is your wife's cousin, George, and all of you are unlisted shareholders. I have a wad of documents to prove it.'

'You dirty bastard,' George Roland said.

'This is blackmail.' Ross was outraged.

'Don't get upset. Nobody is going to blackmail anyone.'

'As long as we back you - you mongrel.'

'That's right, George.'

They made love again after tea, and Hannah was excited and then finally exhausted by the voracity of his passion. Afterwards they bathed together and dressed reluctantly, like young lovers. Then he told her about the events of the day.

'It's far from over yet,' he said, 'but at least I have a fighting chance now. This morning I was cooked.'

'That fighting spirit,' she leaned against him, laughing as her hand found and fondled the start of another bulge forming inside his trousers, 'has produced a very surprising and interesting reaction.'

'I've just begun to fight.' He grinned and kissed her. 'But three times in one afternoon is definitely beyond me.'

They went downstairs, and Hannah walked to the corner with him. She watched his vigorous steps as he strode up Liverpool Street. He would most certainly fight, but no matter how successfully things must inevitably change. They both knew it.

The reporters gathered the following morning at the front gate. Before nine there was a solid cluster visible from the house. William knew there was no likelihood of them leaving, so at 9.30 he sent a parlour maid to invite them to the side lawn. By the time they reached there, he was a picture of domesticity: his extremely attractive daughter sitting beside him and William playing with his grandsons as if hardly aware of the descending press corps, and certainly unconcerned by their arrival. He seemed relaxed, a study in informality. Close to the house, his wife Edith could be seen in her wheelchair, and a baby in a pram was being minded by a young nursemaid.

Very clever, thought Alistair Beames of the *Telegraph. The old dog has a few tricks yet.* The old dog rose from the lawn, holding a three-year-old in his arms. He nodded to Beames and to Quinton Jones of the *Herald*, with whom he had a passing acquaintance. There were other reporters there from the *Sunday Times*, and the *Star*, as well as John Norton's rag, *Truth*, from whom William knew he would get no mercy. Norton was not only sole proprietor and editor whose pungent prose was eagerly read every Sunday, and who published scandalous divorce news under the caption '*Prickly Pairs in the Garden of Life*'; he was also a fierce rival in the Parliament. The two disliked each other intensely.

'Well, gentlemen,' William said, noting there were four photographers with their cumbersome equipment, 'let's make this as pleasant as possible. I've ordered some tea.'

The maids were already on their way from the house, as if to forestall a refusal, bringing teapots and plates of buttered toast. The *Telegraph* and the *Star* exchanged a smirk; the *Herald* looked bored and rather grand.

'Bribed by buttered buns,' murmured the alliterative *Truth* reporter, mentally composing a Norton-style headline: Patterson Parliamentary Pariah: William's Wicked Wexford Wangle.

The *Sunday Times* eyed Elizabeth, and thought he wouldn't half mind hopping into the cot with her.

William stirred his tea, and said, 'Gentlemen, ask any questions you like and I'll do my utmost to answer. If you wish to take photographs, I'm sure you won't mind if they include my family. My daughter is Elizabeth Patterson Muller, married to a hard-working young wine grower in South Australia; this young chap I'm holding is Henry Muller, and his younger brother there is Carl.'

'I is Carl,' Carl piped up with his infectious grin, and several of the reporters smiled and noted down their names.

'Your son-in-law is German?' Alistair Beames asked, thinking *he deserves a friendly one for the tea and toast.*

'He comes from Augsburg, Mr Beames,' William said, 'in Bavaria. That's what is going to make this country of ours great. The influx of other nationalities, bringing their customs and traditions which will enrich our culture. In two months' time, when the Commonwealth is declared, we'll be one people no matter where we originated from. You and I and my son-in-law, Stefan, will all be Australians.'

Jesus Christ, Beames thought incredulously, *I don't believe this. He's making a phony political speech, and two of them are writing it down.*

'But never mind that,' William continued, 'you didn't come here to listen to my views on patriotism or the great future ahead of us, even though most of you know how hard I've fought for Federation. I crossed the floor, and jeopardised my political career, because I couldn't accept the yes-no hypocrisy of Premier Reid. I stumped the country, and stood on soap boxes pleading with people to vote yes in the referendum; I don't need to remind you how hard I worked –' He stopped suddenly, with a modest shrug, as if to say he had not meant to embarrass them with this; they must forget his achievements and get on with the sordid business in hand. *I have done the State some service*, Alistair Beames smiled sardonically; *you clever old prick.*

'Mr Patterson,' he asked, 'are you the principal of the Regal Property Trust?'

'Yes, I am.'

'And does this company own houses in Wexford Street?'

'Yes,' William replied. One of the photographers was ready and waiting beneath his black cloth. A magnesium flare exploded. Heinrich jumped, then giggled, and William smiled reassuringly at him. He had no intention of being photographed without holding the boy, unless someone insisted. There was no risk of being recognised after all this time, but it was best not to take foolish chances.

'Are these slum houses being used for prostitution and gambling?' the *Truth* reporter asked.

'Not to my knowledge,' William said. 'If I were aware of that, I would certainly have the tenants evicted.'

'Chinese tenants,' the reporter persisted.

'Are you prejudiced against Chinese people?' he countered, and turned deliberately to Quinton Jones of the *Herald*. 'Are you, Mr Jones? Is this whole matter a case of racial hatred?'

'I don't think the nationality of your tenants has the slightest thing to do with it,' Jones said, in his rather patronising way. 'What we're talking about is the misuse of parliamentary authority. When you, as the Regal Trust, bought these houses two years ago, you had already served on the Legislative Commission that decided Wexford and Stephen Streets were sub-standard and should be demolished. You knew the amount of compensation to be paid, you –'

'Just a moment, Mr Jones,' William interrupted sharply. 'You're here to ask questions, not make long-winded, defamatory statements. I deny what you've said, and if the *Herald* should stoop so low as to publish that, they'll receive a writ from my lawyers. And so will any other newspaper,' he said, making sure he caught the eye of the *Truth* representative.

There was another half hour of questions. He parried those he was able; disassociated Dr Fairfax from any connection with the company, other than as a nominee; trod a difficult and precarious tightrope between apparent frankness, ingenious equivocation, and occasional bluster. It was every bit as tough as he had predicted, but by the end of it, when they were putting away their notebooks and the photographers were dismantling their cameras, he felt he had done as well as he could. That was when he became aware of Beames looking at him curiously.

'Why did you shave your beard off?' It was a casual question that took him by surprise. He was aware of them observing him, puzzled by his silence, and waiting for an answer.

'Because –' he said, and stopped, feeling a moment of panic.

'Because I asked him to.'

Elizabeth smiled as the reporters turned to her.

'I persuaded him whiskers are going out of fashion, and he'd look years younger.' She singled out the impressionable *Sunday Times* reporter. 'Don't you think I was right?'

The *Sunday Times*, enraptured by her beauty, agreed she was absolutely right.

'Why *did* you shave it off?' Elizabeth asked him, when the press had gone and Sigrid had taken the children to the park. William knew that an evasive answer would not suffice this time.

'You know perfectly well,' he said, 'that I'm no plaster saint. We wouldn't have this house or any money if I had been.'

'Did you do something crooked, Father?'

'Yes,' he admitted. 'I'm ashamed of it now, but they were desperate times,' he said, and was surprised when his daughter rose and hugged him affectionately.

'I hope it wasn't anything too terrible, but I always knew there was *something*. Do you think anyone will recognise you?'

'I hope not.'

She tilted her head to one side, and studied him.

'I doubt it. You look different. Don't you think so, Mama?' she asked as Edith awkwardly propelled her wheelchair into the room.

But Edith had only one interest nowadays.

'Where's Heinrich?' she asked, and on being told Sigrid had taken both children across the road to the park, she rang for Forbes and requested him to wheel her across to join them.

That night, after dinner, William told Elizabeth the full truth about Edith's fall. He did not spare his own behaviour, he admitted his failure as a husband and the debacle of their marriage, although he managed not to mention Hannah.

He begged his daughter to stay a little longer, perhaps till

Christmas, pointing out that if she took the children away, particularly Heinrich, it would break her mother's heart.

The newspapers might have been a great deal worse, William reflected over breakfast the next day, although it was too much to hope they would not make full use of this juicy morsel.

WEXFORD STREET: MR PATTERSON'S STATEMENT, said the *Herald*, and gave a careful and non-defamatory account of his answers.

PATTERSON'S CURSE: THE WEXFORD AFFAIR. The *Star* had a banner headline, and the story below it did him no favours.

MY VIEWS ON PATRIOTISM. A DREAM OF ONE NATION, said the *Telegraph*, and William mentally pigeon-holed Alistair Beames for a crate of whisky at Christmas.

It was relatively quiet until Sunday, when the *Truth* hit at him with a typically lurid headline: SLUM SCANDAL SHOCKS SYDNEY. PREMIER PREDICTS PATTERSON'S POLITICAL PLUNGE.

The next day the Premier, Sir William Lyne, in answer to a question from one of William's political allies, categorically denied having made such a statement. William instantly instructed his lawyers to sue John Norton and *Truth* for defamation, well aware this would render the matter *sub judice* and prohibit comment. There was a delay of at least a year in the courts, by which time he hoped to settle it privately, or failing that, to tactfully drop the action.

The following week, with the far-from-subtle backing of their leader George Reid, the Opposition forced a vote of censure, demanding the resignation of William Patterson for misuse of his parliamentary position, and for a blatant attempt to profit illegally from privileged information. After a torrid debate the division bells were rung, the chamber divided, and the censure motion was lost by four votes.

'We cannot afford to lose men of such initiative and insight from public life,' declared George Roland, MLA, in what many considered was his most convincing speech since his election.

November brought unexpectedly cold winds, but despite the weather William was in good spirits. Elizabeth had made no further mention of her return to the Barossa. In the streets, McCredie's rat catchers were seen no longer, and the battle in the quarantined slums had been won. The bubonic plague was officially declared over. In all, nearly five hundred people had contracted the disease, and one hundred and forty victims had died. Over twenty-eight thousand rats had been destroyed. The city garbage and sanitary systems were radically overhauled, derelict streets and archaic hovels marked for demolition, and the rat catchers went back to the ranks of the unemployed.

Soon afterwards, the worst of the sub-standard premises in Exeter Place and Robertson's Lane were reduced to rubble. It was several more years before the shanty homes in Wexford Street were torn down, and William was able to pocket a substantial profit, but by then people had largely forgotten the accusations against him, and there was little public comment.

The final months of 1900 were a curious time for William Patterson. He had the enjoyment of Elizabeth's prolonged visit, and the pleasure of his grandchildren; his affection for them grew with every week, and he felt a deep, possessive pride that astonished him. He had never been a man with a great deal of time for young children; now he spent a part of every day joining in their games and telling them stories. The boys responded in a most natural way – they both loved him.

Although he tried not to make it too obvious, William had formed a great attachment to Heinrich, who now responded naturally to the name of Henry. Often the little boy and his vigorous and relatively young grandfather were to be seen walking in the park, bringing indulgent smiles to observers noticing the small child hand in hand with his tall and well-known companion.

Because of his daughter and the children, he was happier in the Centennial Park house than he had ever been since its purchase. He found a new affinity with Edith. He sympathised and understood her desperate anxiety at the thought of losing Henry when Elizabeth took the children home. He watched her, sitting in the garden with her elder grandchild, reading to him, playing with him, and he marvelled at the blossoming of this woman he had lived with and disliked for over twenty years. If there was one shadow on his happiness at this time, it was that Elizabeth must soon shatter the pleasure and delight her children had brought them by going home.

Meanwhile he managed to see Hannah almost every day and began to persuade her to appear occasionally in public with him. They went once to the theatre, and another time to a social gathering, and on both occasions he felt a great sense of pride at being seen with her. William Patterson in these final months of the century, had little to complain about in his personal life.

Only he, and Hannah, knew how deeply the Wexford exposure had hurt him. Publicly he had ridden out the storm; but privately

William began to accept the fact that his political ambitions were very likely at an end. He would remain a member of the Legislative Assembly, but he had aspired to a goal far beyond that. William had seen himself standing for election in the new Federal Government. Every day of the last five years had been directed towards that objective.

He had always been a vigorous supporter of Federation and had cultivated the party hierarchy who were staunchly in favour of it, establishing the image of a committed politician with handsome looks and a fine platform presence, and the rare gift in Australian politics of a resonant and fluent speaking voice. He had every reason to believe he would be chosen, and was quietly confident he would be elected.

In the secret moments of the night, when he allowed ambition and imagination to run free, a seat in the Cabinet did not seem beyond him. He knew, without false modesty, that he had the personality and ability for such a position. But now the chance of reaching these heights was virtually impossible. While he had coped with the immediate scandal, the smell of it would remain to taint the rest of his life. As George Roland had said – he had done the unforgivable and been caught. Since he knew, and had made it his business to know, that many of his colleagues were up to their necks in worse corruption, it seemed to him blatantly unfair.

Hannah surmised, better than he realised, the full extent of his ambition. She would have gone one step further and ventured that his sights were even set on eventually becoming Prime Minister. His age was certainly not against him; Edmund Barton, whom most considered the likely candidate for the office, was many years older at fifty-one. Alfred Deakin, another contender, was the same age as William, but there was a body of opinion that being a Victorian would disadvantage him.

She would not have spoken this aloud, for fear of being ridiculed, but Hannah suspected William might have let it be covertly rumoured he would be available, in case there was no clear consensus and a compromise candidate was required.

If it was speculation on her part, it was based on their intimacy of the past five years, and it gave her a unique insight into the depth of his disappointment. That disappointment would be all the more acute, she knew, once Elizabeth took her children home – which must happen any day now.

Stefan's letter was careful not to show reproach, but she could sense it.

> *I do understand your father needs support at such a time, but by now the worst of his troubles must be over, and I hope your mother is better.*

Elizabeth sat with it in her lap, watching the children scamper and shriek with laughter, as her father played Blind Man's Bluff with them around the garden. He had a scarf tied around his face, and pretended to step first into the fish pond, and then to collide with a rhododendron, while the two boys laughed and encouraged his antics. Then he lay down on the grass, and they rushed towards him and jumped on him. *How beautifully the three of them play together*, Elizabeth thought, and the idea of it made her smile. She took up the letter again.

I pruned the grape bushes back in the way that Christian Hubrich taught me they do it at Seppelts and Yalumba, and I think it will benefit us. Even though the winter was the coldest I can recall, there is now good growth on the vines. Everyone misses you, and Gerhardt and Eva-Maria send you their fondest love . . .

It seemed so far away, and she was uncomfortably aware of a sudden feeling of guilt, and what seemed perilously close to disloyalty. She watched her father and the children. Now they were chasing him around the azaleas, and he seemed to have an inexhaustible patience and energy for them. *And how hard he works at it, to keep us here,* she mentally added, for she was perfectly well aware of her father's intent. He had made it transparently clear for weeks now.

She took Stefan's letter into the house, and sat at the writing desk.

Dearest Stefan,

Papa has asked me to stay until the New Year. I do realise that will prolong my absence, but with Federation to be proclaimed on January the first, it is a wonderful time to be here in Sydney. I wish you were with us. There is already great excitement, and much competing for invitations to the festivities and the Grand Ball to be given by the Earl of Hopetoun at Government House. Papa has already met the Earl when he was Governor of Victoria, and pronounces him a 'pommy chinless wonder'. Pommy is a new word everyone is using here this year, which means English.

She broke off for a moment, thinking of what she could not express in a letter; her mother's simple joy when she had announced her decision to stay for Christmas and the New Year. She was more and more uneasily aware Edith's happiness was contingent upon her presence and that of her children.

> *My father expects to be entertaining quite heavily during the proclamation and its celebrations, and has asked me to be his hostess. I really feel it is an opportunity for Heinrich and Carl to see all this – even though they are young. I'm sure it is something they will remember all their lives. Do forgive me, but I have said yes to Papa, knowing that you will understand. We will leave here, I promise you – after the first week in January. Imagine it! 1901 – a new century!*
>
> *With my fondest love,*
> *Your Elizabeth*

She sealed the letter and sent a housemaid with it to the post office. It was better sent, committing her, making the decision she had hesitated over ever since her mother had first broached it.

'Please stay,' Edith had begged, 'it'll be such a special moment in your father's life. To have you stand there with him on the platform. He needs someone. I can't be there. And his mistress certainly can't.'

'His what?' said Elizabeth.

'My darling, he's had one for years,' her mother said, startling her, not only with the news, but with her lack of resentment.

'Who is she?'

'An ex-dancer who lives in a cottage he owns in Paddington. Her name is Hannah Lockwood. I've known for ages.'

She smiled at Elizabeth's shocked face. 'It's never bothered me. Other things have. Not that.'

'What things, Mama?'

There was a silence so long, Elizabeth thought her mother was not going to answer.

'What things?' she asked again. She deeply wanted to know.

At last Edith replied, 'Being - nobody,' she said. 'Being alone in this great big awful house, which I've always hated. And most of all - losing you.'

Elizabeth had not believed she could feel such pain and love for her mother. When Edith asked her once again to stay until the New Year, her answer was interrupted as Sigrid brought Heinrich from the house. He was full of exhilaration as he ran towards his grandmother. It seemed the most natural thing in the world; something she had never been able to do in her own childhood. He embraced Edith as if no one else existed.

Elizabeth saw her mother's face. She could scarcely believe how transformed it was, how animated with delight. In that moment a decision was taken that would influence the rest of her life, although she had no idea then, and in fact, did not realise it for a considerable time to come.

Chapter 16

Towards evening the heat burst in a storm, and the last Christmas of the century was ushered in by driving rain and the sound of thunder. Forbes brought the carriage to the front porch and William, sheltering there, climbed gratefully into it. Forbes, sweating under his heavy oilskins, rivulets of rain running down his face, flicked the reins, and the drenched horse and coachman began the long journey to the parliamentary buildings in Macquarie Street.

Even though the old man treated him well, there were times, Forbes reflected dismally, when the old bastard was a bit bloody unreasonable. And this was one of them. Sodding Christmas Eve. Why in the hell would he have a secret meeting with some geezer at Parliament House on Christmas Eve? And in this weather? As if to demonstrate his point, the wind gusted, and the driving rain blew into Forbes' face, almost blinding him.

The telephone call had come an hour earlier, but William had been waiting in hopeful expectation all day. The male secretary's voice had been ingratiatingly polite, almost obsequious.

'Mr Edmund Barton sends his compliments, and wonders if he might meet with you?'

William, knowing the urgency of the matter, had pretended to consult his diary and suggested a week hence, and had then professed surprise when the secretary asked for the meeting that same evening.

'Tonight? Christmas Eve?'

'If you would be so kind,' the man said, and William once again pretended to deliberate.

'Very well,' he said finally, 'tell Mr Barton I can meet him at seven o'clock.'

And so at last the opportunity had come, the dice had finally fallen his way. The summons could mean only one thing - and he was ready for it. He sat back in the carriage, experiencing a feeling of pleasure and anticipation. The eminent Edmund Barton needed him, and William had no intention of selling himself cheaply.

Barton was there before him, a distinguished figure in formal attire and wing collar, with his silver grey hair and penetrating lawyer's gaze. They greeted each other with careful reserve; William knew that Barton had never liked him.

'Looks like a wet Christmas,' William said, and they ordered drinks, and made small talk about the weather and the forthcoming proclamation of the Commonwealth, a week hence, until the steward went out and shut the door and they were alone.

'I need support,' Barton said.

'So I gather.'

'The British have sent us a fool as our first governor-general. But I have almost enough names to change his mind.'

'Almost?'

'Three more,' Barton said, 'would give me enough.'

'I have these four. And several more if you want to impress His Excellency.' William took a sheet of paper from his pocket and handed it to Barton, who read the list of names and looked at William with a grudging respect.

'You have more influence than I realised.'

William shrugged. He had, ever since the Wexford Street alarm controlled George Roland and his group, and through them was able to count on the support of a number of others. He had been close to the edge, and had no intention of ever being without the numbers again.

'What's the price of your support?'

'I'm a patriot,' William said. 'I believe you would be our best Prime Minister.'

'Thank you,' Edmund Barton said dryly, 'but I suggest we try to avoid hypocrisy. Let's not pretend we particularly care for each other. You're a rich man, and I distrust rich men in politics.'

'Then it's a pity you need me and the support I can command,' William replied curtly.

'I merely asked the price of that support.'

'I said I'm a patriot.'

'There's always a price, Patterson. I want to know yours.'

William got up from his chair and walked to the window. He gazed out at the deepening night, and the gusting rain lashing the Moreton Bay fig trees in the Domain. He could barely see the harbour beyond. It was a moment to savour, making the most powerful political figure in Australia wait for his answer.

'I enjoy politics,' William finally said. 'But the State House will be less exciting once we have Federation.'

'I can't promise you a seat,' Barton told him, 'and you know I can't. I'd be a liar to say I could arrange something like that . . .'

'And I'd be a fool to believe you. But there is the Senate. As the leader of the party, you'll be in a position to nominate.'

'The Senate . . .' Barton said.

William smiled. Barton gazed at him for a few moments, then he nodded his agreement.

'Very well.'

'Senator William Patterson,' William said quietly, almost as if he were testing the sound of it.

Barton made no reply. He rang for their coats, and ordered the carriage.

Less than an hour later they were with His Excellency, John Adrian Louis, the seventh Earl of Hopetoun, Her Majesty's newly arrived vice-regal appointee as the country's first governor-general, revealing to him as tactfully as possible that he was on the verge of making a monumental blunder.

'Impossible,' the Earl said angrily. 'Out of the question.'

He was not a man who took kindly to opposition, or to any hint of criticism, particularly from colonials. He had already had some experience of these people, having been appointed Governor of Victoria at the age of twenty-nine; now, a decade later, invited to preside over the Federation of the rival States, each with their own different laws and diverse rail systems, he had no intention of being dictated to in this fashion. Never mind if the man was a prominent figure, and well regarded in London.

'No,' he repeated, 'it is impossible, Barton.'

'Not impossible, My Lord.' Edmund Barton did his best to remain courteous. 'Merely difficult.'

The rain still fell steadily outside, and in the background of the formal room, William remained a silent onlooker. He saw the aristocrat's pallid face suffuse with indignation.

'I repeat again, Mr Barton, for the last time – what you suggest is impossible. I have invited Sir William Lyne, as the Premier of the senior colony of New South Wales, to form a government and become Prime Minister.'

'Sir William has opposed the idea of a Commonwealth for the past five years,' Barton told him.

'Nevertheless,' the seventh Earl's voice was becoming shrill, 'I am the Viceroy-Elect, and his is the name I have chosen.'

'Then I have to tell you,' Barton spoke so softly his voice was almost drowned by the storm, 'that he has no mandate.'

'I propose to use the powers invested in me by Her Majesty the Queen to announce his mandate.'

'No, Your Excellency.' Barton once again spoke quietly, but with authority. 'You can't do that.'

Hopetoun stared at him, as if he hadn't heard him properly. 'I think you presume too far, Mr Barton. Are you trying to dictate to Her Majesty on procedure?'

But it was a bluster, and they both knew it. William, standing discreetly in the background, also knew it. He watched as Edmund Barton produced a list of names, and handed it to the governor-general.

'We have a constitution,' Barton said, and let the other absorb the long list. 'Procedure under it is clear. Those men refuse to serve under Sir William Lyne.' He took out the list of the names William had provided, and passed it to the startled Viceroy. 'And also these. It gives me a clear mandate.'

'But dammit man,' Hopetoun said almost plaintively, 'it's the eleventh hour.'

'Exactly, Sir,' Barton was as smooth as silk, 'which is why I felt Your Excellency should be informed of the position.'

The Queen's elect frowned over the list of names again, then his gaze encountered William. 'And you - er —'

'Patterson,' William reminded him. 'William Patterson.'

'Quite. Are you a party to this - this - politicking?'

'I merely wish to avoid embarrassment, My Lord,' William said.

'What embarrassment?' Hopetoun snapped at him, starting to lose his temper with these bland and polite colonials.

'The embarrassment,' William said smoothly, 'of Her Imperial Majesty's envoy proclaiming our new Commonwealth, and selecting the wrong man to lead it.'

There was a startled silence, while Hopetoun stared at him. Even Barton almost smiled.

'Are you being clever?' the Earl asked.

'Clever?' William merely looked puzzled.

'All right, dammit,' Hopetoun gave up. 'You may leave us.'

'Yes, Your Excellency.' William bowed. 'May I wish you a Merry Christmas and a Happy New Year.'

He went across the vast panelled room towards the door, and could hear Barton saying, 'Sir William Lyne cannot form a government,' and Hopetoun's testy reply: 'You've made your point, Barton. Confound it, this is hardly an auspicious start for a new nation.'

William went out, closing the door quietly behind him.

An hour later he was in bed with Hannah. He stayed until the early hours of the morning, and woke with reluctance, to find her snuggled against him, her hair tousled, looking pretty and singularly vulnerable, and not for the first time he contemplated what his life might have been if Edith's fall had proved fatal – as she intended.

He had no doubt that he would have asked Hannah to marry him.

He dressed without waking her, left the Christmas present he had chosen for her at the bottom of the stairs where she would find it in the morning, and walked home through the quiet streets. The rain had eased and the night was cooler. It was strange to be going home to decorations and a Christmas tree, and a house lively with the sound of children's excitement. He was going to miss them terribly. In less than a fortnight Elizabeth would be taking them home; there was no way he could persuade her to stay longer. At least before she went would be the day they had all waited for with such expectation.

'I, John Adrian Louis Hope, Seventh Earl of Hopetoun, do here proclaim that on this first day of January, in the year of our Lord nineteen hundred and one, by the Grace of Her Majesty Queen Victoria, Defender of the Faith, that the colonies duly signed and attested shall be Federated to form the Commonwealth of Australia . . .'

The Earl was not a lively speaker, William reflected, as they stood on the platform among an elite group of guests. Invitations for the official pavilion had been a source of speculation and division for weeks past, a social accolade for those who received the embossed cards, a rebuff for others, envious and indignant at being omitted from the select list.

Around them were State Premiers, politicians and their ladies, bankers, businessmen, judges, eminent doctors, lawyers and their wives. The bunyip aristocracy, a wit had once christened them. Sweating in frock coats and top hats for the occasion. The ladies in crinolines and bonnets. He glanced at Elizabeth alongside him, conscious of her youth and vibrant beauty. *I am,* he thought, *escorting the best-looking woman here today.* He saw many eyes, male and female, admiring her, and felt inordinately proud of his daughter.

The city was *en fête*, and had been ever since the wilder than usual New Year's Eve revelry. The end of the nineteenth century went out with a noisy salute to the twentieth - and the first day of Federation. While the churches were full, and patriotic songs sung in theatres, it was in the streets that the people celebrated. Packed crowds produced a ferocious cacophony of sounds; ringing bells, trumpets, whistles, drums, noisy ribald choruses as the night went on, the riotous excitement only dampened towards dawn by a drizzle from overcast skies.

But by mid-morning the rain had cleared, and the sun shone. A lavish procession left the Domain, and traversed the city streets, past privately erected grandstands where the prosperous middle classes had reserved their seats. There were spectacular patriotic floats, regiments of soldiers and a naval brass band, a brigade of Light Horsemen followed by packed carriages with mayors, aldermen, politicians from all sides, and finally the gilded coach of the plumed and uniformed governor-general with an escort of lancers.

The procession was admired and applauded by crowds in Martin Place, and from there it proceeded through the city, festooned with flags, banners and floral arches, past Oxford Square to Centennial Park, where the official guests took their places. As they stood on the platform, William realised he could almost see his house through the trees. They were to proclaim the new Commonwealth on his doorstep, in a park where he often walked, a place he sometimes thought of as an extension of his home, but which today was unrecognisable, crowded with more than one hundred and fifty thousand people, bedecked with flags and bunting, lined with troops and field artillery for the salute.

'... and I do appoint as my Chief Minister with authority to form a government, the Right Honourable Edmund Barton ...'

The roar of cheering almost drowned the name, and Barton nodded in response to the acclaim, as if no other prospect had ever been considered.

A Senator, William thought, and liking the sound of the title, he permitted himself a quiet smile as he took Elizabeth's arm, and wished this particular day would never end.

Her mother's admiration pleased but also disturbed her.

'You look so beautiful,' Edith exclaimed when Elizabeth came home after the long celebratory afternoon; first the reception and official presentation to the Earl in the Centennial pavilion, then the carnival and exhibitions of children's dancing, the band concert followed by a cocktail party, and finally, as it became dark, the massive fireworks display. Her father had delivered her to the door, before having Forbes drive him to State Parliament where there was more festivity that would last long into the night. Her mother had been sitting by the window, waiting for her.

'You look lovely,' she said again. 'Excited. Was it a grand occasion?'

'It was wonderful, Mama. I'm so glad you persuaded me. It was really very special – to be there, at the start of it all. To know that Papa had a hand in shaping it. I felt very privileged.' They had rarely, if ever, spoken so freely to each other.

'The children and I could hear the band,' Edith said, 'and of course the twenty-one gun salute. They both loved all that noise. Carl went to sleep before the fireworks, but Heinrich and I watched until he got tired. Sigrid put him to bed. Sit down and rest, darling. You must be exhausted. Would you like me to ring for some supper?'

'No thanks. There were sandwiches and lots of patisseries, and then we had champagne, and father introduced me to Mr Barton. I'm not a bit tired. It was just a wonderful day.'

'Something to remember for the rest of your life,' Edith said.

'Yes.' Elizabeth nodded.

'And now, any day, you'll be going home.'

'Next week.'

'So soon.'

'I must.'

'Taking your children. Going back to your husband.'

'Mama, be fair. You know I must.'

Her mother gazed at her. Elizabeth felt she had never seen such distress and sadness. Such pain.

'I know. I also know you're going to break my heart, Elizabeth. You can't help it, but you're going to do it – all over again.'

Chapter 17

Stefan woke excited. Today, at last, they would be here. It was hard to believe it had been so long. Almost six months. He had already made arrangements with Gerhardt to borrow their pony and trap, and Eva-Maria was bringing it and had insisted she would stay and clean the house. In vain he told her he had cleaned it.

'I'm talking of *clean* clean,' she said. 'Spotless – so the floors shine and everything looks beautiful. Isn't that how it would be in her big home with all those servants?'

Stefan had to admit, it would no doubt be immaculate in the mansion opposite the park and, in an uneasy moment wondered aloud if six months there, being waited upon and no doubt indulged in all kinds of ways, would have changed her? And what about the children? Maria and Carl were too young to notice, but would Heinrich come home spoilt? Would he find his small home a disappointment after the grandeur of Centennial Park?

Eva-Maria told him not to be such an idiot and to be on his way; it would not be a nice welcome to his wife, leaving her to wait for him at the coach station in Tanunda, while he prattled on with such nonsense.

Watching him drive down to the bridge and cross the creek,

turning the pony and trap southward, Eva-Maria knew he would gladly have driven all the way to Adelaide, to collect her, but Elizabeth had written to say it would be easier and more comfortable for the children if she transferred to the coach, and he met her in Tanunda.

Eva-Maria went inside to clean, and found there was little to do. It was all bright and shining. There were fresh sheets on the bed, and Stefan's washing was ironed and put away. He must have been busy all night to have the place looking like this. Each day he'd been working from dawn to sunset in the vineyard, and toiling to keep the vines moist with the heavy yoke of his watering system, for the harvest was barely a month away, and the hot winds and lack of rain and what they were calling the great drought in the eastern states had begun to affect even their own fertile valley.

She ran a mop over the kitchen floor, although there was little need, and wondered about her friend Elizabeth, and how six months of comfort and luxury might have altered her. It was to have been two, at most three months, but somehow with each letter from her there had been a new reason to stay; some business difficulty for her father, then her mother pleading for her to remain with the children a little longer, and finally, just as Stefan was making plans for a family Christmas, the opportunity to be a guest at the ceremony to proclaim Federation. It had hurt and upset Stefan, she knew that, yet she understood how Elizabeth must have felt.

There would only be one day like that in all their lifetimes. How wonderful to have been there at the heart of it. To have actually been among the invited on the official platform.

Eva-Maria only had one concern, that after the different living style, after the opulence and great events of New Year's

Day, and all the excitement of that city to the east she had heard so much about, Elizabeth might feel deprived or disappointed in her return to this modest house and their small vineyard. It would be a difficult transition. She hoped not too much had happened to make it impossible. Her friends were few, and very dear to her.

She tried to thrust aside the disquiet she had felt all day, telling herself not to be such a fool. A few months apart. Would it be difficult for her and Gerd? She thought not, but then they had never been apart, nor was one of them the child of wealthy parents.

Stop it, she told herself, and decided to scrub the kitchen table, although it was already cleaned to perfection.

Stefan hugged and kissed Elizabeth, exclaimed over how much Carl had grown as he cuddled him, then shook hands with Sigrid and kissed baby Maria, before he realised.

'Where's Heinrich?'

He looked around him, began to move towards the coach to look inside as he saw the nervous glance exchanged between Elizabeth and Sigrid. It caused him to stop and ask again, this time with alarm. 'Where's Heinrich?'

Elizabeth came to take his arm.

'Sigrid will look after the others while I'll explain.'

'For God's sake – explain what? Where is he?'

As his voice rose, a passing couple gave them a curious glance.

'Sigrid,' Elizabeth said, trying to appear calm, 'will you take Carl and Maria into the shade?'

Sigrid, carrying Maria, took Carl by the hand. They went to wait on the cool verandah of the *Australische Zeitung*'s office.

'Where is he?' Stefan could scarcely control his voice. 'What in Christ's name have you done?'

'He's in Sydney.'

'You left him behind?'

'Just for a few weeks.'

'You're insane!'

'Stefan, don't shout. Just give me a chance to explain.'

'I'm waiting for you to explain.'

'I can do it more easily if you'll calm down.'

'I'm calm,' he said through clenched teeth.

Elizabeth had never seen him angry like this. She knew it was going to be worse than she had imagined.

It had been a reckless, impulsive decision; she had admitted it to herself ever since. She had been swayed by the emotion of the day. The exhilaration, the plaudits and admiration of her father's friends, and as he whispered, some of his enemies; a place of honour among the prominent guests, all this excitement had stimulated her in a way she had never before experienced.

It was hardly surprising. She was not yet twenty-two years old, but the Prime Minister-elect had bowed and called her an ornament to the occasion. She had been eagerly sought out by an impressed army captain, the aide-de-camp to the governor-general, who had asked her to be his guest at a garden party, and refused to believe she was a wife and the mother of three small children. Even her father's former friend and now political foe, James North, had complimented her on her elegance. She had come back to her parents' house in a state of dangerous euphoria, her head turned by elation and full of dreams.

Her mother's anguish had profoundly distressed her. The pain and sadness, after all the rapture of the day, had been almost more than she could bear. She had finally pleaded tiredness, and hurried upstairs to her room hearing the words over again: *I know you're going to break my heart, Elizabeth. You can't help it, but you're going to do it – all over again.*

She had sat there for a long time. Remembering so many things. Her own childhood, her natural affinity with her father, her preference for him and the feeling of unease with her mother, who never seemed comfortable in their house with all the servants. She thought of the way Heinrich ran to embrace his grandmother, as if there was no one else so important to him. How he sat and intently watched her face while she read stories to him, smiling when she smiled, responding to each inflection of her voice. Her mother enlivening the childish tales, dramatising, mimicking animals and putting on accents, making him laugh aloud. Enchanting him. This woman who had rarely, if ever, read her a single story when she was young. Who, perhaps, had felt unwelcome, or unwanted. She thought of the way her small son and her mother talked together so naturally, how she spoke to him as if he was an adult, and he responded, and they seemed to have a language all their own.

It might have been an hour, she was hardly aware of time, before she went downstairs again. Her mother was sitting by the window, the room was almost dark, lit only by a small lamp. She went and sat on the floor alongside her wheelchair, leaned against the legs covered by a rug, and told her Heinrich could stay with her a while longer. Her mother had tried to thank her with tears streaming down her cheeks. By the next morning, however, Elizabeth began to realise she had made a serious mistake. But it was not one she could rectify, at least not without causing further pain. Her mother's radiant pleasure, Heinrich's complete and happy acceptance that he would remain a few weeks more with Grandmama – how could she sit there at the breakfast table and tell them it had been a hasty and foolish agreement? The result of an unsettling and stirring day.

On the train home, she had become increasingly nervous. Despite the luxury of their first-class sleeping compartment, she had hated every moment of the journey, wishing she could reverse her decision, or that there had been time to write to Stefan and prepare him. And now, he was waiting for her to explain. Whatever she said, she knew it would upset him.

'My mother pleaded for him to stay just a while longer. And Heinrich wanted to stay with her.'

'Heinrich is four years old. Do four-year-olds make decisions like this?'

'No. I made the decision. Please, Stefan, try to understand how much it meant to her.'

But he couldn't, and they both knew it.

'My father will visit us, and bring him back, the moment the Federal elections are over.'

'Dear God,' Stefan said, and started to stow the suitcases into the pony and trap. He turned and looked at her.

'I missed his birthday. I made him a present,' he added bitterly, as if this was reason for further anger.

'What did you make him?'

He did not answer. Instead he walked to where Sigrid and the children were waiting outside the newspaper office. He picked up Carl and brought him back, with a worried Sigrid following. They climbed aboard, and began the long, unhappy journey home.

~

A group of children were playing near the pond. Hannah sat on a park bench, watching their antics while she read the latest copy of the *Bulletin*. There was a cartoon by Norman Lindsay that made her smile. 'One people, one destiny' it was captioned, and depicted a policeman carting two drunks to gaol, much the worse for wear after the inaugural celebrations. She lowered the magazine, as she saw the two figures approaching; one tall, the other diminutive. They paused near her, and Hannah smiled and nodded as if he was a casual acquaintance. William doffed his hat politely.

'Ma'am,' he said.

'Mr Patterson,' she nodded, and became aware of an alert pair of eyes watching this exchange.

'Hello,' the small boy said.

'Hello,' Hannah answered him. 'Is this your grandfather?'

'Yes,' he nodded.

'And are you taking him for a walk?'

'Yes,' the boy answered. 'My name is Henry.'

Hannah showed her surprise.

'Is it?'

'It is now. Grandpa said so.'

She refrained from a glance at William, and smiled instead at the earnest face of the boy.

'Did he? Well, I'm pleased to meet you - Henry.'

William gave him a bag with scraps of bread.

'Off you go, old chap. Feed the ducks. Say goodbye to the nice lady.'

'Goodbye,' he said politely.

'Goodbye, Henry,' she answered, and watched him scamper off towards the pond, scattering bread for the best fed ducks in town.

'Does your daughter know?'

William had been about to follow his grandson. Now he paused to ask, 'Know what?'

'That her son is no longer Heinrich?'

'No grandson of mine's going to be stuck with a German name,' he said firmly. 'Germans are unpopular. They picked the wrong side in the Boer War. We don't like their damned Kaiser.'

'Willie, dear,' she was unable to prevent a smile, 'don't make a speech to me. Tell Elizabeth.'

'Don't worry,' he replied, 'I intend to.'

He doffed his hat and moved off. She watched him with affection and slight concern, as he joined the boy and they fed the ducks, then walked away, the child running to keep up with his brisk strides until William realised, stopped and reached down – and they continued more sedately, hand in hand.

Eva-Maria knew. She sensed it. She had scrubbed and cleaned the spotless house, and as she saw their pony and trap crossing the creek she could feel trouble. Gerhardt had walked from their farm earlier and Eva-Maria joined him.

'We won't stay,' she said.

'Won't stay? Are you serious?'

'Very serious.'

'Why won't we stay? I want to talk to Elizabeth, to hear about what it was like on Federation day – and see the *kinder*.'

'Later, Gerd. Another time.'

'But they're our friends. We can't leave without seeing the children, and saying welcome.'

'Of course we can't. But we'll say welcome, then leave them to themselves for today.'

She loved him dearly, but sometimes he was *so* slow. There was another word. Elizabeth could tell her, but this was not a time to ask. Then she remembered. *Obtuse*. He was sometimes obtuse.

When they pulled up at the house, Gerhardt called a welcome, and lifted Elizabeth down from the trap. He kissed her, then put out his arms for Carl and baby Maria. He hugged them both.

'Thank God you're home. Stefan's been so depressed. You can't imagine how bad-tempered he's been –' He stopped and looked around, his good-natured face puzzled. 'Where's Heinrich?'

Stefan jumped off the cart, and unloaded the suitcases.

'You tell him,' he said coldly to Elizabeth, and carried the luggage into the house, leaving behind him a threatening silence.

Obtuse. Eva-Maria shook her head at her husband, and came to embrace her closest friend.

'Welcome home.'

Elizabeth kissed her. She seemed close to tears.

'He's staying a little while longer with my parents,' was all she said, but it was enough for Eva-Maria to imagine the agitation this had caused Stefan. Although it had never been discussed in great detail, she knew of his hostility towards his father-in-law. The best thing she could do was take Gerd, and leave them to solve this for themselves.

'Come tomorrow for dinner, yes?'

'Thanks. It's lovely to see you both.'

She looked so absurdly young, Eva-Maria thought, *like a schoolgirl in trouble*. She badly wanted to help, so this homecoming would not be spoiled.

'He's missed you desperately.' She had to be quick, Stefan was coming back. 'Gerd's right. He's been on edge – different.'

'In what way?'

'No laughs. Not many smiles. I think he was afraid.'

'Of what?' There was only just time for Eva-Maria to answer, as he emerged from the house.

'That you might not come back.'

She steered Gerhardt to the pony and trap, waved farewell to them as if it was a normal visit, and nudged him to drive away.

Supper had been silent. After Sigrid washed the plates, then went to her own room, Stefan sat morosely on the front verandah, while Elizabeth dried the last of the dishes. It was, she reflected wryly, a task she had not done for six months. She hung up the tea towel, placed two glasses and a bottle of their best wine on a tray, and took it outside. She lit the lantern. He watched her in silence.

'Lovely night,' she said. 'So tranquil.' When there was no reply forthcoming, she continued, 'I've missed nights like this.' She picked up the corkscrew and opened the wine. 'Will you pour, or shall I?'

'I'm going to bed,' Stefan said, and made as if to rise.

'Don't be so bloody juvenile.'

'Me?' He appeared surprised by her sudden anger, as if considering this *his* emotional domain – being the injured party.

'You. He'll be well looked after. He loves her.'

'You were tricked into this, by that father of yours.'

'Don't be stupid. That isn't true. And stop being so angry.'

'I *am* angry.'

'That's more than obvious.'

'It wasn't right – you shouldn't have allowed it without consulting me.'

'That wasn't possible, since you weren't there.'

She poured the wine. Two glasses. Raised her own, and appeared seemingly oblivious that he ignored his.

'*Prosit*,' she said. 'Welcome home, Lizzie. So good to have you back.' She sipped and nodded approval. 'Or didn't you miss me?'

'Of course I missed you.'

'Is it true what Gerd says? You were depressed?'

'Sometimes Gerhardt talks too much.'

'Were you?'

'Yes,' he said reluctantly.

'Why?'

There was a pause. He picked up his glass, and sipped. It was some moments before he spoke.

'It must have been very luxurious?'

'It was.'

'Servants to make the bed, and clean and cook for you?'

'Yes.'

'He spoiled you, I suppose?'

'If you mean my father – yes, he did.'

'Tried to persuade you to stay?'

'Of course.'

'Made you his guest at the Federation ceremony?'

'You know he did.'

'I expect there were many rich young men to admire you?'

'Heaps.'

'Bastards.'

'They may have been,' she said. 'I didn't ask. But I still want an answer from you. Why were you depressed? Eva-Maria said you were on edge. No laughs. Not many smiles.'

'Everybody in this place talks too much.'

'They're our friends. They're concerned. If I saw Gerhardt behaving like an idiot, I'd try to help.'

'I am not,' he said heatedly, 'behaving like an idiot. I had good reason to be depressed. I knew that bloody father of yours would do everything he could, use all his money and influence to show you what you'd thrown away. What you could have again, just by a nod of your head. Taking you to Parliament, to the theatre, to expensive restaurants. Don't tell me he didn't do those things.'

'Of course he did. I wrote and told you.'

'And made me feel very . . .' he fumbled for a word, and not able to find a substitute, had to use the one he wanted to avoid, '. . . very afraid.'

'That I'd stay?'

'Yes.'

'You fool,' she said affectionately, and felt a debt of gratitude to Eva-Maria for her insight.

'Am I?'

'A galah, I'd call you. There must be a German name for it.'

'Lots,' Stefan said, 'if it means what I think it does.'

'Why on earth would I stay? Of course Papa would have made it easy. And it was all wonderfully exciting, especially January the first. I'm glad I was there. I wouldn't have missed it. But you have to know I missed you, too – so very much. Some nights I couldn't sleep for thinking of you.'

'Truly?' he asked.

'Did you have any nights like that?'

'All the time. Months of them.'

'Then can I ask you a question?'

'Another one?'

'It's more important, this one. Why are we out here, arguing and drinking wine? Why aren't you undressing me, picking me up and carrying me to bed?'

'You're right,' Stefan said, gazing at her. 'I am a galah. Also a *Schwachsinniger.* A *dummkopf.* But first I will carry you inside, and then undress you. And afterwards you must undress me.'

Elizabeth smiled, and felt a wave of desire and anticipation, as he lifted her and kissed her, then carried her inside the house.

They made love twice, the first time with a frenzy that could not be sustained, and she felt him convulsing in her within moments, but her own craving was such that she was already climaxing with him. Then, it seemed only minutes later he entered her again, and this time their movements were slow and gently arousing, taking themselves to the brink, then down again until they could resist no longer, culminating in an ecstasy that left them weak with wonder at the sensations they could arouse in each other. Sometime later in the night, they woke and joined their bodies together again.

Later still, before they finally went to sleep, Elizabeth asked, 'The present for Heinrich – what did you make for him?'

'A small wooden bucket, so he could follow us at this year's harvest, and help us pick the grapes.'

She smiled.

'Next year,' she said. 'There's always next year.'

Chapter 18

'Order,' the Speaker called. 'The House will hear the Right Honourable William Patterson.'

William rose to a mixed reception. There was derision from the Opposition benches, but to his ear it was friendlier than the lack of enthusiasm from his own side of the House. They all knew it was a final appearance before his resignation, and that having been suggested as a candidate for the Senate by Barton, he would certainly be chosen and elected.

'Mr Speaker, thank you. I leave this place with some nostalgia and regret. Above all, I shall miss the Honourable buffoons opposite . . .'

It was greeted by the mocking chorus from those across the chamber, but among them were a number of grinning faces. William glanced up at the public gallery, and saw that Hannah was there.

'However,' he continued, 'I am assured there will be even bigger ratbags in the new Senate. I look forward to it. I am merely here to bid you farewell, and to say I could hardly leave this place, without expressing my gratitude to four Honourable members who have given me such support in this Parliament. I refer, of course, to Mr Cartwright, Mr Shrewsbury, Mr Ross, and Mr George Roland.'

From above, Hannah saw him smile at each of them in turn, and saw each forced to respond. She had enjoyed many occasions here, but few more than this last appearance. As she stood to leave, she saw James North look up and observe her. She knew how dearly he would love to have implicated William in a scandal, and how careful they had been to avoid this. North knew of their liaison, of course, had known for years, since the days when the two men were still friends and he had helped arrange William's entry into politics.

Hannah realised, better than most, James North's ambitions and his capacity for malice. She was glad they were moving from his political orbit. Leaving the public gallery, she experienced a feeling of relief at knowing it would be for the last time.

Later, in Paddington, sitting in the garden she recounted to William her hilarity at the view from what she sometimes referred to, in theatrical parlance, as 'the Gods'. 'The four Honourable supporters were not amused.'

He laughed. William had relished his final appearance in the Assembly. After having been forced to accept his political expectations had been virtually ended by the Wexford Street exposure, he had then had the extraordinarily good fortune to be of use to Barton, and able to strike a deal which would make him a Senator. It was not what he had once envisaged. It was the Upper House, and the constitution which he had helped to draft was such that the Senate had restricted powers and could never produce a Prime Minister. Yet despite these limitations, he was grateful his political life was not entirely over. It was a great deal more than he had expected a few months earlier. In the meantime, he had to keep his promise to Elizabeth and return her son to her. He knew it was going to cause distress and heartbreak.

'When do you leave for the Barossa?' Hannah asked, and her perception was no surprise. She often anticipated his thoughts.

'Soon,' he said. 'Much too soon.'

'His parents will be glad to see him.'

'I expect so. Edith is going to miss him like hell.'

'And so are you,' she told him.

He had no answer for this because it was true. He had come to love the boy, and could hardly bear the thought of the long journey they would be taking together, which would effectively remove him from their lives.

They sat in the shade, near their new plantings, and ate the lunch Elizabeth had packed. On the terrace above, and all the way down to the creek below them the vines were stripped of their grapes; the harvest was over, and they had bottled twice as many gallons of white wine and a little more red than the previous year. Prices for wine had risen, and they should show a profit, although much of it was already committed to be ploughed back into new vines and irrigation.

'Next year,' Stefan said, 'I can start to repay your father.'

Elizabeth avoided a reply. She knew, that while it was of great importance to Stefan, her father would not welcome the repayment of the little money he had expended here. Meanwhile she had another matter on her mind. She said casually, 'Why didn't you tell me about what happened to Eva-Maria? Someone threw a stone at her, didn't they?'

It was a few moments before he answered. 'Who told you?'

'Just someone in town who thought I knew. They said a

drunken man threw stones, and called her a lousy Boer-loving German bitch, while the police stood and watched. Is that true?'

She could see he wanted to lie, but was uncomfortable with the idea of it. 'Yes, it's true,' he said eventually.

'Why didn't you tell me?'

'What was the point of it?'

'You asked them not to mention it. Why, Stefan, did you feel I should be the only one not to know?'

'You were away,' he said evasively.

'That's hardly an answer.'

'It was better not to make a fuss.'

'A fuss? You mean I'm someone who should be protected from this kind of news? I'm not sure I like that.'

'It was nothing of the sort,' he said. 'I asked them not to speak of it – because I felt ashamed.'

The reply puzzled her. 'Ashamed?'

'That they are able to call Eva-Maria such names – and the police do nothing. You know what it means? That we are . . . inferior. Foreigners of no account. They forget Queen Victoria's husband was German, and the British royal family is the House of Saxe-Coburg. They forget and throw stones at a harmless woman, a friend, because to them we are all just German bastards.'

She wanted him to stop. She felt disturbed by his bitterness.

'The war in Africa should soon be over,' she said.

'And let's hope to God,' he replied, 'that there'll never be another.'

~

William could hear the dog barking as he walked home. It sounded young – a puppy. Then, as he opened the gates and walked up his driveway, he heard the excited barking mixing with the sound of happy childish laughter, and Edith's voice calling a name. Whoever owned the pup must be visiting them. Turning down towards the side lawn, he saw the puppy – it definitely was a very young puppy – was black and white. Spotted. He assumed it was a Dalmatian. Edith was sitting in her wheelchair, managing to throw a rubber ball, with both Henry and the puppy scampering in pursuit. The dog barked, the boy laughed, and they rolled around in happy and complete accord.

There was no visitor.

'Grandpa? Grandpa. Look!'

Henry could not manage to lift the tail-wagging animal, so he stroked it instead. William tried not to betray his sense of shock.

'What's this?'

'A puppy dog,' Henry said.

'Where did it come from?'

'From the shop, Grandpa. A dog shop.'

'When?'

The question was directed to his wife, but Henry and the pup were dancing around him, excited.

'He's mine. Grandmama said so.'

'Did she?'

He was aware of Edith, sitting very still, her eyes fixed on his face. He made the effort, clearly expected of him, to stoop and pat the dog.

'Good boy,' William said.

'He's a girl.' Henry laughed.

'Oh. Well, take her for a walk round the garden, old chap.'

'Come on, doggie - walkies.' Henry ran off and the pup jumped up and followed him.

They both watched this.

'Why, Edith?' He asked the question while watching the dog and child run towards the tennis court. 'Why have you done this?'

'He loves animals. You can see he does.'

'So you bought him a dog. And tomorrow evening, is the dog to go home to the Barossa with him? Did you intend it as a farewell present?'

He knew the answer to his question, and her despairing silence confirmed it.

'What does this achieve, except to make it more difficult for him to leave here? It wasn't kind to do that. It helps no one.'

She made no reply to this - just looked down at her hands, and shook her head, as if each word he said was a blow.

'Edith,' he tried to be gentle, 'he has to go back.'

'Not yet,' she said. 'Please.'

'You know perfectly well the reservations are made. I've written to Elizabeth. She's expecting him.'

'No.'

It was a vain, wounded sound, and it moved him more than he thought possible.

'I made a promise to her. We both did.'

'Please, William.'

'Edith, he's not our child. Don't make it more difficult.'

'He loves it here. Loves us.'

'But he can never be ours.'

He knelt beside her, and took her hands. It had been a long time since they had had any physical contact. Her skin felt dry, and her fingers trembled, so desperate was her unhappiness. He realised now that prolonging the boy's stay had been a mistake; far better for them all if he had gone home with Elizabeth and the others. It was a decision his daughter had made, and he had welcomed it then, not only for his wife's sake, but for his own.

He was paying for it now. Because there was nothing he could do for Edith. She had little to look forward to except an arid life, and the one factor that would have made it bearable, he could not obtain for her. For the first time in their joyless years together, he wanted to make her happy, and knew that he could not do so.

Chapter 19

William arrived at the vineyard in the same landau, and with the same driver. As it approached across the creek, Elizabeth began to wave, then realised with bewilderment that Heinrich was not with her father. She saw Stefan start to run down from the top terrace. They converged as the landau pulled up.

'Where is he?' Stefan did not even bother with a greeting.

'Papa . . .?' she started to ask, as William got down from the landau and kissed her.

'Long journey,' he said.

'Where's Heinrich?' Stefan demanded.

'Can we talk at the house? I'm sure my driver would appreciate a cool drink. I know I would.'

'You didn't bring him,' Stefan said.

'Perhaps even a bite to eat, then I'll explain.'

'Father, answer the question.'

The driver said tactfully, 'I'll go on up, Senator, and put the horse out for a spell.'

Senator, Elizabeth thought, amid confusion and her growing alarm. *Of course*. It was the first time she had heard him called that.

'You didn't bring him,' Stefan repeated.

'No,' he agreed, 'I didn't bring him.'

'I expected this.' He clenched his fists, and for an anxious moment Elizabeth thought he might hit her father. If William sensed it, he remained composed and carefully polite.

'You're entitled to be upset, Stefan. You both are. If you insist, after we've talked, I'll go into Tanunda and send a telegraph. He'll be on a train tomorrow – accompanied by a trained nurse, and I'll arrange that you both are driven to Adelaide to meet him on arrival.' He shrugged. 'But first can we sit down and have a glass of wine together? I don't believe we've ever done that, have we?' William Patterson said to his son-in-law.

The driver left them hurriedly, and turned the horse out with hay and water. *A right bit of a to-do*, he thought to himself, as Sigrid brought him a drink and a plate of sandwiches.

'Bit of a row, eh? They were expecting the kid?'

'Mr Patterson, he promise. All week, we say Heinrich comes. His room is clean, his small brother is excited. Elizabeth and Stefan . . . they must be very upset.'

'Some heavy talking going on over there,' the driver said, as they looked towards the verandah, 'but I reckon the Senator's doing most of it.'

At the table where they sat, trying to be civilised, trying to contain their sense of outrage, William was being eloquent about the wine and how impressed he was with all the improvements to the vineyard. Since leaving Adelaide he had acquired what knowledge he could about wine-growing and asked Stefan a number of questions about the grapes, and methods of fermentation. They were knowledgeable and serious questions which showed he had clearly studied the subject and which, not wanting to appear churlish, Stefan felt obliged to answer. Elizabeth watched with disbelief at the way he was trying to blunt their anger with his practised charm. He was waxing expansively, until she could stand it no longer.

'Papa, will you please stop this, and talk to us. And don't ask about what, because you know. We're waiting for you to explain.'

'I'm not sure if I can explain. But I'll try.'

He took another quick sip of his wine. They both watched him intently, and she realised with surprise that he was nervous. It was not a state she associated with her father.

'I'm going to tell you things no one else knows.' He spoke hesitantly, without a trace of his normal vigour. 'I have to say first of all, that you and I, Lizzie, although we never meant to, ruined your mother's life. Although, that's not quite true or fair to you. *I* ruined it. I went off and made a lot of money, and left you in a tiny slum cottage in Glebe, and Edith supported you by taking in washing and mending. You probably don't remember, but I was away for a year – and she kept you alive.'

He took another sip of wine. Elizabeth noticed his hands were shaking.

'I made the money by taking risks – not exactly honestly, if you want the truth, and soon we had a big home, and servants, and rich new friends. Your mother hated it. She could never adapt and was unhappy all the time. It was my ambition for success that did that.'

Elizabeth tried to remember. All she could recall was a tiny house, and then what seemed like a palace, and looking at it, then taking her father's hand and walking inside.

'You went to Miss Arthur's Academy,' he said, 'and learned how to be a young lady – and your mother was never at ease with you after you became one. Then, later on, you fell in love and ran away. I've no doubt you were happy – except for the time in Hahndorf – but you broke our hearts. Especially your mother's – because by then I'd lost all interest in our marriage. So she had no one.'

He went to take another sip of wine, but put the glass down without it reaching his mouth.

'Twice she tried to kill herself. I was told that she was terrified of me. God help me, that's what I'd done to her. And then you came to see us; you brought your children into our lives, especially your eldest son – and you know what happened.'

'Yes,' Elizabeth said, but it was just a whisper. Suddenly her mother's life was exposed like a bleeding wound.

He turned his gaze on Stefan.

'I admit it – I love the boy, too. But Edith . . .' He paused and swallowed. 'She bought him a dog the day before I was due to bring him home to you. I should have been firm. Sent the puppy back. Told her Heinrich must accompany me. Perhaps I'm weak, but I couldn't do it. In front of our daughter, I have to tell you I've never loved my wife – but I feel guilty and ashamed of the way I treated her. The one person in the world she loves is your son.' Again he paused, for what seemed a long time. 'So I'm in your hands.'

'But what,' Stefan tried to control his anger, 'in God's name do you want? What are you asking?'

'To let him stay with us,' William said. 'Even for a short while.'

'No.'

William went on as if he had not spoken. 'Let me educate him – the way you couldn't afford to. I want to give him the kind of education you both had. You did, after all, have the best.' He concentrated on Stefan. 'You've done wonderfully well here, and I congratulate you. No doubt you'll want him to take it over one day. But perhaps he'll want a different kind of life. He may want to go into business, or do medicine - or law. Without an education you give him no choice.'

He rose from the table, and looked at them both.

'I'd send him home. Each school holiday, I'd send him back to you. I'm not trying to take your son - I'm asking you to share him with a woman who has been unhappy most of her life, for which I'm entirely to blame.' He took a document from his pocket, and placed it on the table between them. 'I'm no good at begging. I have no right to ask this, and you're entitled to tell me to go to hell. To be honest, I couldn't blame you if you did. So talk it over. But whatever you decide,' he indicated the document, 'that now belongs to you.'

He walked off and left them alone.

'This is unfair,' Stefan said bitterly.

They felt emotionally drained. Elizabeth opened the envelope he had left, and took out the document. She read it while he watched.

'What is it?'

'A bribe.' She threw it angrily on the table. 'He relinquishes his deed in the vineyard, and puts it in our joint names.'

Stefan picked up the legal agreement, and read it. To him it had a far deeper meaning. The land he had worked so hard for almost three years was now jointly his. There would be no repayments. No longer the insecurity of being little more than a scarcely tolerated tenant.

Yet, of course, she was right; it was a bribe. Blatant and

barefaced. The ultimate corruption. A lease of their child in return for title to the land.

On the hillside, looking out over the creek and adjoining land, William also felt emotionally expended. He had given the impression he'd left them alone so they could make their decision, but the truth was he felt a need to escape from the stress he had generated.

He had not realised it would be so difficult, and now he had to accept the possibility that he had failed. He had a strange intuition that Stefan might agree to his plan, while his daughter would be the one to prove inflexible. Whatever the outcome, he had no arguments left. If the answer was no, he must admit defeat. He, who could debate and filibuster for hours in public forums, had no more words to say. He had, he supposed, the inner consolation, if that was the word, of knowing he had tried his best.

Walking among the vines, he noticed they had already been pruned back for the winter and spring growth. From his quick study of the subject on the train journey, he realised this was good, meticulous viticulture. He examined the grafts and pruned stalks from the main vines, and evidence of the soil tilled by hand. It must take all hours of the day. He wondered about irrigation, and came to the small stone well. Alongside it was Stefan's primitive watering apparatus, with its buckets and yoke, like pictures he had seen of Chinese coolies in their paddy fields. As he studied it, one part of his mind absorbed its details, while the other was becoming more and more certain, as the time passed and there was no sign of them, that he would have to return home defeated.

~

Elizabeth cleared the dishes from the table, stacking them in the kitchen, as if the act of tidying up might help clarify her mind. But why was this necessary? Surely there could be no question. They wanted him home. She went out to where Stefan still sat at the table.

'I'll tell father to go to Tanunda and send his telegraph. He's to make the arrangements for Heinrich to come back home.'

'I was thinking about school,' Stefan said.

'He'll attend the local school.'

'The only one near enough for him to attend is the Lutheran. They teach in German.'

Elizabeth stared at him. It had never occurred to her.

'But you want him home?'

'Of course I do. But your clever, persuasive father has got me very mixed up. I keep hearing what he said, that perhaps Heinrich one day wants a profession, and hasn't the education for it. I've even been thinking about Eva-Maria - the stones, and being called German bastards and dirty names.'

'Then stop it, because that'll never happen to Heinrich,' Elizabeth said determinedly. 'It has nothing whatever to do with this.'

'Perhaps. Perhaps not. If we told him, when he was twenty years old, that he could have been educated at the best colleges in the east and gone to university, and that we rejected it - I wonder what would he think of us?'

'We wouldn't be stupid enough to tell him such a thing.'

'But if he knew? How do you think he would feel?'

'That's an unfair question, Stefan.'

'It's one I've been asking myself. I don't know the answer. So I have to ask you.'

'Oh God,' she said unhappily, and saw the tall figure of her father returning to the house. She had the feeling – and thought it must be her imagination – that he was dejected. His shoulders appeared slumped, and his stride, usually so brisk, seemed sluggish.

Stefan saw him and said, 'So, before he gets here, choose.'

'I can't.'

'An hour ago, we wouldn't have considered this. Now we're not sure. It means he's won, doesn't it?'

'No,' she said vehemently, 'I won't accept that.'

'Then say no. Tell him. And tonight, and next week, and next year, we'll think about this and always wonder if we did right.' He was silent for a moment, then added, 'And I'll ask myself if I denied my son something he might have valued, because of my dislike of your father.'

They watched him approach.

'I'm sorry,' Elizabeth said quietly, 'but because of the way you feel about him, you're the one who has to decide.'

Before he could reply, her father had joined them. He stood at the verandah steps, looking up at them. Elizabeth suddenly realised it was not her imagination. His dejection was palpable. He was about to admit defeat.

'Stefan . . .' But she was already too late.

'Send him home to us –' Stefan began, and she saw her father's dismay and felt her own ambivalence, but then realised he had not finished, '– at Christmas. And each long school holiday. And if we ever feel we were mistaken, we have the right to change our minds. Do you hear?'

'I hear,' William Patterson said.

'If his grandmother dies, then he comes back. Although I don't know her, I respect my wife's opinion of her. I trust her to shape his character. I don't trust you.'

She saw her father flinch.

'Is that acceptable?' Stefan asked him.

My God, thought Elizabeth, *how our lives weave and change. My father a supplicant to a man he once threatened to have arrested, and all because my mother has finally found someone to love. All this because of one small boy.*

She stood and watched, waiting for her father's answer.

'It's acceptable,' he said.

William felt morose and withdrawn all the way back to Adelaide. His driver, after some initial attempts at conversation, accepted the lack of response and lapsed into silence. Whatever it was that had taken place at the vineyard, the Senator was in a dark mood and not at all his usual self.

A suite was booked for William at the hotel in North Terrace. He told the manager he would be remaining for several more days. He asked for a telegraph form, wrote a brief message to Edith, and requested it be taken at once to the central office. She would receive it the following morning. He ordered dinner and a drink to be sent to his room, and went upstairs to wait for it.

His success gave him no sense of triumph. Not even relief. He had a letter to write, and sat down at the desk in his sitting room, to try to put into words his disturbed state of mind and feeling of disquiet and self-disgust for the only person who might understand.

Hannah recognised his handwriting the instant she opened the mailbox. She took the letter to the secluded back garden, and sat down to read it.

My dearest,

There are several things that will detain me for a few days and since the official period of mourning for the death of Queen Victoria ends next week, and the Federal Parliament is to be opened by the Duke of York in Melbourne, it seems logical to travel directly there. It should be a grand occasion. I am told they are determined to outshine Sydney in glitter and ostentation, and that ten thousand electric light globes adorn the Great Exhibition Building and its main cupola, and it is to be the most dazzling set of illuminations ever seen in the southern hemisphere.

I have made arrangements for a suite at the Windsor Hotel, and also reserved an adjoining room in your name. I don't know if this is wise, or if you will agree to join me. I do know I badly need you, and were there some means of transporting you here to Adelaide tonight, I would certainly beg you to come.

Elizabeth and Stefan have agreed to let Henry stay with us. It's done, and I have sent a telegram to Edith to inform her. I have to tell you – and there is nobody else I could tell, or wish to – that today was one of the worst days of my life. I felt ashamed of what I was doing. I began to wonder if I was doing this for Edith, or for Henry's future, or just to assuage my guilty conscience. I suspect the latter.

I think you can gather, my love, that tonight I am not very proud of myself. You will no doubt say, 'You wanted custody of your grandson, and you got it.' Perhaps so. But I got it by using emotional blackmail against my twenty-two-year-old daughter. You would have been ashamed of me. I was like some threadbare and second-rate troubadour, using all his theatrical tricks. Or worse, a shabby politician practising his trade of deception and hypocrisy.

I felt angry at my squalid tactics. I was about to give up, when, to my surprise, Stefan agreed. He managed to make quite clear what he thought of me, and I took it meekly, as beggars must when their pleas are granted and their empty bowls are filled.

It's done, and Edith will be relieved and happy, but I shall not sleep well. Thankfully I can end by telling you this comes with all my love, and know that in a day of deceits and half lies, that that at least is true.

Hannah sat holding the letter long after she had finished reading it. He had not often had occasion to write to her in the past, and certainly never a letter like this. She felt his remorse and pleading in every line. As for Melbourne, she knew it may not be wise, but there could be no question.

She would be there to meet him.

Mrs Forbes sometimes found it hard to believe this was the same nervous, timid woman for whom she had come to be housekeeper over twelve years ago. It had been a strange house, a most unhappy place, and if she and her husband had not been well paid, he as coach driver and in charge of the gardens as well, they would have sought other positions. She had felt sorry for Miss Lizzie; it was a wretched atmosphere for a girl to grow up in, her parents detesting each other, the girl able to make little real contact with her pale shadow of a mother, clearly preferring her father's company. He, while indulging her every whim, was too seldom there. Too frequently engaged in business matters, or else spending time at the house in Paddington, which she and her husband knew all about – the house of the slim good-looking woman who had once been a dancer, and whose name was Hannah Lockwood. There was not much Mr and Mrs Forbes did not know, but they were loyal, and while they speculated in the privacy of their own sitting room on the suicide attempt, Mrs Forbes made it clear she would not tolerate gossip in the servants' quarters, and that any idle talk would lead to instant dismissal.

'The doctor said she had a dizzy spell. And since Dr Fairfax is the leading physician in Sydney, we can assume he knows what he's talking about. So if any reporters pester you, you all know what happened.'

The staff had stood firm, whatever they may have wondered, and Mrs Forbes had assembled them in front of the house several months later to welcome their mistress home from hospital. That had been a mistake. Edith Patterson had seemed frightened, almost terrified at the reception, wanting only to be taken from the ambulance in a stretcher, and upstairs via the small private lift which had been installed for her during her absence. There a newly purchased wheelchair was waiting. She had rarely been seen outside her bedroom in the first few weeks. Half of the top floor had been reconstructed, converting spare rooms to create a private suite for her, including a small sitting room and her own bathroom. It seemed to Mrs Forbes that her employer would spend much of her future time hiding up there.

Then Miss Lizzie had brought the children for the long-awaited visit, and everything had changed. The house, the people in it, and most of all Edith Patterson, had been transformed.

Even now she could hear Henry chattering to his grandmother, her replies to him, and then the sounds of their laughter. It seemed as if they had an inexhaustible fund of things to say to each other, and secrets they shared, more like friends than a small boy and his middle-aged grandma. She doted on the child, that was obvious to them all, but it was the boy's response that was astonishing. Each morning when he woke, his first stop was her room, where he sat on the foot of her bed and talked, until it was time for him to go down to breakfast, leaving the trained nurse to bathe and dress his grandmother. When he came home from a walk, he would immediately go looking for her to relate what he had seen; describing the ducks in the park, or a kookaburra that had swooped and captured a worm in front of his eyes, or how the bellbirds made him think of the chimes of the clock in her room, or else the latest escapade of the dalmatian pup whom they had named Polly. It seemed sometimes as if he went on these walks only to garner such minutiae of news to bring home to her.

It was strange how little he seemed to miss his parents, or his brother Carl, or baby sister Maria. Mrs Forbes wondered how Miss Lizzie and her husband felt about that, and how the Senator had been able to persuade them to part with him. There had been such tension during the time of his journey to South Australia, and almost unbearable anxiety when the telegram came and she had brought it into the drawing room. Henry had been playing with building blocks on the floor, while Mrs Patterson sat in her wheelchair reading the newspaper. She had seen the distinctive envelope, and her hands had trembled so much that she had been unable to open it.

'Please,' she had said, and Mrs Forbes tore it open. 'Read it to me.' Her face had been almost bloodless, her eyes distraught, ready for misery.

He stays, was all the message said. She had read the words out, and heard the long sigh of relief that was like a prayer answered. Mrs Forbes was also thankful. If Henry's presence meant extra work for the staff, she knew they would not complain. None of them would wish a return to the bleak days of the past. Least of all the housekeeper herself, who so well remembered working in that unhappy atmosphere of rigid silence. To her, the laughter of grandmother and grandson was an extraordinary gift, in a house that had known so little of it for so long.

Hymns were sung, and the Archbishop prayed for the Almighty to endow the new King Edward with might and main, with the wisdom and longevity of his mother, and with an abundance of divine gifts. The Duke of York, wearing the uniform of an Admiral of the British Fleet, then declared the Commonwealth's first Parliament open in the name of His Majesty, after which the massive Exhibition Hall was filled with a fanfare of trumpets.

Hannah stood among the invited guests, as they looked down on the pageantry. Below her were the immaculate uniforms of the military escort, guarding the frock-coated and top-hatted elected. Barton and his cabinet occupied the place of honour, and around them were the members of the Protectionist party, then George Reid and his Free Trade opposition, as well as sixteen members of the Labor Party, who would have the balance of power. On the outskirts, as if placed there to show their lack of real authority, were the thirty-six members of the Senate. It was not difficult to pick out William's tall figure as they took the oath of allegiance.

It was true, as he predicted, that Melbourne was determined to show Sydney the real meaning of imperial grandeur. Huge processions, concerts, fireworks, the glitter of the electric globes on the parapets and domes of the Exhibition buildings, all these, the newspapers proclaimed, had shown the rest of the country –

in particular the harbour city to the north – the style with which Federation should be celebrated. Each day brought vast crowds in their thousands to admire the displays, to cheer the Duke and his Duchess, and to confirm Victorian opinion that it had been a wise choice to select Melbourne as the current seat of the Federal Parliament, until a permanent site was found. That, under the agreement between the States, would be in New South Wales, but not within a hundred miles of Sydney.

STILL TOO CLOSE, the Melbourne *Age* thundered, while the Sydney journals made snide comments on the tawdry arches and cheap tinpot decorations of the southern city.

'We're still a bunch of states in search of a national identity,' William said, in the privacy of their compartment as he and Hannah took a train home after the Senate adjourned. 'We can't agree where to build Parliament House, we still play "God Save the King" because no one can compose our own anthem, and we haven't even got a damn flag yet.'

The Union Jack was used on ceremonial occasions, while a nation-wide contest had been launched to select the design of a new flag. All those considered worthy would then be forwarded to London for the approval or rejection of the British Government. William thought it was a disgrace, and had said so, publicly and often loudly. He repeatedly voiced an opinion, not universally popular, that the purpose of Federation was to create a new and independent country, and that while it may keep its allegiances with Britain, he asked why the Commonwealth of Australia should have the anthem and the flag of another nation.

It was an attitude already making him a subject of concern to those on the conservative wing of his own party.

~

Stefan heard it first, a distant noise like an angry bumble-bee; then came the sound of a horse whinnying, cattle lowing, and a series of dogs barking. The noise was moving closer. Elizabeth was painting the new extension to the side verandah, and she turned to listen, wondering what it might be. Sigrid came running, hand in hand with Carl and carrying Maria, and they all stood and watched with amazement as what seemed to be a gleaming metal chariot chugged along the dirt track towards the vineyard.

Elizabeth had seen many horseless carriages in Sydney, but the sight of one here, sturdy and bouncing on its four-wheeled frame, its driver clad in a dustcoat and wearing goggles, was almost bizarre. Their newly purchased cow clearly thought so, looking up from the lush grass by the creek where she was tethered, giving vent to a plaintive bellow. It was answered by a bray from the car horn. A pony in the field on the far side of the creek galloped off in terror. Carl, clinging to Sigrid's hand, began to cry.

Stefan picked him up, laughing, and said, 'Look, it's only a motor carriage. Just like Uncle Gerhardt's cart, only this has an engine instead of a horse.'

Carl was not reassured. He clung desperately to his father, and looked away from the beast as it approached. In front of the house, the driver switched off the engine and all was quiet. While Carl sneaked a look, feeling distinctly braver now all the loud noise had stopped, the man removed his goggles and dustcoat to reveal that beneath it he was wearing a formal suit, winged collar and tie. Elizabeth dared not look at Stefan, in case she got the giggles.

'Mr and Mrs Muller?' he asked, producing a document case and climbing down to meet them.

Stefan found his hand being vigorously shaken.

'Harpur – of Henderson, Hanlon, Potts and Harpur.' He turned to shake Elizabeth's hand with equal vigour. 'Solicitors, of North Terrace, Adelaide.'

'Are you here to see us?'

'Absolutely. Thought I'd give my new Napier a gallop. Four horse power. Marvellous machine.'

He beamed at them both. From somewhere he had produced a bowler hat and now looked like the complete city solicitor.

'Now, shall we talk?'

'What about?' asked Stefan, bemused.

'Quite. That's what I've come to tell you,' said Mr Harpur.

Sigrid watched them talking on the verandah. A funny man, she thought, that Mr Harpur. She hoped he would not stay too long, because it was her afternoon and evening off, and Oscar Schmidt, who was the assistant to the chemist in Bethany, was coming to take her for a drive. Oscar was a nice young man, but rather serious, Sigrid thought. He was almost certainly going to propose to her, but she felt too young for marriage, and had already decided she would say no. She would tell Oscar to ask her again in a few years' time, and if he found someone else meanwhile, then it would be no great loss. There must certainly be more exciting boys than Oscar Schmidt. Her thoughts swung back to what was taking place there on the verandah.

The solicitor was presenting Stefan and Elizabeth with a document. 'One deed of gift, in the joint names of Stefan and Elizabeth Muller,' said Mr Harpur.

'What deed of gift?'

They were both mystified.

Mr Harpur sipped his tea and peered through his glasses at the document in front of him. 'The ten-acre field being lot 21, Folio 11 –'

'Mr Harpur, whatever are you talking about?' Elizabeth interjected.

'The field next door to your vineyard. Wasn't it for sale?'

'It was sold,' Stefan tried to explain to him.

'Indeed it was,' Mr Harpur said. 'You bought it.'

He chuckled as he registered their puzzled faces.

'Or should I say, Senator William Patterson acquired it on your behalf. And it is now deeded to you both. I am also instructed to place to your credit the sum of five hundred pounds –'

They were both astonished. It was a fortune to them.

'Such sum to be expended upon the purchase and installation of a new watering system.'

'Good God,' Stefan said.

William opened the wine, and poured them each a glass.

'Henry's got the measles,' he said, handing Hannah her glass.

'Poor Henry. Badly?'

'You'd think the world was coming to an end. Edith's hired day and night nurses, and gets bulletins on the hour. Try the wine.'

Hannah smiled and tasted the contents of her glass. He could tell she was impressed.

'Rather good,' she said.

'It's wonderful. First class.' He showed her the label on the bottle. It was in copperplate script and read: *Elizabeth Vineyard, 1902.*

'They sent me a case.'

'That was nice of them.'

'I've written to say how good I think it is.'

She was thoughtful for a moment. He studied her.

'What are you thinking about?'

Hannah smiled. 'Who said I was thinking of anything in particular?'

'I can tell. Something's on your mind.'

'Everyone seems to be getting on so well,' she merely said.

'Now what do you mean by a remark like that?'

'Absolutely nothing, William. I'm glad you were generous and helped them. They clearly appreciate it.'

'Generous? It wasn't all that much,' he said. 'The field was an ideal way to increase their acreage. Good piece of land, right on the creek. Let's face it, he deserves it. He's made a go of things. Only needed the chance. And he loves her - which is what really matters.'

He sipped his wine, refilled their glasses, and was disconcerted to find her eyes intent on him, her gaze faintly amused.

'What are you up to, William?'

'Must you always assume I do nothing without an ulterior motive?'

'You rarely do, my darling,' Hannah replied. 'So what is it?'

'I want to help my daughter. What's wrong with that?'

She shook her head and said, 'I can't think of anything wrong with it. Much nicer than when you were forever hoping she'd tire of Stefan and come running back home.'

'I learned a lot in those six months she stayed with us. She won't tire of Stefan. I made everything as comfortable as I could for her, hoping she'd want to remain in Sydney. I said I'd find him a good job, they could live in their own part of the house, or I'd buy them a home. I tried every way possible to tempt her. You know what she told me one night?'

Hannah shook her head.

'She said it could be wonderful. But impossible. Because I would dominate Stefan – make him unhappy. When I tried to protest, she said she wasn't accusing me. It was the way I was, and I wouldn't be able to help myself. I'd make him feel inadequate. She said he needs that vineyard – and she needs him. That's how it is.'

He was silent for a moment.

'There is another reason,' he added finally.

'What reason?'

'I don't want them to change their minds about Henry. It's getting rather difficult.'

'How?'

'He's not so keen on visiting the Barossa for Christmas, but I feel he must – even if I take him in person. It was, after all, the agreement we made. But I can already foresee a time when he'll grow away from them. He'll make friends at school. Going home twice a year, halfway across the country, is going to become a duty and a chore.'

'You mean they might insist he comes home permanently?'

'If they feel they're losing him – yes.'

'And if you're all good friends, that may be less likely?'

'Well – yes.' He shrugged. 'So you're right, of course. I am a conniving bastard. But if we lost him, well, I don't know if Edith could face it. Her whole life revolves around him.'

'And you?'

'I'd miss him like hell. I want him to have the best. The

things I never had as a kid – things Elizabeth could've had, if she hadn't fallen in love and run away. I'd like him to be a lawyer. But whatever he wants, he can have.'

'Do me one special favour, Willie.'

'Of course. What is it?'

'Remember he's a nice, unspoiled small child.'

'Of course he is.'

'Then don't ruin him.'

'Would I?' He felt close to anger, offended.

'I'm not saying you would,' Hannah was undeterred. 'But when you say he can have whatever he wants, you worry me. Don't let him have anything he wants, William – make him earn it. For God's sake, don't make him a rich man's grandson.'

'What the hell are you talking about?'

'Spoiled, superficial, a pampered and indulged brat. I don't have to spell it out. You know what I mean.'

'He won't be that, I promise you,' William said tersely.

'Good,' Hannah replied, equally abrupt.

It was one of their rare quarrels, but Hannah had no regrets that she had provoked it. She loved William; the one thing she feared was that his affection for his grandson might damage not only the child, but family relationships that had suffered such stress, and were slowly being repaired. There was harmony at last in the mansion opposite the park. There was the closer relationship with Elizabeth, and a slowly growing accord with his son-in-law. William was happier than he had been in many years, and she did not want that to change.

PART THREE

Chapter 20

The stout man broke wind so loudly that the two boys behind him heard it, and began to laugh. They took off their boaters and fanned the air, as if to disperse the smell.

'What a fart,' Harry said, and they laughed all the way to the school, where they regaled their classmates with vivid descriptions of the event. Their hilarity was interrupted by the entry of the geography master. Mr Jensen-Clarke was a man who ruled his class with a sarcastic wit, and most of the boys had learned to keep their eyes glued to their work rather than encounter the gaze of the master, always on the prowl for a victim. Today, Harry, having just gone into details about the pong from the year's loudest fart, was not swift enough to wipe the smile from his face. Mr Jensen-Clarke put down his books, surveyed the class and felt an undercurrent of simmering mirth. He had been a teacher in boys' schools for many years, and viewed laughter as the enemy of learning. It had to be stamped out, and the easiest way to do that was to deal with the cause of it.

'Patterson, stand up,' he said.

Harry stood up. At the age of eleven, he was already tall and bore a striking resemblance to his grandfather. Mr Jensen-Clarke was not the least impressed that this was the grandson of a Senator. He had taught the offspring of minor royalty, and the sons of social leaders in England. The descendants of the bunyip aristocracy were of little account, unless they did their homework and secured high marks in their exams, which in due course enhanced his status as a teacher.

He had his favourites, and this boy was not one of them. In his classroom the meek and the studious inherited the best reports, and Patterson was not meek. Nor particularly studious, although his exam results were invariably good. He was the kind of student Jensen-Clarke found aggravating; clearly bright, disinclined to work hard, and far too often the clown at the centre of class commotions.

He left him standing, while he placed textbooks in neat order on the desk, then took up his heavy ruler. He held it in his right hand, like a swagger stick, and tapped his left. He then favoured the boy with a long appraisal, while the class watched and waited expectantly, relieved it was not them facing J-C's wrath.

'Well, Patterson?'

'Yes, thank you, sir,' Harry said, politely but living dangerously. 'Extremely well, sir.'

There was a titter. The geography master turned, too late to see the culprit. The class were all poker-faced, but he knew insubordination when he heard it and beckoned the respondent forward.

'I didn't ask how you were. I'm not in the least concerned with your well-being. I don't like impertinence, Patterson.'

'I'm sorry if I misunderstood you, Mr Jensen-Clarke.'

The master stared at him. He had always found the expectation of punishment an effective way of making his students malleable.

He enjoyed it when they dropped their eyes, and shuffled their feet, showing their fear. This was another aspect of Patterson which annoyed him. The boy looked directly at him. What's more, he was already almost as tall as the stocky schoolmaster.

'When I came into this room, I heard laughter. You were in the process of saying something.'

'Yes, sir.'

'Perhaps you'll oblige me by repeating it, Patterson.'

Harry nodded.

'Certainly, sir.'

The class, and in particular his closest friend, David Brahm, were riveted. He couldn't – he surely wouldn't tell J-C about the fart. It was inconceivable. Not even Harry would go that far.

'Speak up, boy. We haven't got all day.'

'We were talking, sir – about wind.'

David Brahm thought he would wet himself. Those around him bit hard on their lips, trying to remain straight-faced. The entire class were on the verge of disaster, threatened by a gale of laughter which would mean caning, lines, or being kept in. Possibly all three.

'Wind?'

'Yes, sir.'

'What sort of wind?' He was suspicious; he thought he saw a boy in the back row struggling to suppress a snigger.

'All sorts. What I was saying, sir – since this is geography and it's a geographical fact this city is full of wind – there's the cool north-east wind from the sea, the unpleasant west wind from the inland, hot in summer and cold in winter – then there's the south wind which brings storms and is called the southerly buster. There are also occasional other winds, which can be a bit foul —' he knew he was going too far, but could not stop himself '– winds from unexpected quarters, sir –' He could no longer tighten his jaw to prevent smiling, and his shoulders started to shake in spasm.

The class erupted. The roar of laughter could be heard across the quadrangle. Jensen-Clarke felt a moment of panic. He had not had a class out of control for years, ever since his apprentice term as a teacher. He shouted at them to stop, but could not be heard. Then he banged his heavy ruler on the desk, smashing it in half, which sent them into further hysteria. Those who had felt the weight of it on their hands in the past began to cheer.

Jensen-Clarke lost control. He grabbed a cane, seized the boy and directed him to bend over. Harry could not hear the order amid the noise, and was dilatory, so the master began to thrash him around the body and legs, the swish and whack of the cane on his flesh gradually bringing a shocked silence to the class.

Harry was on the floor, hands raised to protect his face and eyes, when the door opened and the headmaster entered.

'Sit down, Patterson.'

'Thank you, sir, but I think I'd better stand.'

'Still painful?'

'Slightly. The liniment Matron put on helped a bit.'

'Good,' the headmaster said. He was at a loss how to deal with this. The boy's grandfather would certainly demand Jensen-Clarke be charged, creating a storm that could well reach the newspapers.

'I'm sorry,' the headmaster told him, and meant it. 'If you go back to the dispensary, Matron will look after you while I telephone your grandfather.'

'Please don't,' Harry said.

'Don't what?'

'Telephone him.'

'The matter must be dealt with. I have to tell him.'

'Why?'

'Better I inform him than you do, Patterson – quite apart from showing him the marks and welts on your body.'

'But I won't do that, sir.'

The headmaster tried to conceal his sudden feeling of hope.

'Why not?'

'I just won't.'

'Are you sure?'

'Yes, sir. It was partly my fault.'

'Really?'

'I was – a bit cheeky. Everyone was laughing. J-C – I mean, Mr Jensen-Clarke, got a bit upset.'

'Mr Jensen-Clarke,' the headmaster now felt able to admit, 'lost his temper.'

'Yes, sir, he did.'

'He won't be teaching here in future.'

Harry nodded. He knew no comment was required.

When he had gone the headmaster felt confused, relieved but perplexed. The boy seemed anxious to conceal the matter. It was most unusual. But the school was reprieved. What might have been a scandal was now a mere incident. A teacher had lost control and been dismissed. In a few days it would be forgotten.

Provided the boy kept silent.

'But why not tell?' David Brahm insisted on knowing.

'It's over, Brahm. It's forgotten.'

The two boys were walking home from school towards their respective homes near the park.

'I'll bet nobody in our class ever forgets it. He belted you at least twenty times with the cane. He should be had up in court.'

'I'd like to see him in gaol,' Harry said.

'Well, there you are. You can do it, easier than anyone. Just tell your grandfather.'

'No.'

'He'd create a hell of a stink.'

'I know he would. And that's why I won't tell him.'

'You're peculiar,' David Brahm said. 'You're my best friend – but sometimes you're really peculiar.'

They continued walking in temporary silence.

'Does it hurt?' David asked finally.

'Yeah.'

'He was using all his strength.'

'You don't have to tell me.'

'Suppose they see the cane marks? At home, I mean.'

'I'll make sure they don't.'

'But why? Why protect that bastard?'

'I'm not protecting him. He's got the sack.'

'He'll go and teach somewhere else. Get a new heavy ruler to make life rotten for some other kids. So you are protecting him.'

'Look, shut up, will you. Just shut up.'

'Don't lose your block.'

'I'm not. It's my way of asking you to talk about something else.'

'What'll we talk about? The weather?'

They entered the park, their normal route to take a short cut, again in silence.

'All right, let's forget it,' David Brahm said eventually.

'No. I'll tell you.'

They stopped beside a silver birch. It was late autumn, and the deciduous trees had shed most of their leaves, making the park resemble a European landscape.

'There's nothing I'd like more than to see him in trouble. He's a bully and a lousy teacher. If I went home and showed Grandad these marks, he'd explode like a firecracker, and there'd be a terrific row. Grandfather likes rows. It might even get in the newspapers.'

'So why not do it?'

'Because of my grandmother.'

'What do you mean?'

'She wouldn't like it. She'd be upset.'

'How do you know?'

'I know Gran. It'd worry her. And I don't want her hurt or upset.'

David Brahm thought it was really strange.

He had two grandmothers, both of whom came to visit and who fussed over him too much for his liking. Sometimes he couldn't understand his friend Patterson's affection for this crippled woman in a wheelchair.

'I'm home,' he called, and fending off the enthusiastic assault of Polly the dalmatian, went upstairs to the small living room that his grandmother preferred in autumn because it was warmed by the afternoon sun. She put aside the new H.G. Wells novel she was reading, and held out her arms to him. He kissed her and tried not to flinch as she hugged him where the cane had bitten deep. Edith felt it.

'What's wrong, darling?'

'An ant bit me,' he lied swiftly. 'It's nothing.'

'Get some balsam and I'll treat it.'

'No, it's just an itch. Come on, I've promised Polly we'll both take her for a walk. Or do you want to finish your chapter?'

'No,' Edith said, smiling. 'Let's go for a walk.'

He wheeled her chair to the small lift, and they descended to the ground floor. Mrs Forbes came to ask if they'd take tea, but Edith said it could wait until they returned, then they'd have it in the library. Harry fitted a shawl around her shoulders, and put a rug across her knees. He told the dog to settle down or she'd be left behind, and attached her lead.

Mrs Forbes stood and watched the boy, as he guided the wheelchair down the driveway. Every afternoon, unless it was wet. Ever since he was old enough to push the chair. And now he was beginning to sprout, and was already inches taller than some of his friends.

Seven years he'd been with them now. Seven years since he'd arrived as a tot with Miss Lizzie, as a child named Heinrich Muller, who had stayed here and become Henry, and then begun prep school and all of a sudden it was Harry. Harry Patterson. The Senator had told them it would be easier – and simpler.

Mrs Forbes sometimes wondered if his parents knew about this.

Chapter 21

There had never been such a harvest. The vines across the hillside were heavy, the grapes ready to burst. On the land her father had bought them, the soil was even richer, and the vines, laden with shiraz grapes, had matured in surprisingly swift time. With money carefully saved, they had also purchased additional acres of land, cut by a meandering stream. In these fields they had planted muscatel. Their vineyard was now one of the few that was self-supporting. Last year they had bottled over a thousand litres and even put money in the bank; while this year Stefan predicted the yield would be twice that.

'You know something?' he said to Elizabeth, as they sat in the shade to eat a picnic lunch, a habit begun when they had first come here and which they still enjoyed. 'There's a secret – but I'm not supposed to tell you.'

'So tell me.'

'I mustn't.'

'But you're dying to.'

'Yes, I am.'

'Now I'm dying to hear it.'

After a moment he said, 'At the *Schutzenfest*, after the harvest, everyone votes that you be the Festival Princess.'

'Don't be ridiculous,' she laughed. 'I was the princess ages ago, in our second year here. Now I'm an old lady. Princess? More like a grand duchess.'

'Who's being ridiculous? Old lady? A grand duchess? Please don't talk such shit.'

'Stefan!'

'Excuse the French,' he said, and she laughed so loudly that Carl and Maria, home from school on their summer holidays, and fishing for yabbies in the creek, heard her and looked towards them.

'Old? How can you be old? You're twenty-nine.'

'I'll soon be thirty.'

'When you were seventeen, you were quite pretty. Now you're soon to be thirty, you're much more beautiful.'

'Nonsense.' But she was pleased. 'When was this great secret decided?'

'They had a meeting in town. Gerhardt said 1909 would be a special vintage, a wonderful year, so they must have the best princess. They all voted for you. Everyone. Even the young girls.'

'That's nice,' she said, feeling warmed and happy.

Carl and his sister came from the creek to join them.

'Don't tell the children,' she said, as they approached.

'Did you tell her, Papa?' Carl asked.

Before Stefan could reply, Maria hugged her mother and said, 'Did you know you were voted the *Schutzenfest* princess, because you're the prettiest person in the valley?'

'Goodness me,' Elizabeth said, 'they need their eyes tested.'

'No, it's true, Mama. You are. I know you are,' nine-year-old Maria said proudly. 'And everyone says I look just like you.'

After supper was over, and Carl and Maria had gone to bed, they took the lantern and a glass of wine each, and went out to sit on the verandah. It had been significantly enlarged since the first porch that Stefan had built, just as the house had grown, and bottling sheds and storage for casks had been added. A great deal had happened, Elizabeth reflected, since they first came here with her father, across the bridge that spanned the creek, and saw the weeds and untended vines and small shabby house.

Nearly eleven years ago.

Sigrid was now married, living in town. She had finally acquiesced to the pleas of the assistant to the chemist, and was Mrs Oscar Schmidt. Elizabeth had been her matron-of-honour, and Gerhardt was chosen as father of the bride, and Oscar, whom they liked but thought the dullest man in town, had surprised everyone by making a very witty speech at his wedding, and then announcing he had bought the chemist shop from his employer, and would be open for business the following morning at eight o'clock – immediately after his honeymoon.

Carl attended the village school, and so he learned his lessons in German and switched from one language to the other with fluent ease. He was an amiable, likable boy, who enjoyed helping his father in the fields, and was extremely protective of his younger sister, who adored him. They were as close as Carl and his elder brother were distant, when, on increasingly rare occasions, Heinrich came home for the holidays.

As for Maria, Elizabeth had her own ideas for her daughter. She wanted her to attend the private school in Tanunda where they taught in English, rather than remain in the village school and graduate from there to the Lutheran Girls Academy. It would mean fees and the added expense of being a weekly boarder. She had not yet proposed it to Stefan, but she felt strongly about it, and thought that this year they could afford it. If the fees were beyond them, then she was prepared to ask her father.

It was something she would have liked to talk about tonight to Stefan, but the letter was like a weight on her conscience. Reluctantly she took it from the pocket of her dress and handed it to him. She had already read it herself several times.

'When did this come?' he asked, glancing at the signature.

'This morning. Mr Carson left it with our groceries.'

The Carsons were a couple who had recently acquired a dairy farm further along the valley. It was small and run down, and while they set about making it viable they supplemented their meagre income by a delivery service that collected stores and mail from town. Although Stefan and Elizabeth had no real need of it, they had agreed, to help their new neighbours get started.

She watched Stefan as he bent his head, and in the lantern light began to read it.

Dear Mama and Papa,

I'm sorry I missed last Christmas with you, but we had a nice month in a holiday cottage at Collaroy with my friend David Brahm and his family. The house was right on the beach, and we spent all the time in the surf. His parents are really nice – his father is something to do with banking, and his mother used to be a musician before they were married, and she played the cello in an orchestra. He has a sister who is called Katherine, and she is two years younger than us. David says she is a pest, but I like her. She also plays the cello.

'He has a girlfriend.'

'Keep reading, Stefan.'

About the mid-winter holidays. Mr and Mrs Brahm have asked me to accompany them to Melbourne, where Katherine is to give a solo in a concert. Grandfather said no, but Gran said the best thing to do was to write and ask you. I will come to the Barossa if you wish, but I really would like to see Kate on stage with her cello.

With love, Heinrich

P.S. Mama, please tell Maria that I got her last letter, and I think what she says is true – she does look like you.

'He sounds like a stranger,' Stefan said later, when they were in bed. 'Like someone from the east coast who I no longer know.'

'I think he's in love,' Elizabeth said.

'Aged thirteen years old? Please, Elizabeth.'

'I married you when I was seventeen.'

'That was different. Besides, he has four years to go. At thirteen, do you fall in love with the girl or the cello?'

She laughed, and kissed him.

'Let's write and tell him he can go. Do you mind, darling?'

'Yes,' Stefan said, after a considerable time. 'I mind.'

'You want him to come home. Why? To argue with Carl? Be surly with us? Is that what you want?'

'I don't want to lose him, *liebchen*.'

'I never wanted him to go,' she said softly, 'remember?'

'I remember you made me choose. And your father was too clever for me. So many promises made, but not always kept. One year he comes home, the next he has friends asking him to spend the holidays.'

'With school, and growing up, that was bound to happen.'

'You know how long it is now?'

'Of course. Two years,' Elizabeth said.

'Two years. Soon he forgets what we look like. Already he prefers his new life to ours.'

'I'll write and say he can go to see his Kate play the cello. But he must come home at Christmas.'

'No. Don't say he *must* come. Say we'd like him to come. We would be happy if he comes. If in the meantime he meets some pretty girl who plays the violin or the mouth organ, we won't expect miracles. But we would feel privileged if he came to spend the Yuletide with us.'

She kissed him, knowing that below his flippancy was a deep disappointment and concern. Heinrich was the first born, the one they had nurtured through the terrible times in the shed at Hahndorf. He had a special place in their lives. Now he wrote bright and lively letters from across the country, the main object of which was to be released from the chore of travelling to the Barossa twice a year to spend school holidays with them. Elizabeth had read between the lines these past few years, but until tonight had not realised that Stefan had also interpreted it so accurately.

'A cello,' Stefan said. 'My Uncle Uhlrich played one, but not well. It's a big instrument for a small girl to carry. So she needs someone to help her.'

I love you, Elizabeth thought. *I just wish your son could be here when you say things like that.*

Edith read Harry's letter sent from Melbourne, and had the same thought as her daughter, although neither would ever know it.

'He's in love,' she told William.

'For God's sake. He's a kid,' William replied, lowering the *Herald*, which had just predicted his political demise.

'Then listen to this,' she said, and read to him.

The hall was crowded, and the orchestra kept tuning up, and if it was me I would have been so frightened. When the curtain rose there was just an empty stage, and then Kate came on with her cello. It looked large and heavy, and made her seem so tiny carrying it, that the audience started to politely applaud, and then it grew louder, and somehow or other they started to cheer. She stood there and bowed her head, and they all went quiet. Then she began to play.

I honestly didn't know strings could sound like that. I never knew she could play so beautifully – so that everyone was silent and you wanted it to go on and not stop – never, ever stop. When she played the Mendelssohn I thought I saw people crying. I wanted to cry myself, only I thought I'd look stupid. At the end they all stood up and clapped and shouted, and made her play an encore, and Kate just stood there and smiled, as if she never expected anything less. I think she will go to London or Vienna and become famous, and we'll never see her again.

We go to Portsea tomorrow, and then start for home in a week. David and Kate and Mr and Mrs Brahm send their regards.

My fondest love,

Harry

In 1910 the old King died, and the Duke of York, who had opened the first Federal Parliament, was in June of 1911 crowned George V.

In London, it was a glorious summer.

In Sydney Harry Patterson and David Brahm were due to sit for their Intermediate Certificate, and had two further years of school before their matriculation. Neither of them had any idea yet what they wanted to do with the rest of their lives, although David's parents hoped he would study medicine.

In the Barossa they looked forward to another abundant crop, but in late November a savage hailstorm ruined the harvest. Stefan and Elizabeth were able to survive it as they had the previous year's shiraz stored in vats and enough cash in the bank to see them through, but it meant economies, and Elizabeth wondered if they could afford to keep Maria at her new school in Tanunda. It would be a pity, because her instinct had been correct and Maria had thrived in the English college, whereas she had not adapted well to the German lessons and Lutheran teaching at the village school. Elizabeth thought about writing to seek her father's help, but was aware he had his own problems, and resolved that they would try to manage on their own.

For William Patterson's political fortunes had fluctuated. In his tenth year in the Senate, the tide of fortune that had charted his career seemed to have deserted him. He had been a member of the Cabinet, one of few Senators to achieve a position of such eminence. When Edmund Barton retired from politics to a place on the bench of the High Court, William was one who helped organise the succession of Alfred Deakin. It was Deakin – with William's encouragement – who believed British paternalism towards Australia must not be allowed to dominate foreign relations, and invited the American fleet to visit. It was no more than a tentative step towards a more independent policy and future alliance, but it infuriated the London colonial office, who still considered themselves in charge of Australia's foreign policy. Senator Patterson encouraged his friend the Prime Minister to write and advise them otherwise.

William was also one of a select few who knew of Deakin's extraordinary secret life. Although qualified as a barrister, he had earned his living as a journalist before entering politics. And as an anonymous freelance correspondent for the *London Morning Post*, he wrote about Australia and its politics during his time as its leader. At times the unnamed journalist approved of the performance of the Prime Minister. Occasionally he was critical. Had his political opponents known, they would have had the ammunition for his destruction. The fact that William Patterson was instrumental in keeping the secret meant he remained close to Deakin, and to the centre of power.

Deakin introduced reforms, including old age pensions, but was able to govern only with the support of the Labor Party. When the fragile coalition split, and Labor took office under Andrew Fisher, the shifts in political allegiances were such that James North, once a conservative, allied himself to Fisher and the Labor Party, and became a minister. He had a long memory, and saw to it no such affiliation was extended to William, whose decline was swift, and by the end of the year he was no longer a shadow minister. Relegated to the back bench, it was rumoured he was unlikely to be preselected again, once his term was served.

At the age of fifty-three, it seemed his public career was over.

It was a difficult fact for him to accept. So much of his life, since his entry into the New South Wales parliament, had been in the public arena. He was an outstanding orator, who loved the cut and thrust of debate and the collusion of politics. He felt he had made his mark, not only in support of Federation, but the equally important achievement of votes for women, and he never tired of pointing out that Australia was the second country in the world to introduce universal suffrage, and the right to vote had still – despite all the efforts of the suffragettes – not been granted to women in Great Britain and most of Europe.

He had also been on the committee that had toured the country in the quest for a national capital, trying to balance interstate rivalry by finding a site convenient to Sydney and Melbourne, but not too close to either to cause resentment. After forty towns were inspected, they had finally chosen a location in the Molonglo Valley – and officially named it Canberra. The public was told it was an Aboriginal word denoting 'meeting place', and the newspapers all expressed approval.

'Thank God I had no part in that,' William said, when it was soon divulged that *Canberra* also meant 'women's breasts'. The disclosure amused him immensely, and he told Edith and Harry at dinner. Since Lady Denman, the wife of the new governor-general, had been invited to name the proposed city, it was too embarrassing and too late to change it.

The story made Harry laugh for the first time in days. He had been deeply despondent, for Katherine Brahm had won a scholarship, and was to study in London. She would leave the following year, when she was fifteen, travel with a family friend as chaperone, then lodge with an aunt in Hampstead. She would study at the Guildhall of Music for four years, by which time he would be twenty-one and no more than a distant memory to her.

Edith, who was the only person who knew how badly he felt, thought the story rather *risqué*, but it made Harry laugh, and therefore she laughed, too. Which pleased and surprised William. In years past she would certainly not have done so.

'We're going to take the same house, at Collaroy,' David Brahm said as they left the school grounds.

Harry's heart sank. He would never be allowed to go, even if he was invited.

'Mother and Dad are going to write officially. They'd love you to join us. Sister Kate seems to like the idea,' David said slyly.

'I don't think I can.'

Harry felt miserable, but after managing to miss last Christmas, which meant he had been to the Barossa only two out of the past four summers, he dare not disappoint them again.

Although, would it be such a disappointment? His mother would miss him, and so would Maria, but all he had done the last time was quarrel incessantly with Carl, who was a year younger but almost the same size, and who after school each day worked in the vineyard, seeming to regard it as his private domain and his brother as an interloper to be resented.

As for his father, Harry always seemed unable to relax and feel at ease. They had so little in common. Stefan Muller was like a stranger with him. Stiff and formal. He was not like that with others. Certainly not with his other children, nor with Gerhardt and Eva-Maria, nor Oscar the chemist who married Sigrid.

Just with him . . .

Remote. Uncomfortable.

Étranger, he recalled from French lessons. *Foreigner*. That's how it was between them. And he would have to give up a holiday at the surf, and walks and kisses on the beach with Kate, to waste the summer in an atmosphere so often tense or even hostile –

'Did you hear me?' David said.

'Sorry. I was thinking about having to go to the Barossa.'

'Princess Katherine will be disappointed.'

'So am I,' Harry muttered.

'I expect she'll find some other boys to cheer her up.'

'You're a prick, Brahm. You know that? You're a bastard.'

In the park, they threw their straw boaters, and tried to make them glide like aeroplanes. Ever since the Wright brothers had made their flight at Kittyhawk, and now a Frenchman, Blériot, had flown across the English Channel, Harry and David and their friends talked incessantly about flying. It was even said that there would soon be airships that would carry dozens of people, and perhaps cross the Atlantic. It was almost possible to imagine that some day they might fly as far as Australia.

David made his boater soar out into the centre of the lake, and a nursemaid minding a child in a pram watched while they tried to retrieve it, and smiled as they threw stones so that the straw hat floated slowly to the far side, where they managed to recover it. David bowed with gallantry to the nursemaid, who waved.

'Not bad, eh.'

'You're too young for her,' Harry said.

David vehemently disagreed, then eyed him carefully. 'So you're not coming to spend Christmas with us?'

'I can't.'

'What's it like in the Barossa?'

'It's all right. There's lots of vineyards.'

'I don't mean that. I heard the people there are Germans.'

'Not all of them.'

'Some are, then?'

'Yes, some.'

'Most?'

'No – about half.'

'Is your mother German?'

'Don't be stupid. She grew up over here – in the house with my grandparents. She's their daughter.'

Too late, he saw the trap into which he had fallen.

'Well, if that's true, then why is your name Patterson? That would have been *her* name. Isn't she married?'

'My grandfather adopted me.' It was all he could think of so quickly. 'You do ask a lot of silly questions, Brahm.'

'It's just that – you're different.'

'I'm not different.'

'Yes, you are.'

Harry was anxious. He considered walking off, to show his annoyance and displeasure, and put an end to this conversation. *Different* was the one thing no boy at school wanted to be.

'Don't talk bloody rubbish,' he said.

'It's not rubbish. You are different,' he repeated. 'Most kids always live with their parents. But you live here – and your parents live there, with all those Germans. So if it's not your mother, is it your father?'

'What do you mean – is it my father?' Though he knew quite well what the question meant.

'Is he a German?'

'Of course not. Don't be ridiculous,' Harry Patterson said.

The words were strange and guttural, although the music of the hymn was familiar. On one side of him in the Lutheran church his brother Carl sang lustily, so Harry, unwilling to stand inept and silent, sang his own version in unison.

'O come all ye faithful, joyful and triumphant, O come ye, O come ye to Bethlehem.'

On the other side of him, his sister Maria heard the English words and looked up and smiled. She began to sing with him. Carl's robust voice took up the challenge as he sang with more vigour, and the congregation seemed enthused by the strength of these young voices, singing with such energy and enthusiasm, the village church resounding to the hymn.

The Pastor beamed. It was not only a packed Christmas Eve congregation, but they were in splendid voice.

The sermon seemed interminable to Harry. It was in German. He thought he saw his mother stifle a yawn, and wondered how much of it she understood. Maria sensed his boredom and smiled in sympathy. He looked down at his sister, and realised how alike she was to Mama. She had the same vivid eyes and blonde hair. The local boys would soon start to take notice. It was difficult for him to believe she was now eleven years old. Or was it twelve?

He nudged her and whispered, 'How old are you?'

She mouthed a reply, and he lip-read it.

Thirteen.

Of course. There were so few years between the three of them. How strange to have a sister, whom he only saw a few weeks at a time, and who grew up so quickly between his visits. But then so had Carl, who was now fifteen. At least he liked Maria – which was more than he could say about Carl, often surly and choosing to speak deliberately to him in their brand of German which was called *Barossa Deutsch.* Carl was already equal to him in height, but sturdier. Built – as his friend Brahm would say – like a brick shithouse.

The thought of David Brahm made him think of Kate, and how last year they had kissed for the first time, and how, having kissed once, they could scarcely bear to stop. He thought about how much he was going to miss her. He thought of their talks, always so much to say, never running out of conversation - and how much they made each other laugh.

He felt a deep longing for her, and a great sadness. He knew, once her studies were complete, she would stay in Europe. She would become a soloist, a celebrity; he had been certain of that since the night he saw her play in Melbourne, the way she accepted the applause that turned into a standing ovation, acknowledging it with grace and humility, yet without surprise, as if it was her due, as if she knew her worth and had no doubts of her success. It would be good to know where you were going in your life, like Kate did.

He felt Maria nudge him, and realised the sermon was over, and their heads were bowed in prayer, although he had not the least idea what they were saying.

'It's another good year,' Elizabeth said, 'More than makes up for the bad one when we lost the harvest to the hailstorm.' She was walking with her eldest son along the paths between the rows of grapes.

'When do you pick them, Mama?'

'In February,' she said, and seemed surprised that he did not know. 'But, of course, you've always been back at school by then. Some day you really must see a harvest.'

I hope not, he thought silently, and then felt disloyal.

She smiled as if she read his thoughts. 'I mean just once. It's fun. Neighbours and the villagers all come to help. At nights we roast a side of beef or a sucking-pig; we drink wine and dance, Sigrid's husband plays the fiddle, and Gerhardt has too much to drink and sings.' She laughed. 'But he sings so beautifully. And some of the village girls are very pretty. Carl can never make up his mind which one to invite to the harvest festival.'

When he nodded and was silent, she changed the subject. 'I had a letter from Father. He says your gran has not been well.'

'She's had some pains. Dr Sinclair says it's rheumatics. He came twice to visit.'

'What happened to Dr Fairfax?'

'I think he and grandfather had a row.'

'That's more than possible.'

They both smiled.

'Grandfather announced one day that Fairfax was an old fogey, a terrible snob and a pompous ass. And he charged too much.'

'That sounds like Grandfather. Also not a bad description of Dr Fairfax,' she laughed. 'And what do you think of Dr Sinclair? More importantly, what does Gran think of him?'

'She likes him. She says he's very handsome, and just the sight of him makes her feel better.'

'Goodness,' Elizabeth said, glad her son and her mother had this remarkable rapport, but sorry she had not known this new Edith, instead of the timid figure of her childhood.

'She's much better. Write more often, Mama. She loves to get letters from you. When Mrs Forbes brings in the mail, and says "there's one from Miss Lizzie", you ought to see the way her face lights up. She enjoys hearing about the vineyard, and how everything is going so well at last. That makes her happy.'

Elizabeth was touched, not only by news of her mother's interest, but by her son's concern.

'Why not send a new photograph of Maria? She has the last one framed beside her bed. She said the pair of you are like twins – when you were Maria's age.'

'Did she? All right, when I take Maria back to school, we'll have a portrait done in Tanunda.'

'Good. I won't mention it. It'll be a surprise.'

'And what about your news?'

'My news?'

'You haven't mentioned your cellist friend. Is she taking the scholarship in London?'

'Yes.'

'You'll miss her.'

'Don't make fun of me, Mother.'

'But I'm not.'

'Some people think it's a big joke. That I'm just seventeen.'

'My dear, I was seventeen when I fell in love and ran away and married your father. Didn't you know that?'

He was astounded – he had never really thought about it.

'I knew you were young. I didn't realise – how young.'

'So I most certainly would not think it a joke. I'd be the last to consider it so. But I want to ask you – will she ever come back to this country? Is there a career for her in music here, as a cellist?'

'I doubt it. Oh, there'd be work. But only in an orchestra, or even worse, a theatre pit. It would be such a waste. She's better than that.'

'Poor Heinrich,' she said.

He wanted to tell her that his name was Harry, but he loved his mother and didn't want to spoil the day.

Chapter 22

The liner *Monarch Star* released a last farewell hoot, a long mournful sound, as it moved slowly from the quay. All the streamers stretched and broke, and a mass of people on the wharf and those aboard lining the ship's rail all began to sing: '*Now is the hour, when we must say goodbye . . .*'

Harry was standing with David Brahm and his family. They were in the midst of the waving and singing crowds, and Kate's mother was crying. He knew for certain Kate was crying too, as the ship moved slowly out into midstream.

He could no longer see her. In an hour she would have passed out of the harbour, and begun the long journey south, via Melbourne and the Great Australian Bight, then north to Colombo, and through the Suez Canal to Europe. In six weeks' time, she would be in London, registered at the Guildhall of Music, where she would spend the next four years.

Harry turned and pushed his way through the crowd. He knew it was abrupt, but he had to leave. There was no choice. If you were seventeen, in your final year of school, after which you were to attend university and study law, there was no way you could remain on a wharf in public view - *and* in full view of your best friend – waving to a skinny girl you would never see again, and bawling your eyes out.

In the late summer of 1913, William Patterson was invited to a private meeting of his party hierarchy at the Melbourne Club, and told he would not be on their Senate ticket in the forthcoming general election. When he asked why, they reluctantly gave their reasons. Divergent opinions, they told him; his strident nationalism, his call for a new flag and a new anthem and more independence in trade policies, all of which conflicted with the accepted view of Australia's place in the world as a dominion of the British Empire. They praised him for his past work, extolling him as a vigorous force in his time – but felt the time was now over.

William called them a bunch of geldings, whose balls had not been surgically removed, because they had never had any in the first place. They were a collection of humbugs, a cabal of meek white mice, and he regretted he could not stand Andrew Fisher or Billy Hughes, or else he would join the Labor Party. One of his former colleagues shouted that the bloody Labor Party wouldn't bloody well have him, which was a pity, because he could go and be a pain in their arse for a change.

The following day, William invited a group of journalists and made a formal statement that the Australian Parliament had been shackled; it was a mere caricature of real democracy, a creature of British foreign policy, and that Federation did not mean nationhood after all – it meant curtsying to Their Lordships in London, and he was therefore resigning from the pathetic petty paradigm of politics. His alliteration was deliberate, and he spoke with some emotion about the loss of impetus in recent years, following the initial flush of national pride.

The newspapers reported him in full. William Foster Patterson had always been good copy.

Dr Sinclair's visits to the house became more frequent. He prescribed tablets, but Edith grew thin and weak. She spent more time upstairs, but she arranged with Mrs Forbes each afternoon to be taken down to the drawing room, or else to the garden if the weather was warm, so that she would be there when her grandson came home from school.

She was concerned about Harry's future. Edith had only loved two people in her life. Her daughter and Heinrich. In her thoughts she often used his given name, because she knew a time would come when he would have to choose between that name and the one William had bestowed on him as a child. Some day he must decide whether he was Heinrich Muller, or Harry Patterson. And now she would not be there to know his choice.

Dr Sinclair had tried to avoid discussing it, but she had insisted. It was ironic, Edith thought, how strong she had become in the years since she was crippled. The doctor had first prevaricated. He had then tried being charming, and when that failed, mumbled about having a chat to William.

'You won't,' she insisted, 'discuss it with my husband. It happens to be *my life* – so you'll have a chat with me.'

In the end she prevailed on him to be concise and clinical – which was all she required. He said his diagnosis of rheumatics had been a way of sparing her and the family concern, and the tablets he prescribed were only a pain relief. The cancer was now widespread and rampant.

'How long?' she asked.

'It's not easy to estimate,' Dr Sinclair said.

'How long?' she repeated more forcefully.

'About three months,' he told her.

'Too short,' Edith said. 'I want to see my grandson pass his leaving certificate. Finish his schooling. The end of the year.'

'I'm sorry. You want me to be honest?'

'Yes, please.'

'The end of the year is not remotely possible.'

For the first time, she felt sorrow that her time had come; she would not see Harry grow up, start law school. She would never know the rest of his life.

'Well, do your best, Doctor,' she said quietly. 'How about October?'

'It's unlikely.'

'You're a hard man.'

'And you're a brave woman.'

'Not particularly.' Edith managed a smile. 'Just showing off. Any advance on three months? I'll take what I can get.'

'If you're very careful it could be a while longer. But you may have to go to hospital.'

'No. Let's get that settled now. No hospital.'

'You'll be in pain.'

'I'm used to pain,' she said, and realised that he thought she meant her shattered spine.

'I can give you pills. But soon they won't control the suffering. You'll need a nurse, day and night.'

'Not yet,' Edith told him. 'When we come to that stage, you

arrange it. In the meantime, I'm anaemic, rheumatic – whatever medical fiction you choose. But I'm not dying.'

'They're going to realise eventually,' Dr Sinclair said.

'Not until I'm ready.'

Harry brought David Brahm home for tea with Edith, and even though it was the last week in May it was still warm and sunny, and they sat in the garden wolfing sandwiches and scones. David kept apologising and telling her how starving he was, because school lunch had been more disgusting than usual, a stew with turnips straight from Paddy's market, which had arrived too late to be cooked, so they were like lumps of wood in thin gravy, and almost tougher than the meat. His stories invariably made Edith laugh – she had become fond of Harry's closest friend.

The liking was mutual. David had discovered you could tell her things; critical things not discussed with parents – such as girlfriends, and whether he really wanted to be a doctor like his father hoped, or not. He had doubts, but felt unable to voice them at home.

'They'd be disappointed,' Edith said, 'but on the other hand, it's your life. You have the rest of the year to decide.'

'What if I decide no?'

'Then you must be gentle with them, David. Tell them how you feel, but remember they're missing Kate, and are bound to have lots of plans for you. So be very sure, before you say anything.'

David nodded. Mrs Patterson was different to most old people. She made you feel grown up. He thought she was looking a bit tired, but perhaps it was just her age, or not being able to walk and do exercise.

'What if I decide not to do law?' Harry said.

'Then you and I would have a most interesting evening, breaking the news to your grandfather.' Edith smiled.

'But would you be on my side?'

'Yes. But only if you found something more important, and believed in it.'

'I probably will do law. I think I will. It's just – difficult.'

'It is. You both have to make a huge decision, and you're only seventeen. You each wonder what the future holds, and don't want to make the wrong choice. I don't blame you in the least for being uncertain.'

David thought that summed it up. He wished he could talk to his parents like this. He now understood why Harry felt so close to her, and regarded her opinion so highly.

'There might even be a war,' he said.

'God forbid,' Edith replied.

'The Kaiser's very jingoistic.' David had read the word in the *Bulletin* that week, where they printed a cartoon that made the German Emperor look like Genghis Khan. 'But Kate writes that nobody in England takes him very seriously. After all, he and King George are cousins.'

'It's politicians and munitions firms who'll start the war,' Harry said, 'not the cousins and uncles of the House of Saxe-Coburg.'

He sounds just like William, Edith thought. *I hope to heaven he's wrong.*

'War?' William said. 'Not if they've got any sense. But then I've come to the conclusion politicians are all cretins.'

'Idiots, without an ounce of brains between them – certainly ever since last month,' Harry agreed, and William chuckled and said he could not have phrased it better himself.

Edith knew he was making the best of the situation, but sensed he was hurt by the party's rebuff. She imagined that Hannah Lockwood could tell her how deeply it had affected him, and stifled a smile at the thought of her telephoning the house in Paddington, and the two of them discussing William's reaction. It was a measure of her contentment, she felt, that she could contemplate such an action and be quietly amused by it. How much her life had changed, and all because of one small boy who, long ago, had looked at her with large brown eyes, while her tears fell, and asked, *'Are you sad, Grandma?'*

'No, Heinrich. I'm happy.'

'If you cry when you're happy, Grandma, what do you do when you're sad?'

She remembered the moment so vividly. She had rarely been unhappy since that day. However brief the remainder of her life, Edith knew she had a lot to be thankful for these past years.

That summer Harry was expected in the Barossa for the holidays. Elizabeth wrote, reminding him, and said it was a kind of anniversary; it would be fifteen years since their first real harvest, and there was to be a larger than usual gathering of friends and neighbours to celebrate the event and make it a specially festive New Year's Eve.

She asked him to use his influence, and persuade her mother and father to accompany him, so that they could all sit down to Christmas dinner together. They had never done this as a family.

She would love her father to see the transformation in the place; he would hardly believe the changes - and most particularly, she wanted her mother to visit her home for the first time.

But by early November Edith had taken to her bed. She could no longer camouflage the pain. Although she had managed to live a normal life many months longer than Dr Sinclair had predicted, the struggle to conceal her condition had eventually become such a strain, it was almost with a sense of relief that she went upstairs to her private suite, knowing it was unlikely she would come down again.

Accepting that further pretence was impossible, she asked Dr Sinclair to inform William, and took it upon herself to tell Harry. She had only one request to them both - that Elizabeth not be forced to leave the rest of her family and come halfway across the continent, by which time Edith would be drugged and unable to communicate with her. She had not seen her daughter for almost thirteen years, and it would be pointless agony for Elizabeth to feel compelled to see her now, when she was dying. With her last act of strength she managed to make them both agree.

In a state of indecision and distress, Harry wrote to his mother. He said he was unable to come for the Christmas holidays, and much as Gran would like to, she felt she could not manage the long journey at present. He gave no other reason for his own non-appearance, and thought it best to ignore his father's reproachful reply, chiding him for a lack of family feeling. Stefan said they were bitterly disappointed, and it was obvious he preferred his friends in the east.

On New Year's Eve, he was invited to several parties, but turned them all down and stayed with his grandmother. She was lucid and calm. She had been overjoyed when he was named dux of the school, and had passed his leaving certificate with Honours. They talked about his future, and he assured her he would study law, not from a sense of duty but because he wanted to, and would do his best.

They watched the display of fireworks in the park, and afterwards he read to her some of her favourite poetry. She tried to insist he go and dance the year in with his friends, but he said he was spending it the way he wished.

Soon after midnight, in the very early hours of 1914, Edith died almost as quietly as she had lived, and her grandson sat holding her hands and feeling desolate. The hours passed, his grief turning to anger as he waited for William to come home from celebrating the New Year with Hannah Lockwood.

Chapter 23

EDITH LOUISE PATTERSON
1858–1914
Aged 56 years

The headstone had been commissioned and completed within days of Edith's funeral. William had acquired a spacious plot in the secluded cemetery, and arranged to have it enclosed with iron railings, and the ground paved with granite. Instructions were given for the work to be done immediately, and fresh flowers were to be placed on the grave each week. The flowers were delivered by a florist, but Harry picked his own and brought them.

He came alone. He thought the site too large, the iron rails forbidding, and in consequence her grave seemed insignificant and lonely. It was not, he felt sure, the kind of resting place she would have chosen. He was deeply troubled; it was both a confusion of sorrow at his loss, and bewilderment that he could feel such a rage towards a man he had loved since childhood.

William wondered what to do about his grandson, and how to repair their former relationship. Harry was like a distant stranger, and had been ever since the early hours of New Year's

Day. William had arrived home to find the boy sitting beside Edith's body. It seemed he had not moved from there since the moment of her death, even to advise the servants, and had to be induced to leave her and come downstairs while they waited for the doctor and ambulance. Though he had not said so, William privately thought such behaviour was unhealthy.

The house was hushed and semi-dark. From some of the neighbouring homes came the end of late parties, the shouts of departing guests, the raucous barking of dogs as motor engines coughed into life, as well as the occasional clatter of horses' hooves and the roll of carriage wheels. There were still some who resisted the automobile, and believed the horse and buggy was the safest and most reliable way to travel.

The library was cold for mid-summer.

'I'm sorry. I had no idea it would be so sudden.'

He waited for a reply, but there was none. William poured himself a drink, and looked at his grandson.

'Small brandy, old chap?'

'No, thank you.'

It was abrupt. Almost curt. He thought he was mistaken, so he tried again.

'I hope – it was peaceful.'

'She just fell asleep. But if you don't mind, I'd rather not talk about it. Especially not today – and not to you, Grandfather.'

William felt shock at the chill, detached voice. 'How could I have guessed it would happen tonight?'

'Would you have bothered to stay, even if you knew?'

William could hardly believe this savage, unforgiving youth was his grandson. They had never quarrelled like this before.

'That's a stupid and unfair thing to say.'

'I expect it is. Before I say anything else, I'd better get some sleep, if you don't mind.'

'You listen to me first. You think she would have wanted me to stay? She'd have seen it for what it was – a token gesture. And she would rather have spent the time with you.'

'While you preferred to spend it with Hannah Lockwood.'

The anger and contempt with which he said Hannah's name was almost as much a shock as the fact of him knowing it.

'Who told you about her?'

'No one in particular.'

'Someone must have. Surely, you understand I had no wish to embarrass your grandmother, so I tried to be discreet.'

'Discreet? You? Don't make me laugh.'

'What the hell do you mean by that remark?'

'You took her to the theatre. To the ballet. You met in public. She went to Melbourne with you when the Senate sat. I used to meet her sometimes when I was a child, didn't I? The nice lady in the park – when we took our walks together. Discreet, Grandfather? Even some of my school friends had heard the gossip. I'd have had to be deaf and blind not to know.'

William studied him, his own anger rising. He felt sorrow for Edith's life, and her death, but he resented being judged like this.

'I'll tell you one thing, Harry. It's none of your damn business.'

'No, it's not. You're right. I'm sorry I even mentioned it.'

There was no contrition in his voice. It was frigidly polite. In that moment, William Patterson felt as if his grandson hated him.

'I understand you made my parents a promise once. That I'd go back there, if Gran died.'

'It was long ago. I doubt if they'd hold us to it.'

'You think promises are made to be broken?'

When William did not reply, Harry said, 'I'll write to my mother, and tell her to expect me.'

Only Hannah knew the extent of William's remorse and depression. He had been deeply hurt in this past year. The end of his parliamentary career had been an unkind blow. Edith's death had brought sadness, for he had grown to appreciate her many qualities, and regret their loveless years. An intimate relationship between them had never been a real possibility, but he had accepted for some time he had misjudged her, and had not treated her well. In recent years he had done his best to make amends, and was left with a sense of loss when she was no longer there.

But it was the third setback – the quarrel and rift with his grandson – which distressed him most. Since Harry left for the Barossa, there had been no communication from him. No decision had been made about whether he would return to begin his law studies when the university year commenced in March. There had been just one letter, from Elizabeth, in which she said he had arrived and how he seemed quiet and despondent, but since he had been closest of them all to Mama, this was understandable. She said in a few weeks they would begin their harvest, and it was always a happy and festive time, so hopefully he would cheer up and enjoy it.

The letter, while not openly stating it, also contained an underlying concern. Hannah knew how deeply William had treasured the boy. She recalled the walks, the tall figure and the tiny one, spending so many hours together, finding so much shared interest to bridge their age gap. William had pleaded for him to be brought up in Sydney, as much for himself as for his wife. Gradually, over the years he had spent less time with him, deferring to Edith whose daily life revolved around her grandson, but his affection for Harry remained. He was able to provide him with the kind of boyhood William himself had wanted; a good school, friends, a home they were encouraged to visit and in which they were made to feel welcome. He had invested so many hopes for the future in him, and Harry, popular with his contemporaries, a prefect and eventually dux of the school, with a law career mapped out, seemed the embodiment of all William's aspirations.

Until now.

He had never felt so disoriented, or so tired. While they bent and stripped the vines, working continuously, filling the wooden buckets with grapes and hauling them to one of the carts that would take them to be crushed, most of the girls and men conversed in *Barossa Deutsch*, the harsh unfamiliar sound alien to his ears. At night, when they cooked a pig or side of beef, drank beer or wine, then played music and danced, he was too exhausted to take part. His limbs throbbed and his back ached, and the first few nights he crawled into his bed and slept, until Carl shook him awake at dawn, and it was time to begin another day.

'Take a day's rest,' his mother said. 'You don't have to do this.' He was sorely tempted, until Carl said, 'Yeah. Go and lie down in the shade. We can manage without you. We always have.'

Harry said nothing and simply began work again. Elizabeth and Maria, as if in support, picked alongside him. Maria had been granted a week's leave from her school to help with the harvest. Fourteen now, Harry realised, and so like their mother it was uncanny. But though she was thirty-five, Elizabeth Muller looked ten years younger. She wore her oldest clothes and a shabby straw hat, but nothing could disguise her beauty. He wondered if it was strange for a son to think of his mother as beautiful, but it was clearly a view shared by many of the male pickers, who glanced at her with conspicuous admiration whenever they had the opportunity.

That night he made the effort to join the others around the fire, and sipped a local ale. Sigrid called for him to join her.

'Heinrich, you remember my husband, Oscar Schmidt?'

'Of course.'

He shook hands with Oscar, who had driven his motorbike and sidecar from town, and later would drive Sigrid back to their quarters above the chemist shop. He was a mild-mannered man in his forties, who wore *pince-nez* glasses, a tie and waistcoat. Harry sat down beside them, wincing as he did so.

Sigrid smiled sympathetically. 'You don't do hard work like this before, Heinrich.'

'No, Sigrid. It's – Harry, by the way.'

'Not to us, *liebchen*. Here you're still Heinrich.'

She meant well, and so it was pointless to persist. It was the same with his parents' closest friends. Gerhardt was as ebullient as ever, his wife Eva-Maria as warm and friendly as he remembered her.

'It's wonderful to see you, Heinrich.'

'Harry.'

'You grew up so fast.' Eva-Maria hugged him. 'And good looking. I think there are lots of girls?'

'No,' he said. 'Only one.'

'She must be nice.'

'Yes. But she's in London.'

She sensed his dejection, and tucked her arm consolingly in his.

Gerhardt noticed nothing amiss. 'One girl. Not like your brother.' He chuckled. 'That Carl – lots of village girls. So much dancing, and some cuddling and kissing when they think nobody looks. But nothing much serious goes on, not with so many. Is yours serious, Heinrich?'

'I suppose it is,' he replied, wondering how to tell them that the name upset him.

'Ach . . . Elisabet. *Guten Tag.*'

'Frau Pabst. Do you know my son? My eldest son?'

'He looks grown up – like he could be your brother, Elisabet. Welcome, Heinrich.'

'Er – Harry. How do you do.'

'It is good to be home, *Ja? Wiedersehen!*' She beamed and crossed the street to a milliner's shop, with hats and gowns displayed beneath the sign: J.W. SCHUBERT'S MODEWAREN GESCHAFT.

'My brother indeed.' Elizabeth was plainly flattered.

He smiled and took her arm as they walked through the foreign town, past the Lutheran church and the strange and unfamiliar names: JOHANN GRAETZ'S DEUTSCHE SCHLACHTERIE, a butcher's shop, the prices of the meat displayed in both English and German; then PASCHKE'S FEINKOST, a smallgoods business, and BRUNO HEUZENROADER, the village blacksmith.

Most people spoke with his mother, but kept their German

to greetings and farewells, conversing otherwise in English. It was clear she was universally known and well liked. They passed the stone and shingled police station, where a fleshy man in a sergeant's uniform stolidly surveyed the street, and seemed satisfied that law and order prevailed. Elizabeth waved. He lifted his hand in semblance of a salute.

'My son Harry,' she called, and paused to introduce them. 'This is Sergeant Delaney.'

'Ah yes,' the policeman said. 'Going to be a lawyer, I hear?'

'I hope so, Sergeant. If I qualify.'

'Good luck then. See you in court someday.'

They moved on, leaving him to scrutinise his domain from the verandah of the police station.

'Thanks, Ma,' he said casually.

'For what?'

'Calling me Harry.'

She glanced at him, and for a moment he thought she was going to avoid a direct reply. Then she nodded and said, 'I know you prefer it. It's difficult for people here. They mean no harm, but they think of you as Heinrich. Always have. And as for your father – it was his father's name. I can't promise to change him, but perhaps we'll slowly convert the others to the idea of Harry.'

She smiled, and all at once he imagined how it might have been, had she been in Sydney while he was at school, able to attend speech days and events like the sports and school games. She would have made all the others there look so dowdy. He wished his friend David Brahm could have met her. The thought of it made him want to laugh. Brahm would have tried to flirt with her, then pronounced his belief it was ridiculous anyone's mother should look like this.

'What is it?'

'Nothing. Just thinking of a friend of mine.'

'Darling, you and I have to talk,' Elizabeth said, deciding that this would be a good time to raise something that had been on her mind. 'I need to know if you're visiting, or intending to stay - or what your plans are.'

'Can I have more time to think about that?'

'Of course. It'll take time. I know how much you miss Gran.'

'I'm sorry I couldn't write to tell you how ill she was,' he said as they walked together. 'She wouldn't let me. She didn't want to force you to come all that way, not when she was dying.'

'Force me? She always underestimated herself.' Elizabeth shook her head, and was silent for a moment. 'I felt desperately sad, not only because she died, but because I wasn't there - to say goodbye.'

'I wish I'd told you the truth.'

'No, darling. Don't feel bad. It was what she wanted.'

They approached Oscar's shop. The window was inscribed: DEUTSCHE APOTHEKE. OSCAR SCHMIDT. DROGERIE. ENGLISCHE SPOKEN. Signs inside the shop amid an array of jars and coloured bottles were in both languages: DRUGS AND MEDICINES. TOILET ARTICLES. VETERINARY SUPPLIES. ENEMAS AND DOUCHES. HAVANA CIGARS.

Harry had never seen such an extraordinary place. Beyond the cluttered premises was a flight of stairs which led to Sigrid and Oscar's home above the store. They went into a living room, where Gerhardt and Eva-Maria were also guests, and Oscar left his apprentice in charge, so he could join them. Sigrid served a huge afternoon tea. On the walls were framed photographs of children; he saw himself as a baby, and others of Carl and Maria. He felt a warmth towards Sigrid, who had been their nursemaid, and still cared enough to keep their pictures in the main room of her home.

The talk flowed unceasingly. They were close friends, a tight-knit group, lacking only his father who was working.

'So you think to study the law, Heinrich?' Oscar asked.

'Yes,' he said.

'You get good results in school?'

'He's the dux, Oscar. The top of the bush.'

'The tree, Gerhardt.'

'Whichever you like,' said Gerhardt, amid smiles. 'Tree or bush. He's bright like you, Oscar. A scholar. Maybe some day a judge.'

'Little Heinrich,' Sigrid said, bringing in a fresh tray of cakes, although the table was already full. 'A judge. I could never imagine such a thing.'

Gerhardt leaned forward.

'So tell us, Heinrich –'

'Gerhardt, will you do me a favour?'

'Any favour, Heinrich. What favour?'

'Will you call me Harry.'

'Of course I will.'

'It's just that – everyone does – in Sydney.'

'So tell me – Harry – what does your grandfather, the Senator think? Will there be a war?'

'No thank you,' Eva-Maria said sharply. 'No more wars.'

'There can't be a war,' Oscar declared. 'Not England and Germany. Out of the question.'

'We all know you don't think so,' Gerhardt told him. 'And my wife don't think so. But what does Harry's grandfather think?'

'He thinks – like everyone in the East – that it's inevitable.'

'No,' Oscar said firmly, 'impossible.' He repeated the now familiar dictum. 'The Kaiser and the King are cousins. It would be like families fighting.'

Well, families do, Harry thought, but said nothing. He was at loggerheads with his grandfather. Ill at ease with his father. While he and Carl – there must have been a time, he imagined, when they were close, but it was too long ago to recall. His brother was aggressively hostile, whenever they were alone.

'Why did you come back, anyway?'

They had been working together, Carl stripped to the waist and wielding a sledgehammer as they fenced a new piece of land. He was muscular and physically powerful. As Harry struggled to bring the heavy wooden posts to him, Carl had kept berating him.

'It's plain as day you think we're a mob of *Schiessers* . . .'

'Of what?'

'Hicks and bloody yokels.'

'What have you got against me, Carl? All I ever get from you is abuse. What is it you object to?'

'You don't belong here. Never have.'

'Even if that's true – why do you resent me?'

Carl leaned on the newly erected fence post.

'Because all I ever heard about, all my whole bloody life, was bloody Heinrich. Every time Papa gets a few drinks aboard, he bores the shit out of everyone by talking about you – as if you're some sort of prodigal son, something special. Whereas you and I know the truth, which is that you don't give a fuck – about him or any of us.'

Harry remembered it, as he accepted another cup of tea from Sigrid. Families fought all the time. Why should the royal cousins be different? He and Carl could generate enough antagonism to start their own war.

Hannah and William had lunch under the shaded trellis at the back of the Paddington house, while she read the letter he had received that morning. It was from Harry, written and sent four days earlier from the Barossa. He watched her while she carefully read again the single page of neat handwriting.

'He says he's enjoying it.'

'I know he does. But what do you think?'

'I'm not sure. I don't really know Harry.'

'You didn't know Elizabeth. Yet years ago –'

'That was different.'

Years ago she had interpreted the hidden feelings in his daughter's letter from Hahndorf that changed all their lives.

'I'm starting to feel like your tame seer. Every time you're unsure about a letter, you consult me.'

'Only twice. And who else can I ask?'

She took his hand, pleased at what he had said, but aware of his concern. She did not want to add to it.

'He writes that he's busy helping around the vineyard. That his muscles have finally stopped aching, all the family are well, and he's met lots of their friends. Why not accept that?'

'Because it's a polite obligatory letter, without even a trace of affection. You know it, Hannah, as well as I do.'

She knew it, but had not wanted to say so.

'He can't forgive me. For what I've done to him.'

'That's unfair,' she said heatedly. 'You gave him so much.'

'I also took. I took him from his parents. It seemed right when

Edith was alive - but now I'm not sure. I don't think he knows where he fits - where he really belongs.'

'He'll make that decision for himself.'

'I feel guilty,' he said. 'I don't know what to do.'

He sounded insecure and, for the first time she could recall, dejected. She wanted to console him. It had been a wretched time, the past months; even the strongest have their breaking points, and Hannah knew he was close to it now.

'I wish I could help, William.'

'You can. Marry me.'

His words were no surprise. She knew he would ask, but had hoped it would not be so soon.

'Darling, Willie –'

'Does that mean yes?'

'It means - shouldn't we go on the way we are?'

'Why?'

'For one thing, it's too early for you to remarry.'

'If you mean public opinion - we know people talk about us already. Marry me and they'd have nothing to gossip about. We'd ruin their malicious tea parties. Doesn't that idea appeal to you?'

She laughed. She rose from her chair, and he put his arms around her, and felt her body tremble against his.

'Do you love me?'

'You know I do.'

'Then why go on this way, when we could be together in the same house, and share each day? Please say you'll marry me.'

'There's something else.'

'Nothing else.'

'There's your grandson. I doubt if he'll accept me.'

'He'll have to.'

'I wouldn't want it like that, William.'

'Hannah, there's something you really must understand.' As she went to speak, he stopped her with a gesture. 'No, I need to make this quite clear. If I have to live without him, I'll manage. But I can't live without you.'

Stefan was pruning the vines. He saw a figure run from the house, and realised he had the book in his hand. Well, it had to come, this moment. He stopped work and waited for Heinrich.

'Father . . .'

Stefan said nothing, watching his eldest son almost warily. He didn't want it to happen, but there was no way it could be avoided.

'Father, this book of Henry Lawson's poems – I lent it to you. The title page is torn out.'

'Yes,' Stefan said. 'I'm sorry.'

'It was a school prize. Why did you do that, Papa?'

'You tell me something. What did it say – this page?'

There was a brief silence.

'Dux of the school – Harry Patterson,' Harry said.

'And who in the name of God,' his father demanded, 'is Harry Patterson?'

'It must be obvious that I am.'

'It was not obvious. Not to me. Yes, I knew he called you Henry – then later it became Harry, I knew that. But Patterson – that I did not know.'

'I always meant to tell you,' Harry said, feeling guilt, 'but each time I tried, I couldn't. I realised you'd be upset.'

'Yes,' Stefan replied, 'I am upset. To disfigure a book, most of all a prize, is not a nice thing to do. But nor is disowning your name. Did your grandfather do that? Was Heinrich Muller too German, even Harry Muller – was it too foreign for him? Did he insist you obliterate Muller and take his name?'

'I wanted it, Father. *I asked him*.'

His father just stared at him and said nothing. For a moment Harry thought he was going to turn and walk away.

'Please listen to me, Papa. Try to understand.'

'I've tried. I tried not to tear out the page. Dux of the school, I should have been proud. Instead I felt ill and angry. But I tried to understand.'

'Then listen to me. *Please*. I had to go to school, Papa. Not here in your quaint German valley – but in the real world, where they'd kick the Christ out of Heinrich Muller, but they accept Harry Patterson. Can't you understand that?'

His father shook his head, looking sad.

'I'm not German, Father.'

'Part of you is.'

'Only by birth. I wasn't brought up to be German. I don't understand them. I'm not sure I even like them . . .' It spilled out in a blind rush, it was blurted out before he could prevent himself, then he realised and was appalled. He took a step towards his father, wanting to repair the damage, but Stefan shook his head, like a boxer hurt by one blow too many, and turned away as if from further punishment. Harry heard a movement behind him, spun around and saw his mother's face.

He had not known, until that moment, she could be so angry.

~

William received the urgent telegram the following day. He was in the library, frowning over the increasingly alarmist newspaper reports from Europe, and in particular the stories of Prussian militarist proclamations in Berlin, as well as disturbances in the Balkan states. He looked up as Mrs Forbes entered with the distinctive envelope. Its short, almost terse message, read: HARRY RETURNING HOME TODAY. WILL WRITE. LOVE ELIZABETH.

The train journey was endless. Harry felt sick and ashamed. He could hardly believe he had spoken that way to his father, and wondered what sort of reception awaited him when he arrived home. He had no idea what his mother had said in her telegram. That she had sent one he knew, because she had gone to the telegraph office while he waited on the platform for the train to Adelaide.

It had been a terrible twenty-four hours.

'I'll explain as best I can to your grandfather. You don't belong with us, Harry. I daresay you realise that?'

'Yes . . .' was all he could manage at first, and then, 'I'm sorry. I did try, Mama.'

She took his hands. She was troubled, and gentle with him. 'I know you did.'

She sent the telegram, and came back. He waited with his suitcases on the almost empty platform.

'What am I going to say to Grandfather?'

'You'll say you prefer to live in Sydney – with him.'

'It may not only be with him,' Harry said.

'You mean he may marry Hannah?'

He gazed at her in total astonishment.

'You know about her?'

'Of course I know about Hannah Lockwood.'

'But how?'

'Your grandmother told me.'

'Gran knew?'

'Certainly she knew.'

He was completely confused. And shocked. Gran, who told him so much, had never said a word. Adults were so complicated.

'Have you ever met Hannah?' he asked.

'No, but I wish I had. I hope she's the right person for him. I do want my father to be happy. It's time he was.'

'Was he so unhappy with Gran?'

'Not entirely. They were unsuited. You kept them together; your living there with them made it possible for them to live with each other, and for that I'm grateful.' She carefully straightened his tie before she spoke again. 'Someday, darling, you might write to your father and tell him you're sorry.'

'I'll do it as soon as I'm home.'

'No,' she said. 'Do it when you feel sad at what you said, and realise how much you hurt him. Don't do it unless you mean it. I don't think either of us want a forced apology. It would be hypocrisy, and I personally would hate that. So would he.'

The train came in. She kissed him goodbye, and waited by the carriage window while he found a seat.

'Goodbye, Mother.'

'Safe trip. My love to Papa. Work hard. Be a good lawyer.'

The train hissed steam. He opened his window and waved until she and the station had receded into the distance. He felt the pain his anger towards his father had caused her, and could not suppress the dismaying thought that he might never see her again.

PART FOUR

Chapter 24

The first rocks smashed the window of PASCHKE'S FEINKOST, then others followed, shattering the glass of JOHANN GRAETZ'S DEUTSCHE SCHLACHTERIE. From the darkened street voices shouted, 'Dirty rotten German bastards.'

'Filthy fucking huns.'

A hail of stones crashed on the rooftops, fracturing the slates, while others broke windows in the neat houses that faced the main street. Most of the occupants, woken in fear and confusion, were too shocked to hide from this unexpected onslaught. Some were cut by flying glass - elderly Mrs Pabst lost the sight of an eye. In the street, a figure with a brick took aim at Oscar Schmidt's APOTHEKE, but when lights in the police station went on, indicating that Sergeant Delaney was awake, the attacker dropped the missile and ran with the others. As they went past the Lutheran church, one hurled a stone. Stained glass cracked, and the figure of Christ splintered and fragmented.

The war was then two days old.

~

In the seaside park cymbals crashed and the brass band played a stirring martial tune. Banners were displayed everywhere – one exhorting the nation's youth to: JOIN UP AND DESTROY THE HUN. Others urged: SAVE CIVILISATION. FIGHT FOR GOD AND COUNTRY. SERVE IN THE WAR TO END ALL WARS.

Young men were queuing to enlist. They had been lining up in towns and cities each day since the declaration.

William and Hannah, there by accident to lunch at a favourite restaurant on the Esplanade, could see the lines of volunteers, and hear the comments.

'It's on,' one said. 'So let's go over there and get stuck in.'

'Bloody oath.'

'Beats working.'

'Beats staying home with Mum and Dad.'

'Beats running the bloody farm.'

'Hope it lasts till we get there.'

'France, eh? Oo-la-la.'

'Bewdy.'

'Where do I sign?'

It was a scene being duplicated all over the country. As events had moved inexorably towards conflict, as Europe's armies mobilised and the Austrian Archduke Ferdinand was assassinated by a Bosnian student at Sarajevo, Australian newspapers had begun to predict the certainty of war. The first act of aggression was on the morning of August 2nd, when German troops crossed the frontier of the tiny Grand Duchy of Luxembourg to seize its railway station.

This tenuous event was the trigger France and Britain required. Winston Churchill, the First Lord of the Admiralty, declared the British navy was ready, and at midnight on August

4th, a state of war was proclaimed. Because of the global time difference, Australia's war began the following morning. No Cabinet decision was required for this. As a part of the British Empire the country had a legal obligation to aid Britain, a fact greeted with wild enthusiasm throughout every State.

Recruitment for a force to be sent overseas began immediately, and eligible men rushed to volunteer. They left their jobs in droves. Some sold their farms or businesses, others arranged for their wives to take over. It was an adventure, the chance of a lifetime, to fight, to wear a uniform and to see the world. Politicians on both sides were unitedly in favour of the war, and some found in its agony their finest hour.

William and Hannah stood and watched as the band music ended. A recruiting officer, smart in tailored uniform, polished shoes and Sam Browne, stepped onto the rotunda to lead the applause of the crowd.

'Thank you, Bandmaster and members of the military band. We will hear more fine music later, but firstly, Mr James North, your Federal Parliamentary Member for this district and a Cabinet Minister in our new government, is here to say a few words.'

William was about to move off. Hannah detained him with a gloved hand on his arm. Though the park was crowded, they had a view of North, as he stepped up to shake hands with the officer amid loud applause. William had not seen him for some time. They were of a similar age, in their mid-fifties, but James North was securely in power since the election, and William was in the political wilderness.

'He's still quite a good-looking man,' Hannah murmured, and received an acerbic glance which made her smile.

'Let's go to the restaurant. I'm hungry,' William retorted.

'Let's wait a minute, and hear what he has to say.'

'Hmmph,' he muttered, but took her arm, conscious as always of the admiring glances she received, and proud to be seen with her. In her late forties, Hannah Lockwood still attracted more than her share of attention.

North was handed a megaphone, which he shunned. He had a strong and powerful voice, and it reached to all sections of the crowd.

'Friends, allies in this dark hour, young men who will save our nation,' he began in ringing tones, 'I bring you a message from our Prime Minister. I have just come from the PM, who said to tell you all: "Keep a good heart – and a stiff upper lip." '

It brought loud patriotic cheers from the crowd, and a glance of incredulity from William. Hannah squeezed his hand; it was by way of an apology for insisting they remain to listen to such drivel.

James North allowed the applause to reach a crescendo, then quelled it with a gesture. He gazed around him. *He's loving this*, William thought. *He's even become a bit better at it.* He wondered whether North had noticed them, and knew that even if he had, there would be no acknowledgement.

'Let me just say this. It is a time for heroes, for our patriotic youth to enlist for the glory of Australia. So step forward, lads. And you older men. We need you all. This is the great moment of your lives, the chance to show the rest of the world our mettle, and to put the fear of God into Kaiser Bill and his filthy German hordes. And above all, remember what Australia promised the mother country – that to defend her – *we will fight to the last man, and the last shilling.*'

The recently coined and highly popular slogan was greeted with a massive roar of approval. Women applauded, men took off their hats and waved them as they loudly cheered this sentiment. James North remained on the rotunda, his head slightly bowed, as if humbled by this deluge of national fervour.

William guessed they had been noticed, but only by a flicker of an eye did North betray it.

'Had enough?'

'I think so,' Hannah said.

They began to move away. Both were aware of curious glances directed at them, leaving as they did amid the enthusiastic and continuing acclaim.

'Lunch,' William asked, 'or have you just lost your appetite?'

The restaurant was a converted boat shed, overlooking the sand and sea. They ate without enjoyment. From the surrounding park they could hear the brass band endlessly playing military tunes.

'John Philip Sousa and his ilk have a lot to answer for, with their wretched martial music,' William said. 'Very stirring. The feet tap. They march. The next thing, some poor devil has signed up to go off and fight, with every chance of getting his head blown off.'

'I daresay the same thing is happening in Berlin,' Hannah said. 'They like to march and sing. But if Europe wants to set itself on fire, why do we insist on being invited to help put out the flames?'

He smiled at her.

'You almost make me wish I was still in politics. I could use that phrase.'

'You wouldn't be popular. Every politician of both parties is in favour of the war. You and I were probably the only people in the park today opposed to that bilge North was spouting.'

'I think he saw us,' William said.

'I'm sure he did. Strange, I used to be afraid of him.'

'Of Jimmy North?' William was startled.

Hannah nodded. 'I always thought he'd do you harm. He hated you.'

'Well, I did use him – then made bunnies out of him and Reid. He never forgave that. And in a way he got his own back. I would've joined the Labor Party if they'd have me, but North got there first and put the boot in.'

'I meant personally harm you. Harm your family. Perhaps through me – while Edith was alive. I was scared of that.'

'You never told me.'

'I supposed I hoped it would never happen. And it never did. But he's still a malicious man. He'd love to hurt you.'

'He no longer needs to care about me. Which brings us to what we came here to talk about. I'm out of politics. I'm alone. And the question with notice is still on the table.'

'William —'

'Please,' he begged her. 'You did agree we'd discuss it.'

'We can discuss it, but nothing changes.'

'You won't marry me?'

'I'd like to marry you. But not now. Not yet. I can't.'

'Because of Harry?'

'You got him back, William. Whatever happened in the Barossa, he came back to you, began his law studies, and you're reconciled. That's very important. And I will not jeopardise it.'

'For God's sake, Hannah, are you saying you want to marry

me, and I want to marry you, and my bloody grandson is stopping us?'

'Will you listen to me? William – listen.'

'I'm listening.'

'Harry must resent me. How could it be otherwise?'

'For God's sake –'

'William, just shut up, and *listen*.'

His mouth opened, and stayed that way. He glanced about him and saw other diners beginning to hear their raised voices, and look in their direction. Hannah ignored them, and reached across the linen cloth and took his hands. She smiled at his expression. It had been a long time since anyone had told William Patterson to shut up, in quite such a public and peremptory way.

'Willie darling, try to see my point of view. If it caused problems, if it meant losing him, you and I'd never forgive ourselves. In the end, our marriage would fail. Whereas we've been happy all these years the way we are. Can't you see, my love, this is best?'

'I want you to be my wife.'

'I have been, in all but name, for a long time.'

'I mean officially. No more hiding. And no more gossip.'

'Who the hell cares about gossip?'

'I do,' William said, 'if it's about you.'

'I'd rather keep what we have, than risk losing everything.'

'I told you before, if it has to come to a choice between you and Harry –'

'You haven't really listened.'

'Of course I listened.'

'Then you haven't heard.'

He stayed silent this time, and she said quietly, 'I don't accept there should ever be a choice. We're not children who must satisfy ourselves, no matter whom we damage. I was angry he walked out – not that I had any right to be, but that's how I felt – because he hurt you. Now I think I understand. Edith's death was the end of a time of stability in his life. He went looking for something else, and didn't find it.'

'You mean in the Barossa?'

She nodded.

'You once said, he doesn't know who he is, or where he belongs. I think he's found out. He's decided he belongs with you. You told me he came back confused and lost. That Elizabeth wrote and said there were family problems, and to be gentle with him.'

'I have been.'

'I know. And he's settled back into his old life. You said you're able to talk like you used to. It seems, since his return, you've become friends again. That's good for you, and terribly important for your grandson.'

He was silent for what seemed a long time.

'And us?'

'One day, perhaps. Give him time. Give us all time.'

'Trouble is, we're getting older and time becomes more precious.'

Carl walked home slowly. He was sick of school. He hated the Lutheran Academy, and the repetitive lessons, which bored him and would be of no possible use, since he intended to work with his father on the vineyard. It was with a feeling of relief that he thought of the end of the spring term, when his school days would finally be over. His mother had not been pleased; she felt he should remain and complete his final year, but Papa had persuaded her.

Let Harry be the scholar, he had said, and there was some bitterness there that Carl did not understand, although he knew his father disapproved of Heinrich calling himself Harry. He silently hoped his brother would not come to the valley again. They would never have anything in common and Heinrich didn't belong here with his different ways; he was an outsider.

The boys from St John's Grammar came out of the bushes at the side of the road, catching him unaware. They were all sixth formers, some almost as big and strong as he was. A few were local, the sons of farmers, others were from Nuriootpa. They stood waiting in a line across the road, grinning with anticipation. He recognised Tom Carson, whose parents ran the dairy farm and did mail deliveries. His own parents had helped the Carsons, and given them work. Now it was his voice that Carl heard first.

'Stinking German spy.'

They all marched a pace forward, then another. They were sniggering. He could not get past them, because the line obstructed the road, so he turned the other way. Another group of St John's boys had come from behind the hedgerow, blocking his retreat.

'I'll fight if you want a fight,' Carl said, 'one at a time.'

They laughed derisively, and began to converge on him.

'Spy. Dirty spy. Filthy hun. Dirty rotten German traitor.'

They came at him in a rush from all sides. He managed to hit one in the nose, and blood spurted, but was assailed by a barrage of fists, as they fell on him like a pack of savage hounds. When he stumbled and fell, they began to kick him.

'German spy,' they chanted. 'German spy.'

~

The university quadrangle was almost deserted. Harry was waiting for David Brahm, and saw his angular figure leaving the medical building. It was a gusty day, and the wind blew a discarded newspaper across the asphalt towards him. It wrapped around his legs, and as he removed it he saw the headlines: GERMANS TAKE BELGIUM CAPITAL. HUN ATROCITIES. NUNS RAPED. Much of the page was taken up with a large cartoon of a bestial figure in German uniform, stamping on the face of a defenceless and frightened girl.

He felt a moment of revulsion at the blatant crudity of the drawing. Was it true, the terrible things he read, that the Germans were supposed to be doing? Was it fair to categorise a whole people as barbaric monsters? His father was hardly that, nor Gerhardt Lippert nor Oscar, nor any other German he had met. He wondered, for the first time how they must feel, seeing their own race depicted as prehistoric and ape-like creatures in brutish caricatures such as this.

'Very nasty,' Brahm said, looking over his shoulder. 'They certainly go the whole hog, don't they? Quite repulsive. Who's the artist?'

'Norman Lindsay.'

'I thought he only painted naked ladies.'

'There's his signature,' Harry said.

'Good God.' David Brahm peered at it. 'So it is. Reprinted with kind permission of the *Bulletin*.'

They walked through the empty grounds towards Cleveland Street, to catch a steam tram home.

'What other news?'

'Antwerp's fallen. It says the Germans are feeding poison to the Belgian men, and raping their wives.'

'Do you believe it?'

'Of course not.'

'Why so vehement, old son?' David put on arm on his shoulder. 'Heaps do believe, I fear. We've just lost our Professor of Biology.'

'What do you mean – lost him?'

'Prof. Beidermann. No longer does he teach us where to find the fibula or the tibia on Sam the skeleton.'

'Why not? What's happened?'

'He's been arrested.'

'Professor Beidermann? For what?'

'Being German, I suppose.'

Harry felt a sudden alarm. A chill of foreboding.

'How can you be arrested for – for being German?'

'Who knows? A paddy wagon came for the professor last night, so the resident students said. Four large members of the constabulary, to arrest one small, inoffensive lecturer.'

'Jesus. But there must be some other reason. It can't just be because he's German.'

'Why not? Lots of them are being interned.'

'Are they?'

They heard the tram approaching.

'Have you heard from my sister?' David asked.

'I had a letter yesterday.'

'Any room on the page for actual news – I mean, after the space taken up by kisses and all that stuff?'

'Shut up,' Harry replied.

'Honestly, what did she say?'

'She said – it had been a lovely summer, and she got Honours in her first year's exams, and so, despite the war, she couldn't possibly come home. Besides, everyone there believes it will be all over by Christmas.'

They boarded the tram. Harry disposed of the newspaper. He wished he had never seen it. They paid their fares and took their places on the hard wooden bench seats.

'What's upset you, Harry? Apart from Kate's being on the other side of the world?'

The tram ride was a slow journey through Surry Hills towards Centennial Park, and he watched the passing terraced houses as he tried to frame an answer.

'I'm worried about some people – friends of my family in the Barossa. German born, but they've lived here for years. Half their lives, some of them.'

'Are they naturalised?'

'Yes. Long ago.'

'So they're Australian,' David said. 'What's the problem? They have nothing to fear.'

'I suppose not,' Harry said.

Oscar Schmidt gave Elizabeth a bottle of liniment, and when she tried to pay he refused to take the money.

'Please, Oscar. This is business.'

'This is not business. This is stupid larrikins. Hooligans. Lucky the doctor says there are no broken ribs. He's to use the liniment three times a day, Elizabeth. And make him rest.'

He saw her to the door of the *Apotheke*.

'Have you reported it to the police?'

'Carl won't let us. Or tell us who did it. He says the police no longer protect people with German names.'

'Silly talk, Elizabeth. He's wrong.'

'Perhaps he is, Oscar. But does Sergeant Delaney stop to chat to you these days, like he used to?'

'The sergeant is a fair man. He'll do his job.'

They went outside. Many of the broken shop windows were still boarded up. Glaziers and carpenters had been in short supply, most of them busy in Adelaide, where the damage had been extensive, while others apparently would not undertake the work. They saw Eva-Maria and Gerhardt across the street, and went to join them.

'How's Carl?'

'Too tough to cry,' Elizabeth said. 'But they hurt him.'

'You see,' Gerhardt said to Oscar, 'it begins.'

'Just stupid kids,' Oscar replied.

'Anti-German feeling,' Gerhardt insisted.

'I keep telling you, this war is nothing to do with us.'

'So everyone keeps telling me.'

'Then be sensible and listen to them. After all, we live here. We don't support the Kaiser. It's just hysteria – things will settle down. Why put ideas in people's heads?'

Eva-Maria was watching her husband.

'Maybe Oscar's right,' she said. 'You should listen to him.'

'I do listen to him,' Gerhardt said. 'The last time I listened to Oscar, he promised me faithfully there wouldn't be a war.'

When the new windows were at last fitted to the line of shops, including JOHANN GRAETZ'S SCHLACHTERIE, PASCHKE'S SMALL-GOODS, SCHUBERT'S MODEWAREN GESCHAFT, as well as most of the houses on the main street, Oscar Schmidt went around reassuring everyone that the hysteria was now definitely over. He was earnest and persuasive, and people began to relax. There had been no more trouble. The town was looking normal again.

Four nights later they came back again, by truck, this time with an arsenal of weapons. Steel bars, clubs and sledge hammers. And this time the lights in the police station stayed dark, despite the clamorous sounds of destruction. When they finally left, not a shop window remained intact, and the street was crystalled with fragments of broken glass.

The following day Johann Graetz, in his striped butcher's apron, was supervising the repairs. While a glazier trimmed putty on the new window, a painter on his ladder was already brushing and obliterating the faded sign that had been on the gable above the shop for forty years. JOHANN GRAETZ & SON. ESTABLISHED 1884 was totally erased. Later that same day a signwriter lettered a new name on the window, and the premises became GRAY'S BUTCHERY. Nearby, Schubert's window simply advertised: ENGLISH GOWNS AND MILLINERY. Paschke sold his business and went to work in a factory.

Gerhardt drove to town for a drink and an argument with Oscar Schmidt. They saw the newly repaired windows, all trace of German names and signs effaced.

'So? You don't have to replace your window yet, Oscar. If you do, if your glass is smashed, do you change your name to Smith?'

Oscar refused to countenance the idea of changing his name. He took Gerhardt upstairs for a glass of schnapps and further argument. He was adamant the situation would be resolved.

'I still say, if we are sensible and don't provoke people, all this will die down.'

~

They were waiting in a thicket along the dusty road. Several groups of boys from St John's school passed, but Carl shook his head. He kept watching, and gestured for them to remain in hiding. When he finally identified Tom Carson approaching with the group of sixth formers, he gave a signal. Before their quarry could realise it, they were surrounded by a number of burly German farm youths.

'This bastard's mine,' Carl said, heading for Carson.

There was a brief but ferocious encounter. When the others had been dealt with, and allowed to run, his friends realised Carl was still battering the terrified dairy farmer's son.

They restrained him, letting Carson stagger to his feet.

'Might've killed him,' Jacob Honneker said in German.

'Fine with me,' Carl said in English. 'At least I used my fists. This pig and his mob used their boots.'

Stefan had tried to ignore the war. He resolutely tilled the soil, tended his vines, and kept away from town as much as possible. He rarely read the newspapers and took no part in the endless arguments between Gerhardt and Oscar. Only at night did he talk of his concerns, to Elizabeth. He felt the best thing they could do was stay calm, obey the law, and in the end reason and sanity would prevail.

Gerhardt tried to provoke him by declaring this was the asinine philosophy of Oscar Schmidt - chemist, optimist and pacifist. Stefan irritated his oldest friend by retorting he also was a pacifist - and why not an optimist? What need was there of another pessimist, with one like Gerhardt around? Eva-Maria had laughed and hugged him, and said if the war lasted, she might have to get a divorce. She complained there was war talk at their table morning and night, and even in their bed, when their minds should be on other things. Stefan smiled and afterwards agreed with Elizabeth there would be no talk of war in their bed.

That had been weeks ago. He worked from daylight until it was dark, and refused to be involved in further debate. It was Europe's affair. He privately thought his adopted country should not be sending troops, offering the British a force of twenty thousand men who would be at their disposal. He felt it was wrong, but kept his silence. It was best that way. A few insults, some racist remarks; he didn't like it, but he could tolerate that sort of thing. But this was different. This time it was his family – Carl had stupidly retaliated.

Elizabeth was cleaning and dabbing liniment on the new cuts around his face, where most of the former bruising had faded, when they saw Mr and Mrs Carson drive across the creek in their new sulky. 'Well, I'm not surprised they're here. You can apologise now.'

'But Ma – he started it.'

'Then you should have told us that, when it happened, and we could have reported it. I daresay you thought this was smarter. Paying them back.' In her indignation at his behaviour, she was far from gentle with the dressing.

'Ouch. That stings.'

'Serves you right. We already have a war – the other side of the world. We don't need one in this valley, thank you very much.'

The Carsons pulled up in front of the house.

They had been neighbours for some years now, and while not close, were on comparatively friendly terms. Stefan and Elizabeth had helped them when they first arrived, using their delivery service, and encouraging others to do the same. The Carsons had improved their herd, and their dairy was now profitable. They no longer had to deliver mail or goods, but had always asserted they were grateful for those early years.

They did not appear grateful now. Both stepped down from the sulky and came uninvited onto the verandah.

Stefan shrugged apologetically, trying to make the best of it.

'Sorry about this,' he said.

'You will be, Muller,' Mr Carson replied, and pointed at Carl. 'Your kid was the bloody ringleader.'

His wife stared with open dislike at Elizabeth.

'Patching him up, are you, Mrs Muller? Well, that makes you a party to this.'

'A party to it?' Elizabeth could feel the personal hostility, and was stunned by it.

'We've had the doctor,' Mrs Carson announced. 'Now I think we should call the police.'

'I'm sorry. Was your son badly hurt?' Carl glanced at his mother, puzzled. Her voice was surprisingly courteous.

'We'd hardly be here if he wasn't.'

'As badly as mine was, weeks ago, when they all set on him?' She was still frigidly polite. 'Eight of them, I think it was.'

'Nine,' Carl said.

'They kicked him when he was down. We had the doctor, too. If you want the police, I think we'd agree. Don't you, Stefan?'

'Definitely. I'll send for them if you wish,' Stefan said.

There was a momentary hiatus. They had not expected this, and there was a hint of apprehension as they exchanged glances.

'Very funny,' Mrs Carson said, unamused.

'It's not the least funny,' Elizabeth said as imperiously as she could. 'Why don't you tell your lout to stop this behaviour –'

'Lout?'

The Carsons were outraged, but Elizabeth took no notice.

'And I'll tell mine the same. Tell yours not to call mine a German spy. Advise him my son was born here - as I was - and my father was. Now get off my verandah, go home and tell him.'

Mrs Carson took a pace backward, but her husband was not so easily dismissed. His face was flushed and threatening.

'I'll tell you one thing, Missus fancy-face Muller. You mob better watch your step.'

'Us mob, Mr Carson? Who exactly are "*us mob*"?'

'Anyone with a German name. Ain't you heard? I could have you arrested?'

'Get off our land,' Stefan told him.

'Read the papers, Muller. The real papers, not your German rag. We could have you in gaol.'

He grinned, and for the first time Stefan felt uneasy. Carson and his wife walked to their horse and sulky. They climbed in. Mrs Carson took the reins. Her husband looked at them and spat.

'Remember what I said. In gaol - any time we like.'

Stefan and Elizabeth watched them drive away. Carl put an arm around his mother, and laughed.

'Ma, you were wonderful. You told the old cow.'

'I don't want another word from you,' Elizabeth said. 'Go away and try to learn some sense. Don't you dare ever put us in this position again.'

'But Ma –' He was shocked at her anger.

'No more retaliation. No stupidity. Have your supper, then go down to Gerhardt's. See if he knows what on earth they are talking about.'

'Have us arrested?' Stefan said. 'They're both crazy. They must be.'

The village church was crowded, but there were no children present. No organist, nor prayer books. The Lutheran Pastor stood at the door in welcome, but he was not in his robes. Eventually, when he felt that everyone was present, he closed the door and locked it. In the experience of most of those present, it was the first time the church doors had ever been locked.

The Pastor went to the pulpit. He surprised them by speaking in English.

'Please be seated. I cannot speak to you in German, except for saying Lutheran prayers. From today the use of German in public places is, by government decree, declared unpatriotic and illegal.'

A shock wave of disbelief ran through the church. It turned to perplexity, as the Pastor stood aside, and Gerhardt Lippert occupied the pulpit. He took from his pocket an Adelaide newspaper. He waited until the murmurs had stopped, and there was silence. He also spoke in English.

'This is a sad day. A terrible day. I feel ashamed to stand here and read you this. But I must. You should all be cautioned of what is happening here. Of what may happen to any one of us.'

He put on his spectacles, and read from the newspaper.

'The government has proclaimed the War Precautions Act, under which anyone of German origin may, on the accusation of any loyal Australian, be taken into police custody and questioned.'

There was a stirring, a sound of collective bewilderment

and doubt, as if none of them could quite credit what they had heard.

'Furthermore, if the circumstances warrant, and the authorities so choose, such persons may be liable to arrest and committed to gaol without trial.'

In the appalled silence there was a growing sense of outrage. Elizabeth reached for Stefan's hand and held it tightly. *No*, she thought. *Surely this could not be happening. There was some mistake, there must be.*

Chapter 25

Everyone is going raving mad, William thought, as he watched a troop of ill-clad recruits drill in the park opposite. None had complete uniforms. Few had rifles, and in response to the sergeant's shouted orders, the majority sloped and presented arms with broom handles.

The rush to enlist had taken the authorities by surprise. Quartermaster's stores could not cope with the unexpected demand. The arms manufacturers were engaged in supplying the major combatants, and it was beyond imagination that an outpost of the Empire (a country only fourteen years old and prior to that a mere collection of colonies) would generate such a stream of volunteers. In early November, with the war a bare three months old, thirty-six packed troopships escorted by three naval cruisers left to emotional scenes of excited enthusiasm. OUR BOYS ARE SAILING OUT TO GLORY, trumpeted a local newspaper.

War fever grew. Enlistments increased with each month. More troopships sailed. Sydney newspapers railed against German wool buyers living in houses overlooking the harbour, demanding such nests of spies be raided. Society women became Red Cross organisers. They called on the women of Australia to knit socks and bake cakes for freedom.

There was joy when the German cruiser *Emden* was sunk but concern Australian troops were not yet in action, being diverted to Egypt for training, when it was expected they would be landing in triumph to support the British in France.

William stood and watched the recruits for a few moments. Their drill was ragged, and the sergeant with his parade-ground voice was not averse to telling them so.

'We do 'ave a lot to learn, don't we?' he bellowed. 'The only way you'll win the war is if the hun sees you trying to slope arms. He might die laughing.'

The men were of all ages, some as young as Harry. He knew many young boys had signed up, especially from country towns. A great deal of pressure was exerted there by recruiting rallies, giving the local males little choice; volunteer to go, or be branded as shirkers.

William left the novice army to their drill sergeant, who was telling them to use their imaginations, and think of their broomsticks as deadly rifles, and if they were really clever, to think of themselves as soldiers, instead of a motley band of no-hopers. He walked on towards the pond, where he would meet Hannah.

Many bizarre things had happened the past few months, he reflected. A school of humpback whales off the coast had been reported as a squadron of German submarines, and rumours of a raid had swept the city. The price of harbourside and beachfront homes had dropped radically because of fear of invasion. In the windows of popular music stores, Steinways and other German pianos were all removed by official order. Orchestral concerts avoided playing the works of Beethoven, Mahler and others considered enemy composers.

Meanwhile, the Department of Defence considered the idea of arming the troops with stockwhips, and building bayonets shaped like boomerangs, so they could come back. The rate of pay for Australian troops - six shillings a day - was criticised by King George V as being excessive for private soldiers. The Ministry of Food and Health decided that processed meat could no longer be called 'German sausage'.

Less ridiculous things had also occurred.

Enemy aliens were interned without trial. Billy Hughes, the Welsh-born attorney-general, passed laws giving the government alarming powers. He imposed rigid censorship. In the universities, students were abandoning their studies to join up. William knew Harry had already discussed this with many of his friends including David Brahm, and was grateful that Brahm was firmly dedicated to finishing his medical degree, and had temporarily diverted his grandson's apparent urge to wear a uniform.

They had already had several confrontations on the issue.

'Not until you're twenty-one,' William had told him.

'But, Grandfather - it'll be over by then.'

'I hope so. Now please, let's drop the subject.'

But the matter would be raised again - if he knew Harry.

As William neared the pond, he noticed a crowd gathered there. A loud voice shouted through a megaphone. A figure hung from what seemed to be an improvised gallows. He saw Hannah sitting waiting for him on a park bench, perceived her discomfort, and hurried towards her.

A spruiker had set up his own sideshow. A busy, cajoling man, he held a dummy bayonet in one hand, while he harangued the crowd that had gathered; mostly young men and girls.

'C'mon, step up. Get a jerry. Kill a German swine. Only a penny a go. Look at him, 'orrible 'un. Bleedin' Kaiser Bill.'

The hanging figure comprised bloated sacking filled with straw. Above the obese body the face was a crude painted replica of an ape with a steel German helmet.

'Come on, boys, show yer sheilas what yer made of. Only a penny to stick him in the guts. Win a prize if you get the target, and hit him fair in his navel base.'

There was laughter, as he incited young men to test their mettle. Hannah rose, clearly distressed as William reached her.

'Thank God. I wanted to leave, but I thought you might worry where I'd gone. Please let's get out of here.'

The spruiker had failed to induce anyone to step up, and saw William put a protective arm around her. They were older, and of a different status to the audience he had collected, so he decided on a new tack. Anything to get the crowd on his side, and fill his pockets.

'What's up, Missus?' he called.

Attention turned towards them, and Hannah tried to ignore him, but this was too good an opportunity for self-promotion.

'Don't like the show? Got an auntie or uncle over there in the Fatherland, 'ave we? We're at war, ain't we?'

'Yes, we're at war,' Hannah said loud and clearly, so they could all hear. 'But that doesn't mean we have to behave like animals.'

'Who're you calling an animal? You better take her home,' he said to William. 'Come on lads, step forward and shove a bayonet up the Kaiser. Show the silly bitch what you're made of.'

'You,' William said, and his voice was like ice. A man on his way forward to accept the challenge froze and changed his mind.

'Something got up your snout has it, old codger?'

'That's correct. You and your sleazy sideshow, you've got well and truly up my snout, you nasty bullying, insulting turd.'

''Ere. That's nice, that is, using disgusting language like that in a public park.'

'Since this *is* a public park, and you're trying to obtain money from these people, I hope you have a permit to operate here?'

'Wait on, mate,' the spruiker said, sensing trouble.

'I won't wait on, and I'm certainly not your mate,' William told him. 'If you and your revolting show aren't out of this park in five minutes, I'm sending for the police.'

'Bit of fun, that's all,' the man said. 'There's a war on.'

'Then why don't you join up,' William said, 'and do your bit for your country.'

Some of the crowd jeered and made ribald comments. William ignored them. He took Hannah's arm and they walked away. Through the sleeve of her silk dress, he could feel her shuddering.

Mrs Forbes brought them tea when they arrived home. She had hurriedly made some sandwiches, and for the first time in many years, seemed flustered.

'Shall I pour, sir?'

'It's all right, thanks, Mrs Forbes. I think Miss Lockwood can manage.'

'Yes, sir.' She bobbed to Hannah. 'Miss – er – Ma'am.'

'Thank you, Mrs Forbes,' Hannah said. 'Such short notice. It's very kind of you.'

Mrs Forbes went back through the labyrinth of passageways to their quarters, where her husband was engrossed in the newspaper.

'Look at this. Our troops still stuck in the desert. Training. Makes you wonder why they took 'em there in such a hurry.'

'Never mind the war,' his wife said. 'She's good looking. And nice. You never told me she was nice.'

'I only ever saw her the once, didn't I? Years ago. The time Mrs Patterson had her accident. I was trying not to look.'

'Why?'

'It was embarrassing. It was daytime, but she had on a nightgown, and – what are they doing in there?'

'Having tea,' Mrs Forbes said, as if it was a silly question.

David and Harry left the tram, and walked home past the pavilions of the Sydney Cricket Ground.

'Have you heard any more from my sister?'

'Nothing – not for weeks.'

'We had a letter yesterday.'

David Brahm seemed ill at ease, and Harry wondered why. Players in white flannels were at practice in the nets. They both waved to one they knew, who played first grade for the university.

'You know she's going to be seventeen,' David said.

'I know.'

'Well, she's growing up. I mean – nearly a woman. What I'm trying to say is, I think she's met someone.'

'I'd better go,' Hannah said. They were on the terrace, where she was admiring the roses.

'No hurry. I want to show you around. Stay and meet Harry, and later on Forbes can drive you home.'

She thought about it, and smiled. 'You mean like a real visitor? Respectable?'

'Why not?' William said. 'It's time we were.'

'Are we by any chance, talking about that same old thing? The matter we agreed not to talk about?' she asked.

'Certainly not. We had an unpleasant experience in the park, and I invited you home to tea. Now I want you to see my garden.'

'Then I accept your kind offer. And if Forbes should drive me home later, that makes it eminently respectable.'

'And perhaps we could even do this again – in a day or two,' he said innocently. 'Next time you might come for lunch.'

She laughed. 'You're a wicked bugger, Willie. You're making overtures.'

'Thoroughly respectable ones.'

'Devious ones. You're machiavellian. Always have been.'

'Don't shower me with compliments, Hannah. Just agree to come to lunch – the day after tomorrow.'

They were both laughing, when Harry walked up the driveway and saw them. William beckoned him.

'Harry, it's time you met. This is Hannah.'

He seemed under a strain, and upset. Hannah smiled and offered her hand. Harry took it without a smile, but nodded politely.

'Miss Lockwood,' he said. 'Excuse me, won't you?'

'Don't run off, old chap,' William said. 'We're about to do a tour of the garden. Won't take long.'

'Sorry, Grandfather. I have to study for exams tomorrow.'

He nodded once more to Hannah, seemed as if he was about to add something, but turned away instead and went inside the house.

Later, Forbes brought the limousine to the front of the house. William kissed Hannah goodbye, a conventional kiss on the cheek, reminded her she was coming to lunch, and waved as the car left. Then he went inside, to confront his grandson.

He tried to tell himself he would not shout, but could already feel his temper rising. Upstairs, he tapped on the door that had once been Elizabeth's room and was now Harry's, but there was no answer. He opened it and went inside. Harry seemed not to have heard him enter. He was at the window, gazing out, as if there was something of importance there. William stood alongside his grandson, before he began to realise he had intruded on some private sorrow.

'That was a lie, of course,' Harry said. 'I'm not studying. And there are no exams tomorrow.'

'I just wanted you to meet.' William spoke quietly, his former anger extinguished by the unmistakable signs of distress.

'I was rude. It was unforgivable.'

'What's up, old lad?'

'Something silly, Grandpa. Bound to happen, I suppose.'

'Anything to do with Kate Brahm?' he asked carefully.

'Seems as if – well, it was inevitable. I expect she'll write and tell me, eventually. Kate's very straight.'

'An awfully nice girl,' William said, sad for his grandson, who was trying so hard to be matter-of-fact and failing dismally.

'Yes, she was – is,' Harry corrected himself. 'Always will be. One day she'll be famous. She'll have to live overseas. So it might as well end now before – before we get too attached.'

William put a hand on his shoulder. It was an odd moment to realise it, but Harry was almost the same height.

'Come down and have a drink with me in the library when you feel like it,' he said. He went to the door.

'I'm truly sorry about Hannah,' Harry said.

'I'll explain to her. We'd had a disagreeable incident – some bloody man in the park insulted her. We came back here for tea, and . . .' he shrugged, and smiled. 'I suppose I thought it was a good opportunity for you two to meet.'

'Oh.'

'Never mind. Right people, wrong day. She'll understand.'

'I'd like to write and apologise. That is if you'll give me her address, Grandfather.'

'Gladly.'

'Tell me about the park. I don't know about you, but I'd quite like that drink now.'

William nodded, and they went downstairs together.

He had often wondered what it would be like, tried to picture it. Perhaps the love nest – that was the word that always came to his mind, the one the scandal sheets would use – perhaps it was in one of the new blocks of flats being built, which were still rare except around the Darlinghurst area, and considered rather racy. Or perhaps a house on the water. Something rather grand.

But this secluded small house at the end of the cul-de-sac, this wasn't grand. Charming, yes. Private, certainly. But not grand. And not the least bit racy. The courtyard was vivid and lively, enhanced with ceramic pots of petunias and a blaze of marigolds. Overhanging the house was the blue canopy of a huge jacaranda in full summer flower. He rang the bell, and after a moment Hannah answered it. She was wearing a long skirt and silk blouse, and for a moment did not seem to recognise him. Then, with a start, she realised who it was.

'Harry?'

'Yes,' he said. 'Hello, Hannah.'

She looked anxious – fearful.

'It's not your grandfather – nothing's wrong?'

Too late he realised that his sudden appearance here might alarm her.

'No, no, he's fine,' he assured her. 'He gave me your address so I could write to apologise for the way I behaved yesterday. Only I felt it would be best if I came in person. I also wrote you a letter too, so it's not actually deceiving Grandfather. Well, not quite. I hope you don't mind.'

He gave her the sealed letter. She glanced at the envelope, her name and address written there, then looked intently at him for so long he was unsure if she was pleased or offended.

'Has anyone ever told you how much like him you are?'

'Lots of people say I look like him.'

'Not only look.' Hannah laughed, and took his arm. 'You sound like him and you think like him. You're an absolute chip off that old block. My dear boy, come in.'

It was going to be all right. He was glad he'd come here.

Later, after he'd elected to have a lemon drink, because it was too hot for tea and too early for wine or beer, and she'd made savouries on thin biscuits, and they'd taken them into the back garden, he felt he could tell Hannah Lockwood almost anything. It was strange, because it was like Gran in that way, only different; she was younger and laughed more easily, but had the same way of listening, so that you said things, and didn't feel embarrassed.

He told her about Kate, and how there had been a letter from her that very morning, which undoubtedly came by the same ship as David's letter, but had been delayed, so that he got the news from her brother first, instead of the way she wanted. He said Kate promised that they'd always be close, but they had never deceived each other, and she thought she was in love with a student from Cambridge - and not that it had anything to do with her feelings, but he actually rowed in the Eights against Oxford - and she'd watched the finish from Hammersmith Bridge. That was not a factor, just an aside so he'd know she hadn't fallen for a complete dill. But she had fallen for him, and she had to be honest about that - and since the chances of her and Harry meeting again were unlikely, he ought to find someone for himself. She hoped he would, hoped he'd be happy, and hoped especially he'd forgive her.

'And do you forgive her?' Hannah asked, when he paused for breath.

'I'm trying to,' he said. 'I'm really trying. Of course I'll hope like mad that Oxford wins next year's boat race, and he catches a crab, loses his oar, falls in, and makes a complete goose of himself.'

She smiled.

'But you felt she was going out of your life, didn't you?'

'Yes. I howled my eyes out, the day her ship left.' After a moment he said, 'I've never told anyone else that.'

'Nothing wrong with a good howl.'

'But men - aren't supposed to cry.'

'The nice ones do,' Hannah said. 'Stiff upper lips are all very well, but sometimes they're attached to vacant faces.'

'Or a Cambridge goose,' Harry laughed.

'Indeed. On the other hand, if Kate likes him, he's probably not too bad.'

'I expect you're right,' he admitted. 'In fact I know you are. He'll probably be the hero of the boat race.'

They both smiled.

'I like your house,' he said, suddenly. 'I like you.'

'That's a nice thing to say, Harry.'

'Can I tell you why I really came to see you today?'

'Not just to bring a letter?'

'I could've sent it. But I did want to meet you – and I'm glad I did. I've been thinking about you. Rather a lot – ever since my mother mentioned you, the last time I saw her.'

Hannah blinked. 'Your mother knew about me?'

'Gran knew. She told Mama.'

'Oh God,' Hannah said.

'No, please, you mustn't feel like that. I'm putting this badly, but Mama – well, she said she wished she'd met you.'

'Elizabeth said that?'

'Truly.'

'Good Lord.' After a moment, she said, 'We did almost meet once. When she brought you all home – after your gran's accident. She came to watch her father in the State House.' She smiled at the memory. 'It was one of his great days. He was in tremendous form, determined to impress his daughter in the gallery. I sat a discreet distance away, and watched her. I thought she was the loveliest looking girl I'd ever seen. Is she still beautiful?'

'I think so. Even if she is getting older.'

'My dear, she's only thirty-six – despite having a grown-up son. One of the few advantages of eloping and having a baby so young.'

'Was it a big scandal?'

'More of a private one. A lot of pain and sadness.'

'No one's ever told me much.'

'It's the past, Harry. I hope she's happy.'

'She and my father seem to be. And my brother Carl, he's left school and works on the vineyard. And my sister's at a weekly boarding school. She's fourteen, and looks like Ma.'

'Lucky girl.'

'Maria and I get on. Carl and I don't.' He hesitated. 'Pa and I don't, either.'

She said nothing.

'It's funny how I seem to be able to tell you things.'

'Now tell me why you *really* came.'

'It's a bit personal – and you might think it rude or cheeky.'

'Tell me anyway.'

'I felt you and Grandfather would marry. I told Mama and she said she hoped so. She said it was time he was happy.'

Hannah thought if she tried to speak she might weep for joy.

'This is the personal part. Tell me to go if you're angry. But Gran's been dead almost a year, and by now – what I mean is – what I'm trying to say is – Hannah, hasn't he asked you?'

'Oh, my darling boy,' Hannah said. The tears began to flow, and there was nothing she could do to prevent them.

'I'm a fool. I've upset you and made a mess of this.'

She blew her nose and wiped her eyes. 'No, you haven't. You'll never know how glad I am you came here today. It's one of the best things that's ever happened in my entire life.'

Chapter 26

Elizabeth sat smiling over the letter. What a cheek! He told her everything about his visit to the house in Paddington, pages of it in his swift and scrawling handwriting; even Hannah's comment on her looks! She tried to remember back to that day, watching her father on his feet in the Parliament, deriding and scorning the Opposition and drawing applause for his own supporters, so passionate about Federation. The King Canute speech, she had always called it in her mind since.

'If the gentleman, and I use the word with caution . . . chooses to align with other dullards, dinosaurs and die-hards who wish to emulate King Canute . . . I suggest this House repair to the nearest beach . . . to watch the waves of history wash them into obscurity . . . beware the tide of public opinion . . . ignore it and it may drown you.'

She laughed aloud, recalling the angry faces of James North and Mr Reid. But most of her attention had been focused on her father. There had been several well-dressed, attractive women there, and one of them must have been Hannah. She turned back to the letter.

I felt terrible making her cry like that, but she kept saying she was happy, then bursting into tears again, and finally, I don't know why, but we both started to laugh. She asked me to wait while she went and fixed her face – I said it didn't need fixing because she's very attractive, even though she must be almost fifty, and has a lovely sense of humour. Anyway, she went off and came back with a glass of wine each, and said this was the last of the very best vintage, the 1909 Elizabeth that she'd been saving for a special day, and this was it. And so we toasted each other – and Grandfather – and you and Papa for making it.

I'm sure that Grandpa is going to ask her again any day now to marry him, and it makes me laugh to think I know something he doesn't – that this time she will say 'yes'. Goodness knows what we will do if he's become discouraged and doesn't ask: I told Hannah she'll have to send him a card on Valentine's Day! I wish you could meet her, Ma. I know you'd get on together. They'll be awfully happy if only he'll pop the question. I'll send you a telegram when he does. Mr and Mrs Forbes also liked her when she came to the house for afternoon tea, and twice since for lunch – so that's good.

I've talked all about Hannah, and nothing about you. I worry when I hear about anti-German displays, and people being interned. I do hope you're not having any trouble over there. But then you're you, and Pa is naturalised, so there shouldn't be any difficulty. Only I would like to hear from you that everything is in order and there's no antagonism, and that Gerhardt and Eva-Maria, and Sigrid and Oscar are all fine. Give father my fondest affection, and tell him Hannah (and also Grandfather) think he is one of the best winemakers in the country.

Much love to Maria, and to you,

Harry

P.S. I think my childish infatuation for Kate Brahm is over, and it seems she has met someone in England. I was upset at first – but we all have to grow up, don't we?

She enjoyed the letter. He writes like he talks, she thought: I can hear his voice in every line. And he and Hannah - weaving webs for her father. How the world turns and spins. She would like to have shown the letter to Stefan, but was hesitant. It was such a contrast to the polite, almost stilted letter Harry had written to him in apology, almost a year ago. Stefan had said little, but she had been disappointed at the careful formality. It was the one disturbing element in her life, that her eldest son and her husband could find no rapport. And yet, Hannah Lockwood, whom he had almost hated as a threat to his beloved Gran - here they were, friends and confidantes. Edith Patterson would have been quite bemused. Perhaps the woman her mother had become, particularly in her latter years, might have even enjoyed the irony.

She heard the sound of an approaching motorbike, and came out onto the verandah, thinking it might be Sigrid and Oscar. But it was a single machine with no sidecar. It stopped near the house, and the rider took off his helmet, goggles and protective coat. She saw the stripes on his uniform, as he put on his police cap.

'Sergeant Delaney,' she said.

'Ma'am.' He nodded.

'We haven't seen you in ages.'

'No.' He seemed ill at ease. 'Husband about?'

'Yes, he's just switching on the irrigator.'

They heard the sound of the petrol-driven pump from a tin shed behind the house. The trenched irrigation hoses Stefan had installed over the years pumped water from the dam, to trickle along the rows and moisten the roots of the vines. It was what had made their harvests so abundant, and had brought them comparative wealth in this quiet part of the valley.

'Stefan!' she called over the noise of the motor, and he came around the corner of the house and nodded a greeting to Delaney, who did not return it.

'Mr Muller, I'm here on official business.'

'What is it, Sergeant?'

'I've got a list somewhere.' He searched in his pockets and produced a crumpled sheet of paper.

'What list?'

Stefan was puzzled by the sergeant's manner. Despite what some people claimed about the police being biased, Stefan had always thought Delaney a decent man.

'List of aliens. Enemy subjects.'

'I beg your pardon,' Elizabeth said, with incredulity.

'Enemy aliens,' Delaney repeated, louder, as if she might be infirm and hard of hearing.

Stefan intervened. He could see Elizabeth start to fume.

'Please explain, Sergeant. My name is on this list?'

Delaney became more aggressive.

'Stefan Muller. That's you, isn't it?'

'You know it is.'

'It's a matter of identification. Are you Stefan Muller?'

'You've known me for ten years.'

'Well, listen to this.' He read from an official document. 'War Precautions Act. All names listed here as enemy subjects are to report to the police station as required, at noon tomorrow.'

'This is ridiculous,' Elizabeth said angrily.

'It's official,' the police sergeant said.

'It's effrontery. My husband's naturalised. He's Australian. The whole idea is absurd.'

'Don't try to tell me. Argue with the government, Mrs Muller. But until they change their minds, he reports tomorrow.'

'For what purpose?' Stefan asked.

'To answer questions. To do whatever you're told to do.'

'But this is stupid,' Stefan said.

'Look, Muller,' Delaney was fast losing patience, 'just be there. Or else you're in big trouble.'

They stood numbly, watching him return to his motorcycle. He had been the rather pleasant, unimaginative village police sergeant for more than half the time they had lived there. He had assimilated into their community; indeed, they had been one of the first families to go out of their way to make him welcome.

Now he was informing Stefan he was an enemy.

The hubbub of bewildered complaints began to quieten, as the two men emerged. By the time they mounted the boxes set up to form a dais, there was silence. The inspector was unknown, new to the district. His uniform was smartly tailored; in contrast to Delaney's rather ill-fitting tunic and casual appearance, this was a man who gave the impression of neatness and precision. He had sharp, penetrating eyes that surveyed the perplexed and uneasy crowd.

There was no more room in the yard behind the station. Surrounded by high brick walls, it was a place where police vans parked to pick up and discharge prisoners, rather than accommodate so many people. The streets of the town were strangely empty; most of the shops closed, their owners and assistants summoned to attend. Pastor Hubrich was there, along with all the teachers from the Lutheran schools. The rest of the crowd were tradesmen, or from farms and vineyards. Their parked horses and carts, sulkies, trucks and automobiles filling the streets gave a false impression of a fete or a market day.

'This is Inspector Lucas,' Delaney announced. 'He'll tell you why you're here.'

Lucas's gaze swept the crowd, as though seeking out any likely malcontents. He was in no hurry, making them wait, and Stefan had the feeling he enjoyed creating the tension. Beside him Gerhardt muttered, and Eva-Maria anxiously whispered to him to be quiet.

'I hope you can all understand English,' Lucas started, speaking slowly and loudly, 'because I will say this once – and once only. You are all registered as enemy aliens.'

It provoked a storm of protest. Lucas made no attempt to quell it; he waited, surveying them, until it died to a murmur.

'You are required to swear an oath, not to take up arms against the Commonwealth of Australia or the British Empire. Any person refusing to so swear, will be arrested.'

'Sir!' Gerhardt Lippert raised his arm.

'No questions,' the inspector said.

'Surely a mistake has been made,' Gerhardt persisted, while Eva-Maria tried to hush him.

'Gerd, *halt den Mund!*'

'A mistake, sir,' Gerhardt persisted, ignoring his wife. 'Half the people here are naturalised.'

'There's no mistake,' Lucas replied. 'But since you've raised the matter, let me make it clear. The government has stated this makes not the slightest difference.'

'But naturalised means that we are Australians.'

'Don't argue with me. You swear the oath, or go to gaol.'

They were made to queue. It was hot in the confined yard. There was no shelter from the sun, and most of them were thirsty. The process was deliberately slow, with only Sergeant Delaney and one of his constables administering the oaths. Those sworn were then required to wait, and told in due course they would be advised of their legal standing before being allowed to leave. From time to time Inspector Lucas emerged from the police station to see what progress had been made. Once he was eating a sandwich. Another time he had a drink in his hand, and seemed amused at their resentment.

'Name?'

The constable was middle-aged. In years past, the summer of 1909, he had been a paid picker at the Muller's harvest, and a guest at the feast of thanksgiving. Now he stared at Stefan and repeated the question.

'Name? We haven't got all day.'

'Stefan Muller.'

'Put your hand on the Bible. Do you, Muller, solemnly swear not to take up arms, or engage in activity against the interests of this country or the British Empire? Say – I so swear.'

'I so swear,' Stefan said, hating the other's enjoyment.

'Louder please.'

'I so swear.'

'Be sure you remember it. Now wait over there with the others. Next.'

'Am I an enemy alien?' Carl asked his mother.

'Don't be stupid,' she said quite sharply, anxious because

Stefan should have been home long since. 'You were all born here.'

'Our name's still Muller. At least mine is – and Maria's.'

'Carl, stop it,' she snapped, then regretted her tone. She kissed his cheek. 'Sorry. I'm worried.'

'They've been a long time.'

'Too long. I wanted to go with him, but he wouldn't let me. He said I'd get too angry. I told him the trouble with him is – he doesn't get angry enough.'

They were still waiting. Crowded together, standing. Some of the women were in tears. The men were seething with a helpless and growing impotence. The afternoon sun was hotter, and no one had been given food or drink. One inadequate latrine had been unable to cope with the numbers, and many stood with close to bursting bladders rather than face the queue and the smell of the primitive toilet.

Finally Lucas appeared, flanked by Sergeant Delaney.

Two men had refused to sign, he told them, and were already on their way to gaol. Stefan knew the two. Brothers who ran a business sharpening ploughshares. Solitary, obstinate men who refused to speak English, and made no secret of their hope that the Fatherland would win. He had little sympathy for them.

'Now the rest of you listen carefully,' Lucas said. 'You have sworn an oath, and don't you forget it. From now on, you are all officially prisoners of war.'

A wave of puzzled murmurs became a storm of outrage, as they began to realise what he had said. *Prisoners of war*. The anger grew into a tumult of protest. This was the final indignity of an infamous day.

'Be quiet.' Lucas's voice sliced through the hubbub until he had their attention again. 'Shut up and listen. The government is prepared to be reasonable. You are all granted parole.'

Parole?

They tried to translate it in their minds. Parole meant what? First they were summoned, made to sign an oath and told they were all aliens, even though they were naturalised. Then they were categorised as prisoners of war, and now they were paroled. As they became silent, some comprehending, others still grappling with the complexity of it, there was no relief in their faces. There was just confusion, and a great deal of anger.

'Do you hear me?' Lucas looked down at them from the dais with impatience. 'Don't you even understand English? You're on parole. You can go home.'

'For how long?'

Without having to turn around, Stefan knew it was Gerhardt.

'For as long as you behave,' Lucas said. 'Any trouble and you go to prison.'

'Without a trial?'

Lucas stared at him.

'Sergeant, what's this man's name?'

Stefan could hear Eva-Maria murmur in German, pleading with him to shut up, for God's sake. Not to bring attention to himself.

'My name is Gerhardt Lippert,' Gerhardt said.

Lucas left the platform, and pushed through the crowd, until he reached Gerhardt. He stared long and hard at him, then looked at Eva-Maria and Stefan, on either side, intent on remembering them.

'You listen to me, Mister Gerhardt Lippert. Did you say trial? We don't need trials. All we do is revoke your parole.'

'Which has been unlawfully imposed.'

'Unlawfully?'

'Of course it's unlawful. We're on parole, but we've committed no crime. If that's your so-called British justice, it's just a heap of shit.'

They thought Lucas was going to strike him. Instead he kept staring at Gerhardt. A muscle twitched in his cheek, and his eyes were like ice. Stefan knew the policeman was never going to forget this.

'Harry,' his grandfather was unusually diffident. 'I'd like you to hear the news - that is, I feel you should be first to know —'

'What news, Grandfather?'

'I've asked Hannah to marry me.'

'Have you really?' Harry looked surprised and ingenuous.

'I have. And I'm glad to say that she's finally said yes.'

'That's wonderful. Marvellous.'

'You mean it, old son?'

'I truly mean it, Grandpa. Congratulations.'

William was pleased by the unquestionably sincere response. They had a celebratory drink together, then Harry left the house and went eagerly to the post office in Oxford Street. Smiling, he wrote out a telegram form to his mother, in his own ebullient style: HE HAS FINALLY POPPED THE QUESTION. HANNAH SAID YES. I'M VERY PLEASED AND HOPE YOU ARE TOO. ALL MY LOVE, HARRY.

He asked for it to be sent at the urgent rate, and the friendly, middle-aged lady at the counter assured him it would be there later that same day.

It was such good news, but the timing of it could hardly have been worse, Elizabeth reflected, although she could not blame her son for that. He had no knowledge of what was happening. Stefan and a group of friends had gathered at Oscar's shop after they were allowed to leave the police station, and since the post office was just across the street, Eva-Maria had gone to enquire if there was any mail. The clerk, who knew they were neighbours, had given her the telegram.

It had been almost dark before they'd arrived home. By then, Elizabeth had walked several times to the bridge over the creek to look along the road, for she was becoming increasingly alarmed. Once, Carl had accompanied her, and that was when Mr and Mrs Carson passed with a load of hay. They were driving a new truck.

Doing well, Elizabeth thought. *A new sulky and now a truck*. Some people were not finding the war a hardship. The truck went past, and stopped. It slowly reversed until it was beside them.

'Rounding up the huns, I hear,' Carson said. 'Good thing, too. Mob of traitors. I'd shoot 'em.'

'Mrs Muller,' his wife taunted, 'is it true, you're gunna change yer name to Miller?'

Elizabeth ignored her. It was her only way of dealing with people so offensive, and she waited for them to drive on, but before they could Carl ran to confront the dairy farmer.

'Clear off,' he said. 'Clear off and leave my mother alone.'

'Or what, sonny?' Carson said.

'Or I'll beat the hell out of you, you great fat slob. And I could do it, too.'

Carson assessed him, reluctant to back off from this threat. Mrs Carson was more realistic, aware Carl was taller and tougher than her husband. She nudged him.

'C'mon, Jim. Leave her and her snotty-nosed kid. We might catch German measles.'

They drove off.

'To think you used to help them,' Carl said bitterly.

'We all make mistakes, darling. I must say, they seem in the money. That's an expensive truck.'

'Hadn't you heard? Their dairy's got a contract to supply army camps in Adelaide. Mr and Mrs Carson are going to do very nicely out of the war.'

Gerhardt and Eva-Maria stayed for supper. He was still fuming, and she was trying to calm him. Elizabeth was shocked by the news of the day's events, and felt surely what the police inspector had done was unlawful.

'Not with this War Precautions Act,' Gerhardt said. 'It means the government can do what they like. It's called "prosecuting the war", and it gives people like Mr Lucas powers they should never be allowed to have. He is not a nice man, that Lucas, believe me.'

'We believe you,' Eva-Maria said. 'We just have to be careful. No fuss, nobody trying to be a hero. We work our land and attend to our own affairs.'

'Put our heads in the sand like dogs in the manger,' Gerhardt said, mixing metaphors in his agitation.

When they had gone, and Carl had gone to bed, Elizabeth told Stefan the news contained in the telegram.

'It was from Harry –' she corrected herself, 'Heinrich.'

'Harry,' Stefan said. 'His life, his choice, so Harry it is. Also, it makes it easier for you.'

'Thank you.'

They sat in silence for a moment.

'Was today awful?'

'Not nice. Let's not talk about it. Please. Gerhardt's done more than enough talking for all of us.'

'Too much, you mean?'

'I hope not. Not if he does what's sensible and keeps quiet.'

She poured them each a glass of wine, and they took it out to the verandah. The sky was a mass of bright stars. A crescent moon profiled the vines, the robust tendrils shorn of their fruit for another year. It was difficult to imagine a more peaceful place.

'Fancy Papa marrying again.'

'His long-time love.'

'Yes, she is. That's a nice way of putting it, Stefan.'

'Would you like to be there?'

'You mean for the wedding?' She was startled.

'If there is time? Would you?'

'Stefan –'

'Perhaps as a surprise. He'd like it.'

'He would, but –'

'Well, then - send a telegraph tomorrow. Find out when the ceremony is. No point in arriving if they are on honeymoon.'

'But Stefan –'

'We can afford it. By first-class sleeper, what's more.'

'That's madly extravagant,' Elizabeth said.

'First-class sleeping car, or you don't go.'

'Heavens,' Elizabeth said, starting to feel excitement at the prospect. 'You really do mean it?'

'On one condition. Don't stay so long as last time.'

'I promise.' She laughed. 'A month, at most.'

'Good. Time to see Harry. Meet his friends.'

'I'd like that.' She thought about it. 'How wonderful. Stefan, how surprising and absolutely lovely.'

'You should be there. He made all this possible. Perhaps not for me, but certainly for you. He would never let me repay him. So – when you arrive – tell him it is a wedding present from me.' He smiled and added, 'Unless you think it might spoil his day.'

She leaned against him. She loved the feel of her face against his, the warmth of their cheeks touching, the quiet affectionate moments that later might culminate in lovemaking.

'It won't spoil his day,' she said. 'As for making all this possible, of course Papa helped. But you did it. You created what's here. You made this vineyard.'

'We did it together,' Stefan said.

Chapter 27

'No fuss,' William said. 'Next week on the twenty-third. We'll just duck off to the registry office.'

Harry was dismayed. *No,* he thought, *that's too soon. That won't work at all.*

'Aren't I invited to this wedding?' he asked.

'My dear chap, of course you're invited. And Mr and Mrs Forbes have asked if they can come as witnesses.'

'No one else?'

'That's how Hannah wants it. And the next day, a discreet announcement in the *Sydney Morning Herald* and the *Age*.'

'Would it be a nuisance to make it the twenty-sixth?'

'What's wrong with the date we've chosen?'

'I've got exams all that week,' Harry said, hastily improvising a story that sounded plausible. 'While you're being married, I'll be doing a paper on common law.'

'Blast,' his grandfather said, and telephoned Hannah, who said that if Harry was doing exams, then they could certainly make it three days later – since she wanted him to give the bride away. When he heard this, Harry asked to speak to the bride.

'Hannah, did you know that sort of thing doesn't happen

in registry offices? They're cheerless places. And registrars are mostly indifferent, rather seedy characters, like something out of Dickens. Fustian, that's the word for them. You want some fustian Dickensian character to garble your marriage vows?' He heard her laughter on the other end of the line.

'Harry dear, whatever are you talking about?'

'Some atmosphere, something to remember.'

'You mean a church?'

'What about the university chapel? The vicar and I play football in the same team. He doesn't mind if neither of you are religious. He even thinks – I don't know how you feel about this, but there's a big silky oak tree just outside – he thinks it would be legal to be married there, provided you do all the signing in the vestry.'

'A silky oak tree?'

'Yes.'

'And the vicar plays rugby?'

'Yes – he's on the wing.'

'It sounds perfect,' Hannah said.

A troop train was pulling out, khaki-clad youths waving and whistling, a crowd on the platform blowing farewell kisses and shedding tears, but apart from that Central Station had hardly changed at all. Still noisy and smoky, engines stoking up, hissing steam, guards shouting and whistling as doors slammed for departure. She could see the familiar billboards as her train crawled into the station. BEX POWDERS FOR HEADACHES; DOCTOR MACKENZIE'S MENTHOIDS FOR COUGHS AND COLDS; AEROPLANE JELLY; ARNOTT'S BISCUITS – PROUDLY AUSTRALIAN.

She saw Harry running along the platform, trying to spot her, and she waved. He burst into the carriage as the train stopped, and hugged her, collected her suitcases, and shepherded her out past the other passengers, excusing the rush, but they had a wedding to attend.

'But it's not till tomorrow,' Elizabeth said.

'They don't know that. First out gets a taxi.'

She laughed, and insisted on taking her smaller suitcase, so she could link arms with him.

'I've booked you into the Castlereagh Hotel for the night, Ma. We'll have dinner, after you've settled in. I wish you could be at home, but it would spoil the surprise.'

'And you really mean it's going to be under a tree?'

'Yes, my friend Tim's managed to persuade the bishop. Isn't it wonderful?'

They were walking out through the colonnades that overlooked Belmore Park, where the hackney cabs plied for hire, when the pleasant middle-aged woman approached.

'Excuse me', she said. 'It seems hard to realise on such a nice sunny afternoon, but we're fighting for survival. And young men like you who refuse to volunteer are shirkers who put our country at risk.' She handed Harry a white feather.

That evening they had picked a quiet place for dinner, in Glebe Point Road near the university. Harry knew the Italian family who ran the restaurant. When he introduced his mother, they first expressed disbelief, then gave them the best table, and kept bringing small appetisers accompanied by smiles of approval.

'It happens now and then,' Harry said. 'Usually the nice, well-educated women are the ones.'

'How dare she,' Elizabeth said.

The incident had spoiled the pleasure of her arrival. She had wanted to remonstrate with the woman, ask if she expected to be defended by under-age boys, but the woman with her white feathers had walked swiftly away and been lost amid the crowd.

'I look big enough and strong enough,' Harry said.

'But not old enough, darling,' his mother said carefully.

'Lots of my friends have joined up. Their parents gave them permission.'

'A lot of young men went into the services, because they had no other careers.' Elizabeth knew she had to tread warily. To so many of the young, the distant war seemed like a chance of glory.

'Grandfather refuses to even discuss it.'

'He wants you to get your law degree first. He's right, Harry. It would be such a waste –'

'But you heard and saw that woman.'

'I saw a well-dressed creature, with a handbag full of white feathers, who thinks she's winning the war handing them out. If she's so concerned, why isn't she a nurse or working for the Red Cross?'

The proprietor brought a carafe of his best wine, compliments of the house, for Harry Patterson's *molto bella* mother. Harry told him this would be a test, because his mother and father owned a vineyard.

The proprietor called his wife, to tell her this. He wanted to know where, how many acres?

'About a hundred acres now,' Elizabeth said. 'We started with twenty. It's in South Australia – in the Barossa Valley.'

'Barossa? But they say many Germans are there.'

'You have any trouble?' his wife asked.

'We try to avoid it,' Elizabeth Muller said.

At the end of their meal, and after effusive farewells, they left to walk to a tram that would take them back into the city.

'Nice people,' Harry said. 'Brahm and our crowd go there for a meal most Friday nights. The family came from Naples about ten years ago.'

'Lovely people. But so concerned about me going back to the Barossa – with all those Germans.' Elizabeth sighed. 'It just won't go away, will it?'

'Forget it, Ma. Just be happy. Tomorrow's a special day.'

'It most certainly is. Not everyone has a father getting married under a tree.'

Harry laughed, and took her arm. They decided to walk for a while, since it was a lovely mild April evening.

The Dardanelles is a bleak stretch of water that leads past Cape Helles and the Gallipoli peninsula in the direction of the Balkans and the Black Sea. On the morning of the 25th, at the time Elizabeth's train reached Sydney, dawn broke in Gallipoli. The first light revealed troop transports that had crept in under cover of night.

The Turks were expecting them.

A British division landed at Helles, while the 3rd Australian Brigade led an assault twenty kilometres to the north. Together with New Zealand troops, they stormed ashore under ferocious Turkish gunfire, at a beach forever after called Anzac Cove. It was a long and desperate day, and a foothold was secured on the ridges, but casualties were high. News of the attack was sent to Lemnos, and a cable dispatched to the Colonial Office in London announcing a successful landing had taken place. By the morning of the 26th, rumours were circulating that Australian forces had engaged the enemy, and it was a gallant, triumphant victory.

They waited self-consciously outside the chapel, in the shade of the silky oak tree. Harry was late. Forbes had driven to collect the bride, who was elegant in a slim grey dress, and he showed her into the roomy back seat of the sedan, asking in his customary deferential way if Miss Lockwood would mind him saying how charming and attractive she looked.

Miss Lockwood did not mind in the least, and complimented Mr Forbes on how polished and shining the car looked, and how well he drove it. Forbes, who had once been terrified at the idea of converting from carriages to motor cars, felt no nostalgia for the days of harnessing horses, or cleaning up the stables after them, and was delighted at his new mistress's approval.

At the house, they collected William and Mrs Forbes, who sat in the front with her husband. Harry was to meet them at the university. They arrived to find he had not yet appeared, and they waited with mounting impatience alongside his friend, the Reverend Tim Swanson, while William looked at the large silky oak, and wondered what people would say if they knew he was being married beneath a tree.

'We're holding you up,' William said to the minister, after a wait of ten minutes that seemed infinitely longer.

'Not at all. I'd say that's him now,' the Reverend Swanson said, unperturbed by the delay.

A taxi had approached. It stopped a short way off. Two people emerged, and the cab drove off. One of them was unmistakably

Harry, accompanied by the slim figure of a smartly dressed woman.

'Good God,' William said. He thought his heart might stop.

He heard Hannah's gasp, then Mrs Forbes's incredulous, 'It's Miss Lizzie.'

William saw his daughter smile at their astonishment, and knew it was no dream. 'Elizabeth!'

He ran to her, and they hugged, and for the second time in his life, William Patterson shed tears. But these were tears of joy.

Elizabeth turned to Hannah. They exchanged smiles like old friends, and warmly embraced. She kissed Mrs Forbes and her husband, who thought he should shake hands, but Elizabeth insisted, while Harry and the parson watched and enjoyed the astounded faces.

'Good heavens,' William said, and blew his nose noisily, and tried to wipe his eyes. 'I just can't believe it.' He felt he had made an utter fool of himself, but was so happy he did not care. But how had it all been arranged? He remembered the three-day postponement for law exams. He looked at his grandson.

'You young bugger,' he said, then with an apologetic glance at the minister. 'Sorry, Reverend.'

'Perfectly all right,' the minister said cheerfully. 'He is a young bugger at times. Jolly good five-eighth, though. Safe pair of hands. Well, the bishop was not altogether approving, but he stretched a theological point since it's my last wedding. I'm joining up tomorrow, so he said that provided we observed all the rituals, he'd allow it.'

'What exactly happens?'

'The same as would happen if we were in the chapel.' He looked at Elizabeth. 'I'm told you have a request to make, Mrs Muller.'

'If the bride agrees, I'd like to be her matron of honour.'

'I can think of nothing I'd like more,' Hannah said.

Afterwards, at the house, Forbes opened the champagne, and William asked them to drink to his wife. He said it was a joyous day, and that he was a happy and lucky man. And that the surprise appearance of his daughter had been like an added jewel in the crown of what was a magic moment in his life. If he sounded overwrought, he told them, he was sure they would understand. He expressed his gratitude to his son-in-law, for what had been a perfect wedding present. It would be his pleasure to write to Stefan and thank him.

He thanked the Reverend Swanson for an enjoyable and unique wedding ceremony, and wished him luck and a safe return from the war. He told Mr and Mrs Forbes it was good they were a part of this day, for they had shared his life for over twenty-five years. They were friends.

'I think that takes care of everyone,' he concluded, gazing around, and then as if he had forgotten – 'Ah, yes. My grandson. I'm told he's a good rugby five-eighth, with safe hands. I think we've all been in his safe hands today. Hannah and I were going to slip off to a registry office, but Harry thought otherwise. He's so devious he should go into politics. He turned our quiet wedding into a real family celebration, for which we thank him with all our hearts. So I think that Hannah and I would like to drink – to Harry.'

'To Harry,' Hannah said.

Elizabeth echoed it, and they all drank.

The following day came the first word of the Gallipoli landing, and by the end of the week the headlines were trumpeting news of a glorious victory. DAWN LANDING. AUSTRALIAN VALOUR.

It was a time of high excitement. People were thrilled; the general opinion was that our boys had been given their chance and had shown what they were made of. News was slow, but the Turks by now must be in headlong flight. The Anzacs, as they were being called, would sweep along the peninsula and into the Balkan states, implementing Winston Churchill's glorious plan.

In May, before Elizabeth returned home, came the first casualty lists. She looked through the *Herald* in a state of mounting shock. Page after page was filled with the names of the dead and wounded. Her father and Hannah joined her, and their breakfast turned cold while they absorbed the implications.

'Dear God,' William said, 'if this is supposed to be a victory, what do they call a defeat?'

Each day it became more apparent, that while the invasion forces had secured a foothold, the price had been a dreadful carnage. In Cairo and on Lemnos, Australian nurses tended the wounded. Packed hospital ships brought them further casualties each day. The Light Horsemen were sent as reinforcements, but without their prized mounts, for this was a war in trenches and on hillsides.

The initial surge of national pride and patriotism brought an immediate rise in enlistments, then as the toll mounted, there was an equally sudden fall. It was slowly beginning to sink in. Courageous it may have been, but this was no victory. No triumph. This was an ill-conceived debacle. In certain parts of the country it fuelled anger, and people looked for scapegoats.

~

The editor's name was Gottfried Johanning. He was a man in his fifties, who had begun as a copy boy, then a reporter, until he finally took over the modest German language weekly. He had been editor now for twenty years. When a crowd began to gather, he looked nervously out at the street. But after all, this was Tanunda, where he had grown up, where all his friends and his family lived, and had done so for a lifetime.

The crowd grew. Someone must have spread the word, for by the time the platoon of soldiers came there were over a hundred people watching in the street. The soldiers stood guard on the premises until a police van drew up. It had been planned as a joint operation. These people were printing a newspaper in an enemy language. There were rumours it contained anti-Empire sentiments and fuelled opposition to the war. It was considered a clear case; the proof was there in pages of German typeface, which no loyal Australian could read, and was therefore a perfect instrument for treason.

Gottfried Johanning was arrested. No charge was read; he was grabbed and marched out to the waiting van. The crowd cheered the police and booed Johanning. They kept up a chorus of boos as other employees were brought out. A printer and a linotype setter. A young female cadet who wrote the social news. She was pushed into the van with the others. It drove away, but not before many of the crowd hammered their fists against its sides.

Soldiers and police emerged, carrying out print trays and forms with the linotype already set. These were smashed by a constable with a mallet. The crowd cheered his every stroke. Inside, the machines were destroyed. A match was struck and thrown onto a pile of newsprint.

Gerhardt Lippert was visiting friends in Tanunda. He reached the scene, wondering what all the excitement was about, as the first sign of fire could be seen through the windows. The last of the troops ran out, as the flames became a conflagration.

'Are you all insane?' Gerhardt shouted, but no one heard him over the loud cheers as the fire destroyed the premises.

By the evening he was too drunk to walk. Stefan carried him into a spare room, and Eva-Maria covered him with a blanket. She said she should go home, because their chooks had to be fed and the eggs collected, not to mention the dogs unchained, and after the morning chores she would come to collect Gerhardt in the cart, because he would be too sick to walk. Stefan tried to dissuade her from going back to an empty house, pointing out there was another spare bed with her goddaughter Maria away at school. When she insisted, he took a lantern and walked with her.

'I worry, Stefan,' she said. 'I've never seen him like this. It is a stupid, dreadful thing they do, but he gets so angry.'

'I get angry,' Stefan said.

'But you control it.'

'I try.'

'Not Gerhardt. He wants to go and shout at the police, to tell them they destroy freedom of the press. That terrible day, when we're made to swear an oath, who was the only one that talks back to the police inspector?'

'I know.' Stefan sighed. He was starting to worry they might not be able to constrain Gerhardt. It had been a long, noisy argument that night, with Gerhardt appalled by what he had witnessed in Tanunda, and Stefan pouring him glasses of wine so that eventually he was too drunk to fulfil his promise to ride into town to lodge a complaint with the authorities.

They hardly needed the lantern. The moon lit their way and the sky was lustrous with stars.

'Any more news from Elizabeth?'

'Just the one letter. It sounded like a wonderful day.'

'Nice if you could have been with her.'

'I'm not sure I'd have been welcome.'

'I think you misjudge her father. People change.'

'He had such plans for his daughter. I'm the one who spoiled them. Even if he no longer hates me, I doubt if he can ever forget or forgive.'

'At least, by the sound of her, that would not be the case with his new wife.'

'She seems nice. Elizabeth is fond of her.'

'You should invite them here one day.'

'I'd like that. To show him what we've done. And to meet Hannah. But after the war, I think. When it's peaceful.'

'You think he's anti-German?'

He was silent for a moment.

'Who knows? As you said, people change. But he once called me a dirty fortune-hunting foreigner – and worse.'

Eva-Maria did not know what to say. Stefan shrugged.

'I don't hold it against him. I was shabby – and I hardly had a penny. And it was a very grand house. Servants and gardeners. Stables and a tennis court. Perhaps the tennis court is still there, and Harry and his friends play on it.'

'You call him Harry?' She did not know this.

'I bow to the inevitable.' Stefan smiled, as they crossed the front paddock to the Lippert house, and he held the lantern high for her to use her latchkey.

There was blood on the front door.

'*Mein Gott,*' Eva-Maria said, and started to shake.

The blood was wet and fresh. Crude lettering formed the words: GERMAN PIGS.

She began to cry, shivering distressed cries, and Stefan held her, and told her he was taking her back with him. He would listen to no argument. She could not stay here alone.

'But the dogs . . .'

'I'll unchain them,' he said, then each realised the dogs had not barked or made a sound at their approach.

They found both the dogs dead, still chained, with their throats cut. The blood disfiguring the front door had been theirs. It had happened only recently; the bodies were still warm.

In the chicken run behind the house, the light from Stefan's lantern revealed the bloodstained feathers and crushed shapes of over fifty hens. They had all been bludgeoned to death.

Chapter 28

'It's ridiculous,' David Brahm said. 'How could anyone's mother look like she does?'

Harry laughed. He remembered that long ago he had predicted this response with remarkable accuracy. The comment pleased him, and made him feel proud, but it also posed a problem.

They had been having a practice hit on the tennis court, and his mother had paused to watch, and after a rally which Brahm won, she had applauded. They stopped play for a moment, and Harry said, 'Ma, this is David Brahm. David, my mother.'

He had not introduced her by name, because he was suddenly aware what it would mean. He could hardly introduce her as 'Elizabeth', not to a friend of his own age. 'Mrs Muller' was the correct wording, but by so doing, he would expose the truth that he had kept private for so long. It was made all the more awkward by David coming to shake hands, saying they were about to stop for a lemonade, and would she please join them? He had been, as Harry expected, greatly impressed, and if aware he had not been given a name, he called her Ma'am with considerable charm.

His mother asked after David's sister. Was she safe in England, and had there been any Zeppelin bomb raids? David said she wrote often. She had seen Zeppelins, but while the idea of bombs being dropped from the air was alarming, the delivery had apparently not been very successful. He also said Kate had become an ardent member of Mrs Pankhurst's campaign on votes for women, because strange as it seemed, women in England did not yet have the vote. Harry learned more about Kate's recent life in those few minutes, than he had in months.

When his mother went into the house, they poured more cold drinks before resuming practice. That was when Brahm had passed the admiring compliment about her looks. It was also when Harry came to a decision. He had lived with evasions and deceit for too long.

'I should have introduced my mother properly,' he said, hoping his voice was steady. 'Her married name is Muller. My father's name is Stefan Muller, and he comes from Bavaria. In Germany,' he added.

'I know where Bavaria is,' David said. 'Now tell me something I don't know.'

'I'm half-German. You didn't know that.'

'I knew you were peculiar. I always said so. Why didn't you tell me ages ago?'

'Because I felt ashamed.'

'Don't talk rubbish,' Brahm said. 'Ashamed? Why the hell should you feel that?'

'We're fighting them.'

'So what did you do? Or your father? Did you do something terrible? Did you shoot someone? Are you a spy?'

'Don't be a stupid prick.'

'Who's the stupid prick here? So you're half-German?'

'Yes.'

'What does that matter?'

'It matters to me,' Harry said, although he could not say why.

'I'm Jewish,' David announced.

'I know. What's that got to do with it?'

'Well, put it this way. Every now and then, I meet some great hulking bastard who tells me I killed Jesus Christ.'

'Anti-Semites,' Harry said. 'Ignorant people. Nobody cares about them.'

'*We* care. You should try being Jewish. If you're German, so they hate you for a while – till this war's over. But we're different. Everyone has hated us for two thousand years.' He shrugged and said, 'Never mind all that. I don't care what you say, your mother is still too young and pretty to be anyone's mother.'

Harry wanted to hug him. But it was not the done thing. He wanted to say that in his entire life he would never have another friend like him. He was afraid it would sound mawkish. Instead, they finished the drinks and went back on court to play tennis.

Elizabeth had already made her return train reservation for a week hence, when the letter arrived. She opened it eagerly. When she had read it, she went upstairs to her room, the bedroom that had been her mother's, for her own childhood room had long since become Harry's, and she sat by the window and carefully read again what Stefan had written. She was still sitting there an hour later, when there was a tap on the door. It was Hannah.

'We're all downstairs –' she began to say, then realised that something was wrong. Elizabeth held out the letter to her, and

Hannah sat beside her to read it.

My darling,

All of a sudden some terrible things happen here. We don't know who, but someone slaughtered Maria's dogs, and all their chickens. Soldiers and police closed down the local newspaper, and arrested the editor, Mr Johanning, who was two years old when his family brought him to South Australia. Gerhardt tried to make the police explain the accusation against the editor: they said there need be no charge – since there will be no trial. He is considered guilty. The inspector ordered Gerhardt to leave before he was also arrested.

Several houses have been burnt down in Gawler, and two families attacked. Some of our friends have been arrested, and once again we do not know why.

I hate to tell you these things, but it is a madness, and it will not last. Oscar convinces me the war will be over this year. He says neither Britain nor Germany can afford this terrible loss of their youth, and they must make peace by the end of 1915. So I wonder if it would be best for you to stay there, in Sydney, where such things don't seem to happen, and if they ever did then your father's position would be a protection. Carl and I can look after ourselves here, and Maria can stay at school – or else come to join you in Sydney. I wanted you to receive this so you have time to think about it very carefully. With all the bitterness that is developing here, it might be best – at least for now. Whatever you decide, my dearest love to you always.

Stefan

Hannah handed back the letter. They sat by the window, while they talked about what Elizabeth should do. By the time they finished, the sun had set behind the cluster of box trees and it was growing cold.

Each day seemed unbearably slow. She would certainly have had the letter by now, Stefan knew, and today or tomorrow at the latest there must be a reply. Since he had written there had been several other incidents. A barn had been burnt, and a German farmer's cattle poisoned. The police investigation in both cases had been less than adequate, and no arrests had been made.

Stefan had also received a letter from a neighbour in Hahndorf, saying his Uncle Johann and Aunt Anna had been interned, and their children had left the farm, which had been acquired by a local land agent at a bargain price. It was an unwelcome letter, the first news he had received of the Ritter family since he and Elizabeth had left there. *Grossmutter* was long dead, and the man asked if Stefan, whom he had heard was a prosperous vintner, could use his influence to have his aunt and uncle released into his care. His uncle believed such arrangements were sometimes agreed, if the custodian was of sufficient standing.

Stefan wrote politely back, saying he was very sorry to hear about their suffering, but the man had been misinformed. No such deals were ever made, unless bribes were exchanged, and if this was what his uncle was suggesting, it was quite impossible. He could not even contemplate it. Such an act would achieve nothing; it would not help the Ritters, and might harm his own family. Also, the rumours of his success were greatly overestimated, but he enclosed five pounds for his relatives, in the hope it might help ease conditions for them in their internment.

He did not add that any idea of bringing them here to live

was completely abhorrent, and something he would never contemplate. He had only bitter memories of them, and knew Elizabeth would be appalled at the thought of seeing them again. *If* she returned. He had asked her to stay where it was safe. He tried hard to convince himself that it was the best thing for her to do.

'Of course you must stay,' William said. 'I think he's being prudent and sensible. It's the logical thing to do.'

'You think so, Papa?'

'Stefan wants you to be safe. It's clearly unstable over there.'

'Maria could join you, like father says. She could even attend your old school.' Harry was enthusiastic. 'What do you think, Hannah?'

'Elizabeth knows how welcome she'd be. Here with us, or else she could take over the house in Paddington. Make it her own, as long as she wants. We discussed both possibilities.'

'Yes, we did,' Elizabeth said.

They were in the living room, and the portrait of her, painted by Tom Roberts when she was sixteen, hung above the mantelpiece behind her. It created a strange mirror image, the youthful painting and its subject, twenty years older, yet still so alike.

'I'm grateful for the offers, and touched that you all want me to remain. I've loved being here with you – it's been a happy time – and it would be nice to stay. But I can't. I think you all realise I can't. It may be prudent and sensible, Father – but you above all people know how little that counts with me. If it is unstable, there might be some awkward times ahead, but I couldn't leave him to face them alone. Not because he's incapable, but because I'd rather be there with him. As for being safe – that's not me at all, is it, Papa?'

'No, it's not,' her father said sadly. 'But sometimes, how I wish to God it was.'

The train moved off, and even after it had cleared the tiny village station Elizabeth and Stefan stood there alone on the platform, their bodies pressed together, their lips reluctant to part.

'Didn't you want me home?' she said eventually.

'Of course I did.'

'You made out a very good case for the opposite.'

'I was trying to be honest. Things are bad. And they're getting worse.'

'They'd be worse still, if I was in Sydney worrying about you.'

They went arm in arm to their recently acquired Ford sedan, parked in the station yard. On the drive home, she told him all about the wedding, what a splendid day it had been, and the way she felt about Hannah. How strange that she and her son, and even Mr and Mrs Forbes who had worked there for so long, all felt such a liking for this woman who had taken her mother's place. Had in fact been her father's mistress all those years.

'They belong together,' Elizabeth said. 'I don't know how else to say it. Papa's a different person. They really love each other.'

'And what of Harry? I hope you notice I give him his correct name?'

'I notice,' Elizabeth said, and leaned against him, wishing they were already home and could make love. He seemed to sense it. He took one hand from the wheel and put an arm around her.

'Can you drive like that?'

'I think it's against the law, but there is nobody to see. Tell me Harry's news. He works at being a lawyer?'

'He tries.'

'What does that mean?'

'It means his mind is on other matters.'

'This girl? Kate?'

'No, I think he's given up on Kate.'

'Then what is it?'

'He goes through the motions of studying for the law. I believe what he wants, Stefan – what he really wants – is to enlist.'

'Dear Gott, no.'

'His closest friend, David Brahm thinks this is what he wants. He told me. So does Hannah. She's sure of it. I trust her judgement.'

'And your father? What does he say?'

'He's opposed to the whole war. He says it's Europe's squabble and if we had leaders with guts, we'd be neutral. He's completely against the idea of Harry joining up.'

'Good,' Stefan said. 'I agree with your father. It shouldn't be our war.'

'You and Papa in agreement? Wonders will never cease.'

'But I'll be twenty next birthday, Grandfather.'

'I've told you often enough,' William said. 'It's too young. Wait till you're twenty-one, Harry. And by then I hope it's over.'

Hannah looked up from the newspaper she was reading. The three were in the library, having coffee after dinner. William was pacing restlessly up and down. A coal fire was burning in the grate.

'Will you please explain to me,' he demanded, 'what in God's name is so important about going to war and getting your head shot off?'

'Well, for one thing, I keep being given these.' He produced a white feather from his pocket and tossed it on the table. 'That's the fourth time.'

'Who gave it to you?'

'Some young, well-dressed woman.'

'Obviously a silly, vicious woman,' Hannah said angrily.

'She didn't look it. I expect she thought I seemed old enough to defend her. Even if I am half-German.'

William stared at him. It was very quiet in the room.

'Is that what this is all about?'

Harry rose and stood beside his grandfather.

'Grandfather, try to understand. I have to be on one side or the other. Heinrich Muller or Harry Patterson.'

'That's utter and complete bloody rubbish,' William said firmly. 'Young lawyers are supposed to be intelligent. Being half-German is of no relevance. You were born here, brought up here, your father's settled here and been naturalised - you're Australian.'

'Then I should do what other Australians are doing. Join up and fight for this country.'

'And how would your parents feel?'

'I don't know.'

'Then ask them. Because I'm sorry, I understand your feelings, but please respect mine. Not at the age of nineteen.'

Harry nodded, as if he had expected this. He picked up the feather from the table, and dropped it in the fire. He leaned down to kiss Hannah on the forehead, said goodnight to them both and went upstairs to his room. William shook his head. He watched the last of the white plume curling as it burnt amid the coals.

'It's an outrage,' he said. 'A bloody disgrace – these women going around, demanding young men go off to die for them. Trying to shame them into it, when they're not even old enough to be allowed to vote.'

'Yes, it is. And it's a terrible irony he feels this need to go and fight, when his father and friends are being so ill-treated. What would Stefan say, if he knew?'

'I think he'd be as much against it as I am. I think we'd be on the same side.'

'You know something, my darling? There are times when you sound as if you're starting to like him.'

'He makes good wine. And he loves Elizabeth,' was all he said, gazing into the flickering glow of the coal fire.

The truth was, more and more of late he wished he had acted differently. He had been wrong about Stefan; had categorised him as a fortune-hunter, which was untrue. If he had shaken hands that day, invited him into the house, accepted the unpalatable fact that Lizzie loved him, they would have settled in Sydney, and his grandchildren would have grown up around him. All three. He sometimes forgot there were two others, and Maria, from her photographs, looked exactly like Elizabeth had looked when she was fifteen.

'Maria's at boarding school, isn't she?'

Hannah had begun to read about the Turkish counter-attack on Gallipoli, where so many had been killed that both sides had declared a day's truce to bury their dead. She looked up with relief from the graphic description of bloated bodies and the fear of cholera.

'Yes.'

'In Adelaide?'

'She was a weekly boarder at a school in Tanunda, but they moved her to Adelaide. They felt it was safer.'

'Does she go home for weekends?'

'Not any more. Or half terms. It's a shame, but they want to protect her from any chance of trouble.'

'Stefan suggested in his letter, if Lizzie stayed she might like Maria to join her here. Go to school in Sydney.'

'Yes, he did.'

'Harry was keen on the idea.'

'He's fond of his sister. And you're up to something.'

'I was just wondering how they'd feel, if we offered to take her until things are more settled? They hardly see her, and she'd be safe here, and could attend Miss Arthur's, where Elizabeth went.'

'You were just wondering?'

'Yes,' he said innocently.

'Why don't you write and ask?'

'I thought you might. That is, if you agree?'

'I agree.'

'You wouldn't mind having her here?'

'If she's anything like her mother, I'd love it.' Hannah smiled. 'And Harry would be pleased. It might stop him doing anything rash – like joining up,' she said, glancing at him.

'Exactly what I was thinking.' William nodded.

'You're as conniving as ever.' Hannah shook her head and laughed. 'I'll write – and we'll see what happens.'

Chapter 29

There were four soldiers. All young, in their militia uniforms. They marched in a tight group, in the charge of a corporal. Their rifles were at the slope, and their tan boots shone. The Sunday morning street was deserted, the shop windows with their names all anglicised now, except for Oscar Schmidt's *Apotheke* which had still managed to remain defiantly traditional and avoid being vandalised. The corporal gave an order; the squad turned smartly right, towards the steeple and the bell tower of the Lutheran church.

As they drew closer, they could hear the massed voices of the congregation singing a hymn. The soldiers knew the tune, but not these words, for they were in German. As they reached the steps, the hymn ended, and the sound of the minister's voice was heard, requesting his parishioners to pray.

'*Lasst uns beten.*'

The congregation knelt, as the corporal pushed open the heavy oak door. His squad stamped to a halt on the stone floor of the church. The butts of their rifles grounded like revolver shots. Startled faces turned to see the source of the interruption. The minister's voice faltered; he tried to continue with the prayer.

The corporal's loud voice stopped him.

'Pastor Thomas Hubrich?'

'Yes?'

'Step down from the pulpit.'

'Please – can this wait? You are interrupting our service.'

'The service is over. My orders are to take you into custody.'

'Custody?' The minister looked bewildered.

'You're under arrest.'

A shocked ripple ran through the crowded church. Oscar and Sigrid, who were present, turned to look at each other in perplexity. In the pew beside them were Eva-Maria and Gerhardt, and before anyone could realise what he intended to do or prevent him, Gerhardt stepped into the aisle between the soldiers and the minister.

'Why?' he demanded. 'Why do you bring guns into the church? Why is he under arrest?'

'Orders. Preaching in German is an offence.'

'He was not preaching – he was saying a prayer.'

'In German.'

'Lutheran prayers are in the language of Martin Luther. Our pastor's sermons are preached in English, as the law insists.'

'Stop arguing and get out of the way,' the corporal said, pushing Gerhardt back into the pew, where Eva-Maria clung to him.

'He was breaking no law,' Gerhardt insisted.

'Stop it,' she whispered fiercely to him. 'Stop. Be quiet.'

'Escort, remove the prisoner.'

The corporal snapped the order, and they all watched, as Pastor Hubrich walked slowly out, surrounded by the four soldiers.

'You barbarians,' Gerhardt said loudly and bitterly. 'How can a man on his knees, saying prayers to his God be your enemy? This is an act of shame.'

The corporal murmured to one of his men, who returned to where Gerhardt stood.

'You silly old bugger,' the young soldier said so softly that only Gerhardt heard it. Then he kneed him in the groin so swiftly that hardly anyone realised what had happened, until Gerhardt doubled up in agony. The soldier grabbed him by the arm, dragged him along the aisle and out the church door, as Eva-Maria cried out in protest.

'No, please.'

She ran after him. The door was slammed shut in her face. She tried to open it, but it was securely held from outside. There was no response to her frightened pleas to be allowed to talk to her husband.

Outside the church, one solider guarded the pastor and another kept a hold on the door, while the rest encircled Gerhardt.

'Barbarians?' the corporal said. 'You're the barbarian, you fucking German bastard.'

The first blow was to his kidneys, from behind, making him gasp; the second a hard punch into the solar plexus, which almost doubled him up in agony. They cuffed and slapped his face. He tried to remain silent, to spare Eva-Maria, and they hit harder, as though goaded by this tacit resistance. When he fell to the ground from their blows, they began to kick him.

Stefan and Elizabeth were in Adelaide where they had driven to spend the weekend with Maria. On the Saturday night they took her to dinner, and booked a single room for her at the Gresham Hotel, where they were staying. It was a habit they had grown to enjoy, ever since they had moved her school, and it was some compensation for not having her home at weekends or half term. Maria understood their reluctance. There seemed to be far more hostility in the small towns and districts like the Adelaide Hills and the Barossa, than here in the city.

She had experienced no trouble at school. The headmistress, Miss Shillington, had addressed all the girls at assembly one morning, and had made several concise points. The first of these was that their state of South Australia had a greater percentage of German immigrants than the rest of the country, many of whom had been here for generations, raised families, contributed to the community and become part of the fabric of the society. They had no liking for their national counterparts on the other side of the world, nor any wish to join them. The second point made was that she ran a most selective school, her pupils chosen not only for scholarly achievements, but also for their impartiality, understanding and commonsense. She felt sure nothing more need be said on the matter, they were all much too sensible - but if there was the least sign of bigotry or any sort of racially biased behaviour, then the girls concerned would no longer be welcome at her academy.

Maria was vivacious over dinner with her parents. She regaled them with news of the past few weeks. It had been an eventful time. She had been made class captain, and selected for the hockey team. She really loved the school much more than the one in Tanunda, had heaps of friends, and hoped her parents could afford to keep her there until she was eighteen, when she would like to go to university.

'And study what?' Stefan asked.

He adored this bright and spirited girl, so engagingly like the one he had met and fallen in love with aboard a ship years ago. Of the three children, she was by far his favourite. He knew parents should not have favourites, but Carl was a pleasant, hard-working lad with little sense of humour, and Harry was virtually a stranger, so who else could it be but this gamine replica of his wife?

'Medicine,' Maria replied, and laughed at the startled expression on his face.

'Medicine? A doctor – or a nurse?'

'A doctor, of course, Papa.'

'But it's unusual,' he said.

'Then it's time that changed,' Elizabeth said.

'But are there many women doctors?'

'Some, Papa. Not enough yet, but one day there will be. Did you know that back in the 1880s, the first university medical school to admit women was here in Adelaide?'

'I didn't,' Stefan said.

'And that there are two hospitals actually founded by women in Australia. The Rachel Forster in Sydney, and Queen Victoria Memorial Hospital in Melbourne.'

'I didn't know that, either.'

'And the doctors there are all women.'

'There seems to be a lot I don't know.'

'You know a great deal about making wine.' Maria laughed.

'Was it difficult for these women to become doctors?'

'Very, specially at first. Some were refused admission. They went to Canada to get their degree. It's still not easy. Still a men's club. But I'm going to hammer on the doors until they let me in.'

Stefan thought about it. He smiled.

'Good,' he said. 'I'll help you in any way I can.'

Elizabeth sat watching them fondly. Stefan, still only in his early forties, and their daughter, in the transition years between leaving childhood and becoming a woman. She knew Maria was his favourite. No one could doubt this, seeing their affectionate rapport, the way she made him relax and smile.

Months ago she had received a letter from Hannah, suggesting that if the situation got worse, Maria could go to Sydney to complete her education and stay with them. She had replied expressing her gratitude, but saying that of them all, Maria was the one most settled, and very attached to her school. If anything changed, she would gladly accept their offer. They had written regularly since, and she looked forward to the letters. Hannah's correspondence was very like her own - a series of brief jottings with exclamation marks - and diary-style notes in which the big house opposite the park and all the people in it seemed to come alive.

Harry, she learned, had done well in his first year of law. The exam results would not be out until after Christmas, but his tutors were pleased and he was confident - which in Hannah's opinion meant a lot, because he wasn't the type to arouse false hopes. He was seeing a new girl, a fellow student. Quite pretty! He and Kate no longer wrote. He never mentioned joining up any more and seemed to have come to terms with remaining at university and completing his degree. Thank heaven! There was every chance it would all be well and truly over long before then.

Hannah also wrote that William was back in the limelight! Although still out of parliament, and unlikely to be re-elected, he was an active opponent of a campaign to introduce conscription which the government was trying to introduce by stealth. Had Elizabeth heard of this? It had hardly received any newspaper coverage yet, but a most enormous row was brewing. Ever since Gallipoli and the terrible casualty lists, there had been a big drop in enlistments – way below expectations – and Billy Hughes was in London making lots of promises Australia could not possibly keep. William was gathering information to take on the Prime Minister – whom he called a dangerous Welsh gnome. (*But more of this anon!*) Hannah had scrawled at the end of her most recent letter, and made Elizabeth smile. Her father was girding up his loins for his own war.

'Elizabeth, did you hear that?' Stefan's voice broke into her thoughts.

'Yes, I heard. Maria wants to study medicine.'

'Not that. I mean what she just told me, about patients?'

Elizabeth had to admit her mind had been wandering.

'It seems many people won't go to women doctors.'

'Why on earth not?'

'Prejudice, Mum. Men get embarrassed at the thought of us examining them. Asking them to take their trousers off.'

'But nurses do the same thing.'

'I know. They don't mind women emptying bedpans, but don't want us to be physicians or surgeons. It's infuriating. What's more disappointing is that even other women seem to be reluctant. They like the image of the venerable masculine figure in a white coat.'

'Well, darling, we can buy you a white coat,' Elizabeth said, 'but I doubt if you'll ever look venerable. Or masculine. At least I hope not.'

Maria laughed. 'Anyway, it's years off. One and a half

more in school, then my medical course. Time for attitudes to change.'

'And if not, you'll have to help change them – by being as good as, or better than your male colleagues.'

'You bet I will,' Maria said.

They left the restaurant early, for they planned to spend the following day driving to Glenelg, to picnic on the beach and swim. Maria was due back in school by six o'clock. Stefan and Elizabeth intended to spend Sunday night at the Gresham, and drive home early on the Monday morning. Now that they had a car, the Barossa was not such a distance. They would be home for lunch. Meanwhile the vineyard was in Carl's care, and Eva-Maria and Gerhardt were close by if he needed them.

The Gresham was their favourite hotel. It stood on King William Road, overlooking Elder Park, and was a landmark. The foyer was spacious, with brocade furnishings and lamps of etched glass. A large crystal chandelier lit the ornate drawing room, where guests met for coffee, or read newspapers in which their names were likely to be featured. It was a place Stefan could not have contemplated or afforded a few years ago but now, as regular visitors, they were known to the staff and management.

The receptionist gave them their room keys, and wondered if Mr Muller would be kind enough to spare Mr Barrington a moment. He could be found in his office.

Stefan had discussed the possibility of the hotel placing a forward order on his new vintage, at a discount to be arranged, so he left Elizabeth and Maria to take the lift upstairs, while he went to talk to the manager, doing swift calculations on the price he could offer if the hotel took a thousand bottles of the 1916 claret.

He knocked on the door, and was asked to sit down.

'It's really rather awkward,' Mr Barrington said. 'I don't quite know how to put this.'

He was English, and had been assistant manager of the Hyde Park Hotel in London's Knightsbridge, before emigrating and taking over as the manager of the Gresham almost ten years ago. He was in his late forties, and believed in cultivating frequent guests, and on several occasions Elizabeth and Stefan had been invited to drinks in his suite. It was there Barrington had first broached the idea of the hotel bulk-buying some of the vineyard's next harvest.

'If we're talking about the wine purchase, don't let it concern you, Mr Barrington. I have extensive orders. And what we don't sell, I'll be happy to put down.'

'It's not about the wine,' Barrington said, frowning and clearly ill at ease. 'I had a guest complain.'

'About what?'

'About you. Your family. Staying here.'

'Complain?'

'It's the most damnable business, and I'm deeply sorry. I'm placed in the awful position of having to ask you to leave in the morning, and not to stay here in future.'

Stefan simply stared at him. He could already guess what this was about, and felt numb.

'A guest saw your name in the visitor's book. He came to me and objected. He said it was a foreign name, and that he'd made enquiries and found out you were German.'

'I've never made a secret of it,' Stefan said. 'Why should I? After all, I'm a naturalised Australian.'

'I told him you and your wife are regular guests. I'm afraid he became rather unpleasant.'

'Oh?'

'He insisted on using my telephone to ring our chairman of directors. It seems they're friends, members of the same club. The chairman instructed me to move you from your room, today. I said it would upset your wife and daughter, and was told it would damage the hotel if it was known we allowed Germans here. I'm to be more careful in future, if I wish to keep my job. I'm ashamed, Mr Muller. At least I managed to insist you be allowed to remain tonight.'

'Thank you, Mr Barrington,' Stefan said.

'It's a disgrace,' the manager said. 'Please give my apologies to your wife and daughter.'

It was, Stefan thought, like a treacherous icy slope. Just when he took a few paces upward, when the vineyard prospered and he could afford small luxuries to compensate her for all the hard years, for the rigour of their penniless days and the cruelty of the Ritter farm, when after all the work and careful saving he could at last redress the balance, repay her for almost twenty years of loyalty and hardship shared, it was as if the ground crumbled beneath his feet and he slid back. The climb, the effort, had all been in vain.

As he returned to their room he knew the receptionist was watching him, while trying not to give the impression of doing so. Stefan felt angry that by morning they would be the object of gossip and debate. No doubt the staff would take sides. Some might say they weren't so bad really – for Germans – while others who had served them and accepted their tips would doubtless speak of them as if they were the carriers of a plague.

He decided not to tell Elizabeth. Why upset and humiliate her? And certainly it was better that Maria did not know.

'Did he want to buy the wine?'

She was curled up in bed. He started to undress.

'Not this year. Something to do with his board of directors. They've contracted with Penfolds.'

'Oh, well. We won't hold it against them.'

'He was most apologetic.'

'I like Mr Barrington. And his comfy, lovely old hotel.'

'Yes.'

'Something wrong, Stefan?'

'No, darling.'

He put on his pyjamas, and went into the adjoining bathroom to brush his teeth.

'I was thinking,' he said, 'after we take Maria back to school, we could really drive home. Provided you don't mind?'

'I don't mind. We wouldn't get back until very late, though. I thought the idea of taking an extra day was to give you a holiday?'

'You know me. Can't keep away from those vines.'

He felt relieved. He had managed it without her suspecting. Now he yawned and kissed her goodnight.

'Sleep well.'

'You, too,' Elizabeth said.

'I'll dream about our daughter, the doctor.'

Elizabeth didn't dream. She lay awake, wondering what had happened, and why he was lying? He was such a bad liar.

An ambulance had to be sent for, to transport Gerhardt to the police station, for he was unable to walk. The three assailants, one of whom was the corporal, were afterwards to swear they did no more than restrain the prisoner, who was abusive and violent. The soldier who had gone back into the church to keep the congregation from leaving at rifle point said he could hear nothing because of the cries and screams from the man's wife, who seemed to be hysterical and had to be prevented from trying to assault him by her friends.

Thomas Hubrich, the pastor, said it was a brutal unprovoked attack by three young army thugs upon a man in his fifties, but the pastor was by then in prison, and his testimony was declared biased and unreliable.

The young soldier guarding him said the minister was obviously confused or lying, because he, the man's escort, had seen and heard nothing – apart, of course, from the other prisoner being abusive and violent as his comrades had already stated.

The congregation had remained for a few minutes in confusion and were told to wait while the soldier went to see if it was safe for them to leave. Eva-Maria led a rush to the door, by which time the detail was driving away on board the ambulance, along with the pastor and the unconscious Gerhardt. The street was otherwise empty and no one had any real idea what had happened.

Oscar Schmidt took Eva-Maria back to his shop, where he made her take a sedative powder, and he and Sigrid insisted she lie down and rest. He knew the ambulance driver, and promised he would find out where they had taken Gerhardt, and what had really occurred.

It was dark before Oscar returned, and he was worried. The driver, a Geordie from Tynemouth, was usually friendly. But today, he and his vehicle had been missing until late in the afternoon, and when Oscar finally found him, he was far from pleased to be met by questions. He replied that he had delivered the soldiers, the minister and Gerhardt to the local police station, as ordered by the army corporal.

'How was Gerhardt?' Oscar asked.

Upset and abusive, but otherwise unharmed, he was told.

'Then why did the soldiers need to send for you and the ambulance?'

The driver took a careful look at Oscar. He said the inspector of the police and the military had both warned him not to discuss this matter. Gerhardt was under arrest, and the incident was covered by the National Security Act. So if Oscar knew what was good for him, he'd shut up and stop asking so many bloody questions, or else they might all be in the shit.

'But why should it be difficult to explain what happened? All I want to know is some news to tell his wife,' Oscar persisted.

'Tell her not to expect him home,' the driver said, now considerably less friendly, as he opened a bottle of whisky and made no attempt to offer his visitor a drink.

Stefan was silent on the drive home, watching the headlights pick out potholes on the road, and the occasional rabbits or kangaroos held perilously mesmerised in the car's glare. It was the first time they had made the journey at night, and she was still wondering why.

She knew he was upset. It had been a warm day, glorious sunshine, the beach uncrowded, and Maria so happy and talkative while they picnicked, that his subdued mood had not been so apparent. They had all tried a swim but pronounced the water still too cold, and had gone walking and looking for shellfish instead. Maria had declared it a perfect weekend when she hugged them both at the school gates.

But it had not been perfect, and Elizabeth knew it. She pretended to doze for a time, allowing him his silence. She could see his face in dark silhouette, eyes fixed on the road, so different from his almost boyish anticipation on the trip down. She would wait for him to tell her. If not, before they went to sleep she would ask.

But an hour later when they arrived home, such concerns were swept aside by the news that Gerhardt Lippert was arrested, almost certainly injured, and Carl had brought Eva-Maria from town, shocked and exhausted, and she was asleep in their spare room.

Inspector Lucas was enraged. A cold man, he rarely showed emotion, finding a constrained impersonal approach and full control far more effective in his job. In his experience, a frigid appraisal and a quiet manner had always proved more menacing than threats. Now for the first time, certainly since he had taken over this district, he was in a white hot fury, shouting at his subordinates, unable to curb his temper, losing all restraint.

He had never been so angry.

A bunch of young imbeciles, half-trained bloody militia had brought real trouble. What had possessed them to kill the wretched man? And why here, of all places, right on his doorstep? For the prisoner had died after the transfer from the ambulance. He had died in one of their police cells, either from the beating he had received, or a heart attack - a discreet post mortem had yet to determine which - and since the death had occurred while he was in custody, it became their mess to clear up.

He had no choice but to telephone his superintendent in

Adelaide, privately, ruining his chief's Sunday afternoon, and being forced to listen to a long tirade on what might happen if certain of the newspapers unfriendly to the government got hold of this. He was told – quite unnecessarily, he thought – it could be dynamite, and to handle it with the utmost care.

And he had done so. Or thought he had. The ambulance driver, the army fools, they had all been instructed what to say. By late Sunday night he was able to advise his superior that the immediate crisis had been contained. And now here was his sergeant, telling him some friend of the dead man had come to make enquiries.

'What's his name?' he asked.

'Muller. Stefan Muller,' Delaney said.

'Keep him outside until I'm ready. Tell him I'm busy and have more important matters to deal with. Make him wait.'

'I used to tell him, don't be a hero,' Eva-Maria said. 'Leave it to someone younger. He never listened. In the church, I try to make him keep quiet. I'm so afraid, Elizabeth. I know they hurt him.'

Elizabeth thought so too, from all the evidence gathered from talking to Sigrid and Oscar, as well as others at the service, but she tried not to reveal her disquiet.

'Just because they called an ambulance?'

'Why else would they do that? Even Oscar has to admit he thinks it's strange.'

'Knowing Gerd, he probably refused to move. Sat down and defied them. They didn't have a truck, so they called for transport . . .'

It sounded lame, even to herself. Something had happened

outside the church, and she hoped Stefan could find out what – without placing himself in danger by antagonising the police. That such a risk could now exist in this country seemed unreal to her.

'You'll stay with us,' she said, 'until we find out more about it. Carl can keep an eye on your farm. Now no arguments, please.'

'Maybe I have to sell the place, if they keep him in a camp.'

'You mustn't do that.'

'Not if I can help it. Perhaps later on there's no choice.'

'We'll lend you money.'

'I can't accept it.'

'Listen, we're friends. Best friends, ever since Stefan and I came here. If necessary, I'll ask my father. He can buy the farm, and lease it back to you for a peppercorn rent. Papa would do that for me, and he can afford it.'

Eva-Maria had tears in her eyes.

'It would be nice to know, whatever happens, I can keep the farm safe for that stupid hero.'

'I promise you will.'

'Thank you. It would also be good to know I needn't sell it to those people.'

'What people?'

'Carsons. The dairy farmer,' Eva-Maria said.

'Why should you sell to them?'

'When I went to the house to collect my clothes, he came past. He said he and his wife would buy our place.'

'What? Buy it?'

'One hundred pounds, he offered.'

'How dare he,' Elizabeth said with astonishment and anger. 'Why, that's not a quarter of what the land is worth.'

'One hundred. He said he was doing me a favour.'

'You tell him to go to hell.'

It was not the first time the Carsons had bought land at cheap prices, after arrests. She wondered uneasily what Carson knew this time, and who so obligingly supplied his information?

Stefan realised he was being kept waiting deliberately. It was at least an hour before Inspector Lucas strolled onto the police station verandah. By then the midday sun was directly overhead, the day was hot and still, and the galvanised iron roof held the heat like a furnace. Stefan mopped sweat from his face, and nodded in greeting. Lucas said nothing, merely stood surveying him, a long and probing scrutiny. It was clearly a tactic he employed; from a position of authority he used silence to force others into speaking, and thus dominated them.

'I came about my friend Gerhardt Lippert.'

Lucas continued to stare. It had a disconcerting effect. Stefan knew he was expected to continue.

'I gather he was stupid and unwise, but the remarks he made were in the heat of the moment.'

'You were there, were you?'

'No, Inspector. I was in Adelaide.'

'Then how can you know about the remarks he made?'

'I've been told.'

'I'm surprised, someone like yourself, claiming friendship with this troublemaker.'

'He's a good man. He means no harm,' Stefan said. 'If there is any way you could give him another chance?'

'Are you serious? You expect me to give him another chance to abuse soldiers who are protecting this country?'

Protecting the country? By arresting a minister saying his prayers, Stefan wanted to reply – but knew he must not.

'Perhaps I could see him?'

'I'm afraid that's out of the question.'

At least they were talking. Lucas appeared to have relaxed a little. There was even the trace of a smile on his last remark. Stefan felt encouraged enough to say, 'Or if I could stand bail . . .'

'You can afford that sort of thing, can you? That's right, of course – you're the one with a daughter in college, a new car, and a big vineyard. Well, I'm sorry but the law won't permit bail in these cases.'

'What *will* the law permit, Inspector?'

'The law won't permit anything, Mr Muller. Not a thing.'

'Then what's to happen to Gerhardt Lippert?'

'He'll be imprisoned until the war is over.'

'May I ask where?'

'You may – but you won't receive an answer.'

'Then can you assure his friends that he's safe? People are worried.'

'Germans, you mean,' Lucas said, and there was no mistaking the hostility. 'Germans are worried.'

'All of his friends would be greatly relieved if we knew he had not been harmed.'

'That sounds like a threat to me, Muller,' the inspector said.

'It wasn't meant to be.'

'It sounded like it. A man of your standing, with your assets, it would be stupid to threaten people in authority. You could have your land confiscated. All sorts of awkward things could happen.'

'Are you *threatening* me, Inspector?'

There was a silence. Stefan sensed, although he could never be sure, that there was a change in the policeman's attitude.

'Nobody is threatening anyone,' Lucas said. 'Your friend took on the army, who arrested him. They brought him to us.'

'By ambulance? Why?' Stefan asked.

'They had no transport. Mr Lippert was being abusive and violent. It says so in the arrest statements. A troublemaker. As requested, we took custody of him, and last night we ordered a police van. He was transferred to Adelaide.'

'I see.'

'I'm glad you do.'

'But last night,' Stefan said, 'I was on the road back from Adelaide. I didn't pass a police van.'

Lucas shrugged. He appeared unconcerned.

'What time would that have been?'

'Between seven o'clock and nine.'

'Ah, well. The police van left at ten.'

'You could prove that, could you, Inspector?'

'I'm sure there'd be paperwork, Mr Muller,' Lucas said.

'But you can't – or won't – tell me where he was taken?'

'I'd have no particular reason not to – assuming I knew. But once he left here, he was out of our jurisdiction. It could have been Torrens or Langley Islands, or even interstate. Trial Bay or Berrima? There are so many camps.' He sounded almost conciliatory.

'Is there some higher authority I can see about this case?'

'You've seen me, Mr Muller. That's as high as you get.'

'Your superior? A superintendent?'

'I'm sorry,' Lucas said, 'I've told you all I can.'

He went back inside.

Stefan walked away. He felt sick.

It was false. Totally false. This man hated Germans. But today he had been almost docile, allowing Stefan to argue and contradict him. It made no sense. Unless – and that was what made him feel ill and afraid – unless Lucas had something crucial to hide.

He was possessed of a terrible apprehension, and wondered if he should confide his fear to Oscar Schmidt. But Oscar was not good at facing reality. For the moment, until he could find out more, he would have to bear this alone.

'We buried him,' the superintendent said. 'The coroner was difficult, but he finally agreed it could be called a heart attack. Brought on, mind you, by blows and the soldiers kicking him, which did not go on the death certificate. I'd like to hang the bastards, but we're not allowed to say a word. How is it at your end?'

'Under control,' Lucas said. 'I suspect Muller doesn't believe a word I said, but there's nothing he can do about it.'

'Is he a danger?'

'Not yet, sir.'

'Should we take him in? Invoke the emergency powers?'

'With respect, Superintendent, I think it might be unwise.'

'Really?'

The voice on the telephone became cool. He was not a man who liked being given direction by subordinates.

'Only a personal opinion, sir,' Lucas hastily assured him. 'We don't want more rumours. Let this matter settle down for a while. If we need to act, I'd prefer a clear and obvious reason for Muller's detention.'

'Why is he different to any of the others?'

'He has a wealthy and prominent father-in-law. He was a senator, and we don't know how much pull he still has.'

The superintendent thought about it. Perhaps his inspector had a point, after all.

'If he does become a problem,' he asked, 'what then?'

'No one's influence would count in a more serious charge. For instance, provoking trouble. An act against the Crown. Then he'd be a menace, a danger to the country.'

'But how would you be able to manage that?'

'We have a dog on a leash,' Lucas said.

Some nights later, a motorcycle sped along the Nuriootpa road. It was late, and there were no other vehicles about. It turned into a gateway, and pulled up outside the milking shed at the Carson's dairy. The rider remained on his machine, wearing a coat, his helmet and goggles forming a protective mask, as Carson joined him from the house. He listened carefully, as the rider spoke, explaining in detail what was to be done, the splutter of the two-cylinder engine covering the sound of their voices.

Before he left, Carson gave the motorcycle rider a wrapped bundle of notes, payment for details that had led to the cheap acquisition of a local farm, the owner of which had been interned.

Sergeant Delaney put the money in his saddlebag. He kicked the throttle of his motorbike, and rode away.

Stefan felt a deep and growing melancholy, but he had to try to conceal it. He was convinced that Gerhardt was dead. It was terrible to feel this about his closest friend, and not be able to discuss it, or to openly mourn him. He felt he could not tell Eva-Maria, because he was afraid of what she might be driven to do. Nor did he fully confide in Elizabeth. He feared her reaction, perhaps even more.

It was a time of fear, as the war that everyone had said would be over by the first Christmas ended its second year.

The initial surge of recruits had fallen to such an extent that the hastily promised quota of troops to the Empire was endangered. A referendum was called by the government, for the right to introduce conscription. It was fiercely opposed by a diverse group across the political spectrum, including Dr Mannix, the Catholic Archbishop of Melbourne, and former Senator William Patterson, whose grandson, having by now received eight white feathers, could wait no longer.

Two months before his twentieth birthday, he abruptly left university and joined up.

Harry had expected an enormous row. Ready to stand his ground, he predicted a strident scene with violent objections, but he was wrong.

They were at lunch when he walked in wearing his uniform.

'Oh my God,' Hannah said.

His grandfather said nothing, only looked at him for quite a long time, with a strange expression. He shook his head.

'I'm sorry,' Harry said.

He stood waiting for a response, but there was none.

'I did defer it for a long time. When they bring in conscription I'd be called up, anyway.'

'You'd better tell Mrs Forbes to set you a place,' Hannah

said, because William did not look as if he was going to speak, but clearly Mrs Forbes had been informed of his arrival, for she entered and laid out cutlery for him on the linen tablecloth. He smiled his thanks, but no one said a word until she was gone.

Harry sat down. He wished there had been a protest. Some of his grandfather's ranting and raving would be a great deal more comfortable than this.

'I said I'm sorry, Grandfather.'

'I heard you,' William replied. 'I also heard you say there'll be conscription – well, you're wrong. There won't be.'

'People are going to vote on it.'

'They'll vote No – if commonsense prevails.'

'What about patriotism, Grandpa?'

'It's still the last refuge of a scoundrel,' William declared with relish. 'We're going to beat that Welsh bastard. Conscripting the young to go and fight his war is an outrage.'

'If you feel that strongly about conscripts, then you really can't object to volunteers.'

'Hmmph,' was all he said, as the maid brought in Harry's lunch. When she had gone, William folded his napkin, and stood up.

'Point taken,' he said. 'But if the volunteers get killed, it's an awful waste. It leaves a gap in the lives of people who love them.'

'I won't get killed,' Harry said quietly.

'Did you, by chance, have the courtesy to advise your mother and your father?'

'I wrote to them two days ago.'

'I don't suppose you'd accept a commission, if I managed to arrange it?'

'I'd rather do it my way, Grandfather. Like everyone else.'

'Bugger it,' William said, and paused in the doorway as if he wanted to say more, but for once could not find the words. 'Bugger it,' he repeated, and walked out.

Harry tried to eat his meal. He looked up at Hannah.

'Don't cry, please, Hannah.'

'Who's crying?' she said, eyes wet. 'When do you report?'

'Tomorrow,' Harry said.

Six weeks later he was gone. They were allowed a two-day final leave. At dinner the last night, Harry admitted they were untrained, but there was an urgent need for reinforcements, and the voyage and a brief time in England would be spent making them into soldiers.

William said this was bloody insanity, and promised he was going to do his best to prevent Prime Minister Billy-bloody-Hughes from dragooning others into being cannon fodder.

Hannah asked him to please not use that term. It was a phrase she kept reading, and it distressed her.

William apologised. If Harry had only allowed him to arrange a commission, he wouldn't be marched off like this, to an infantry troop so clearly unready and ill-equipped.

Was his grandson quite sure he couldn't exert some influence and get him at least one pip?

Harry said he was certain – and if he had second thoughts it was too late. He told them he had written again to his parents, and would write to his sister from somewhere romantic, like Cairo.

It had been a strange time for the Mullers. A series of small incidents, not all happening at once, but extending over several months. Nothing to put a finger on, but they made Stefan uneasy.

An irrigation hose cut. A window broken. A fence dismantled, allowing neighbouring cattle to invade the burgeoning vines. Amid these nocturnal events – they did seem to happen at night – came the disturbing news about Harry.

'I always knew it,' Elizabeth said. 'I just hoped the war would be over before he could join.'

'Such a waste,' Stefan brooded. 'Giving up his law studies.'

'He'll go back to it – afterwards.'

But neither of them felt comfortable discussing it. They were acutely aware of the casualty lists. The news from the trenches in France had grown progressively worse. Thousands of lives sacrificed to gain a few metres. Thousands more lost when the same metres were retaken. Elderly generals in warm greatcoats and braided caps, playing lethal chess; a deadly endgame with the youth of so many nations.

In their own distant world, other things were happening. Risible, ridiculous things.

'You know the latest edict?' Stefan asked. 'Every place with a German name is to be obliterated from the map.'

'What?'

'It's in the paper. All dangerous, unpatriotic names must be changed. The government says Hahndorf must be called Ambleside. Mount Kaiser Stuhl is to be Mount Kitchener. Krondorf has become Kabminye. Heidelberg is most unsuitable. It is now Kobandilla.'

She started to smile.

'You can't be serious?'

'Rhine Hill is gone – changed to Mons. Seppelts is not Seppelts any more. It's Dorien. They were going to change Tanunda. Too Germanic. In the nick of time, they found out it's Aboriginal.'

'They're all crazy,' she said, laughing, yet knowing this was not funny; it was out of control. Blind prejudice, becoming blinder.

'Also,' he said, 'I heard they wanted to abolish Barossa. It was considered a seriously Prussian name.'

'And is it?'

'No – it's Spanish. It means a hill of roses.'

'I like that.'

They spent most of the morning in the fermentation shed, where they bottled some of last summer's stored vintage. Elizabeth enjoyed the days when they worked together. She packed a basket for lunch, and they walked up to the crest of their property, to the magnolia tree, where they spread a rug in the shade. The view was spectacular. They could see their land right down to the creek, and the paddocks beyond belonging to the Lippert farm, where Carl was spending the day ploughing for Eva-Maria. She had insisted on returning home to live, refusing financial help, accepting occasional work by Carl, on condition she fed him. Knowing his appetite, Elizabeth said she might be the loser, but was relieved her friend had begun to plan for the future, and decided not to sell the farm. Although they tried not to discuss it, the feeling of dread about what had happened to Gerhardt remained.

She lay with her head pillowed on Stefan's lap, as she gazed up at the canopy of the magnolia, with its large dark green leaves and creamy white flowers that heralded the spring and lasted throughout summer. Someone before them had planted it here, positioning it perfectly on the hilltop, but it had been only half this size when they first arrived. The tree – like their children, like themselves – had grown and matured.

She was thirty-eight years old, and had now been married to

Stefan more than half her life. If it were not for the war, there would be only one shadow on her happiness; the lack of accord between her eldest son and his father, and the actual feeling of dislike between the two boys. Carl and Harry would never be the same sort of people; their upbringing had been so entirely different, but she wished they could at least be friends. She tried to imagine where Harry was, this minute. On his way towards Aden and the Suez, perhaps, crossing the same ocean where she had flirted with the officers, and fallen in love with the thin-faced young man from Augsburg in Bavaria.

Elizabeth wondered if there were people in Augsburg with sons at war, as fearful about the future as she was?

She sat up, determined to stop this kind of thinking. Stefan helped her pack up the lunch basket, and he carried it as they linked arms and began to make their way down the slope towards the house and the cluster of sheds behind it. Then he paused.

'What is it, darling?'

'I don't know.'

He pointed, and she saw it. Way below them, near the road. It seemed to be a figure, like a scarecrow, but too far away to be distinct.

'Perhaps Carl put something up, to keep off the birds. I'll have a look.'

'I'll come with you,' Elizabeth said.

When they drew closer it was a scarecrow, or appeared to be. It faced towards the road. Unsuspectingly, they circled the figure to look at it. The buzz of blowflies should have been a warning.

'Oh, Jesus Christ,' Stefan said, with shocked disbelief.

Elizabeth thought she was going to be sick.

The front of it was a cruel and lifelike dummy of a hun figure, gross and barbaric like the savage newspaper cartoons, with a bayonet stuck in its midriff, from which animal entrails and blood spilled out. The blowflies were feeding on the blood, and swarming all over it.

Then she was sick. She felt the rush of bile into her mouth, and could not control it, as she retched and fell to the ground on hands and knees, turning from the sight, from the grotesque savagery, feeling terrified and revolted.

Stefan picked her up, heedless of the vomit staining his shirt, holding her tightly. She could feel his body against hers, racked by shudders, and realised he was sobbing with a helpless rage.

Oscar was cleaning the window of his shop. He saw Stefan's car pull up across the street. He waved, but Stefan did not respond, as he took a hessian bag and went towards the police station.

'Sigrid?'

'I saw him,' she said, emerging from the shop. She called down the street, 'Stefan, come in for *kaffee*.'

Stefan kept walking. He seemed not to hear.

Inspector Lucas came out the screen door of the station, aggrieved and impatient. 'You again? What the hell do you want this time?'

Stefan made no reply. He emptied the gruesome figure onto the tiled verandah floor, the entrails, dried blood and bayonet with it. Lucas stepped back from the repellent stench.

'Shit!'

'I sent my son, asking you to come and see what was in my paddock. What some maniac put there to scare my wife.'

'Get this bloody mess out of here,' Lucas said.

'Sorry, Inspector, it's evidence.'

'It's filthy. It stinks.'

'My son was told you were too busy – and if I had a complaint to bring it here. Well, there it is.'

Lucas stared at the offensive sight with acute distaste.

'Animal guts, blood, and – is that a real bayonet?'

'Yes.'

'Is it yours?'

'Of course it's not mine.'

'Are you sure?'

'Inspector, I'm the one making a complaint.'

'Against who?'

'Whoever did this.'

'And who might that be?' Lucas asked.

'I don't know.'

'Then how can you make a complaint?'

'Isn't it your job to find out who left this?'

'My job, Muller,' Lucas said with deliberate arrogance, 'is to keep the peace. Not waste time on squabbles between neighbours. I'll keep the bayonet, and you clean up this filth and get rid of it. And don't bother me again.' He extricated the bloodstained bayonet and took it inside.

Stefan knew that further protest was pointless. He cleaned up the putrid mess, and after he had disposed of it, crossed the street to the chemist shop. In their living quarters Sigrid provided him with hot water and carbolic soap, then handing him a cup of steaming coffee, insisted he remain. Oscar had come upstairs from the shop, so they could talk. He looked at Stefan with a deepening concern. He could tell how the incident had affected him. But despite the provocation, Oscar still felt any response was a mistake.

'It's unwise to attract attention these days. Best to stay quiet.'

'I won't stay quiet,' Stefan said. 'I've been quiet since the war started. What has it got me?'

'Freedom.'

'Is that what you call it?'

'It's safest not to antagonise,' Oscar insisted.

'And what? Hope no one notices you?'

'It may not be very brave,' Oscar said, 'but it's sensible.'

Stefan sipped his coffee with difficulty, barely able to hold the cup, his hands were shaking so uncontrollably with anger.

They came in the night. Weeks later. Two of them. They stopped at the *Apotheke* and slapped paste on the window. They affixed caricatures of bestial ape-like German soldiers, stamping on the faces of cowering girls. When they had covered the window with these, they forced the lock and went inside. One held a torch, while the other began to smash the medicine jars and dispensing bottles.

There was no attempt to do this surreptitiously. Quite the contrary. They heard a movement from above, and the light on the landing came on. Oscar Schmidt appeared in his pyjamas, fitting on his rimless glasses as he came down the stairs. He only had time to see that the two intruders wore sacking hoods, with eye holes cut in them, time barely to begin shouting a protest, before the glasses were ripped from his face and crunched beneath a foot. Then he was punched and knocked to the floor, where a heavy boot kicked him.

Sigrid screamed, and one of the assailants looked up to see her on the landing. He ran swiftly to reach her, two steps at a time, and held her by the hair while he punched her until her cries of terror became whimpers of pain. Before they left, the two smashed all the plate-glass shelves, leaving a carpet of crystal shards. They walked out to the silent street, where the sounds of destruction and Sigrid's screams must have been audible to half the town - but windows stayed dark, and the street remained empty.

It was a town frozen into paralysis by fear. People stayed inside their houses, ashamed, trying to reassure themselves, trying to believe that if the chemist or his wife were hurt, they would seek help. After all, they were one of the very few in the district who had a telephone. They did not know the instrument had been ripped from the wall.

When daylight came and townsfolk emerged nervously from their homes, they saw the shop window blanketed with the odious caricatures, and the door to the premises wide open. The less timid approached, to witness the devastation inside. Bruno Heuzenroader, the blacksmith, crunched across the broken glass in his heavy boots, and found Oscar Schmidt unconscious beneath a debris of smashed medicine bottles. He found Sigrid, her face barely recognisable, her arm broken, lying on the stairs. She was conscious, but in a state of disabled shock. He ran to fetch the local doctor, Keith Hardy, who took one look and requested the police be called immediately.

It was Sergeant Delaney who arrived an hour later, claiming he had been busy investigating a prowler reported at the Carsons' dairy. By this time, Dr Hardy had sent for an ambulance, and treated the cuts and bruises on Sigrid's face, trying to comfort her. He assured her all the lacerations would heal, but privately doubted if the scars would fade.

Hardy was young, and new to the district. He had been in

the first landing at Anzac Cove, and later wounded and invalided home. He had seen a great deal of horror on the heights of Gallipoli, but the callous and spiteful savagery of the attack on the chemist's wife shocked him deeply. Making a temporary splint for her broken arm, which would suffice until she could be admitted to hospital, he then examined Oscar and found he was severely concussed, cut by fragments of glass, and three of his ribs were almost certainly broken.

He saw them both into the ambulance, and gave instructions for their removal to the cottage hospital. He was about to follow in his own car, when Inspector Lucas arrived to join Delaney. Lucas shook hands with him.

'Very glad of this opportunity to meet you, Doctor.'

He asked for the details. Dr Hardy said that he was needed at the hospital. Enough time had already been wasted and both required urgent treatment. The sergeant had the necessary facts.

Lucas pronounced it a nasty business. A lot of bad blood between these German people, he explained. This was typical of how they behaved. The doctor would no doubt understand, Lucas said, since he had apparently been in the army and fought the hun at Gallipoli.

'We fought Turks,' Hardy said abruptly. 'I think you ought to be searching for the thugs who did this, Inspector, not drawing unlikely conclusions. It's obvious that whoever attacked the Schmidts was not a German. Take a look at the window.'

'Could be deliberate,' Lucas said. 'Put there to confuse us.'

Hardy gazed at him with growing dislike. 'You're a bloody idiot,' he said, ignoring the other's look of outrage as he went to his car.

'Just a moment, Doctor,' Lucas called. 'We don't use that sort of language here. Perhaps you've forgotten, but swearing in public in this country is a punishable offence. And swearing at a police officer on duty will land you in a lot of trouble.'

Dr Hardy drove off without a reply, following the ambulance and his patients to the hospital.

'So *that's* the new doctor,' Lucas said, staring after him. 'Looks like the war might have left him a bit shell-shocked.'

Elizabeth sat with Sigrid and tried to comfort her. She and Stefan had not heard the news until late morning, and had driven to the hospital. They were horrified at the sight of her battered face. The swelling had increased until she was almost unrecognisable, and in great pain.

It was in the ward that they met the new doctor, who had completed his rounds, and returned to check on their condition. Dr Hardy reluctantly agreed that Oscar, now his ribs were strapped and his cuts treated, could go home, but he wanted Sigrid to remain overnight. He was worried about her, not so much her injuries, which were serious, but more her reaction to the night's attack. He was relieved when Elizabeth said she would sit with her for as long as she was needed, and sleep at the hospital if a bed could be found. She explained Sigrid had been her friend for years, since she came to work for them in Hahndorf; had helped bring up their children and they regarded her as one of the family. If the doctor could use his influence to get her a private room, Elizabeth personally would be very grateful.

The doctor used his influence. Within the hour, Sigrid was given her own small room, with an extra bed for Elizabeth to stay overnight. Stefan drove Oscar back to the *Apotheke*. Dr Hardy watched them leave through the window of Sigrid's room.

'He should really be staying. He still has slight concussion.'

'Then why let him leave?'

'Some patients fret more in here. Any good I do will be offset by worry about his pharmacy, so it's better he goes there to look after things. He'll have a shocking headache tonight.'

'At least he'll have lots of aspirin close by,' Elizabeth said.

They both smiled, and the new doctor, who needed to confide in someone, felt he could tell her about his first encounter with the police.

'You weren't impressed?'

'They didn't give a damn. How can they behave that way?'

Elizabeth asked him where he had been lately.

The Dardanelles, he told her. Then a long spell in a Cairo hospital - as a patient.

'You were in the Medical Corps on Gallipoli?'

'Yes.'

'It must have been terrible.'

'Thank God,' he said, surprising her.

'For what?'

'To find someone who actually realises it was terrible. Most of the people I meet think it was exciting, something not to be missed. I've even had some say they wished they'd been there.'

'I'm afraid that's because the newspapers here told us it was a great triumph.'

He was silent for a moment. Then he said, 'It was, in its own particular way. A triumph of courage over impossible odds. It was very heroic. But heroism isn't enough, not when the plan is so flawed and stupid that the enemy is waiting.'

'As bad as that?'

'Worse. A debacle, apart from the evacuation, but I can't tell many people the truth. It's not what they want to hear.'

When he had left, promising to visit again after evening surgery, Elizabeth thought the district had done rather well with their new physician. The previous doctor had been there many years; he had grown obstinate and combative, and would certainly not have shown such concern for Sigrid. This man was an agreeable change.

Bruno Heuzenroader had constructed a new steel bolt for the front door, and cajoled some of the neighbours into helping clear up the mass of broken glass. They were scrubbing the window, when Stefan arrived with Oscar. Against his protests, Stefan made him go upstairs to rest, then went to assist with the tidying up. It took them another hour before the worst of the damage was repaired, and some order restored. The stock losses would be considerable.

Stefan wrote out a sign that the shop would be open for business in the morning as usual. He asked Bruno if the police had any idea who did it. Bruno looked at him with incredulity, then he laughed. It was a laugh without humour.

'If they knew, you think the pigs that did this would come to any harm, Stefan? Do you really imagine anything would happen to them – like being brought to court and charged?'

They saw Lucas approach.

'This slimy bastard would pin a medal on 'em,' Bruno said, deliberately speaking loudly in German, then spat and walked away.

Lucas studied Stefan, with his same intent scrutiny.

'What was that he said, Muller?'

'You'd have to ask him, Inspector.'

'I'm asking you.'

'Sorry. It was a private discussion,' Stefan said, surprising himself with his own boldness.

'I'll remind you speaking German is against the law.'

'Thank you,' Stefan answered. 'I'll do my best to remember. But when laws seem so unjust, it's difficult to obey them, because we don't know why they exist. A priest says his prayers; a man talks to another – are these now acts of treason?'

Lucas kept staring at him, hearing the anger and contempt, and unable to believe it. Stefan gazed back, refusing to be cowed.

'I wouldn't talk like that, if I were you,' Lucas advised.

'Don't you think the police would be better employed trying to find who vandalised this shop, and battered a defenceless woman?'

'I think you'd better shut up, Muller – right now, before you get yourself into real trouble.'

'So nothing will be done? No real attempt to find the criminals?'

'There are no suspects. If I were you, I'd leave. Go home.'

'Is this another new law? I'm not permitted to visit and help friends who are attacked?'

'I'm trying to say, keep out of things that don't concern you.'

'My friends being violently assaulted – this concerns me, Inspector. Especially since there are, as you appear to be insisting, no suspects.'

'You're a bloody idiot, Muller.' Inspector Lucas stared at him angrily.

He turned and strode away. Johann Graetz came from his shop, together with others who had witnessed the encounter.

'Stefan, Stefan,' Graetz shook his head. 'That was madness.'

'It's best to stay quiet,' said Elsa Schubert, the milliner.

'Staying quiet,' Stefan said, 'is what Oscar did.'

'Calm down, Stefan,' another shopkeeper told him.

'We don't need trouble,' Graetz said.

'Johann, you've already got trouble. How many broken windows, how much humiliation does it take to realise that?'

'What do you ask of us?'

'A little courage. Some guts. Enough to say – stop. You're not going to frighten us any longer.'

'Easy to talk, Stefan,' another shopkeeper said angrily. 'But how do we do this?'

'Complain.'

'To who?'

'The government,' Stefan said. 'The people we elect. Make them hear us. Tell them every time we are attacked, the police look the other way.'

There was a chorus of disapproving murmurs. A small crowd had gathered around him. A far from amiable crowd.

'Go home, Stefan,' someone said.

'Yes, go home. Stick to making wine.'

'Leave us out of it,' said another.

'That's good advice.' Graetz nodded. 'Stay out of trouble.'

'Johann, you make me sick. You all make me sick. Every one of you is frightened.'

'Maybe we have good reason.'

'What hope have we got,' Stefan demanded passionately, 'if we turn the other cheek? We're people, for God's sake. This is our country. We chose to make our homes here, didn't we?'

There was barely any response. They wanted to be left alone.

'Now they take away our rights. Blame us for a war on the other side of the world. How can that be just? How can we allow it?'

That evening when he came to the hospital, they sat with Sigrid for a time, then walking to the car with him, Elizabeth expressed her concern.

'Why are you saying these things?'

'Someone has to.'

'No, Stefan. Not you.'

'Yes, Elizabeth, me. It made me ashamed – seeing them all so afraid.'

'I'm afraid,' she said.

'Of what?'

'Of you. And what you intend to do.'

'It is a time for heroes . . . the great moment of your lives . . . put the fear of God into Kaiser Bill . . . don't forget, Australia promised the mother country: "to the last man and the last shilling".'

It was almost the same speech, William thought cynically, as he stood in the Domain and listened to James North's ringing voice.

There was a cheer from the crowd, but the spark, the enthusiasm was lacking. In the several years since William had first heard that speech, the country had sickened of the slaughter. Such phrases were no longer stirring people to enlist. 'The last man and the last shilling' had become a regrettable slogan, to many a colonial cringe never quite shaken off.

William hated the phrase. He hated the perception the wording itself suggested, that Australia was still a mere possession of the Empire, and when those in Whitehall said Britain was at war, then by implication and legal allegiance, Australia must follow. It was a slap in the face to him and all the others who had fought so hard for Federation and renounced imperialism. It enraged him the Labor Party so subscribed to this mythology. They were in power and had been since the war's beginning. Andrew Fisher had coined the phrase. Now he was gone and Billy Hughes was Prime Minister, and James North, who stepped so deftly from one political philosophy to another, was in Hughes's Cabinet.

William, at the back of the crowd, remembered the time he was in the Cabinet, when the concept of decimal currency had been proposed, and how Britain had vetoed it. That was back in 1904. It had been one of the first indications the Colonial Office in London had not given up; they had simply shrugged and indicated that the game would henceforth be played by new rules.

He waited for the crowd to drift away, and the organisers to leave. It had been a long time since he and North had met, and they had scarcely parted as friends. The constraint was still visible, as they met and shook hands.

'A good speech, James.'

'I think you've heard it before. The same old flag-waving clichés.'

'Even so. It seems effective.'

'One does one's best,' North said. 'We all have to help.'

More pompous than ever, William thought, trying to conceal his dislike. He managed a smile of agreement.

James North studied him, not deceived by this apparent truce between them, as he enquired, 'You want a favour I take it?'

'Hardly a favour,' William said.

'Then what?'

'This War Precautions Act. It's being abused. Surely you can see it's penal and unjust?'

'It's very popular around the electorates.' North smiled.

'Germans are being persecuted. Losing their jobs – and their homes. Being wrongly arrested. Beaten up in the streets.'

'I can't control the popular mood. Nor can the government.'

'The bill's immoral, and a complete travesty of justice.'

'What's your special interest?' Then, as if remembering, he said, 'Yes, of course. Your daughter married one, didn't she?'

'You used to be fond of Elizabeth,' William replied, feeling suddenly ineffectual.

'I used to be friends with you, William. Perhaps you recall how you exploited that? Well, it can never happen again. Your time is over. I'm back in government and you're history . . .'

The malice was palpable. It had been a mistake to come here. He realised North was smiling at some private joke.

'I never even needed to use the details. Your own party got rid of you. Ours didn't want you. If they had I could've used it to crush you.'

'Use what details? What are you talking about?'

'Broken Hill.'

William felt his mind freeze with shock; he was unable to suppress an involuntary gasp, it was so devastatingly unexpected. He could only stare at North, who was patently gratified by the reaction.

'What was it called? Oh yes . . . The Silver City Trust . . .'

'Never heard of it,' he said, struggling for calm.

'Naturally not.' North was amused. 'A long time ago, you feel, and difficult to prove. But if you were still in politics, I'd use it to get rid of you. As I will in the future, if you ever give me trouble. I'd have them gossiping about you in every club and bar in town. Your name would be dirt – not very pleasant for your new wife.'

William knew he had to keep his temper, and try to bluff this out. 'You'd find yourself in court, fighting an action for slander.'

'Which would merely compound the damage. You know how easily dirt turns to mud, and how it sticks. There are a lot of people ready to believe the worst of you. Take it to court and you'd bring joy to the newspapers – and pleasure to your many enemies.'

'Until the verdict. You'd pay a heavy price – without proof.'

North smiled again.

'The jury would decide that. I'd simply tell the court what happened. That a few years ago a man came to see me – a miner, he was. He'd been in Broken Hill in 1886 – he was very precise about the date – where he was persuaded to buy shares in a fraudulent company called the Silver City Trust. Amusing, isn't it,' North said, 'how these frauds always use the word Trust in their titles? Of course it collapsed, like so many of its kind, and the promoter – his name was McIntosh – he was certain of that, too – promptly vanished. It was assumed he was dead, but my informant said he'd seen you at a meeting, and something about you, some mannerism made him curious. He found out where you lived, saw you again, several times, even looked up newspaper files to study photographs of you. He's prepared to swear you were McIntosh. He said although it was thirty years ago, there could be people in Broken Hill who still remembered the fraud. This is what I'd tell the judge and jury – to be reported in the press, of course, in great detail – if you were stupid enough to sue.'

'And you paid him for this ridiculous, fanciful story?'

'I paid. It was worth every penny. To know I could cause you such harm if I chose – and will if you ever cross me again.'

'The threat is unnecessary. I'm out of politics, thank God, which means that I no longer have to associate with reptiles like you.'

He saw North's face flush with anger, and knew he had just lost whatever remote hope he had of helping Elizabeth.

As if to confirm this, North said, 'I'm afraid this War Precautions Act is essential.'

'Why?'

'To weed out the enemy in our midst.'

'Enemy? What enemy? Half the people being victimised were born here. Thousands more are naturalised.'

'You're missing the point,' North said. 'Not as sharp as you used to be. We need an enemy. The war's too far away. If we want recruits, this country has to feel threatened. Nothing like a bit of hatred to foment patriotism.'

'Good God. You bunch of bastards.'

'It's in a good cause. Defending the flag. Raising money and troops to help the mother country. And if a few huns suffer, it's all in the best interests of Australia.'

'For Christ's sake,' William said, aware he had been naive to approach this former friend, 'you and your manufactured loyalty, and genuflecting to the "mother country" make me sick.'

'Better be careful, William. Quite apart from antagonising me unnecessarily – if you talk like that, people may start to ask which side you're on. Especially since you have a German son-in-law.'

As he walked back past the cathedral towards College Street, William felt angry and dismayed. North's threat and the chance of future blackmail had deeply disturbed him. It had been a foolish error of judgement. Hannah had warned against giving him an opportunity to indulge his long-held resentment.

'I'd rather you see anyone else. Even Billy Hughes.'

'The Welsh gnome? He knows I campaigned against his first attempt at conscription. I'd never get through the door.'

'Well, go if you must. But James North has a long memory, William. He's a good hater. I've no idea how – or what he could do any longer – but I've always felt he'd harm you if he could.'

Well, she'd been proved right. More than either of them had realised. But he'd been so anxious, after receiving a telephone call from Elizabeth, who had driven all the way to the post office in Gawler to make it in secret, that he felt he had to try to help.

His daughter had said she was frightened. It was something she had never said before.

Chapter 30

The petition was carefully drawn up. It must be beyond reproach, Elizabeth insisted, no wording that could be construed as being against the government's War Act, nothing that could be labelled treason. If Stefan was going to pursue this, then they must be careful.

He agreed.

They wrote it out, and when they were satisfied with the wording, she drove to Adelaide for an appointment with Mr Harpur, of Henderson, Hanlon, Potts and Harpur, in their offices on North Terrace. He had become their solicitor: ever since his visit years ago with her father's gift of the ten-acre paddock, he had done their conveyancing whenever they bought more land. Mr Harpur now wore stronger spectacles, and was in his fifties, but was otherwise recognisably the same man who had arrived in his Napier Four to startle the animals and the children.

She smiled. She liked Mr Harpur, who insisted on coming out to examine their motor, and showing her his recent acquisition of a sports roadster. Then his clerk served tea and biscuits, while she told him the news, and apologised that none of it was good.

Sigrid was out of hospital, but the new doctor had confided

that some of her facial scars might be permanent. Oscar was a worry to them all; for so long such a cheerful and determined optimist, he was now silent and morose, and it would be months before his ribs mended.

And Gerhardt Lippert? Mr Harpur asked.

She told him nothing more had been heard. They had already begun to accept the worst. Mr Harpur shook his head. He had met all these people over the years of visits to the valley, and was shocked at the way their lives were being ruined.

Finally, he took the petition and studied it carefully. It was silent in the cluttered room as he thoughtfully read it again.

'Mrs Muller, I'm no expert on these matters, I warn you.'

'I understand that, Mr Harpur. I just want an opinion.'

'Well, my opinion would be not to circulate it.'

'You mean, it's treasonable?'

'On the contrary, I can see nothing whatever wrong, not a word or a sentiment which could bring any action against you, or anyone who signs it. You've been very careful. It's just that, in these times, any people who draw attention to themselves are inviting danger.'

'I'm afraid if you told Stefan that, he'd say that's why he must do this. He's determined, Mr Harpur – all I can do is try to make sure there's nothing in the petition which could be used against him.'

'In normal times, this is a harmless appeal. It's respectful, and it breaks no laws. Everyone should have the right to sign it.' He paused and sighed. 'Unfortunately, these are not normal times.'

'I'll tell him what you said. But I don't think I can change his mind. I've tried. He was docile for too long, he says. You see, apart from Gerhardt and this attack, there've been other incidents.'

She told him about the blood-splattered scarecrow figure that had so distressed her, and about the Gresham Hotel, where Stefan had eventually revealed to her they were no longer welcome.

'Dear God,' Harpur said, visibly shaken.

That a prominent city hotel could shut its doors to Senator Patterson's daughter because her married name was Muller, seemed somehow closer to the world he lived in, and therefore more disturbing than the other distant events, no matter how brutal. The Gresham was only two streets away, a favourite lawyer's meeting place for lunch.

'Would it help if I spoke to the manager?'

'I gather it wasn't his fault. He was very upset.'

'Where will you stay, whenever you come to see Maria?'

'We haven't worked it out. Last time we came for the day. We told our daughter we were busy in the vineyard, and couldn't stop over.'

'Next time, you'll stay with my wife and me,' Harpur said. 'We have a large house with many spare rooms since the boys went. And I won't allow any excuses.'

Elizabeth smiled, and surprised him by kissing his cheek. 'You won't hear any,' she said.

He walked outside with her. 'Any news of Harry?'

'He's in England by now, I imagine. Or else France - although I hope not. And your two?'

'David's transferred to the Royal Flying Corps. A pilot. Loves it, he says.'

'And Frank?'

The moment she asked, she dreaded the answer.

'Frank was killed at Amiens.'

'Oh, I'm sorry.'

'About three months ago,' Mr Harpur said.

'I had no idea. I'll write to your wife.'

'Would you mind very much - would you take it amiss, if I asked you not to?'

Elizabeth shook her head. She didn't know how to respond to this.

'It's just that - she won't allow herself to believe it. She pretends it's all a mistake, and he's not dead. It would have been his twenty-second birthday last week. She sent him a present, and a birthday cake.'

All the way home, Elizabeth thought of Mr Harpur. She knew from their correspondence and the signatures on documents that his name was Charles, but somehow he had always been 'Mr Harpur', just as they had remained Mr and Mrs Muller. Yet despite the formality, they were friends.

She had felt his hand tremble as she held it, then he insisted on cranking the engine for her, and had stood there in the street outside his office, waving as she drove off. She had never met his sons, only seen their school photographs in his chambers, and heard the news that they had both enlisted.

'Oh God,' she said vehemently and out loud, 'I hate this war.'

Mr Harpur, after watching her drive away, returned to his office. He also hated the war. It had taken one boy, and might take his wife's mind. He feared for the safety of his older son, who was inclined to recklessness, and who loved speed and fast cars. David shared his own passion for engines, and would be a skilful flier, but it was the risks, the bravado that concerned him - and the thought of aerial combat against other equally skilled young men flying planes also armed with machine guns.

He thought about the awful events unfolding around Mr and

Mrs Muller; a friend disappearing, Sigrid and her husband both attacked, the series of disturbing incidents that had brought no protection from the local police. He reflected also on the incident at the hotel and the way they had been treated here in Adelaide, and asked his clerk to ring up the Gresham and cancel his table for lunch.

It was bitterly disappointing. There were barely thirty people, and Stefan had hoped for at least a hundred. He stood on the improvised platform in front of the church, wondering if he should wait in case others arrived, but alert to the nervousness of those already there. If he did wait, they might easily drift away.

'I'm sorry there are so few here,' he began. 'There should be more. If we felt free, unafraid, then everyone would be here, every single person in this valley who has been victimised, discriminated against, or made to feel an alien.'

He could see, emerging from the police station, two constables and Sergeant Delaney, and behind them like a ventriloquist manipulating his dummies, the uniformed figure of Inspector Lucas.

'But thank you for your courage and support. Your being here today is important.' As the police approached, some of the crowd began to glance at them uneasily.

Delaney smothered a grin. He and the constables strolled to positions behind various people. They had pencils and notebooks, and began to take down the names of those they recognised.

Stefan could feel the wave of fear this produced. As he continued to speak, he realised Lucas was writing down his words.

'Don't be afraid. We are not breaking any laws. We aren't speaking in a forbidden language. This is a peaceful gathering. I'm not going to criticise the authorities. I promised my wife not to. I promised her to obey the law, and so I shall. All we want to say to the gentlemen of the police and the government is this – we are not your enemy. We're no one's enemy. We just want to be left in peace, to raise our families, farm our lands, grow our crops or our grapes. But if we're attacked, if we're hurt, we surely are entitled to protection. We vote. We pay our taxes. That is our simple right.'

He became more confident. His voice rose.

'I want you to take copies of this petition. Have your friends and neighbours sign it. We need hundreds of names. After the villages of the Barossa, perhaps we can gather more names in the Hills district, then in Clare, even Adelaide. Enough names to take to the Commissioner of Police, to the Premier of the State, and say to them, "Please read this, and see that we mean no harm. We are not against this country. We are a part of it. It is our native land, by choice." Some of you were born here, others of us chose to make the journey – to make this our home.'

When Stefan finished speaking, there was scattered applause. It might have been more positive, but for the police presence. Lucas and his men finishing writing down names, put away their notebooks and watched, as a few people queued to sign the petition. Others took copies, with promises to get signatures from those unable to be there.

Elizabeth kept watching Lucas, nervously waiting for something to happen, but to her relief she saw him gesture, and the police moved away, back to the station. One constable stopped a farmer who had a copy of the petition, and took it from him.

'We would have given him one, if he'd asked,' Elizabeth said, and went to hand the farmer another copy. 'Don't be afraid,' she told him. 'It's quite safe to sign this. We had it checked by a lawyer in Adelaide.'

'Thank you, Frau Muller,' the farmer said. 'I'll sign it. Even so, nothing is really safe. These people in uniform have torn up the law.'

He drove off in a creaking bullock cart.

'He's right, of course. How can anyone be safe?' Elizabeth told her friends.

'But thanks to you and the lawyer, Stefan said nothing wrong,' Eva-Maria assured her. 'Not even Inspector Lucas could complain.'

The response to the petition was a bigger disappointment than the size of the meeting had been. In the following two days, Elizabeth and Eva-Maria visited those who had promised to collect signatures. They grew progressively more despondent. It was clear that people were very afraid. Many just shrugged, unwilling to discuss it as they handed back the unsigned paper. Some were candid enough to admit it was a risk, and said they were not prepared to take it. By mid-afternoon on the second day they had collected all the copies and counted the number of people who had signed. The total was less than a hundred. They had hoped for a thousand.

Elizabeth drove into town where they shopped for groceries and she picked up her mail. There was a letter from her father, recounting the lack of success in his meeting with James North, but assuring her he would try other avenues. It was a difficult matter, because the newspapers were prejudiced, and few people had any real idea that the police and militia were behaving with such intransigence. He begged her to avoid any sort of confrontation. Hannah was concerned and sent her love. They had received a letter from Harry, who was in Aldershot, England, and had apparently been made a sergeant. She smiled as she read her father's acid comment – that if he hadn't been so damned *independent* – she could see him at his desk underlining the word – he could have been an officer by now, but had clearly inherited his streak of stubbornness from his mother.

There was also a short note from Mr Harpur, on his personal stationery, inviting them to come and stay the following weekend, if they were able. It would greatly cheer up his wife, who was looking forward to meeting them, and he hoped they might bring Maria, because it would be his great pleasure to have them all to dinner.

'That's nice,' Eva-Maria said when Elizabeth showed her the letter on their way home. 'You should go.'

'We will.' She thought for a moment. 'It'll do Stefan good to get away – after this fiasco.'

'It wasn't his fault people didn't sign.'

'I know it wasn't. But he'll feel let down.'

'And how do you feel?' Eva-Maria asked shrewdly.

'Relieved.'

'I thought so. Make him stick to his vines. That's what he does best. No more speeches. It's enough not knowing about Gerhardt. We don't want more trouble.'

Elizabeth was grateful for a friend who knew her so well.

The van left soon after it was dark. It was a twenty-minute journey. Inspector Lucas sat in front with the constable who drove, and Sergeant Delaney and another policeman occupied the rear seats. They turned off the road when their lights picked out the distinctive wooden planked bridge that spanned the creek.

In the house the Mullers had finished their meal, and were washing up when the first flicker from the approaching headlights of the vehicle touched the windows. They could hear the van bounce on potholes in the dirt road, and the squeak of the brakes as it pulled up.

Elizabeth snatched up the pitifully small bundle of petitions, and put them in the meat safe. She came back to the table with a pack of cards, and spilled them out in front of Carl and Stefan.

'Elizabeth – we have nothing to hide,' he protested.

'Perhaps not, but take some cards anyway.'

They each took a hand, and held them self-consciously. With mounting tension they heard footsteps cross the verandah. They waited for a knock at the door, but instead it was abruptly pushed open, and Lucas entered, followed by Delaney and the constables. He stood there, his cold eyes surveying them, amused.

'Friendly game of cards, is that the idea?'

'What do you want, Inspector?' Elizabeth asked.

'We didn't hear you knock,' Stefan said.

'I don't believe, under the emergency powers, I need to state what I want,' Lucas said. 'And I most certainly don't have to knock.'

Stefan tossed aside his cards, and rose.

'In that case, if your intrusion is lawful, will you please state your business, and then go.'

'You're either very brave,' Lucas said, 'or extremely stupid.'

'We've broken no law.'

'That remains to be seen. You've been a public nuisance. On your soapbox, making speeches against the authorities.'

'You wrote down what I said. It was nothing illegal.'

'Well, that may be decided, in due course. For now, we're here to search your property, to see if you're hiding any weapons.'

He gestured to Delaney, who produced a torch and went outside accompanied by the driver. The other constable made what seemed like a pretence of searching the house.

'This is ridiculous, Inspector, and you know it,' Elizabeth said, trying to remain calm.

'Just doing my duty, Mrs Muller.'

'We have no weapons.'

'I'd hardly expect you to admit it, would I? Your husband did have a bayonet, which I confiscated at the police station.'

'That wasn't his.'

'It was in his possession.'

'But it belonged to whoever put that revolting figure on our land. You've never attempted to find out who did that. It might tell you who owned the bayonet - just supposing you want to know.'

Lucas made no reply. He seemed to be waiting for something, as he moved about the room, looking into cupboards and drawers. They watched with helpless fury. Elizabeth saw Stefan's hands clench into fists, and she silently begged him not to lose his temper. Sergeant Delaney pushed open the door and came inside. He was carrying a dusty rifle.

'Inspector –'

'Well, well,' Lucas said. 'Where did you find that?'

'Hidden under the verandah steps.'

'That's a lie,' Stefan said heatedly.

'Of course it's a lie.' Elizabeth rose to her feet alongside him. 'We all know it's a lie. You planted it there - as evidence.'

'Now why should we do a thing like that?' Lucas asked. 'There won't be a trial – so we don't need evidence.'

There was a stunned silence, as his words began to register. Of course there'd be no trial, she realised. No one was tried under the War Precautions Act. There was no need for the rifle as evidence.

So why had they done this? It was a device, so they would have a ready explanation for the arrest. In case questions were asked. But by whom? Stefan was now a well-known vintner, but reputation had not helped others. Then why the unnecessary charade of finding the rifle? In case her father . . . That was it! She saw Lucas's eyes probing her with quiet triumph, and knew he had decided to handle this with unusual care.

'This so-called charge is as false and dishonest as you are,' she said, and felt the immediate antagonism directed at her. It chilled her. It was like the venom of a snake.

'Take the prisoner out to the van.'

He snapped the order, and the constables each took an arm, giving Stefan no chance to speak as they marched him out. He made no attempt to resist, but was treated as if he was armed and dangerous. Carl started to rise, inflamed by the sight. Elizabeth put a restraining hand on his arm. Lucas, whose eyes missed nothing, saw this.

'Very sensible. We don't want anyone else arrested, do we?'

'You're not going to get away with this, Inspector. I hope you realise that,' she said, with more conviction than she felt.

'Of course,' he managed to make it sound as if he had only just remembered. 'Your father's some sort of bigwig, isn't he? Or used to be.'

'I intend to ask him to use all his influence.'

'I expect you will. But what have we done? Arrested a known

troublemaker, who's tried to get people to sign petitions. Disturbing the peace, you might call it, in time of war. And now found to be concealing arms. You say I won't get away with it? Get away with what, Madam? I'm just doing my lawful duty.'

He went out. Elizabeth followed, and gasped as she saw Stefan now handcuffed, being flung roughly into the back of the van.

Lucas observed her obvious distress.

'Steady,' he called. 'Not so rough with the prisoner. We must do our duty, but there's no cause to upset his wife.' He turned to her, with exaggerated politeness. 'Very patriotic, these men. I'm afraid they get a bit narked with foreign agitators.'

Elizabeth stared at him. The smile did not reach his eyes. His look of satisfaction was unmistakable.

'You malicious hypocrite,' she said.

'Get in the van, Sergeant,' Lucas ordered, and when Delaney was gone and they were alone, he said, his voice quiet and cold, 'Did you people really think he'd be allowed to stand up there, making speeches like that about us, in public? Threatening us. You should've had more sense, Mrs Muller. A woman like you – I'd have thought at least you would've known better.'

He climbed into the front of the prison van. The headlights dazzled her. She realised Carl had come out to join her. They stood distraught and helpless, as the van drove off into the night.

There was half an hour's time difference to the eastern states, and William and Hannah were in bed when the telephone rang. Grumbling, William got up and found his dressing gown. He went out to pick up the extension that had recently been installed, then realised Mrs Forbes had answered the main telephone downstairs.

He could hear his daughter's voice. Then there was distortion and crackling, and he couldn't understand what she was saying.

'What is it? Is that Elizabeth?'

'Yes, sir,' Mrs Forbes said. 'It's a very bad line, but I think she was saying something has happened.'

'Lizzie?' he shouted into the phone. 'Are you there?'

'Just a moment, please,' an operator's voice said, 'we're trying to contact the caller. Hold the line.'

'I'm holding the line.'

Hannah came out wrapped in a silk robe, trying to calm him.

'Don't bellow into the phone, darling. It doesn't help.'

'Bloody invention,' he said, now concerned at her late call and thoroughly agitated. 'They keep telling us how marvellous it is. If you ask my opinion, the whole system is one big fucking muddle.'

'Sir!' came the shocked voice of the woman at the exchange.

'I beg your pardon. I didn't realise you were there.'

'We are doing our best.'

'I'm sure you are. Shall I keep holding on?'

'I think we may have to ring you again – that is if the caller gets through.'

'But what's wrong?'

'There must be a storm between here and Tanunda, from where the call is being made. I'm afraid we've lost contact.'

'I'll sit and wait then,' William said.

'It may be a long wait.'

'Never mind. It's my daughter. She wouldn't be phoning so late, unless there was something wrong. I heard her voice, but couldn't understand what she was saying. I don't suppose you . . .' he tailed off.

'I heard something,' the operator said.

'Could you tell me what it was? Or is it against the rules?'

'It's against the rules.'

'Oh, well . . .'

'But I distinctly heard her say, "Daddy, please help me."'

Please help me.

She hadn't called him Daddy in years. He felt a sense of dread. He and Hannah made a cup of tea and waited.

In Tanunda the telephone exchange closed down for the night. By then Elizabeth and Carl could see the electrical storm over the eastern hills. There was nothing they could do, except go home and wait for the morning.

They took him into a large cell at the back of the police station, where they undid the handcuffs on one wrist, and before he realised what they intended, his hands were again secured, but this time behind his back. That was when he knew what to expect.

The constables each had a truncheon. He could see Lucas, a figure at the doorway, almost in silhouette as Sergeant Delaney turned out the main overhead lights, and they began to hit him.

'Not his face, boys. No marks on his face,' Delaney warned, and then he turned and joined Lucas. They stood watching the first flurry of blows. The policemen were both country boys, strong and physical. They began by using their fists, and occasionally their boots, and after that came the sickening thud of the truncheons.

Lucas and Delaney went out and shut the door behind them.

PART FIVE

Chapter 31

The shell landed like a damp squib and then exploded, spraying earth over the men crowded in the trench. But the shower of dirt and even the shrapnel was less of a problem than the fetid water and the mud they stood in, day after day, so their boots were always sodden and the feet inside them grew septic and abscessed. The mud lived on them and their uniforms, and would not go away.

Harry sometimes wondered at his insane ambition to be a part of this battlefield, to join this ragged army of hollow-eyed, shell-shocked and disgusted men, angry at the patriotic fervour that had brought them here to this awful piece of ground in France, which had already been won, then lost, then won again, at the cost of over two hundred thousand lives.

They were talking of half a kilometre.

Five hundred metres of pock-marked ground, where nothing grew, or would grow for a generation. Five hundred metres of blood, and the ghosts of young men on both sides who had died, some in agony, some without warning, all hoping they were fighting and dying for a better world.

Harry and those few of his friends still alive no longer accepted that. They confessed to themselves, in their cramped, stinking dugouts, that it was a heap of bullshit. They had been lied to, and misled. The politicians who exhorted them to do their duty should be here, and made to die, face down in the putrid mud.

They were all very angry. They felt completely betrayed.

He never wrote of this in his letters home - just supposing they ever reached home. To his parents he wrote of the vineyard, and how he hoped 1917 had been a good harvest, and he expected by now the vines would be pruned back and bare of leaves. These were things he could speak of, from this unspeakable place. He sent best wishes to Carl, his love to Maria, and hoped that all was well in the valley. He felt sure it was. It was such a peaceful part of the world.

Sitting in the mud, in the stink of death, among the lice and the rats that were a part of their daily life, he believed the Barossa remained pristine and untouched; he saw it as a terraced paradise, where the rows of grapes grew thick like bushes, and the creek meandered through the rich and abundant landscape dominated by the magnolia on the hill. From where he sat, with a tiny patch of dank sky and dripping rain, the valley he once disliked now seemed like heaven.

He wrote to Hannah and his grandfather of his last leave in England, and meeting Kate Brahm by extraordinary chance at a concert at the Albert Hall in Kensington, and how they had only recognised each other after much scrutiny - on her part, because she could not believe he might be here in Europe, and on his, because she had changed so much and looked very grown up, and attractive. He added, casually, that she was with her fiancé, Rupert, and they had all had supper together.

The letters home were not about the way he felt, or the days he lived through. They were circumspect, designed not to cause alarm. It was only to Kate that he wrote the truth.

It was easier now that he could write purely as a friend, knowing she was committed to her Englishman who had helped win the boat race for Cambridge, and was now a captain instructing troops at Camberley – who would undoubtedly survive the war, go into the city like his father, and marry Kate. Rupert was amiable and friendly: he confided to Harry that while he wanted her to continue her career, he felt that two children, a flat in London, and a country house in Oxfordshire were the ingredients for an ideal marriage.

Harry didn't mention in his letters that he hated this cheerful paragon – instead he wrote, just to her, about the way things really were.

Dear Kate,

Yet another dreadful day along the line to hell. Yesterday we gained one hundred yards and lost five thousand men. I expect the Germans have lost the same. That's a lot of men for such a small amount of territory. I used to run the hundred yards at school, in about eleven seconds. Yesterday it took us fourteen hours.

I keep seeing these photographs of old men in heavy trenchcoats with medalled caps, and I realise they are our generals. What most concerns me is the inevitable question: do they care? After all, their lives are nearly over. Ours are – we hope – just beginning. Although if you look around here, you might doubt that.

A month or so later he wrote:

I look at the grotesque caricatures of Germans in the Bulletin *and newspapers sent from home, and feel revolted. I think*

Norman Lindsay and his drawings are a disgrace. I hear he struts around Sydney as a Bohemian, but I think he has much to answer for in his depictions of German people. The ones I know are not like that. My father's not like that. Not a scrap like that. He's a civilised and decent and rather gentle man, who loves my mother. But I haven't the guts to come out and say so. I've only ever told one of my friends apart from you. I finally plucked up courage to tell David. Of course, as his sister you're going to ask what he said. Well, I'll tell you. He refused to be surprised. Typical David. Told me it was worse being Jewish. (I can't agree with that, though it was meant kindly, and probably the reason why we've always been closest and best friends.) God knows what the brass here would say, if they found out I was half-German. I'd probably be relieved of my command of this platoon, and sent back in disgrace to Aldershot. It sounds marvellous. Should I summon the troops and inform them my dad's a Kraut?

Affectionately,

Harry

P.S. Re: mention of my platoon above, did I tell you I've been made a lieutenant? It's only because we've run out of officers. They all love to polish their Sam Browne belts and their pips, and the enemy snipers have such a field day picking them out, that God's square mile is full of officers and gents. However, I don't intend to polish anything, or make myself a target. I'm not really an officer, or a gent. I take after my grandfather, who'd be deeply offended to be described as either.

P.P.S. If you're writing to your brother, tell him to ignore any sweet old ladies with white feathers, and finish his medical degree. Tell him this is a dreadful place, and anyone who volunteers to come here is totally barmy. Which very much applies to yours truly . . .

He explained that he could freely write such things, because he was now in charge of censoring the mail for their battalion. *We're not supposed to inform the loved ones at home what a mess this is,* he told her, and admitted he hated the job of reading private letters and trying to censor them. He rarely did read the letters, let alone use a pencil to edit, but his platoon, not knowing this, forced themselves to be cheerful and optimistic to their families. He told her they sometimes made the war sound like a combination of a training exercise and a bush picnic.

Harry needed the solace he found in expressing the exact way it was, and there was no one else he could confide in but Kate. He knew it was unfair on her, and he sometimes tore up the letters, but it was like the release of writing a diary in which he was able to put down the truth. As conditions deteriorated, his letters grew more intemperate.

> *We are lousy, stinking, ragged, unshaven, sleepless. I have one puttee, a dead man's helmet, a dead man's gas protector, a German's bayonet. My tunic is rotten with other men's blood, and partly splattered with a comrade's brains. I hate to write such things, but I cannot tell my family – yet I feel someone must know. If only to inform people when I'm dead. Why should some of those safe at home not be told what it's like. I mean the ones who were so keen to send us here. I want the middle-class ladies who hand out white feathers to know that several of my friends are raving mad. One lived for two days with his head split open and his brains visible. Thank Christ he's dead now. I'd like to tell politicians that I met three officers out in no-man's-land the other night, all rambling and completely insane.*

He went to England on leave. Kate met him at Victoria, when the troop train came in, and at first glance thought he looked the same. Although the letters of the past months belied that. So did his manner, she discovered. By the time they had finished tea at the nearest Lyons Corner House, she thought he should be invalided out because of an alarming mental instability. He was like an exhausted worn-out old man, convinced he would not live to see his twenty-second birthday. Trying desperately to cope, she asked him why he thought this?

'Johnno worked it out,' he said.

Johnno, it appeared, was a schoolteacher. Maths. Taught at North Sydney Boys High School, and a bit of a genius.

'What about him?'

'He has this system. Very complex. You multiply the number of men in the platoon by the average number of shells per day, plus add in a quotient for sniper fire and machine guns, and by a ratio over seven - being the seven days in the week - you get this convoluted algebraic answer, which gives you your estimated L.S.'

'Harry, what on earth are you talking about?'

'L.S. Life span. Otherwise known as D.L.T.L - Days Left To Live. I'm already on minus fifteen. Which means borrowed time. I should have been dead two weeks ago.'

'It sounds quite mad.'

'Here in Joe Lyons, with tea and sandwiches, it does. I admit in here it sounds a bit loonie. You'd be surprised how logical it sounds over there. Johnno's very rarely wrong. He was plus six when he told me all about it. Then, six nights later, someone gave us an order to attack. Someone else told the French the Germans were advancing. Out in no-man's-land, the French gunners managed to kill Johnno and about ten others, before we put up a flare.'

'Oh God,' she said, feeling this was impossible, it was going to be an absolute disaster. She wished David was here with them. Or else Rupert. Either of them might know how to deal with this. There was no way she could.

'Kate?'

She looked across the table at him. He tried and almost managed a smile.

'Sorry,' he said.

'For what?'

'I'm a mess. No, don't try to deny it,' he said, as she was about to. 'I know I'm a mess. But you can't just switch off. Give me a few days to stop the shells exploding in my head.'

'It must have been terrible.'

'I want to forget it – not talk about it.'

'How long is your leave?'

'A week. I've got a room at one of the officers' billets. Here's the address. Do you know where it is?'

She looked at the printed details.

'Yes, in Chelsea. Near the Embankment.'

'I'd better go and find it. Can we meet tomorrow? Will you have any spare time?'

'Of course,' she said.

She was due to sit for her trial finals in a month, and this was the fourth year, the one that really counted. She needed to rehearse every waking hour.

'I'll have lots of spare time,' Kate said.

It was late summer in London, but drizzling with rain, and people were rugged up against the cold. Kate walked with him, through the back streets of Pimlico, past Sloane Square and into the Kings Road.

'It's filthy weather for the end of August,' she said. 'Fancy calling this summer.'

'I'm used to it. Just as bad in northern France.'

'Do you remember,' she tucked her arm into his as they skirted dog droppings on the pavement, 'how one August in Sydney we all went swimming? Midwinter, and the water was freezing, but the sun was so warm, and we ran miles along the beach to get the blood circulating.'

Harry nodded.

'Do you ever miss it?' he asked. 'The sun?'

'Often. But I didn't really come here for the climate. Mind you, we've had at least one lovely summer. Nineteen fourteen was the best, people say. But if you're busy, and, well, happy I suppose – who cares about the weather?'

He felt a moment of envy for Rupert – whose second name he could not remember, and had no intention of asking.

The officers' billet was a cluster of houses that overlooked the gardens of the Chelsea Hospital.

'It's where they hold the flower show,' Kate told him, as he gave his name at the desk.

A rather stern middle-aged lady requested his paybook or any suitable identification, scrutinised it, glanced interrogatively at Kate, and then checked the register and admitted he was indeed booked in for the week. Single room, she said and, with another glance at Kate, regretted there was a strict rule that officers were not allowed guests on the premises. She asked if Lieutenant Patterson would be good enough to sign the book.

Lieutenant Patterson signed, and said he quite understood the rules. But this lady was not a guest, he said. This was Katherine Brahm, the renowned cellist, who had been kind enough to show him the way. It was such a friendly city, London, he said, and Miss Brahm had been telling him about her fiancé, a captain in the British army – and had insisted on guiding him here, and without her help he would have been hopelessly lost. He said to the lady behind the desk that she obviously knew of Katherine Brahm, the cellist, and the lady thought deeply for a moment and then assured him she did.

'I'll just see Miss Brahm to a hackney cab,' he said, and they went out, barely able to control their laughter.

'You galah,' Kate said. 'That's the kind of mad thing we used to do when we were kids.'

'Remember when you and David and I unscrewed all the street signs and changed them around?'

'God, we were larrikins.'

'Great days, Kate.'

'They were indeed,' she said, and kissed him on the cheek.

He wanted to hold her, but instead he took her hand for a moment and said goodnight. He went back to the doorway of the billet, watching her slim figure walk away, suddenly realising they had completely forgotten to hail a taxi.

The professor was less than cordial. He was Polish, and had been Kate's tutor for the past four years. He predicted a brilliant future. On the other hand, if she wished to spend one of the most important weeks of her life attending to some childhood sweetheart from the Antipodes, then she had best find another tutor, because this was not proper behaviour, and she was not a serious person. Any fool could play a cello. It took energy and strict discipline to succeed, to reach the top, the highest pinnacle, where it mattered. The shallow emotion of being concerned about some soldier was not for the likes of her.

Kate apologised that she was apparently so facile. On the other hand, she pointed out, she could well have sent him a note saying she had a cold and could not study for a week. It would have been far less disagreeable. But she had this peculiar trait of preferring the truth, and she'd make up the time, but this was her brother's closest friend who had been in the thick of the war and needed help - and if the professor didn't want her in his course any longer, then that was a pity. But there were several tutors who did.

The professor, not known for his graciousness, stalked off. Kate went home to Swiss Cottage, and the tiny flat she shared with a student actress from Cardiff. Later that day she waited in Kensington Gardens by the Albert Memorial, where they had arranged to meet. It was once again drizzling rain. He was late. Almost an hour late, and she was becoming angry and was about to leave, when she saw him. He was running from the direction of Queens Gate. He dashed across busy Kensington Gore without even a glance, and almost went beneath the wheels of an omnibus. It hooted in protest. A car braked suddenly to avoid him, and in a moment the entire street was a cacophony of tooting horns and squealing tyres. Harry gave them a cheerful wave and a bow, as if they were applauding him, and reached the gates opposite the Albert Hall.

She laughed, and knew then, despite any misgivings, that she had done the right thing.

Much later, when they had dinner, he explained that he had

slept almost twenty hours, and woken in a panic to realise he was late to meet her – and had run all the way from the Kings Road, through Chelsea, skirting South Kensington tube station and pounding his way past the museums in Cromwell Road before turning towards the park, hoping to God he was travelling in the right direction – and fortunately he was, because he glimpsed her by the Albert Memorial, tapping her foot and about to leave.

'You could have taken a bus,' Kate said.

'I didn't know which bus – or which way. Besides, after all that sleep I needed the exercise.'

'Twenty hours? How could you sleep twenty hours?'

'With no difficulty at all.'

'How was the officers' billet?'

'Spotless,' he said.

'Her ladyship on the desk wouldn't have it otherwise.'

'Too bloody right, mate. Not even a mozzie would dare cross her threshold.'

'Not to mention an officer's *guest*,' Kate said.

Harry smiled. 'In my brief acquaintance with this country, I've learned there is nothing quite so ferocious as the almost upper-class Englishwoman.'

Kate cupped her face in both hands. She looked at him for what seemed a long time.

'Let's pay the bill,' she said, 'and go back to my place.'

'Would that be a good idea?' Harry asked.

'I don't know. I'm proposing it.'

'What about the girl who shares your flat?'

'She's gone to stay with her family in Wales. I asked her if she'd mind. For a week.'

Harry's blood began to race. He could hardly believe it.

'But Kate –'

'What?'

'This isn't – it isn't because you feel sorry for me?'

'Don't be such a stupid bugger.'

'All right, then. But what about Rupert?'

He could not remember her looking so beautiful.

'This has nothing whatsoever to do with Rupert,' she said.

He had made love with other women, but never before with Kate. Slept with other girls, seductive, attractive girls, but it was not like this. Nothing was ever like this. When they were in their teens – children – they had kissed and touched each other, and felt as if they were in love, but that was adolescence, this was real. This was the culmination of his life. For two days they never left the tiny flat. In that brief time he lived as if there had never been trenches or mud, as though nothing had changed since he was thirteen, and his friend David had invited him home, and he had, for the first time, seen Kate Brahm.

He had been in love with her ever since then.

He would have loved her if she was plain and untalented, and it would have been a great deal easier. No scholarship to the Guildhall in London. No Rupert. They might even have been married by now; his mother told him she had married before she was eighteen years old. It was futile to even think of it. He was happy and grateful to be in bed with her, their naked flesh vibrant and thrilling. He accepted something he had not allowed himself to admit for years: in the entire world there was no one who even came close to Kate.

It was not easy to concede this. She had committed herself

to someone else. This was transient – wonderful, but ephemeral. They both knew it. Kate would always have to live in Europe or America. There was no future for her as a solo cellist in Australia; Harry had understood that ever since he realised the extent of her talent. But in the meantime they made love as if nothing in the world mattered. There was no tomorrow. Certainly for him there was none, because when he returned to the front there was Johnno's prediction. He was fifteen days over his lifetime.

If there was no Rupert, if Kate was free, he would have gone absent without leave and to hell with military police, or desertion in the face of the enemy. He would have walked away from the war, taken Kate and gone. There was no chance this could happen – but he fantasised about it. It was part of the joy of making love with her.

On their third day together she told him of his father's arrest.

It was something she had dreaded. She had learned of it in a letter from his grandfather. William Patterson had obtained her address from David. He stated Harry's father, Stefan Muller, had been summarily taken into custody, imprisoned without a trial, and that it was a travesty of justice. They were going to try to secure his release, but it could take time, because of the complex wartime laws. Both he and Harry's mother felt it was wrong to convey this news to him in a letter. He had gone on to say that, while it was asking a great deal of her, if she was to see him again on his next leave and felt able to tell him, then they would be very grateful. On the other hand, if she felt it was not a task she wanted to undertake, he would understand. It was asking a great deal but, knowing Kate, he was certain she would handle it sensitively, or else advise him it was beyond her. In conclusion, he congratulated her on her engagement, and wished her luck for her future. It would give he and his wife, Hannah, great joy if she became a concert artist, and some day they were able to hear her play.

It was a nice letter. Kate had always liked Senator Patterson. She replied, agreeing with their decision; that under no circumstances should Harry be sent this news. It would be unfair and would disturb him. (She did not say he was already deeply disturbed, writing erratic letters that distressed her.) When he came on leave, which might not be for some time, she would do her best to tell him. If it proved impossible, she would write to say so. She asked the Senator to let her know if there was any change in the situation, and to convey her sympathy to Harry's mother. She congratulated him on his marriage, which she had heard about and which seemed like a truly lovely day - and sent her regards to Hannah, of whom Harry spoke so fondly.

There had been a grateful reply, in which his grandfather said there had been no success as yet in freeing Stefan. He would wait to hear from Kate, and left it entirely to her decision whether she felt it wise to tell his grandson, or not.

When she first met him, off the troop train, that awful first day when she wondered if he was mad, she felt certain she could not possibly give him this news. He would be unable to cope with it. After three days he was like a different person, like the Harry of the past, only now they were lovers, however fleetingly, and she did not want to hurt him and had no real idea how to break such tidings. In the end, she simply gave him his grandfather's first letter to read.

He finished reading it, and there was silence. She looked at him across the table, his coffee going cold, his face registering the shock, wondering if she had done the right thing.

'Jesus Christ,' he finally said, 'what kind of a sick world do we live in, Kate?'

'No one wanted to tell you - not even me - but I think you had to know. You can't do anything to help, and it'll upset you and make you angry, but it's your right to be told.'

'And I'm a big boy now,' he said.

'That's right. You are.'

'Poor bastard. Poor Papa.'

He handed her back the letter. His eyes were wet with unshed tears. He brushed his sleeve angrily across them.

'Fancy being considered a threat to national security. A man who loves his wife, tends his vines, and is a success, a citizen proud of the country that's now imprisoned him. That's an irony, isn't it?'

She knew him so well, she simply put her hands in his, let him hold them tight as he talked.

'I'm glad Grandfather decided you were the one to tell me. I'm glad he's trying to help - because he never really liked my father. They didn't get on. The awful thing I have to say is - neither did I. I don't mean I disliked him, but we never understood each other.'

'You were brought up in a different way.'

'I still adored my mother. I'm very fond of my sister. But Papa and Carl . . .' He shook his head. 'I wonder why it was?'

They went for a walk in the park, and held hands. It felt as if they were lovers, but he knew it was only four more days, and then her life would return to her musical studies and to Rupert. In an odd way he did not begrudge this. He had tasted heaven, and it was sweeter than he had ever dreamed of. He tried to think of his father, in some prison or internment camp, unjustly held there, but his mind could not absorb it. He could only think about Kate's hand in his, that there were three more nights their naked bodies could touch each other, at moments in passion but mostly in great tenderness, and that if he were by some mischance and against Johnno's law to live beyond his allotted time, he would find life empty without Kate Brahm.

They walked by the Serpentine, and watched a family rowing a boat much too small for them, all the children splashing their oars and shouting loudly with delight. They bought sandwiches, and sat on a bench to eat them, and soon the pigeons came strutting and cooing. They laughed and threw them the crusts the birds were demanding.

'I'll write to Grandfather, and my mother. I can't believe that Grandpa won't get him out.'

'I'm sure he will,' Kate said, although from a letter David had written her, she was not sure at all.

'It's hard to understand. They're so far away. Yet they behave as if the war's on their doorstep.'

'We always did what England did. Why are we fighting, anyway? Ask yourself that.'

'I dare not,' Harry said, 'or else I'd never go back there.'

Kate threw the final sandwich crust to the pigeons, who fought over it, as if instinct told them this was the last offering.

Their days were so very few; they sped by in a blur of ecstasy and happiness. It hardly seemed believable that they were at Victoria Station again, the platform crowded with seasoned troops returning reluctantly from leave, or new recruits looking eager and vulnerable in unspoiled uniforms.

Harry found a window seat. The guard was blowing his whistle, carriage doors slamming, the great engine impatiently hissing steam amid shouted goodbyes and tears. He pushed open the grimy window, looked down at her on the platform, took her hand briefly as the train began to move.

'Dearest Kate,' he said, 'it was the best week of my life.'

Kate went back to the flat. It seemed lifeless without him. On the table were the letters he had written that morning, to be sent to his mother and grandfather. Folded with them was another sheet of paper with his handwriting.

I love you. I always have. Always will. Tell Rupert to be good to you, or I'll haunt him – that is presuming there's some sort of a life after. I don't want you to think I'm falling back into black pessimism; it's just that I have to be realistic. I count my blessings that we had these days together, yet I'm sad the world couldn't be different, so we'd live happily ever after – like in the best of magic fairy tales.

If you should ever meet my father, tell him I'm sorry. I didn't mean to hurt him. We were different people, going our different ways. I know he's strong; he'll survive. And my mother – you should meet her. David said nobody's mother should look as young and beautiful as she does. God bless, my love.

It was a wondrous time.

Chapter 32

'I'm sorry,' the attorney-general said, 'my department advises there can be no question of a writ of habeas corpus. The prerogative to enquire into the lawfulness of restraint does not exist.'

William Patterson tried to contain his anger.

'What do you mean, does not exist? If you consider yourself a lawyer, you know perfectly well habeas corpus is a right that has existed since Magna Carta.'

'The National War Precautions Act overrules common law in this case.'

'But that's a Federal act. We're applying under State law.'

The attorney studied the man sitting opposite him. Tall and vigorous, still in his late fifties with neatly groomed greying hair, accompanied by a well-dressed and handsome wife, ex-Senator Patterson was a complication the State Attorney could well have done without. No one in Adelaide quite knew the extent of his influence these days. The file on his son-in-law was in front of him, the police reports blunt and unambiguous.

The man was an agitator, and had threatened the local police inspector with a bayonet, while a rifle was later discovered hidden on his property. He ran what was apparently a thriving vineyard, but had been a constant source of trouble for some time. It was all closely documented. He had also made defamatory speeches against the Crown, and tried to circulate a petition that would have undermined police and government authority. There would certainly be no habeas corpus here.

On the other hand, the file had a note in the Premier's own handwriting. *Handle this with courtesy and caution.*

'I'm truly very sorry, Senator –'

'You're not the least bit sorry, and I'm not a senator any longer,' William interrupted frostily, 'so let's stop this humbug and hypocrisy.'

'I think you're being unfair, sir,' the attorney said, trying not to show his resentment. 'I didn't create this law. I may not even be in favour of it. But my department has to administer it.'

'Your department that decided Stefan Muller has no rights.'

'I wouldn't exactly put it like that.'

'Well, how would you put it?'

'I've done my best to accommodate you. I've allowed you to see copies of the police reports.'

'My daughter says they're untrue.'

'She may well be biased.'

'I expect she is, Mr Langford, since they've had a friend vanish and others attacked, without the police showing any interest.'

'I'm afraid my decision stands. The case is closed.'

'It can hardly be closed, while the man remains imprisoned. If you want to talk legalities, at least speak like a lawyer.'

'I mean,' the attorney was becoming terse, 'there will be no further enquiries. No more meetings. No application for release.'

'May I see the Premier?'

'He's delegated the matter to me.'

'Washing his hands. Well, that's apt. The Pontius Pilate of the City of Churches.'

Hannah could feel the anger in his voice, his rising temper, just as she could see the attorney-general's growing intransigence. Nothing would be achieved here. It was the end of a long and bitter battle, ever since the night of the first telephone call interrupted by the storm, and a tense thirty-hour wait until the line had been repaired and Elizabeth was able to inform them of what had happened. There followed months of frustration which had seen William rebuffed by former political colleagues, first in Sydney and Melbourne, now here in Adelaide, as he vainly tried to seek help.

In this spring of 1917, with a second referendum on conscription due, nobody was interested in the plight of any German emigrant, not even one well connected by marriage and long since naturalised, whose wines were known on affluent tables. As for William – those in power knew he had been active in the narrow defeat of the first vote on conscription. Others had personal vendettas. In his heyday he had been a ruthless debater in New South Wales's notorious parliamentary bearpit, a noted performer with an acerbic wit and a sharp and corrosive tongue, and some who had felt his trenchant invective had long memories.

Hannah badly wanted to salvage something from this debacle, for William's sake. They had come so far for such a total failure.

'Mr Langford,' she asked politely, 'perhaps my step-daughter could at least visit her husband?'

'It's not normally allowed, Ma'am.'

'Which is a pity, because then it leaves us with the feeling nothing is normal about this case. Whereas if she was able to visit, she could at least assure us he was being fairly treated.'

The attorney hesitated. She was a gracious and charming woman, and it might get this political albatross off his back.

'I'll have to take advice, Mrs Patterson,' he said. 'But I promise you I'll do my best.'

Stefan still remembered the day he came to the island. He wore the same clothing in which he had been arrested, and moved stiffly and in great pain from the repeated beatings the police had given him. The last of them had been two days earlier, and apart from having a bucket of water thrown over him each time they had battered him unconscious, he had not been allowed to wash. He felt grimy, and knew he smelled. He was handcuffed, and his feet were manacled. It was chilly on deck, the wind off the river was brisk, and the small craft rolled and plunged. The engine slowed, as they drifted in towards an isolated landing stage. A deck hand caught a rope thrown from the wooden jetty, and secured it to a bollard. Stefan was told to step ashore. He found it difficult, with the riverboat swaying and his legs chained, and when it seemed as if he might slip between the boat and the mooring, two guards grabbed his arms and hauled him onto the wooden planks.

Thus he arrived on Langley Island face down. He had already been warned it was to be Langley and not Torrens Island, and informed with relish that the latter was a holiday camp. Langley was where the intractable cases were sent. Guards dragged him to his feet, unchained his legs, and told him to proceed. There was a pathway that led towards a compound strung with barbed wire. Inside the prison area were wooden huts. Prisoners sat around with looks of despair or sullen defiance. Stefan saw a familiar face; for a wild, hopeful moment he thought it was Gerhardt, but the man turned and it was Horst Krausen, a shopkeeper from Nuriootpa.

The man nodded in recognition.

'Horst,' Stefan said involuntarily, but before he could continue, received a jolt in the small of his back.

'Keep moving, you German bastard,' the guard ordered. 'And no talking.'

He was made to wait until more new prisoners arrived later in the day, and they were all ordered to strip naked. Warders hosed them, laughing as they directed the powerful streams of water at their genitals. When the hoses were finally turned off, they were each thrown a strip of rough towelling.

A craggy-faced man who had been watching this, and who was clearly in charge, shouted at them in a broad Scottish accent that was difficult to understand.

'Ye've got thirty seconds to get dry, get dressed, and get the fuck oot of here.'

He came past Stefan, and paused as he saw the livid bruises all over his body. He studied them, as if they might be of future interest.

'A troublemaker, are yer, laddie? Well, for your sake, ye'd best not cause trouble here.'

Since that day Stefan had lost track of how many months had passed. He had heard nothing from Elizabeth, nothing of the outside world. Clearly the war continued, because they all remained prisoners. In his first weeks, he learned the rules the hard way. To speak in German, if overheard by the guards, was punishable by a hundred metre run, barefoot, over coiled barbed wire laid out like an obstacle course. It had happened to Stefan once; he hoped it never would again. The pain was extreme, excruciating, his feet raw and bleeding by the time he reached the end of it. He could barely walk on them for weeks, and there remained scars that would be permanent on his soles and ankles.

It was one of many disciplines for minor infringements.

The chief warder, McVeigh, was a despot, who ran the camp in the most stringent and authoritarian way. He informed Stefan that as he had been arrested and not merely interned, he was confined to a hut that contained the dangerous subversives. The traitors' quarters, McVeigh labelled it, and its occupants were allowed only an hour of exercise daily in a caged yard.

Boredom was their greatest enemy. Sometimes they were marched out to other parts of the island, and put to work digging ditches. When they were dug to the satisfaction of the supervising warder, the party was ordered to fill them in again. To men who had worked long and hard to achieve positions in the community, as many of them had, this fruitless endeavour caused anger and distress. Which was, they soon realised, the intention. Among the group of 'traitors' there was a Lutheran missionary, a teacher of music, and a wealthy pastoralist. Daily, they were bullied and humiliated by guards their social and intellectual inferiors.

After one harangue by McVeigh because a prisoner had kept a diary in German, they were paraded to witness its destruction, an act which took an hour, while each page was ripped from the diary and burnt. The man was then stripped naked, and bound with barbed wire. Prodded by sticks, he was forced to move about the camp, and Stefan and his group were made to watch. Each step was agony; he bled copiously and screamed with pain, until eventually convulsing.

A former lecturer, Professor Adolph Linke, dismissed from the Adelaide University because it was alleged he was indoctrinating the young with Prussian principles, risked a dose of the same punishment by murmuring to Stefan a translation from Goethe:

'In time of war, the devil makes more room in hell.'

Elizabeth could still not believe it. She was going to see him in a few minutes. Hannah - dear, wonderful Hannah - had worked the miracle. And a miracle it was, for no one was allowed to see or correspond with those in custody. Even her father admitted he had been able to achieve nothing, and it had been Hannah's quick thinking which brought about the agreement for her visit.

She stood on the deck of the small river craft, and watched as it approached the jetty. On the wooden landing stage was a smart, uniformed figure, who saluted as she prepared to step ashore.

'Mrs Muller? Chief prison officer McVeigh. The Governor has asked me to supervise your meeting with the inmate.'

At first glance she felt instant dislike. *Inmate?*

'Thank you,' she said formally. He extended his arm, but she stepped ashore without his help.

'This way, Ma'am.'

He conducted her to an administration building. She was asked to sign a document attesting that she was the legal wife of the prisoner, Stefan Muller, and she did so with a feeling of distaste, certain that this was a charade designed to humiliate her.

'There are certain rules, since this is irregular,' McVeigh said in his Scottish accent, and she knew then that he resented her. 'You will not touch the inmate. You will not make statements relating to his crime or anything other than personal remarks. Is that clear?'

Inmate, she thought again. *I distrust this man already.*

'Did you hear me, Mrs Muller?'

'I heard. You said my visit is irregular. On the contrary, it was sanctioned by the State Attorney-General.'

'If you're ready,' he said, avoiding a reply, 'we'll proceed.'

He opened the door and walked ahead of her into a room. Stefan sat on a chair in the far corner. A guard stood close beside him. As he rose, and Elizabeth instinctively moved towards him, McVeigh was between them.

'Personal contact is forbidden. Muller, resume your seat.'

The guard already had hold of his arm. Stefan subsided into the chair.

'Mrs Muller, please take this chair.'

It was on the opposite side of the room.

'Can't we sit together?'

'Sorry.' McVeigh did not sound it. 'Official instructions.'

She sat down. There could hardly have been more distance between them. The guard and McVeigh remained.

'For God's sake,' she said, 'aren't we to have any privacy?'

'Regulations.'

McVeigh was poker-faced, but she sensed he was smiling.

'Try to pretend they're not there,' Stefan said. 'That's what I often do. You look wonderful - lovely.'

You look pale and thin and threatened, she wanted to say, but knew it would not be wise. She could feel the gaze of the senior warder, waiting for her to respond.

'Maria sends her love. So does Carl.'

'How are they?'

'Angry. My father's doing his best. And Hannah - she was the one who managed to arrange this.'

'Thank them both. Tell them - it must be over soon. When it

is, there'll be enquiries made, and questions to be answered about places like this.'

'Careful, Muller,' McVeigh said. His hand tapped his thigh with nervous regularity. Like a metronome. It betrayed his inward anger that this visit was taking place at all.

'Is Gerhardt here?' Elizabeth asked.

'No. If Gerhardt had been arrested like they said, then this is where he'd surely be. Which means that Gerhardt's dead.'

'I'll tell my father.'

'What can he do?'

'I don't know. Make a fuss, perhaps. He's good at that.'

'Tell him then. Gerhardt was a kind, decent man, with the courage to speak his mind. A fuss should certainly be made.'

McVeigh stepped forward. 'This is not personal conversation,' he said. 'You will speak only of domestic matters.'

'There was a letter from Harry. He said he met Kate Brahm by chance in London,' Elizabeth said, hating the way they were being made to talk in front of these men.

'I'm glad. Does she still play the cello?'

'Even better, he says.'

'What other news?'

'Sigrid's a bit better, but she still has the scars. Dr Hardy is worried about Oscar. He's deeply depressed. We all miss you. People in the town feel ashamed now, wishing they'd been braver and supported you. Everyone is angry that our corrupt police tricked you into being arrested, and sent to this place.'

'All right, Mrs Muller!' McVeigh shouted. 'Time's up.'

'What do you mean, time's up? I've only just got here.'

'And now you're leaving. Say goodbye to him.' He gestured, and the guard hauled Stefan to his feet.

'This is a farce.' She was incredulous.

'Rules. I told yer. Yer were warned.' The warder's voice became shrill, his Glaswegian accent so pronounced, it was difficult to decipher. 'I said only to talk of personal matters. Yer fault, woman, ye' broke the rules. Get him out,' he shouted at the guard.

'Elizabeth –'

McVeigh yelled violently, drowning whatever Stefan was trying to say. 'Go on, out! Get the bastard out!'

The guard secured Stefan with an arm tight around his throat; pulled open a door beside them, shoved his prisoner forward, then used his foot to propel him into the adjacent room. Stefan went sprawling and landed heavily on the floor. It took only seconds. Elizabeth could see nothing more, as the door slammed, but she heard a cry of pain. She stared at McVeigh, and realised with revulsion that he was not even trying to conceal his satisfaction.

'What are you? Some kind of filthy sadist?'

Now he was in control of his voice again he ignored her anger. 'Now you see, lassie, why we don't approve of visits. Why it was unwise to allow it. Some silly emotional female like yourself just brings the laddie a whole lot of trouble. The Good Lord alone knows how much trouble.'

It was even worse when he smiled.

She felt an animal hatred for him – and pure terror for Stefan.

'Listen to this,' Marty Renshaw said, reading from a torn and mud-stained copy of *The Times.*

'Too late in moving here, too late in arriving there, too late in coming to decisions, too late in starting enterprises, too late in preparing. In this

war the footsteps of the Allied Forces have been dogged by the mocking spectre of too late. *Unless we quicken our movements, damnation will fall on the sacred cause for which so much gallant blood has flowed.'*

'Bloody right,' Corporal Shortland said. 'Who said it?'

'Lloyd George, in the House of Commons.'

'Good for Lloyd George,' Harry Patterson said, 'but we could have told him that. Everything in this theatre of war – as Shakespeare used to call it – has been a fuck-up. When you get a good general like Monash, they try to give him the push.'

'Who did?'

'The British. And King George V.'

'You're kidding? Tried to get rid of Monash. He's the only bastard who gives a stuff about us cannon fodder.'

'Why did they try to get rid of him, skip?' Shortland asked. They were cramped together in a dugout, waiting for the guns to begin. Harry, Sergeant Renshaw, Corporal Shortland and the platoon. Thirty minutes from now, when it was dusk, they would go over the wire. The enemy – since the artillery barrage and charge was a tactic used constantly by General Haig – would be cleaning the barrels of their rifles and oiling their machine guns in readiness.

'The King didn't like the idea of having a Jew command the Australian and New Zealand Army Corps.'

Harry had heard it at division headquarters.

'C'mon, skipper. Are you serious?'

'Absolutely. His Majesty said, "But the man's a Jew. A bloody German Jew, to boot."'

General Monash's father had come from Bavaria. Harry had met the general only once, when he was promoted to captain, and saw no reason to raise their common German heritage. He wondered if Monash's father was alive, but doubted it – and whether he might have been interned if he had been. He rather doubted that, too.

'It stinks,' Marty Renshaw said.

'Why?' Shortland asked him.

'Because the fucking King himself comes from Germany. He's a hun like those buggers over there.'

Harry moved away from them. He had been back in the line a month, and still unable to fully comprehend the news Kate had given him. His father was interned. Somehow – even if they had always been remote and estranged – he had to write to him. He had tried several times, but now he realised he must. Johnno's law would catch up with him soon, and not to have written, knowing the truth, was unthinkable.

He sat in the corner of the sodden dugout, and took a pad and pencil from his pack. There was a fountain pen somewhere, but it had long since run out of ink.

My dear father . . . he began – and wondered what else he could say.

Chapter 33

William had never known total defeat. Not like this. Not the humiliating and thinly veiled indifference of bland bureaucrats, to whom he was no longer a person of importance, merely the relative of an internee, importuning for his release – while also asking questions about another missing alien, claiming he was possibly killed by troops who had arrested a pastor of the Lutheran church.

He could sense their disbelief. What date did this occur, he was asked? What was the name of the minister? He consulted Elizabeth and her friend Eva-Maria Lippert, and provided the authorities with the details.

Nothing whatever known about the matter, the army replied so promptly that William knew no real enquiry could have taken place. He asked if he could interrogate the troops concerned in the pastor's arrest, but was told they were serving overseas. When he said he doubted this, since they were militia and not A.I.F., he was asked to meet with a colonel, who informed him the army was not in the habit of lying, and the men had volunteered for service abroad and were no longer in Australia. If he wished, the colonel said, he should put his concerns in writing, and the area officer would consider if it required further investigation. He was left in no doubt that there was more important work to hand - a war to be won - and his intrusion with these questions was a waste of the colonel's and everyone else's very valuable time.

During this period of frustration in Adelaide, his few moments of pleasure were the meetings with his granddaughter, Maria. He was startled by her resemblance to Elizabeth. It was not merely that they looked alike - he already knew that from her photographs - but her expressions, the sound of her voice, everything was like turning back the clock to be confronted with a perfect replica of Elizabeth at that same age. It was uncanny.

He and Hannah tried to appear encouraging, when they spoke to her of attempts to secure Stefan's release. Maria was upset - she had not told her friends or teachers, and it was affecting her school work. She was trying to concentrate, knowing failure to get into medical school would only cause her father additional distress. But it was difficult, she said, and she was feeling very insecure. It was clear Stefan's imprisonment had come at a critical time in her life.

Maria came with them, when he and Hannah went to spend a few days in the Barossa, where he marvelled at the transformation of the vineyard. The once shabby house on a twenty-acre patch had become an elegant home blending into the landscape, and surrounded by well-built storage and fermentation buildings, some of timber and others of stone. There were neatly clipped rows of vines terraced all the way up the hill, and on the land acquired beyond. The original block he had given them had grown to over a hundred acres, and everywhere the nurtured bushes were flourishing, bursting into new growth. He walked the property with Carl, who was eager to show him everything. William was impressed by the tidiness, the obvious love and care that had been lavished on the place.

'So who's looked after it, ever since your father . . . ?'

'I have,' said Carl.

'Without help?'

'We can't get help. Mama sometimes insists she and I prune the vines together.' He smiled. 'I manage, but it would be a lot harder without the watering system that Pa said you gave us.'

They walked to the crest of the hill and stood beneath the magnolia tree, so they could look at the land falling gently down to the creek on one side, and abutting the Lippert farm on the other. The vines ran in perfect symmetry. The soil between was ploughed and free of weeds. With the late afternoon sun slanting on the leaves, it looked like a picture postcard.

'I never dreamed it could develop like this,' William said. 'It's just remarkable.'

'He worked hard. That's why it's so unfair, what's happened. Do you think he'll be released soon?'

William hesitated. This boy wanted the truth, not promises or glib false hopes.

'I wish I could say yes, Carl. But I don't have the influence any more. Our best hope is for this damn war to end soon, then they'll all come home.'

After the brief few days, Maria was due to return to school. William and Hannah drove her. It was goodbye; he knew he could accomplish nothing further by remaining in Adelaide, but promised they would visit again soon. Carl shook hands with them both, and kissed his sister. He stood waving as they left.

That night at supper, he said to Elizabeth, 'It was strange, meeting my grandfather.'

'I gather it wasn't as bad as you expected?'

'I always thought I'd hate him. But I didn't.'

'He's not really very hateable.' She smiled.

'He doesn't think Pa can get out.'

'I know.'

'Is it terrible in there? You didn't say very much about your visit, Mama. Just that he was well.'

'He is well. So much better than I expected. And as for being terrible – after all, it's a prison camp, and so it's rather strict and bleak, but he's managing,' Elizabeth said, hoping he believed her.

The letter arrived two days later. It was in pencil, with an accompanying note to Elizabeth, dated two months earlier.

My dear father,

I'm told you're in a prison camp, accused of being some sort of enemy. What kind of people, in God's name, are making this accusation? We have not been close, you and I, for which I apologise. I should have tried harder. Perhaps you should have, also. But an enemy alien? Are they all mad? You came to Australia as a penniless emigrant, met my mother, eloped with her and rejected what could have been an easy and an affluent life. I have to be proud of you, Papa. I am proud, and want you to know it.

Now I'm fighting in this wet and muddy corner of France, and I hear the news you are imprisoned as an enemy. I wish the people who did this to you were here, so I could point out the enemy to them. I could say – climb out of this dirty hole in the ground, look across the dead bodies and the barbed wire – the enemy are over there. They are mostly young – like us; sick and tired of death – like us; misled, lied to, provoked to war – just like us. Our enemy is not so different to us. Unlike yours.

Your enemy seems to be people who call themselves patriots, who insist they are on the side of the Almighty – for both sides in this insane war claim the allegiance of God. If God were half of what we were taught, he must turn aside in horror. I am appalled, Father – I am sad beyond words of mine, that the country you sought as a refuge and loved, the country that should be proud of your achievements, has done this to you. I have long been convinced – and we have these crazy thoughts here in this hellish place – that I would die here. That I could not survive. Well, now I must. I must come home, first to make my peace with you, and after that to find out who is to blame for this outrage – and try to make them accountable.

Your son,
Harry

As battalion censor, he had cleared the letter himself, and it went back with the mail to headquarters. A week later it was on board a cargo ship, and six weeks after that reached Perth. It took another week to cross the Nullarbor to Adelaide.

Elizabeth read it and wept.

She knew she could not post this to Stefan. It was too precious, too important to risk someone intercepting or destroying it. Much as she feared the prospect of another visit to Langley Island, she must somehow obtain permission to deliver this in person.

Mr Harpur toyed with legal papers on his desk, apologetic with bad news. The photos of his two dead sons gazed at Elizabeth.

She had heard, weeks ago, that Lieutenant David Harpur of the Royal Flying Corps had been killed in action over the Hindenberg line. She had written to Mr Harpur at his office, rather than his home, grieving for this kindly man who had always hoped at least one son would someday become a partner in the family firm. She dreaded to think how Mrs Harpur might be feeling.

'I only heard officially yesterday. Since you'd written to say you were coming to Adelaide, I thought it best to tell you in person.'

'They've refused to let me visit?'

'I'm afraid so. They say last time you caused trouble, which we know is untrue. But I have no recourse – no way I can take them to any court to appeal. This is becoming an awful world, Mrs Muller.'

'It is, Mr Harpur.'

She rose and looked out the french windows. Across the square were the sedate, fashionable buildings of the North Terrace. She did not see the view, filled only with despair.

'A son wants to make peace with his father, and I don't dare send the letter. Am I wrong? Do you think they'd let him read it?'

'Not a chance.'

'Then how can Stefan know? Unless I take it in person, and read it to him. There's no other way. I have to do this. It would mean so much to him to be reconciled, to hear what Harry says.'

'When they turned down your application, I applied to visit, as his legal adviser, hoping I could convey the sentiments of the letter. But they rejected that. It's grossly unfair.'

'It is,' Elizabeth said, 'and I'm not going to accept it.'

'But what can you do?'

'Fight.'

'How?'

'I've no idea, Mr Harpur – not the remotest. They arrested my husband on false evidence, and I can't contest that, because they'll manufacture more lies to support their action. But I can challenge the concept that in this day and age, they can imprison a man and prevent anyone from seeing him. It's not just unfair – it's inhumane – and I've no notion how, but I'm going to fight it. I'm going to make them wish they'd never heard of me.'

Mr Harpur looked at her, and felt a stirring in his heart. It was impossible, of course, that she could achieve anything, but if he had been granted a daughter, he would certainly have wanted one like this.

Elizabeth waited most of the day in the cheerless room, one of many people sitting and waiting there. She read the magazines, all months out of date, then pondered over a copy of the *Bulletin* with one of Norman Lindsay's vicious anti-German cartoons in it. She was truly puzzled by Lindsay. This Bohemian, this free spirit who painted so well had adopted the stance of British magazines, but gone far beyond the English cartoonists with his unrelentingly spiteful illustrations. His drawings had become a leading force in the widespread hatred of anyone with German ancestry.

My children, she thought, *are victims of Mr Lindsay's pen and ink.* It was all the more astonishing, because artists were generally supposed to be liberal, to have a measure of understanding. She felt that Lindsay was either well paid for his savagery, or had no real compassion.

Leaning back, she studied the notices covering the gaunt walls. CARELESS TALK COSTS LIVES. CONSCRIPTION – VOTE YES. BUY WAR BONDS. Elizabeth wanted to close her eyes. She was weary with waiting. At the reception desk, a middle-aged woman in charge sat endlessly knitting. A man carrying a bulky file came from an office. He enquired of the receptionist, whose needles paused to aim in the direction of Elizabeth. The public servant approached and introduced himself as an under-secretary.

'I'm sorry you had to wait so long,' he said. 'The matter has been very carefully investigated. I regret your request to visit the prisoner is denied.'

'I asked for an appointment with the Premier.'

'There's no hope of that, I'm afraid.'

'All I wish to do is state my case.'

'He's busy. It's completely out of the question.' He returned to his office, without bothering to wait for her response.

Elizabeth left the building. There was a park opposite, and she sat on a bench there, wondering if she should go home. It was probably the sensible thing to do, but it seemed too much like failure. She thought of telephoning the school, to ask if Maria could have time off. For what? To console her mother, who could not cope with the complication of being married to the enemy?

Elizabeth shook her head angrily, determined not to allow herself to think in those terms. But what could she do? It was all very well to make brave statements to Mr Harpur, fine to declaim that she would fight, but how? And who would she fight?

She watched a group of children playing on a swing and a seesaw. Their excited voices bonded them, whereas she felt utterly alone. Even in the worst days, at the Ritter's farm in Hahndorf, there had always been Stefan and herself; always the two of them. And at that time she had been nineteen years old and no matter how bad the present, there was always expectation of a future. At thirty-nine, she was no longer so confident of what lay ahead.

Across the park, beyond the playground, she could see lines of delivery vans, where men were carrying out bundles of newspapers. It was a large Queen Anne building, with massive lettering across the facade: SOUTH AUSTRALIAN PRESS LIMITED. THE ADELAIDE HERALD. THE WEEKLY STAR.

She hesitated, then rose from the bench. *What have I to lose?* she thought, and began to walk towards it.

'No,' the secretary said, 'I'm certain that you can't see him. I really must insist you leave.'

'I can hear you insisting,' Elizabeth said tenaciously, 'but I'll wait and let him tell me.'

She had, by a blend of audacity and good fortune, walked right through the busy newspaper office without being challenged, and found the frosted glass door with JAMES BOOTHBY, EDITOR inscribed across it. But her luck had lasted only briefly; now his protective private secretary had discovered her, and in a moment would call for someone to eject her from the premises.

She turned as the door opened, and Boothby entered. At the sight of him, her heart sank. She had wildly hoped for someone young, who might be sympathetic. James Boothby was in his fifties, short, thickset and dour.

'Mr Boothby,' the secretary said, 'I've told this person you can't possibly see her without an appointment.'

'That's correct.' Boothby did not even bother to glance at Elizabeth.

'She just walked in here – and now refuses to leave.'

'Then call the security people,' he said, now turning to study her. 'Do I know you, Madam?'

'Not yet,' Elizabeth replied.

'Then please do as my secretary requested. You don't look like the usual type of ratbag we get in here. I'm sure you wouldn't want the embarrassment of being removed from the premises.'

'I simply ask you to spare a few minutes to listen to me.' She felt her courage evaporating with every passing moment.

'I'm too busy,' Boothby said.

'My name is Elizabeth Muller. My husband is a prisoner on Langley Island.'

She saw the secretary's face grow crimson with outrage.

'Mr Boothby – I had no idea she was a German! I'll call someone immediately.'

'My father,' Elizabeth continued rapidly, 'is former Senator William Patterson. More importantly, my husband is a naturalised Australian, imprisoned on false evidence supplied by the local police.'

Boothby stared at Elizabeth. He ignored his secretary, poised at the door, awaiting orders.

'False evidence?'

'You've only my word for that, but please believe I'm not in the habit of lying.'

'Patterson's daughter? "Federation" Patterson?'

'He'd enjoy hearing you call him that.'

'Married to a German?'

'Stefan was born there. He came here twenty-two years ago.'

'When did you marry?'

'Back then – twenty-two years ago. We have three children. We own a vineyard. If you're beset by ratbags, Mr Boothby – I'm most assuredly not one of them.'

Boothby was by now well aware of this. 'Look, I'm sorry. We were rather hasty, eh, Miss Bain?'

'Yes,' the secretary said, chastened.

'And I deeply sympathise. I daresay there are many cases of injustice. No doubt about it.'

'Then let me tell you –' Elizabeth began to say, but was interrupted.

'Sorry, Mrs Muller. But it would be a waste of your time. This newspaper can't show support for anyone with a German name.'

'Are you serious?'

'Totally,' he said. 'We wouldn't dare.'

'Why not?'

'We'd lose half our readers, have our newsstands burnt, and our windows broken.'

Elizabeth was genuinely shocked.

'Are you saying you're afraid?'

'I'm saying yesterday, in France, a thousand Aussie boys died gaining a strip of land that may well be lost again tomorrow. It's a dreadful war, Mrs Muller. If people are unfair and irrational about the Germans, who can blame them?'

'I can,' Elizabeth said.

'I'm truly sorry.' He sounded as if he meant it.

'I'll show you out,' Miss Bain said, now also sympathetic.

Elizabeth took no notice.

'It is a dreadful war, Mr Boothby. My eldest son is one of those Aussie boys in France. So you ask who can blame people for their blind and ignorant prejudice. Well, I can – and I do.'

'Mrs Muller, please –' The secretary tried to take her arm.

Boothby gestured at her to stop. He gazed at Elizabeth. 'What did you say? Your son?'

'Yes.'

'Your son's in the army? In Flanders?'

'Wherever the war is now, that's where he is.'

'And your husband's imprisoned as an enemy?'

'Yes.'

'And your father was an original Senator? One of the founders of Federation.'

'Yes.'

'Good God.'

She decided she might as well use the truth to make a further impact, since he was at last listening to her.

'The real founder of Federation, Sir Henry Parkes, came to my tenth birthday party.'

'Jesus Christ. I do beg your pardon - but - good heavens, Mrs Muller, why didn't you tell me all this?' Boothby shook his head. He seemed to realise Elizabeth was still standing. He jumped to his feet and brought a chair for her.

'Please sit down.' He turned to his secretary. 'Miss Bain?'

'Yes, Mr Boothby?'

'Bring us a pot of tea - and - and biscuits. Cakes. Whatever you can manage. And ask one of the photographers to step in here, and bring his camera and flashbulb apparatus.'

'Yes, Mr Boothby.'

She went out. Boothby sat down again.

'Parkes,' he said, looking at Elizabeth with what seemed like awe. 'Sir Henry.'

''Enery. Couldn't pronounce his aitches.'

'So I heard. Was it true?'

'Yes,' Elizabeth said, smiling, 'although sometimes I think he exaggerated it. By then it was legend.'

'He was my hero,' Mr Boothby said. 'When I was starting out, just a young reporter. Perhaps we could manage to use a picture of him in this story?'

'You mean you're going to help me?'

'I wouldn't dare mislead you, Mrs Muller. Would you object if I call you Elizabeth?'

'Not at all.'

'It's just that - you seem so awfully young. If you don't mind me saying so.'

'I don't mind in the least. But I'm thirty-nine.'

He shook his head, as if this surprised him, too. He wrote it down. She supposed he thought her young to have a son at the front.

'I was eighteen when he was born,' she explained, 'and he joined up under age.'

'It gets better,' Mr Boothby said.

'In what way?'

'In every way. People will read this, and shed tears. That's what I meant about not misleading you, Elizabeth. We're an afternoon paper, in the business of selling stories. We're not quite as grand as some of the morning newspapers. Not as conservative. We use large type and your name will be in headlines. It's a very good story, and it will sell lots of our newspapers. But I'm not sure how you'll feel, about being exposed to public view like this.'

'I have no choice,' she said, and made a decision. She took Harry's letter from her handbag.

'I can't read you all of this, but my son wrote these words to his father: *"I am appalled, Father – I am sad beyond any words of mine, that the country you sought as a refuge and loved, the country that should be proud of your achievements, has done this to you. I have long been convinced – and we have these crazy thoughts in this hellish place – that I would die here. That I could not survive. Well, now I must. I must come home, first to make my peace with you, and after that to find out who is to blame for this outrage – and try to make them accountable.*"'

'Can I use that part of it?' Boothby asked quietly.

She nodded.

'We'll need the front and both centre pages,' he said. 'Box the letter. A photograph of you, one of your son, perhaps your father, certainly Sir Henry. But you do realise, people are going to take sides. No one will be neutral. You'll be both famous and notorious.'

'Famous and notorious?' They felt like strange words.

'I'm afraid so. I hope that doesn't frighten you.'

That afternoon she took Maria to afternoon tea, by special permission of the headmistress, and told her what to expect.

'When's it being published, Mama?'

'The day after tomorrow.'

'Are you nervous?'

'A bit. I'm more concerned for you.'

'Why?'

'It'll be all over Adelaide. So everyone at school will know.'

'Let them.'

'It won't be easy, Maria. People take sides. Even your friends might do so.'

'If they side against me, then they're not my friends.'

'I nearly backed out of it – because of you. I think it's too late now, but you're the one who'll be hurt most.'

'That's not true,' Maria said. 'Papa's the one who's hurt most. He didn't commit any crime, did he?'

'No.'

'And he's imprisoned. So what else could you do, but this?'

'Thank you, darling,' Elizabeth said.

'And, anyway, it's not going to be easy for you.'

'But I have to stay. You don't.'

'Where could I go?'

'I spoke to Hannah by telephone. She and your grandfather would love to have you – either until this dies down, or you could finish school there, and try for Sydney University medical school.'

'That's nice of them.'

'They mean it.'

'I know.'

'But you want to stay here?'

'I think so.'

'That may not be easy. The school could end up being bothered by reporters. Miss Shillington wouldn't like that.'

Maria shrugged and smiled. 'Then we'll see how progressive and tolerant the old Shilling really is.'

'I think you're as stubborn as I was at your age.'

'That sounds almost like a compliment, Mama.'

'It's meant to be,' Elizabeth said, taking her daughter's hand.

It was far bigger than she expected. Worse in some ways. Her name on street placards. Her photograph on the front page, with a banner headline: SENATOR'S DAUGHTER PLEADS FOR JUSTICE, it said, ignoring her father's retirement. HUSBAND IMPRISONED WITHOUT TRIAL. SON WITH THE AIF ON THE WESTERN FRONT.

In the centre of the paper, the story of her life extended over both pages. This was headlined: THE AGONY OF A WIFE AND MOTHER.

There were prominent photographs of William Patterson and Sir Henry Parkes, with the caption: *He attended her birthday parties.*

There was an artist's sketch of Harry done from snapshots, resplendent in his uniform as a captain. Boothby had also sent a photographer to the vineyard, so there was a picture of that. He seemed to have overlooked nothing. There was even mention of January the 1st, 1901, when Federation had been proclaimed, and Elizabeth Patterson Muller had been the youngest guest of honour on the official dais in Centennial Park. A guest, the story said, of Prime Minister Edward Barton himself.

By the following day, other newspapers had tried to follow up the story, but Boothby had anticipated this and taken precautions. Did she have friends, he asked Elizabeth, here in Adelaide where she could stay in obscurity? Elizabeth at once telephoned Mr Harpur, and received the first intimation of what her future might be like.

'I'm most desperately sorry, Mrs Muller. I don't know quite how to put this.'

'If the invitation to stay is withdrawn, Mr Harpur, all you have to do is say so.'

'It's my wife. I feel mortified, but I must think of her first.'

'Of course you must.'

'She now accepts both the boys were killed. Unfortunately, it's brought about an almost pathological feeling towards Germans. She read your story in the paper - and feels unable to ask you here.'

'I'm sorry to have caused you embarrassment, Mr Harpur,' she said sadly, and hung up at once, before he could reply.

If this was the first reaction, she felt a sense of foreboding. Famous and notorious, James Boothby had warned her. He hadn't mentioned losing friendships, or having to find a new lawyer. But that could wait. First, she had to find somewhere to spend the night.

Evelyn Shillington had always prided herself on a reputation for being strict, but fair. She had been headmistress for sixteen years now. She had only distant family, she was single, and had no partner or lover to share her life. The school, where she had come as a novice teacher, then graduated to house mistress, deputy head, and finally headmistress, was in fact her life. 'The Shilling', as she knew her girls called her, was straightforward and scrupulously ethical, and because of it was well liked. Now she had a problem to solve, unlike any she had previously encountered. Since the publication of the story on Maria Muller's family, the office had received almost fifty letters from parents, requesting the girl leave, or they would withdraw their daughters.

Miss Shillington had walked in the quadrangle, visited the classrooms, and seen not the slightest trace of prejudice towards Maria. It was not the girls who were the problem; it was their middle-class, affluent parents, who paid the fees that kept the school solvent in these uneasy times. She knew fifty letters was only the start. By the end of the week the number would double. And if fifty left, others would soon follow. In a school of three hundred girls, she might well lose over a third of them. The Board would have no option but to dismiss her, ask Maria to leave, and request the parents to reconsider.

It would be reported in the newspapers, and would certainly be the end of her career. She could hardly expect another position, not at her age, and not in the present poisonous climate. She might be forced to earn a precarious living by private tuition, a prospect which she dreaded.

It was disgracefully unfair. Maria was one of the school's most promising pupils, and had an ambition far beyond her peers'. No pupil had ever aspired to be a doctor; it was more than aspiration, for the Shilling knew Maria had the intellect and determination to succeed. It would have been a tremendous cachet for the school, and for her as headmistress. Something of which to be proud.

Miss Shillington liked the parents. She felt sympathy for their predicament, the appalling way events had treated them. And Elizabeth Muller - what a glittering background, that astonishingly had never been known until now. She would have been pleased to invite her to dinner, to ask about Sir Henry Parkes, and about her own father who had so strongly advocated votes for women, and helped to bring about Federation. In normal times, Mrs Muller was the kind of woman who might well have presented the prizes on speech day. No one else she knew in this city had been on the official platform with Edmund Barton and the Earl of Hopetoun, the day they proclaimed the Commonwealth.

Instead, with a feeling of sick despair, Miss Shillington knew she would have to ask Elizabeth Muller to withdraw her daughter from the school. No matter how biased and unjust, it was the only way that she could avoid complete catastrophe.

Chapter 34

The day was windless and hot on the island. A work party was erecting new fences of barbed wire. The roll of new wire was sprung tight, and ripped their skin as they tried to handle it. Stefan worked with Adolph Linke. Professors of philosophy are unused to fencing, and so the pair were constantly berated by a young warder, relishing his power.

'Get on with it, you stupid, idle bastards, or I'll wrap some of that barbed wire around your balls.'

'At least it would prevent a population explosion,' Linke said in an aside, and Stefan tried not to laugh. It was dangerous to laugh at these humourless bullies, but without the professor's caustic asides and determined refusal to be coerced, life would have been intolerable.

'You . . . Muller,' another warder shouted, and Stefan turned towards the sound. 'Yes, you. You're wanted in the office.'

He and the Professor looked at each other with concern. Being wanted in the office meant a confrontation with McVeigh. It was not a summons to be welcomed.

'Take care,' Linke murmured.

Stefan was escorted to the administration hut, where

another warder took charge of him, barked an order to smarten himself up, and marched him into the office where McVeigh was studying files. There was no attempt by the chief warder to acknowledge his presence for the next few minutes, while Stefan stood in front of his desk, sweating with apprehension and an impotent anger.

When he knew he had achieved his objective of instilling fear, McVeigh looked up.

'You're in luck, laddie.'

'Luck?'

'Aye. It seems someone likes you.'

For a delirious moment, he thought he was to be released. The warder, enjoying this deception, smiled humourlessly.

'No, not quite that lucky. But you are being privileged. You're being allowed another visit from your wife.'

All Stefan could remember was the humiliation and pain of their last meeting. He was not certain he wanted to subject Elizabeth to that again.

'No happy smile? No joy? That's not very loving, Muller. Not very romantic, laddie. She's been getting talked about, getting herself in the newspapers, your wife has.'

McVeigh handed him several newspaper clippings. On the top was a front page, which contained a photo of Elizabeth with a headline: 'INJUSTICE' CRIES SENATOR'S DAUGHTER.

'Stand over there and read them. Tomorrow, when she visits, you'll know the kind of nonsense she's talking, and you'll be in a position to put things right, won't you?'

'How?' But he already knew.

'Don't be thick, Muller. You're going to tell her there mustn't be any more stories like this. Do you understand, laddie? That's why the visit's allowed. It's orders, from higher up. You're going to tell her – if she ever wants to see you again, she has to stop.'

Like her mother many years before her, Maria Muller looked out the train window, and watched the shabby gateway to Sydney, as the express from Melbourne went slowly through the inner suburbs, past the squalid tenement backyards that led to Central Station. Unlike her mother, she did not know the surprises contained in the rest of this city. It was Hannah, perhaps sensing her disappointment, who suggested they might make a brief detour to see part of the town on the way home.

Maria sat between them in the back of the large sedan, while Forbes drove past the emporiums of Grace Bros and Anthony Hordern's, more like palatial pavilions than department stores, then towards Hyde Park and into Macquarie Street, passing the barracks built by the convict architect Francis Greenway a hundred years earlier. There seemed to be one grand building after another; Sydney Hospital, the Parliament where her grandfather had begun his political career, the Conservatorium of Music where Kate Brahm had studied before she went to England, and finally they parked above Bennelong Point, and stopped the car to look at the view.

She felt her breath catch.

Long ago, unknown to Maria, her father had felt the same emotion when he first saw this harbour, its rippling sunlit water, blue as a Vermeer painting. She looked out towards the small fort of Pinchgut, and beyond it to the foreshores of Cremorne, where Hannah told her they would take a trip one day soon, and visit the famous Cremorne Gardens, and afterwards go to Mosman to see the new Taronga Park Zoo. She watched the ferries docking, the projecting fingers of wharves in Sydney Cove, the bulky shape of the warehouses and wool stores dominating Miller's Point, not knowing that long ago her father had lived in the mean streets of that neighbourhood, penniless and alone.

On the point below them were the sheds that housed the city trams, and across the water was Kirribilli. A crowded punt carried cars and their drivers to the Alfred Street jetty.

'They're going to build a bridge one day,' her grandfather said, pointing to where it was supposed to span. 'Mind you, we were debating it nearly twenty years ago. I'll believe it when I see it.'

They went back to the car. She was grateful to them both, not only for offering refuge, but for not smothering her with sympathy. She had had more than enough of that from her headmistress, teachers and school friends. After the long, unhappy journey, she had arrived prepared for further pity. Instead, they had hugged her, welcomed her, taken her to see the sights, and behaved as if she would make her home with them here in this city - at least until the war's end. Their natural acceptance of this was strangely comforting.

It had been an unpleasant shock, the news that her presence in the school was such an offence to so many parents. She had been prepared for divisions among some of the girls, but had never imagined their parents would force her removal. The poor old Shilling had been almost in tears, and tried to express her support, and her distaste for what had happened. The girls in the dormitory had watched in ashamed silence while she packed, though by now perceptive to the sentiments of others, she felt some of them were not altogether displeased. In the end she left the school where she had been so happy for so long with a distinct feeling of relief.

Her mother had taken her to a small suburban house where she was a guest. It was owned by an aunt of Oscar Schmidt, and Sigrid had made the arrangements. Elizabeth had already explained the difficulty with Mr Harpur, and that she did not want to risk further humiliation by trying to take rooms in a boarding house or a hotel. She told Maria of the incident at the Gresham on the weekend which now seemed a distant unpleasant memory, and tried to apologise for the dislocation to her daughter's life.

'Mum, you're not to blame. You had to do it.'

'I thought so. Now I'm not so sure.'

'Well, you mustn't feel like that. I'd have done it, too. I think Harry's letter is wonderful, and Papa has to know about it.'

'That's why I'm staying in Adelaide. If we make enough fuss, and all the newspapers have taken this up now, they might let me see him. Just to shut me up.'

'And if they don't let you?'

'Then I won't shut up.'

Maria laughed and embraced her emotionally. 'I'll miss you,' she said.

Elizabeth remembered it vividly, as the same boat idled in towards the jetty of Langley Island. She felt desperately unhappy about Maria. When she had warned her it might create an upset, she had never dreamed the parents of so many girls would behave the way they had. Nor, of course, had she known that all the other newspapers would feature the story, so that in the past week it had become difficult for her to walk in the Adelaide streets unrecognised.

It had been a salutary experience. A smartly dressed woman

had spat at her. A group of office girls, on the way to the park to spend their lunch hour, had shaken her hand and wished her luck. A number of city businessmen whom she knew had snubbed her, making audible disparaging comments, while a uniformed soldier on crutches, had paused and managed, with difficulty, to salute her.

There seemed no predictable response. She knew her story had divided groups of people, and certainly caused eruptions in her own life. At moments all she wanted to do was return to the vineyard, and remain there in obscurity. The limelight, whether it be fame or notoriety, was not something she relished. *Perhaps*, she thought, *I'm more my mother's daughter than I realised.*

The chief warder was waiting on the landing stage, with an older man. Once again he offered a hand to assist her ashore, and again she deftly avoided any contact with him.

'Mr Lawrenson is from the Department of Prisons,' McVeigh said. 'He wishes to speak to you.'

'Mrs Muller,' the older man seemed anxious to make a good impression. 'A visit to a prisoner here is a rare privilege. It is granted to very few. This is the second time you've been allowed to see your husband. I do hope you'll remember that, when you next find yourself pursued by members of the press.'

'I hope,' Elizabeth said, 'I'll be able to tell them it was more agreeable than the first visit.'

'I understand you made a scene?'

'If you believe that, there's little point in having this discussion. May I see my husband under more pleasant conditions than last time?'

'I'm sure Mr McVeigh will do his best.'

'I hope I'll be able to tell the reporters so, when I leave.'

She could see McVeigh was livid with her, and while she nursed fear for Stefan, she realised she held one huge advantage.

They were afraid of what she might say to the newspapers.

She was determined to make full use of this. If she had to endure this tribulation of being in the public eye, so be it. Her sights were now set higher. It had begun to seem to her, if you had strength of purpose, almost anything was possible. If she could prolong her ordeal of being on the front pages for a short while longer, then it was not beyond question that she could force them to free him.

'I have to tell you, Mr Lawrenson, I intend to read my husband a letter from our son, who is fighting in France. If I'm prevented from doing so, the *Adelaide Herald* has a copy, and will publish it in its entirety.'

'Letters are subject to censorship by my office,' McVeigh said.

She interpreted the look the man from the Prisons Department gave him. He told McVeigh to take Mrs Muller to meet her husband, and allow her to read the letter - provided it was purely personal and there was no information in there to jeopardise the security of the nation. She wanted to laugh, but had an awful feeling the man was serious.

This visit was such a contrast, even though it was the same bleak room, with McVeigh and the same warder both still radiating hostility, preventing any hope of privacy. But the previous time she had been intimidated. Today, when she and Stefan were ordered to sit on opposite sides of the room, and the two men took up their intrusive positions, Elizabeth immediately requested the chief warder send for Mr Lawrenson.

'Why?'

McVeigh was distinctly less abrasive, almost wary. She felt

certain he had been told to handle this with more care, and it gave her assurance.

'If his department wishes me to say I had a satisfactory visit, I can't. I want him to see for himself, so that when I tell journalists we were forced to sit apart like this, stared at, listened to, treated worse than thieves or common criminals, he won't be able to deny it. Not without lying.'

'You want to sit a wee bit closer to him, is that it, lassie?'

'I want five minutes of privacy.'

'Impossible.' McVeigh knew he was on safer ground here.

'Five minutes.'

'Rules, Mrs Muller. Dear me. Lord knows what the prisoner might get up to, if we locked you in here with him for five minutes.'

The guard sniggered. Elizabeth ignored him, her gaze fixed on McVeigh. Her contempt for the cheap jibe was obvious, and she meant him to know it. He was under some outside pressure and could not behave with the same aggressive malice he had shown the last time.

'I'll make one concession – to prove I'm not as bad as you may think,' McVeigh said. He told the junior warder to leave, but remain on guard outside – and he waited until the man had gone.

'You can put your chairs nearer, but you don't touch, you don't embrace or do anything of that nature. I'll be in the next room with the door open. I'll be able to hear your conversation – it's my duty to monitor discussion, but you won't be distracted by my presence or able to declare you were not left alone. I don't think I can be fairer than that, Mrs Muller.'

'Thank you.'

Even if he was under instruction, she was surprised he was being quite so conciliatory. It seemed unnatural, but she was not going to complain. He went into the adjoining room, leaving the door wide open. They moved as close as they dared. They wanted to reach out and touch hands, to hold each other urgently, but knew McVeigh was liable to return no matter what he promised, so they forced themselves to resist. He feasted his eyes on her, and she felt the strength of his love.

'You look so beautiful. Not a day older.'

'Oh yes I am, darling.'

'Not to me. I can't bear it much longer, not being with you.'

'When this nightmare is over,' she said, 'we'll never be apart again. Stefan, I want to read you a letter.'

'From Harry?'

'Yes,' she said, surprised, 'how did you know?'

'Read it. Afterwards I'll tell you.'

'My dear father,' she began, *'I'm told you're in a prison camp, accused of being some sort of enemy. What kind of people, in God's name, are making this accusation?'*

She continued to read it quietly to him, at moments having to pause because her throat filled and her eyes stung with emotion. It was the letter she had always hoped he would write to his father, ever since their quarrel, yet it was so much more. Harry poured out his feelings, spoke of his pride in Stefan, his anger at those who accused him, his horror of the war which surrounded him. Nothing was held back in this letter. It was from the heart, and therefore, certainly to her, unbearably touching.

When she finished he remained silent, nodding his head but unable to trust his voice to express how deeply it had moved him.

'What was the last bit?' he finally managed to ask.

'I have long been convinced – and we have these crazy thoughts here in this hellish place – that I would die here. That I could not survive. Well, now I must. I must come home, first to make my peace with you, and after that to find out who is to blame for this outrage – and try to make them accountable. Your son, Harry.'

'My son, Harry.' Stefan whispered it. 'I also want him to survive. Not to make anyone accountable, just to come home and live the rest of his life. To find a girl nearly as wonderful as I did. To have children, nearly as nice as mine. I want to spend time with him, *liebchen*. I want to make up for the years we lost. This letter – I know now why you fought so hard – this letter is something truly special to me.'

'Now tell me how you knew about it?'

'A few lines were quoted in a newspaper.'

'You saw them?'

'Yes. All newspapers are banned here – but they made an exception. They allowed me to read about you. It's why they let you visit. Why they left us alone, instead of sitting in here, listening to every word and smirking at us.'

Now she understood McVeigh's uncharacteristic conduct. His surprising docility. She was angry at herself for imagining she had won: nothing had been won, she had merely been used.

'What do they want?'

'I'm to ask you not to go to the newspapers with more stories like that. I'm to tell you to stop making trouble.'

'I understand,' she said, feeling deflated. Feeling a fool for imagining she could beat these faceless people.

'At least, that's what they'd like me to say,' Stefan said. 'What I say, my love, is make more trouble. Lots more. All the trouble you can. People in here are on your side – they think you're wonderful. And so do I.'

From the corner of her eye, she saw McVeigh moving into the room, moving past her, jerking his knee into Stefan's groin, and bunching his fist as he hit him in the region of the solar-plexus. Stefan went down in agony, and McVeigh flung open the door and yelled for the warder to smarten himself, to wake up for Christ's sake, the fucking prisoner had just attempted an assault and had been dealt with. So what was he doing outside the door, the dumb prick, hearing nothing, while his senior officer was in jeopardy? And the bloody prisoner's wife egging him on.

'Get the fucking bitch out of here,' he yelled – and the warder, by now convinced he actually *had* heard something that was dangerous, shouted at Elizabeth to hurry and get herself down to the island jetty, where he would guard her until the next boat arrived, in an hour or two. McVeigh was blowing a shrill whistle that summoned more guards, and she was hustled outside, but not before she glimpsed a boot kick Stefan as he tried to rise, and saw McVeigh's unforgiving face.

'The stupid bastard had his chance,' he snapped at her. 'All he had to do was make you shut up. Ye'll not get another chance to see him, that I promise you.'

Someone slammed the door, and mercifully she could no longer see them beating Stefan, or hear McVeigh's malignant voice.

'I can't print that,' Boothby said the following day. 'I wish I could, but we're no longer a free press. Guards kicking prisoners in the ribs while they're on the ground. The chief warder of the camp speaking to you that way. The censor would put his pencil straight through it, but our own board would themselves disallow it before that.'

Elizabeth nodded. She felt sick with what she had seen.

'It was all a ploy to make me stop,' she said. 'Allowing the visit was simply that. I feel so angry - and helpless - and such a fool. I even thought I might be able to make them release Stefan. I was stupid enough to imagine I had that kind of power.'

'But you have,' James Boothby said suddenly. 'You have.'

William came down to breakfast. Mrs Forbes brought in his grapefruit, and said Maria had already been down, hardly even bothering to sit, just a piece of toast and a cup of tea and was on her way to school. She worried that she worked too hard, that one, and ate too little. It was very nice to be ambitious, and to get into Sydney University like her brother, but success was no benefit if you didn't have your health. Without your health you had nothing, didn't he agree?

William dutifully agreed. Mrs Forbes, in her late middle years, had become decidedly more garrulous, but he couldn't imagine this house without her. She gave him the morning paper, and said Maria had marked a story on page three about Miss Lizzie, and for her grandpa to be sure to read it. Mrs Forbes said she hoped the Senator didn't mind, but she herself had read it, and wasn't it wonderful the way Miss Lizzie was standing up to people.

William, who was eager to read it, agreed it was wonderful, and thought again about telling Mrs Forbes he was no longer in the Senate, and therefore plain Mr Patterson would do - but he knew it was a lost cause. To Mr and Mrs Forbes, who had been here almost thirty years and had seen all the changes in his life, he would always be the Senator.

He began to read the story, and, if he hadn't been so concerned, might have smiled. SENATOR'S DAUGHTER, the headline said: PETITION TO THE SUPREME COURT.

The report was from Adelaide, dated the previous day, and stated Mrs Elizabeth Patterson Muller, who described her father as one of the architects of Federation, and thus one of the founders of democracy in this country, had petitioned the South Australian Supreme Court for the release of her husband.

He realised Hannah had come in, and was reading it over his shoulder. She kissed the nape of his neck, and he slipped an arm around her trim waist.

'Maria marked it for us, as compulsory reading.'

'I should say so. Clever girl,' Hannah remarked.

'Maria?'

'No question. But in this instance I meant Elizabeth. It's smart. What I'd call a tactical ploy. Very enterprising.'

'My darling, she hasn't a snowball's chance in hell.'

'Surely that's not the point, William.'

'She wants him released. They won't grant a writ of habeas corpus. We already know that.'

'So does Elizabeth.'

'Then what will she achieve, apart from further humiliation and more pain?'

'She's already achieved it.'

'I must be missing something. I don't see how?'

'She's put the matter back in the newspapers. As the daughter of – what does she say? – *one of the architects of Federation, and thus one of the founders of democracy in this country*.'

'People don't care. Even if it's half true. They've forgotten.'

'She's reminding them. Lizzie is making sure that she can't be dismissed as some crackpot – or a nobody.'

'Good God,' he said. 'How do you know all this?'

'Women's intuition. If she loses, it gives her an opportunity to protest, to make another speech. There'll be a great many reporters keeping an eye on the outcome. This virtually guarantees it.'

'Devious.'

'Wonderfully so. Truly her father's daughter.' Hannah laughed, and kissed him again.

They asked her to pose on the steps outside the Supreme Court building, and she patiently did so while the photographers set up their tripods. The reporters shouted a barrage of questions.

'Any comments, Mrs Muller?'

'How long has your husband been imprisoned?'

'When did he come to this country?'

'How did you first meet?'

She answered them all in turn. She refused smiles for the photographers despite their requests; she had no intention of being seen with a smile in any newspaper.

'Did the court's refusal to even hear your case surprise you?'

'It deeply disappointed me. My husband was arrested without a charge – he's being held without a trial – and the Court chooses not to hear my petition for his release.'

She looked towards the reporter who had asked the question. He worked for Boothby, and it gave her the opportunity she needed.

'But the real answer is, no it didn't surprise me. I'm no longer surprised at the failure of decency and justice. But I have to wonder how my son feels, there in France fighting for his country – a country which imprisons his father, and will not tell us why.'

The photographers clicked. Lights popped. The reporters busily wrote it down. It was a good story, and this Mrs Muller was one hell of an attractive woman. If the pictures were any good, if those clowns with the cameras did their job, it should get a run on the front page.

It did far more than that. During the following few days the story was extensively reported by newspapers right across the continent.

The *Sun* ran a very large photograph of Elizabeth, and a banner headline: SENATOR'S DAUGHTER CONDEMNS SUPREME COURT. The *Herald* was more sedate, but probably more persuasive. FAILURE OF DECENCY AND JUSTICE. MRS MULLER'S STATEMENT.

The *Telegraph*, where Alistair Beames was now editor, suggested there were a number of questions which should be answered, and that since the complainant was not only reputable, but related to a man who had helped frame the constitution, the very least the justices could do was to hear her. If not, it was more than reasonable to ask why.

William read them all. There was even a leader in the *Star*, and while it was equivocal, determined not to risk appearing sympathetic to any German-Australians, it also thought the public were entitled to know the facts of the case, and whether there was any truth in these startling accusations being raised by the daughter of a former but prominent politician.

Christ Almighty, he thought incredulously, with a rush of emotional pride, *she might just win.*

~

Elizabeth went back to the vineyard, but only for a day. Carl was running it alone, managing to keep things going, he said, but warning her that when the harvest time arrived next February they may not have any pickers for the grapes. A few of his friends would help, but some would be busy on their own family vineyards, and the seasonal pickers they had used in the past would no longer work for Germans. Especially not for them. That was when she began to notice he was restless, almost distant.

'The harvest is still four months away,' she told him, 'and who knows what may happen by then?'

He seemed not to have heard the determined optimism.

'What is it, Carl?'

'Nothing.'

'Trouble?'

'No more than usual.'

'Please tell me.'

'Nothing, I said.' There was a silence, then he shrugged. 'That bastard Carson's been stirring things up.'

'They're so vindictive,' Elizabeth said, 'yet we helped them when they started their dairy farm. When they were poor.'

'He's rich now. They have even more contracts for army milk supplies.'

'What happened?'

'He's been round again, trying to make Eva-Maria sell her land. He keeps offering less, scaring her into practically giving it to him. She was in tears, so I went and told him to keep away.'

'How did he respond to that?'

'Laughed. "What'll you do?", he said. "Go to the police?" He kept laughing like it was a great big joke. Said he'd have our vines ripped out and his cows grazing here before long.'

'*Here*? He most certainly will not.'

'He swore there'll be a government order soon, saying no criminals can own land. Reckoned Pa's a criminal. I nearly hit him.'

'I'm glad you didn't. It's a silly lie, Carl, a bluff to scare you.'

'I sort of knew that. And anyway – you own it, too. But the way things are lately – just about anything could be true.'

He looked away from her searching gaze, and she knew there was something else. What he had told her was merely camouflage for what mattered.

They were all so different, her children. Of the three, Carl was the one with whom she had spent the most time, yet the one she knew the least. There was a private, withdrawn side to him that she had never been able to penetrate.

'That's not all, is it?'

'All?' He pretended not to understand.

'What else is worrying you?'

'You are, Ma,' he said after a long time.

'Me?'

'What you're doing. Not everyone agrees it's right. I don't mean people like the Carsons and their mob. I'm talking about people in the town, friends, folk you've known for years – they're divided. Some are in favour. Some think . . .'

'What do they think?' she prompted, as he faltered.

'That every time you make a speech or get yourself in the newspapers, the prison guards will take it out on Pa. That you might be making it worse for him.'

'Is that what you feel?' she asked him gently.

He finally nodded.

'Yes, I do.'

'That I'm making it worse?'

'That you've never stopped to think what you're doing. What you've done. Maria forced to leave school, living in Sydney, so we won't see her again. You in Adelaide, so busy with speeches that you hardly ever come home. So many people gossiping about you.'

It poured out of him, a flood of pent-up anxieties, of doubts and mistrusts engendered by years of encountering hostility. Since the day war broke out, a schoolboy of barely sixteen, his life had been its own battlefield.

'Nobody meets in town these days, without them all talking about you. "What's she done now? What's she said? Is she in the papers again?" Some think you're really pleased at being so famous . . .'

'Oh my God,' she whispered.

'I'm sorry, Ma, but you asked me. I've heard them say it.'

Famous or notorious, James Boothby had warned her, but no one could have warned her of this. Her own son, disapproving, almost hating her she felt, voicing the secret rancour he harboured. She felt sad at the enormous gulf between them, and knew she must try to bridge it.

'I was foolish,' she said. 'It was wrong, not to talk to you first, to tell you what I planned to do. I told Maria, because I thought it might affect her at school, and she insisted I go ahead, do what I've done. The same as your father did.'

She saw him turn and stare at her.

'When did he say that?'

'On the last visit. When I read him Harry's letter.'

'Harry's letter,' Carl said accusingly. 'That's why all this happened.'

'Don't you think he was entitled to see it? You need something in that hell hole to give you hope.'

'I thought it was just a prison camp – strict and bleak, not so terrible. That's what you said, Mama.'

'I know. I tried to spare you. I should've told the truth. If you think anything I do could make it worse for him, I assure you that's not possible. Not in there. The treatment is inhuman. The chief warder is a filthy sadist, the guards are brutes, and the place is cold and dirty and barbaric.'

She unconsciously repressed a shudder.

'As for those people who think I enjoy being "famous", as they call it, I'm sorry. They won't believe me, but I hate it. I'm scared. I feel sick every time I stand up and make a speech, but I'll go on doing it as often as I can – because it's the only chance of getting your father out of that dreadful, disgusting place.'

She drove away soon afterwards. Carl had a lot to think about, and he would do it in his own time. That was his way, and always had been. Carl was far more his father's son, just as Harry was hers. She wondered if he even resented the references she often made to Harry fighting for his country in France. She should have told Carl she loved him, and without him there to run the vineyard she would be lost. But instead she had an uneasy feeling the void existing between them still remained.

It was wintry cold in London, and the afternoon had barely seemed to begin before it was over, and the twilight, as swift in winter as it was leisurely in summer, turned into dense night. The street lamps were few in number, and dim in case of any aerial bombing. The German airships had already made many raids, but ever since some had been shot down in flames, the attacks had been made by twin engine biplanes.

Kate sat by her window, and watched the searchlights scan the clouds. Like most people, she felt little fear of the bombs, even though the raids had killed over a thousand people since the war began. Much of the damage had occurred in Kent and Essex, and the recent raid in the City of London which destroyed the central telegraph office. One night she and Rupert had stood on Hampstead Heath, with hundreds of others, and watched the artillery guns and a searchlight trap a Zeppelin, and felt a shiver of horror as the airship burned, a spectacular conflagration that detonated the sky. The crowd cheered, then the sound died to a shocked whisper as they could see the outline of burning figures in the blazing craft, and one, trailing flames, hurled himself into oblivion. The others were etched in their dying agony, as the struts of the Zeppelin's fiery skeleton fell slowly towards the heath and the ponds.

'Bloody good shot,' Rupert said, and looked around for Kate, but she was in a nearby clump of bushes being noisily sick. He calmed her and explained that war was hell, and the dead men would have dropped a bomb on the crowd, if they'd had the chance. She asked him to please shut up, and he did, and they walked across the heath to The Spaniard where he made her drink a brandy.

Soon afterwards the pub started to fill up, people excitedly regaling those who had missed it with the details of what had happened. A group of males, wrapped in thick coats, with public school scarves that advertised their old Harrovian origins, came in and ordered pints.

'Beats the hell out of Guy Fawkes,' one of them said.

'Should've put up a sign saying, "Frying tonight".'

There was a burst of laughter.

'Oh God,' Kate said, 'what a disgusting, filthy thing to say.'

The laughter had ended. Her voice sounded loud and clear in the lull. Faces of the group turned to look at her. Rupert touched her arm, and stood, ready to leave.

'We'll be off, I think. The lady's upset.' He gave them a nod in token apology. 'She didn't mean it.'

'Oh, yes she did,' Kate insisted.

'Take the bitch away, old boy,' one of the group advised. 'Or else we might take offence.'

'Might take down her drawers and give her a slap.'

'And a tickle.'

They all laughed again, and she realised they were drunk.

'Not a bad idea, eh, Toby?' another said to the man who had made the offensive remark.

'Bang a beat on a beautiful bum.'

'Alliteration!' they all chorused, and thought it hilarious.

'For Christ's sake, Kate, let's get out of here,' Rupert hissed.

'Tickle the tits. Top that, Toby.'

'Tease the tottie's twinkling twat,' the one called Toby shouted, and Kate picked up an almost full pint of bitter and flung it in his face. There was a sudden silence, and then uproar, as the startled and drunken Toby made a lunge at her and Rupert hit him. The proprietor and a barman vaulted the counter and tried to restore order, shouting at Kate and Rupert to get out, and warning the old Harrovians that the police had been called and were on their way.

'Please, Kate,' Rupert said, then Toby's fist found his eye. Kate lashed out and kicked his shins. Toby fell like a wounded buffalo, trying to claw at her legs, and she stamped on his hand and emptied another pint all over his mottled face.

'Kate! Please.'

'Oh, all right,' she said to Rupert, and they dodged past the barman and out the door, as a police car with its strident bell came up Spaniards Road. It pulled up in front of them. Uniformed police with truncheons emerged like Keystone Cops at the cinema. Kate stifled an urgent desire to giggle.

'Thank goodness,' Rupert gasped, as though expecting them. In his best Camberley instructing officer's voice he said, 'In there. Drunken bunch of civilians, trying to pick fights and wreck the place. Well done.'

They watched the police run in, and the hubbub inside quieten. Then they saw a bus coming, and ran to catch it.

Later on, in bed, she bathed his eye.

'Is it black?' he asked.

'More red and swollen. Like a carbuncle. But it definitely will be black by the morning.'

'Oh Christ,' he said, 'I've got the General coming to address the graduating officers.'

She had started to laugh, and Rupert had joined in, and mutual hysteria enveloped them. After that she could no longer tell him what she had been bracing herself to say for weeks. That she was no longer certain. That perhaps they ought to just leave things a while, and not get married quite as soon as they planned.

Kate remembered that night as she sat by the window, watching the lights sweeping the sky and seeking German planes. The silly scene in the pub that had suddenly turned nasty. Rupert, directing the police. Making her laugh. Making love in this bed afterwards, and not being able to explain that she might, just *might* be in love with Harry Patterson after all – but since she wasn't sure if he was alive or dead, that perhaps they could wait and see if he ever turned up, and then she could hopefully sort things out. That was what she had intended to say.

She hadn't said a word, because he was really so nice, Rupert, and Harry was just a miraculous few days that felt like part of a dream, and it might never be like that again. So Rupert's mother had begun to make plans, generously glad to be able to give the wedding since her own parents were unable to, and the church had been booked, bridesmaids chosen, a date set.

Six weeks from now.

In the meantime, her brother had written to say the family would drink a toast to her on the big day, and sent a batch of newspaper cuttings with photographs of Harry's mother, and amazing headlines. She was being talked about a lot, David said, people were taking sides, and he was completely on hers. He wished Kate had met her. She was far more beautiful than her photos, and marvellous. Had she heard from H? He'd had a letter saying they'd met when he was on leave in London, but no details and nothing since. Anyway, he would keep her posted on the battle of Elizabeth Muller against the oafs of officialdom. His regards to Rupert, and a wedding present was on the way which he hoped would escape being torpedoed by a German sub.

Kate read all the newspaper stories. She remembered vividly the day she had been the one to break the news of his father's imprisonment, his sadness for the man he had never been able to love, the anxious belief that his grandfather would have enough influence to secure his freedom. She had known then that it was unlikely. And now his mother was having a go! Making speeches. Challenging the court. *Good on her!* she said aloud.

In the days that followed, she thought about it endlessly, and finally she wrote to Elizabeth Muller. She enclosed the letters she had kept and never shown anyone, letters from Harry's moments of despair in France, and she asked Mrs Muller to make use of them if she thought they could help. She added a P.S., saying that she believed she loved Harry, but things didn't always work out the right way, and she was marrying someone else.

Chapter 35

The small hall was packed. There was a sprinkling of men present, but they were scarcely noticeable among more than two hundred women. Despite the nervousness she had expressed to Carl, Elizabeth was becoming increasingly more confident each time she faced an audience, and she spoke with an impassioned sincerity that reached to all corners of the local School of Arts.

'There are thousands - and I mean it literally - thousands of men and women being held in internment camps. Langley and Torrens Islands are only two such prisons. Trial Bay, Holdsworthy, Langwarrin and Berrima are others. How many thousands are held captive in these places? I can't tell you that. We simply don't know.

'We can never know, because there are no records. No courts. No juries. And no convictions ever recorded. People are just taken away in the night - without warning, without reason, without proof. It is a shameful record of persecution and prejudice, and a stain on our history.'

From the back of the hall, a man rose and shouted at her. 'Shut up. You lousy traitor. Dirty, stupid German-loving bitch!'

'Keep quiet,' a woman told him.

'Sit down,' another advised him. 'Either sit and listen – or clear out.'

'Thank you, ladies,' Elizabeth said, 'all I ask is a fair hearing in our land of free speech.'

But the heckler was not to be silenced.

'Stinking German tart.'

'Go away,' other women started to call at him.

'He's drunk.'

'Throw him out.'

'Your husband's a lousy bloody spy,' the heckler yelled, and left amid a chorus of boos and disapproval. A middle-aged lady rose from her seat and whacked him with a furled parasol as he went past, raising a gale of approving laughter. Elizabeth laughed with them, then seized on his parting words.

'If my husband's a German spy, then let me be the first to say he deserves to rot in gaol. Let me challenge them here and now – bring him to court, and accuse him. They won't. They can't. Because you know – in your hearts you all know – he and all those imprisoned people are innocent victims. Their only offence is to be caught up in the hysteria and the tyranny of this war.'

In the front row, an old lady stared up at her. Elizabeth could feel her intent gaze. The old lady nodded – and then put her gloved hands together. She began to gently clap. Around her, people saw her and followed suit. In a matter of moments the hall was enlivened by the sound of their applause.

Some weeks later Elizabeth was opening her ever-increasing batch of mail, much of it supportive and laudatory, some abusively offensive and obscene – you never knew which it would be until the envelope was open. In the pile there was a bulky overseas letter with an English stamp. The address was correct, the hand that wrote it unfamiliar to her. She opened it, and saw it contained several pages with Harry's handwriting, and for a terrible heart-stopping moment thought he must be dead, and the mail had been forwarded on. Then she found the note that came with them, from Kate Brahm, and began to read it.

There was an even larger crowd this time. An amateur theatre, glad to rent the hall, filled at lunchtime with all ages, young office girls with their sandwiches, nurses in uniform, even soldiers. Perhaps four hundred people in all. It was her biggest audience so far.

'This is a letter from my son,' she spoke quietly, but they could all hear her. 'It was sent to me by a friend of his. It was written in the trenches in France. It's a cruel, unhappy, angry letter, but I make no apologies for reading it. This is what he and his comrades endure every day, while his father is imprisoned without a charge.'

She had carefully studied all of the letters from Kate, and never doubted which she would choose. She took the crumpled paper and began to read: '*We are lousy, stinking, ragged, unshaven, sleepless. I have one puttee, a dead man's helmet, a dead man's gas protector, a German's bayonet. My tunic is rotten with other men's blood, and partly splattered with a comrade's brains. I hate to write such things, but I cannot tell my family – yet I feel someone must know. If only to inform people when I'm dead. Why should some of those safe at home not be told what it's like. I mean the ones who were so keen to send us here. I want the middle-class ladies who hand out white feathers to know that several of my friends are raving mad. One lived for two days with his head split open and his brains visible. Thank Christ he's dead now. I'd like to tell the politicians that I met three officers out in no-man's-land the other night, all rambling and completely insane . . .'*

She stopped there, because she could no longer see the writing or bear the pain. There was utter silence, until somewhere among the crowd, a woman began to sob.

In the cooler days of summer, they often had their breakfast on the side terrace. It was one of those fine and calm Sydney mornings, and even Maria, now that her leaving certificate was done and her fate in the hands of the examiners, agreed to put down her books and join them.

Hannah had been out early and bought hot bread rolls from the bakery, and made a pot of tea. She had somehow persuaded Mrs Forbes she was unused to being waited on hand and foot, and did not enjoy it, and in this fourth year of the war it was wrong to have a large staff, when the factories and shop floors were desperate for people.

They no longer had a squad of servants. They closed sections of the house. In the evenings they used the cosy library rather than the formal and draughty drawing room. William marvelled at the way his wife had convinced Mrs Forbes to accept change, and found the simpler lifestyle so much more enjoyable. They often worked together in the garden, and if it had not been for Elizabeth's problems and his fear for Harry, he would have said he was happier than at any time in his life.

'Good heavens,' Maria said. She was immersed in the *Sydney Morning Herald*.

William nodded with some satisfaction. 'Yes, your mother's

in the news again. MRS MULLER GAINS SUPPORT. Not bad for the *Herald*. I read it earlier.'

'The Letters to the Editor, Grandfather. Did you read those?'

'Not yet,' he said. 'You nabbed the paper.'

Maria looked at Hannah, who smiled.

'When did you send this, Hannah?'

'I took it around by hand yesterday. And posted off copies to the *Age*, and the *Adelaide Advertiser*.'

'Copies of what?' William asked.

'*I would like to publicly make known*,' Maria read aloud, her eyes shining, '*my total support for my step-daughter, Elizabeth Muller, and her attempts to free her husband, Stefan Muller. He is not merely interned, which would be unfair enough, since he is a respected member of the community and a naturalised Australian of many years standing, but is imprisoned without any charge being proved. He has never faced a court or a jury, and his "crime" seems to have been asking the police to give adequate protection to acts of vandalism against his friends. If a plea for law and order is a crime, then I for one should be locked up. And so, I expect, should many decent and right-minded people.*

'*This case is particularly unfortunate, since Mrs Muller's son is an infantry captain in the A.I.F. in France. Imagine the feelings of a young man who volunteered to fight for his country, being informed that country has now imprisoned his father without a trial. Yours, etc. (Mrs) Hannah Patterson.*'

Maria threw her arms around Hannah and hugged her tightly. 'I love you,' she said.

William blew his nose noisily. 'Bloody good,' he said. 'Bloody marvellous. Well done.'

An hour later the telephone call came. Mrs Forbes hurried out to the garden, where Hannah was planting out seedlings, and William was clipping the lawn edges.

'It's Mr James North's office wishing to speak to you, Senator.'

'Thank you, Mrs Forbes. Tell them I'm busy at present, and to try again in half an hour. You might explain there are journalists here and I'm unable to speak to anyone.'

'Sir?' Mrs Forbes looked askance.

'Half an hour, Mrs Forbes. Do you think you could perjure yourself for me?'

'How many journalists, Senator?'

'Rather a lot, I think, don't you? Shall we say . . . a crowd?'

Hannah laughed. Mrs Forbes nodded, smiling, and went back into the house to convey the message. William watched her, knowing this was dangerous, but he had no choice. *So what, if it was to be made known he had been a villain in the past. Was he so different from many other politicians, or a former Lord Mayor of Sydney*? This was for his daughter: he was prepared to be vilified, or indicted if that was necessary.

The telephone rang again, exactly half an hour later.

'Mr Patterson? The Honourable James North's parliamentary secretary here. The Minister wonders if you would care to visit him at his office. Say, this afternoon at four?'

'Tell the Honourable Mr North,' William said, 'I have no reason to visit him. But if the Minister cares to call on me at four, I'll give him a drink and hear whatever it is he has to say.'

He put down the telephone.

'That'll get his goat. I'm damned if I'm going to call on him. That's an old ploy, giving him home ground advantage.'

'Besides, you're far too busy,' Hannah said. 'Trimming the edges and weeding the garden with me.'

He nodded and smiled, hoping she did not sense his fear.

The ministerial sedan arrived promptly at four. James North

was in formal wear that some parliamentarians were favouring; a stiff collar, morning coat and striped trousers.

William, in his oldest gardening slacks, open-necked shirt, and favourite cardigan, later said his visitor looked like a pox doctor's clerk. North, who knew William had purposely not dressed for the occasion, told his wife Patterson looked like some old codger from the potting shed. They shook hands, exchanged pleasantries, and William poured drinks, while North admired the portrait of Elizabeth that still hung above the mantelpiece.

'Splendid painting. Grand house this, William. It's very decent of you to receive me.'

'Always glad to see old friends, James.'

He handed a somewhat embarrassed North his drink.

'I regret our last meeting,' North said.

'Heat of the moment. I've forgotten it.'

'I rather doubt it. But it's generous of you to say so.'

They raised their glasses to each other, and sipped the drinks.

'Ever miss the old days, the State Parliament?' North asked.

'Often,' William said. 'I haven't been called a class traitor or a rotten conniving bastard in years.'

North forced a smile. He glanced again at the portrait.

'Elizabeth was only seventeen, when we got you elected, Reid and I, remember?'

'Yes.'

'Abroad on her world trip. Hadn't even met the fellow.'

William said nothing. He waited.

'Look, William - can't you put a stop to this nonsense?'

'Which nonsense?'

'Come on, man. The newspaper interviews, the damn speeches, your own wife writing a letter of support –'

'You read it?'

'Of course I read it. First bloody thing I saw when I opened today's paper.'

'If you're in Melbourne soon, you can read it in the *Age*.'

'Very amusing.'

'And the *Adelaide Advertiser,* I'm told, a day or two later.'

'Confound the letter. I came here to talk about Elizabeth. Haven't you any control over how she behaves?'

'None at all,' William said. 'Never did have.'

'I can't believe you approve. Not even you could approve of the way she's going on.'

William smiled, and said, 'If you must know, I'm proud of her. Immensely proud.'

'Good God!'

'She's got guts and spirit - and the gift of making people listen. Approve, James? I'm bloody delighted.'

'And I'm shocked,' North tried to control his anger, 'at your lack of patriotism.'

'I assure you I'm a patriot. So is my daughter.'

'Be buggered. She's a ranting and dangerous subversive.'

'I'll write and tell her. She'll be flattered.'

'She's talking treason. Undermining the war effort.'

'Balls,' William said. 'In the privacy of this room, do me the courtesy of not treating me like an idiot.'

'I mean it. She's influencing people,' North insisted. 'Women, in particular, are listening to her. They're the key to the coming referendum on conscription - we can't afford to lose votes.'

William smiled.

'You know where I stand on that. My daughter's trying to correct a personal injustice. If she costs you votes in your immoral crusade that the people have already rejected once, that's a bonus.'

North sighed. He finished his drink.

'The P.M. will be extremely disappointed at your attitude.'

'The little digger? I expect his lilting Welsh snarl was in your ear bright and early, once he saw Hannah's letter. Told you to get off your arse and meet me, no matter how distasteful the idea. And as you've achieved high office obeying your master's voice – that's why you're here and why we've had no unpleasant threats like last time.'

North said stiffly, 'You misjudge Billy Hughes. He admires you. He had hoped to include you in the next Birthday Honours.'

Before William could reply to this, there was a tap on the door and Hannah entered. She smiled at them.

'Mr North, will you stay for dinner?'

'Thank you, no. I'm expected home,' he added, to make it sound less ungracious.

'Mr North has just told me I've chucked away the chance of Knighthood,' William said. 'You'll never be Lady Patterson.'

'I expect we'll manage. Plain old Mister and Missus is good enough for me.' She gave a most deliberate dazzling smile at North.

'The government wants an end to this stupidity,' North said, unable to conceal his irritation. 'If your daughter agrees to stop, I'll set up an inquiry into her husband's case.'

'That won't satisfy her.'

'Dammit, William, don't push me too far.'

'I'm not pushing you at all, James. I do wish you'd realise, this is nothing to do with me.'

'What do you mean – nothing?' North asked heatedly.

'I mean,' William said, 'that I have a very independent daughter – and an equally independent wife. What do you expect me to do? Give them orders? That's not how we live in this family.'

North glared at him, making an effort to restrain his temper.

'I want her pledge. No more speeches. No newspapers.'

They waited, determinedly showing no outward emotion.

'In return –' he paused. It began to seem to them he would never say it. 'In return – after a suitable time – the bloody man will be released.'

'A suitable time?'

'A month or two.'

'Not a hope. She'd refuse – unless he's out immediately.'

Again they waited while North inwardly fumed and debated.

'Very well,' he said finally, 'within forty-eight hours.'

'She'd want it in writing.'

'You know perfectly well I can't put it on paper.'

'You're asking her to trust you?'

'It's the best I can do.'

'If you renege, James, you'll have me to reckon with.'

North stared at him with naked dislike. The deal was done; he had been told to resolve it. There was no longer need for pretence.

'Who the hell are you any longer?'

'A parent – used to dealing with political bastards like you.'

'I'd be extremely careful, William. Or you'll regret it.'

'You mean once this is over and Hughes is satisfied, I'm fair game?' William turned to Hannah. 'He has some material on me, to do with a fraud years ago in Broken Hill.'

'Will he use it?' Hannah asked, ignoring North. 'If so, it won't make any difference to you and me.'

'He'd love to, but he can't,' William said, wanting to put his arms around her, but feeling she knew that. To North he said, 'You see how it is, James. My wife likes me, warts and all. I no longer have a political career for you to ruin. Whereas you're a Cabinet Minister – with lots to lose. Ever since you threatened me, I decided to protect myself. I have a dossier, with enough dirt to make you an electoral liability. Hughes would unload you so fast you wouldn't know if you were North – or South.'

North was livid. 'Very droll. Let's have no stupid threats.'

'I entirely agree. This is about Elizabeth.'

'If she accepts – I give you my word. And despite what you may think, I'm not in the habit of breaking it.'

'I'll talk to her. See what she has to say.'

'I suggest by telephone – and tonight. This has to stop, or we could lose the referendum.'

'Indeed you could,' William murmured.

North ignored the remark. He nodded abruptly to Hannah, and went out of the room.

She made no attempt to accompany him. Mrs Forbes would be there to give him his hat and coat, and observe the courtesies. She was always relieved to see the back of James North, and she knew that this would certainly be the last time.

William came and put his arm around her. They watched as he was ushered into the ministerial car, and it drove away.

'Have you really got a file on him?' Hannah asked, as the car passed through the iron gates at the end of the driveway.

'No.' William grinned. 'But he doesn't know that.'

She laughed and hugged him. Then they went to telephone

Elizabeth, who was in James Boothby's Adelaide office, waiting to hear from them.

It was a tumultuous month. The nation had never been so divided. Violence and bitterness grew as the day of the second vote on conscription approached. The hostility between both sides became extreme. Crowds engaged in angry abuse that turned into fights and street riots. There were bonfires; brigades were kept busy, as people burnt leaflets expressing the rival point of view, or set fire to speaker's platforms. The government resorted to the use of obscure censorship laws to ruthlessly intimidate those advocating the NO vote. Daily there were raids on printers, and pamphlets confiscated. Premises were vandalised; many of the owners were prosecuted and heavy fines forced some to close.

Almost without exception newspapers campaigned strongly in favour of compulsory military service, and used artists and cartoonists to ridicule those in opposition. Lurid posters and crude caricatures were distributed to libraries, and even given to children in schools.

Influenced by this stream of propaganda, in which murder and rape were constantly featured, and babies and old women depicted being bayoneted by bestial creatures in German helmets, groups of women stepped up their campaign, harassing men in the streets of almost any age, demanding that they join the army.

The discord had its lighter moments. In the Sydney Domain at a massed rally against conscription, a vast women's choir sang:

I didn't raise my son to be a soldier
I brought him up to be my pride and joy,

Who dares to put a musket to his shoulder,
To kill some other mother's darling boy?

In response, Dame Nellie Melba appealed to all women to vote YES. If Germany won, she asserted, the Kaiser's first demand would be for the Australian continent to be handed over to him! Certain newspapers rushed to print this, informing their readers the world-famous diva would certainly be in a position to know.

'How can the bloody woman sing like an angel and speak like such a fool?' William demanded, reading it in the *Argus.*

'How can smart, well-educated editors praise her wisdom?' His wife laughed, and Maria, busy writing a letter, smiled and thought that Hannah Patterson was the sunniest person she had ever known.

Dearest Mama and Papa, she wrote, *it must be wonderful for Papa to be safe home again . . .*

Elizabeth was afraid, from the moment she left the river boat and stepped on to the island jetty, that they might change their minds. But Stefan was waiting. He stood defensively between two guards, while McVeigh sat at his desk and smiled, as if they were old friends and this was a welcome visit.

'Mrs Muller,' he said, 'the laddie's ready. Washed and cleaned up and ready for you. All we have to do is sign the release.'

'What release?'

'This piece of paper. Can he read English?'

'Of course he can read. What's wrong, Stefan?'

'He refuses to sign it. I thought perhaps he was a wee bit thick, or couldn't understand. Why would he refuse to sign?'

She ignored him, and asked again: 'Stefan, what's the matter?'

'Read it,' Stefan said. 'Read the lies they insist I sign.'

McVeigh pushed it across the desk. Elizabeth picked it up. It was a statutory declaration. Short, and crudely drawn up.

I, Stefan Muller, herewith acknowledge that while at Langley Island as a prisoner, I have been properly and fairly treated, and have no complaint whatsoever to make against any of the staff of the said camp. I do so swear, this first day of December, nineteen hundred and seventeen, that I was correctly and justly imprisoned on the evidence available, and before God swear not to offend in like manner again.

'Either he signs it, or he stays,' McVeigh said.

Stefan almost imperceptibly shook his head. Her eyes pleaded with him. Her mouth framed the word *please*. She thought of all the nights she had been alone, all the insults she had endured, the speeches spoken, the statements made. *Famous and notorious*. She was both, and sick to death of being lauded by some and snubbed and abused by others. She had fought and won, and no scrap of paper was going to defeat her now.

She picked up a pen from the desk, dipped it in the inkwell, and put the statement on the desk in front of him. She was not going to beg – not in front of McVeigh and the guards – but she *had* to make him sign. She had to choose her words, so that he would want to attach his signature and not feel humiliated.

'Sign it,' she said, 'and we need never see this sadistic creature again.'

~

It was a silent journey home. When the river boat docked they disembarked with relief. Their car was parked waiting for them. It had been tacitly understood that there would be no wide press coverage, no exhibition of triumph, but James Boothby had sent a reporter and a photographer, and Elizabeth felt they could not deny him that. Stefan stood beside her while a photo was taken, and said little in response to the reporter's questions. Elizabeth found herself answering for him. Yes, he was greatly relieved to be released, and was going home to rest. On the matter of his treatment in the camp, he had no comment.

They left and drove back to the Barossa, arriving in the late afternoon. Carl was waiting to meet them, eager to show his father the vineyard and the ripening grapes. Stefan pleaded tiredness, and Elizabeth became increasingly aware how little he spoke during the evening meal, his replies to Carl and herself almost monosyllabic. Later, in their bedroom, she saw with consternation the physical evidence of his ill-treatment in the prison camp. His body was scarred with the lacerations caused by barbed wire; his back and buttocks bore the ribboned welts of floggings that had gone untreated, and must have meant days and weeks of agony. The skin was permanently marked and ridged with reminders of the brutality he had endured. She saw the soles of his feet, scarred from being forced to walk across the sharp wire. There were fading purpled bruises where he had been hit by fists, and kicked by the boots of the warders.

'Dear God,' she whispered, and kissed the mutilated flesh as if she could somehow restore it, 'how did you stand it?'

'Hatred was a help,' he answered, strangely, and she thought she had misheard. 'I used to lie awake thinking of how McVeigh would some day be accused of what he allowed to happen in that place. That he would go to prison, and the prison would be full of us –'

'Stefan, don't darling.'

'We'd be the guards. We'd hit him if he dared look at us, make him sleep on broken glass, starve him – fill his cell with rats –'

'Stefan, please . . .'

'You asked how I stood it. That's how. All night, planning, dreaming fantasies in revenge. It's unhealthy, like a poison, but if you're abused and degraded every day, that's how you become.'

'It's over, my darling.'

'It will never be over,' he said coldly.

In the days that followed, she began to fear, not the injuries to his body, but the damage to his mind.

Meanwhile, the referendum to introduce conscription, despite being fought ferociously by the government, and supported by the press, was lost by two hundred thousand votes. It was also lost in four of the six states, therefore failing in every respect. The Prime Minister, William Morris Hughes, having declared he would resign if the vote was unsuccessful, did so, and was promptly asked by his party to reconsider. He said if that was the country's wish, he must resume the heavy burden of leadership – and accepted.

Accusation for the defeat was laid at many doors. Among those to be blamed were the Irish, prejudiced by the Easter Rising. Farmers reluctant to lose their workers were also held responsible, as were men due for conscription if the vote was passed. Few refused to face reality – that vast numbers of people had become disenchanted, and begun to recognise that only the legality of Empire bound Australia to a conflict that was someone else's war.

In some communities, zealots laid individual blame. Most of all in isolated rural districts, the condemnation was often personal and bitter. In the Barossa, there were some who considered Elizabeth Muller a factor in the scandalous repudiation of the war, and felt she had contributed to the outrage of voting against conscripted aid to the Mother Country. Such rabid patriots were mostly entirely Australian born, and often too old or unfit for military service.

But there was another, far less obvious group who resented her. There were German families with some of their members still interned, jealous of the way she had somehow managed to secure her husband's release. Concerned only with Stefan's recovery, Elizabeth was unaware quite how much envy and seething malice she had aroused.

Her father wrote - delighted about the referendum defeat - and expressing the wish that he and Hannah could visit soon. She replied, asking him to delay for a short while, to allow Stefan time to recover. She said nothing else. It was something she had to cope with alone. Carl was aware of the long despondent silences, as well as an apathy and a listlessness in his father. When he broached the subject, she tried to reassure him it was a natural reaction to being imprisoned for so long, and that he would soon regain his vitality.

Friends were worried, but she asked them not to display their concern. It was best not to dwell on the events of the past year, she said - telling them he was badly run down, and needed only a period of rest. Oscar and Sigrid wanted her to talk to Keith Hardy, no longer new, now the accepted General Practitioner in the district. She raised it with Stefan, but he said there was no reason to do so. His wounds would heal in time, he told her: the scars inside would remain for life.

He had dreams that made him wake, sweating and babbling in the night. She thought they would become less frequent, but this did not happen. He continually fretted that McVeigh and the warders were criminal thugs who had terrorised people, even driven some to suicide, and that they would escape justice. He expressed these fears to her only when they were alone; no one else knew of his turmoil. He even, in one respect, blamed her. He regretted, above anything else, not being able to accuse McVeigh and the warders on the island.

'We'll go to the authorities, if you wish,' Elizabeth said.

'There's no evidence.'

'We can show them. Your whole body is evidence.'

'It means nothing.' He shrugged. 'I signed that declaration. You wanted me to, so I signed away any chance of retribution.'

She was angry, but held back any retort. No retribution was worth being held in there for the rest of the war, she wanted to say, no matter how long it might last. She tried not to feel resentment that he barely acknowledged the part she had played in gaining his freedom, nor conceded her father and Hannah had helped secure his release. It was as if, in the emotional storm caused by prolonged torture and torment, no one was entirely free from guilt.

During much of the time they spent together, he was silent and remote. He walked alone a lot, and where once he would have wanted her to join him, now he paced with restless strides between the vines, heavy with ripening grapes, showing little interest in them, hardly bothering to examine them, while she watched in growing distress from the verandah.

They made love rarely; when they did it was brief and without passion, unrelated to their once joyous encounters. She had been married and deeply in love for twenty-two of her thirty-nine years. Now it was like sharing her bed and daily life with a stranger.

Elizabeth recognised the Ford as it crossed the bridge over the creek. There had been few visitors in the weeks since Stefan's return, and she wondered why Dr Hardy was calling unannounced, until she realised Eva-Maria Lippert was in the front seat beside him.

'I was on my way to see you. The doctor gave me a ride.'

'Just finished my rounds,' Hardy said as he shook hands with them both, 'and it seemed a perfect opportunity.'

'To give Eva-Maria a ride?' Elizabeth hoped their obvious subterfuge would not be too apparent to Stefan.

'To see your renowned vineyard,' the doctor smiled. 'And to say I'm glad you're out of there, Mr Muller. Welcome home.'

'Thank you,' Stefan said. 'Although opinion seems to be divided on that issue. If half the local people are pleased at my release, the other half seem to think I should have been left to rot.'

'There are always bigots and fools,' the doctor replied. 'The most ferocious soldiers are the armchair ones, who've never worn a uniform or seen a gun fired.'

Stefan remembered the doctor's compassion after the attack on Sigrid and Oscar. He gave a brief and rare smile.

'Will you stay for coffee, Doctor?' Elizabeth asked.

'Gladly.' He turned to Stefan. 'Any chance of a look round the vineyard in the meantime?'

Elizabeth watched them move off. She turned to Eva-Maria and asked, 'Your idea?'

'My idea.'

'What did you tell him?'

'The truth. That you and I've been friends too long for me not to know something's badly wrong.'

'Yes, something is.'

'So he's a doctor. He likes you both. Maybe he can help.'

'I hope to God he can,' Elizabeth said. 'I need help.'

A few days later she met Hardy in town, at a meeting contrived by Eva-Maria.

'He'll be making some purchases at Oscar's pharmacy when his morning surgery finishes. At noon tomorrow.'

'I don't want Oscar or anyone else, not even Sigrid, to know about this,' Elizabeth insisted.

'They won't. We're just doing our shopping,' her friend said. 'When he leaves the *Apotheke*, we'll happen to meet. Then you and he will stop and have a friendly talk – pass the time of day – while I have to go to the milliner's and see about a hat.'

'Oh, God. You and your plots!'

'It's not a plot. It's an accidental encounter.'

'Eva-Maria – honestly!'

But Elizabeth made sure she was there.

'He should be in hospital,' Hardy told her, while they went through the charade of their casual encounter. 'But I don't think he'll go. He's been physically and mentally tortured, as you know. He was also badly beaten here after his arrest.'

'I never knew that. Stefan told you?'

'Yes.' He hesitated. He had debated whether to confide this, and decided he must. 'He was beaten unconscious. He was kept here for a week, and beaten every day.'

She shut her eyes, to block out the image and stop any tears.

'It's a wonder they didn't kill him. Lucas should be charged, but there'd be no proof,' the doctor said. 'They'd all deny it.'

'And he's learned the hard way, there's no future in protest. But he trusted you, telling you that.'

'He told me quite a lot.'

'Then you might be able to treat him.'

'I'm just a country doctor, Mrs Muller. Broken bones, babies, and some surgery from my army days. Stefan is the closest thing I've seen to total shell shock since Gallipoli.'

'Shell shock?'

'It's the only way I can explain it. Each day in that prison was like – like an explosion in his mind.' He hesitated, then went on, carefully, 'They stripped away his self-esteem. He'd built a good life here. A fine vineyard, beautiful wife, children, good friends. He worked hard, he was prosperous. His world was a nice place; decent and secure. Each moment in there, every humiliation was a blow to his self-respect. He began to doubt his worth, doubt you, his friends, most of all himself. I don't want to be cruel, but he's been reduced to a shell.'

'You're not being cruel. You're telling me exactly what I felt, and couldn't bear to admit. Now tell me the rest.'

'His whole character, his identity is damaged. If he looks the same man, you and I know he isn't.'

She nodded. People passed. She managed to respond to greetings, to appear normal, to pretend this was a normal day.

'Is it his mind?'

'Nature, temperament, it all stems from the mind, and must be carefully restored, by someone qualified to put his life back together. If it was a broken leg, I could put it in plaster. This needs a doctor who specialises in mental treatment. They call them psychotherapists. Or psychiatrists. It's relatively new, at least outside of Europe.'

'There are some problems,' Elizabeth said. 'First, I don't know where we'd find someone like that.'

'Certainly in Sydney. Your father could find out.'

'Second and more important, I doubt if Stefan would agree. I'm sure if we were to confront him with this – and I'd find that very difficult – he'd say that rest would soon make him his old self again.'

'I'm sure he would, but I don't think it can. Any more than in the war, kind nurses with words of comfort could cure shell shock.'

'Oh God.' She spoke so softly he wondered if it was a rhetorical question, or did she require an answer? 'What am I going to do?'

Chapter 36

London's Victoria Station seemed far busier than he remembered. It was crowded with embarking troops, mostly raw recruits by the newness of their uniforms, as his train came in. Another was about to depart, so that one side of the platform was filled with people waving tearful farewells, while on his side others scanned the carriage windows for arriving faces. A hospital train bringing the wounded was already in the station, and the uniforms of nurses could be seen all over the vast concourse. Some men were being assisted to the rows of waiting ambulances, others carried on stretchers by bearers wearing Red Cross armbands. A few – blinded – were being led.

Harry felt lonely, knowing there would be no one in the crowd waiting for him. He wished Marty Renshaw or Ted Shortland were there on leave with him. They could get pissed at the Grenadier near Hyde Park Corner, and go on a pub crawl all the way to the Kings Arms at the World's End. End up full as boots, and try to pick up a girl each at the YWCA, or the nurses' home in Battersea.

But Marty was dead, from a sniper's bullet, and Shortland wounded and home by now. Only he and Harry knew he had shot himself in the leg, because he had been in the trenches too long, and his nerve had gone. Harry did the paperwork that saved him from a charge and military prison, but when Ted tried to offer thanks, Harry could not look at him. He understood why it had been done - he had made sure no one guessed, and perjured himself to save Ted from a court martial - but was unable to accept his thanks, or look at his face. Yet, he badly missed Ted Shortland. He would have been a comfort. Because there would be no Kate to share this leave with him.

He had not written to tell her he would be back in England this time. His final letter to her, three months ago, had been painful and difficult to write. He had delayed until almost the week of her marriage, and ultimately managed a polite but cheerful note to wish her well; long life and happiness, apologising he was unable to send a wedding present, but when next on leave he would remedy that.

He realised, as he thought about it now, in a taxi on his way to the same officers' billet in Chelsea, that he did not know her address. No doubt he could find out, for she would be housed in the married quarters at Camberley, where Rupert trained public schoolboys to be sent as officers, immature and untried, into the cauldron across the Channel. He could telephone the adjutant's office there, once he found a suitable gift.

The row of terraces that comprised the billet was unchanged. If not the same lady, a counterpart on the desk, who explained the rules. No drinking in the rooms, no female guests, no undue noise after ten p.m. He went up to a neat, spartan room, a replica of last time, although he had little memory of it, having spent six of his seven days in Kate's tiny shared flat at Swiss Cottage. It seemed a lifetime ago. Six months - one hundred and eighty something days that he had managed to cheat from the late Johnno's mathematical theory of survival.

He unpacked, and looked out of the window. The same view; but a different season. Then, the trees of the hospital garden had been in full leaf; now, in winter, they were bare and gaunt against a pale watery sky. He felt cold; the heating was inadequate. He realised, with a trace of nostalgia, that it would still be summer in Australia. In Sydney, the beaches would be crowded, the girls wearing the daring new one-piece bathing suits instead of frumpish neck to knee costumes. The sea would be warm, with foam-crested waves washing onto soft white sand.

He longed to be there. Or else in the Barossa, where very soon they would harvest the grapes, and where his father was free at last. It must have been a happy Christmas, he thought enviously, and wondered who had been instrumental in securing his release.

The good news had come by telegram, which had somehow reached him in the line beyond the Somme at Villers Bretonneux, where they were huddled in masks, waiting for intelligence to confirm that the Germans would be shelling their position with mustard gas. A dispatch rider had brought a sealed communication to field headquarters, and it had been sent through the labyrinth of trenches and handed to him where he waited with the battalion. Ever since the major who was the senior officer had been killed, Harry was in temporary command, and he assumed this official-looking envelope was from Intelligence, who had apparently come to believe that using field telephones was unsafe. But inside he found a telegram, opened by a censor, who had then scrawled 'Personal' on it. It simply said: YOUR FATHER HOME. ALL WELL. TAKE CARE. GRANDFATHER.

He had written, expressing his relief at the news, but they

would not have received the letter yet. Gazing out at the hibernating trees and the dead winter landscape, he tried to visualise the terraces of vines, the lush grapes, the noisy celebrations after the picking was done. Once he had hated it; how he would love to be there now, instead of spending this dismal leave in London. He could have chosen Paris, and been mad not to. Every step he took, every corner of this city was crowded with joyful memories, and full of pain.

At an art dealer's in the old Brompton Road, he found a set of framed and numbered prints of Arthur Streeton's Sydney sketches, and knew immediately that Kate would adore them. He was unsure about Rupert's taste, but the wedding present was for her. They were far too expensive, but he haggled and tried to convince the dealer he was spending most of his leave pay on them - which was true - and they finally agreed on a price. He then located a public telephone, and began the business of attempting to obtain a number for the officers' training college in Surrey.

'Camberley,' he said yet again, being passed from one operator to another, repeatedly interrogated on why he required this information, and told eventually the matter could not possibly be dealt with over the telephone, and he must present himself at the Central Post Office, with suitable identity, and fill in a form. If the authorities were satisfied it was a genuine request, and he was who he claimed to be, the number could possibly be given to him. When he protested that he was only trying to trace a friend, he was reminded there was a war on.

He hung up, frustrated, the simple pleasure of purchasing the prints spoiled by this officious intransigence. He decided it would be simpler to go to Swiss Cottage if Kate's former flatmate still lived there, obtain an address from her and send the damned things. He wrapped them and took them with him.

He rang the doorbell, hoping the girl would be home, and trying to remember her name. When there was no answer, he thought of leaving a note. Not knowing her name was awkward; he'd simply write that he needed the address, and would call back later in the day. Anything to avoid the ordeal of more telephones and pompous bureaucracy and having to present himself to fill in forms, trying to prove he was who he claimed to be, not someone trying to infiltrate Camberley Officers' Training College with treasonable intent.

He gave the doorbell one last try for luck, then began to go down the stairs, hoping to find a neighbour to ask for paper and a pen. That was when he heard the door open. He turned and saw a figure on the tiny landing above him.

It was Kate.

'Harry?'

'Good God.'

She looked confused, as if the bell had woken her. She wore a floppy robe, and seemed startled and bewildered to see him.

'Where did you come from? What are you doing here?'

'I came to see your friend – the girl you shared with –'

'Joanna? Why?'

'To find out where you were living.'

'She's moved. I still live here.'

'I thought you'd be in Camberley. In digs there. Has he been transferred?'

'Who?'

'Rupert.'

'You woke me up,' she said, and he thought this was one of the strangest conversations he had ever had with her.

'I can see that. May I come in?'

He realised he was still holding the wrapped prints, and gave them to her, as she stepped back for him to enter.

'This is for you.'

'Thank you. What is it?'

'Your wedding present.'

She shut the door.

'Didn't you get my letter?' Kate asked.

'What letter?'

'The one I wrote, when I decided not to marry Rupert.'

He wasn't sure which he wanted to do first – hug her or shout for joy. In the event, he did neither. He just stared at her.

'You decided not to marry Rupert?'

'That's right.'

'But it was all arranged, wasn't it?'

'Yes.'

' The church, bridesmaids, all that stuff?'

'All that stuff. Flowers, caterers, bridal car, everything.'

'So what happened?'

'His mother got upset. Well, awfully upset. But she had every reason to be.'

'No, I mean what changed your mind? *When* did you change it?'

'About two weeks before the event.'

'No wonder she was upset.'

'It was worse than that. It took another week bracing myself to tell Rupert. You see, I was very fond of him. Then it took days before he could convince his family. No one would listen. They just smiled and said it was the usual nerves. And then there were the relatives – *his* relatives, starting to arrive from all over England.'

'Oh, God. Must've been absolute hell.'

'It was. In another way it was like a terrible farce, out of control. At one stage I thought I'd have to go through with it, to save all their faces. So that was when I told his parents.'

'Told them what?'

'That I was pregnant.'

He suddenly realised what he had thought was a robe was in fact a loose-fitting maternity dress. As if to confirm it, she smoothed it against her body, and in profile the bulge was clearly prominent.

'Rupert was a sweet man. He insisted he wanted to do the right thing. I had to explain to them all it would be the wrong thing – because it wasn't his child.'

'Jesus Christ,' Harry said.

'And that was finally the end of the wedding.'

'You wrote and told me all this?'

'No. Only that it was off. I didn't want any nonsense about having to marry me, just because you were going to be a father.'

'And it's really mine?'

'Half yours. Yours and mine. I can tell by the way it kicks.'

'Can I feel?'

She nodded, and he held his hand against her body. He looked startled and laughed aloud.

'It does kick. I just felt it.'

'Of course it kicks. Little bugger.'

'Little bastard – unless we do something about it. If I kneel, cap in hand and ask you nicely, will you marry me?'

'I might.'

'Tomorrow?'

'I think it takes three days. Don't you need permission from your commanding officer?'

'I'm the temporary C.O. I've just given my approval.'

'Aren't you going to kiss me?'

He did so, gently at first, then with a growing passion. When they reluctantly paused for breath, he remembered.

'I nearly went to Paris,' he said.

'Why?'

'Because I thought London would be unbearable without you. I contemplated spending all my leave in bed with a French tart.'

'I may be six months pregnant,' Kate said, 'but there is nothing a French tart can do that I can't.'

'Six months. Of course.'

He smiled, and remembered. Six days and nights in this room, six months ago.

'So when did you – realise? How long afterwards?'

'Victoria Station when I waved you goodbye.'

'A few days! That's impossible.'

'You may think so. But I had a firm feeling that you'd left something behind.'

Late that night there was an air raid, but it was far to the south, over Crystal Palace, Kate thought, and they stayed snug in bed, with the lamp switched off and the curtains open so they could watch the probing searchlights. There was so much to talk about.

Above all, the letter he had never received.

'You must have wondered why I didn't write back?'

She was silent for a moment.

'It's the only time in my life I've been really afraid. All those weeks, then months, and no answer. Every day waiting for the mail to arrive. I began to think you must be dead.'

'I suppose there was no way to find out?'

'None. Unless I wrote home to ask your grandfather or your mother. I couldn't do that.'

'Why not?'

'I don't know. I thought if you were, they'd write. On the other hand, if I was going to marry someone else, why would they? And they had their own problems. They didn't need mine.'

'David would have written.'

'I know. But mail gets sunk, or goes astray. I got myself into a bit of a state, but it's not as if you can telephone Australia, is it? And I didn't want to send a telegram, asking if you were all right, or mentioning the baby.'

'When you opened the door today and saw me – you seemed so strange.'

'I felt as if I was having a dream. That I'd look again, and find out it was another illusion.'

He could suddenly, painfully visualise what it had been like.

'Poor Kate.'

'Not any more.'

'What about your music?'

'That's another story – for another time,' she said.

He applied for compassionate leave. At the Australian army headquarters in Horseferry Road a brigadier studied his application.

'You must mean marital leave, Captain. And permission to wed.'

'No, sir. I have permission to wed. My Commanding Officer granted it. I'm applying for extra compassionate leave, because

I'm about to become a father – as well as a husband.'

'I see,' the brigadier said, frowning. 'Rather a lot of this sort of thing going on. Giving us Australians a bad name.'

'We already have a bad name, sir. They say we're useful soldiers, who get drunk and behave badly in Trafalgar Square.'

'Quite,' the brigadier said. 'Well, at least you're tying the knot in time. Any other reasons why I should grant this?'

'Yes, sir. I've been at the front for too long, and it's starting to show. Also, my father is German, just released from an internment camp at home. It's been a period of great strain – and I need this.'

'German. Steady on, Patterson. You're not German.'

'My father says my name is really Muller. He says I'm nearly as German as the King.'

'What King?'

'The King of England, sir.'

'That's quite enough, Captain Patterson.'

'I agree, sir. But try telling my dad.'

'You can't be German. It says here you were recommended for the military medal.'

'That just proves I'm a bit barmy, sir. Anyone who wants to be brave in the trenches has got to be crackers.'

'Are you trying to be funny, Patterson?'

'No, sir. I'm trying to make you realise how much I desperately need a month's passionate or compassionate leave. Call it what you like. Not a week. A month is the least my wife and I deserve; anything less is unfair and I'll shoot through and take my chances going A.W.L.'

'Don't talk to me like that, man. I could have you charged and in the slammer.'

'That would do nicely, Brigadier. I'd survive in there.'

'A month. And what about the war, while you have a month's nesting with your new wife?'

'May I be frank, sir?'

'If you must.'

'Fuck the war.'

'Hmm,' the brigadier said. He grunted and signed the form.

'One month's compassionate leave, Captain. Even though I know it's complete bullshit that your father is German.'

'Thank you, sir,' Harry said.

'I see by your record you're twenty-one. Too young to be a major, although promotion was suggested. You've done well. Any ambitions for the future?'

'Only one, sir. To be a civilian.'

They queued for hours at Caxton Hall, where busy registrars were trying to cope with the rush of American soldiers marrying English girls, and where the state of Kate's advancing pregnancy drew knowing glances. The next day they took a train to Swanage and a bus to Studland Bay in Dorset. Many of the guesthouses were closed for the winter, but they found one, where a cordial couple made them welcome, and where they spent the nights entwined in a double bed, and the days walking along the crescent sand. Except that the sea was slate-grey, the long empty beach reminded them of Australia.

'So what about your music?' he asked her. 'Every time I ask, you change the subject. What's happened?'

'Nothing's happened,' Kate said, and took his hand. 'I topped my finals at the Guildhall, even if I was preggers.'

'That's wonderful.'

'Pablo Casals came to hear me. It was for an audition, to play as a guest cellist with him in Barcelona.'

'Casals? Isn't he world famous?'

'The best. I didn't get it. He preferred a girl who came third to me in our finals.'

'Were you very disappointed?'

'Very. And angry. I even wondered if he fancied her. Which was stupid, because that wasn't it at all.'

She tucked her hand into the crook of his arm. The breeze off the bay was getting chilly.

'He asked to see me. Told me I played beautifully. From the head - not the heart. The other girl would never be technically as good, but she made him feel sad and want to cry. She had emotion.'

'You had emotion. You made me want to cry, up there on stage when you were about the same size as the cello.'

'Thank you, darling,' she said.

'People stood and cheered you. That was emotion.'

'I was fourteen. A home crowd, who wanted me to succeed.'

'So what are you saying? Bloody Casals says you're not good enough for him. Does that mean you're going to chuck it?'

'Of course I'm not going to chuck it. I was grateful to him.'

'Why?'

'Because he was honest. He helped me.'

'To do what?'

'Sort out my life. I'll never give up music, but I won't mortgage the future for it. I'm not going to live in Europe, be an exile, run the risk of losing you. He made me realise I can be good, but not the best in the world.' She smiled at his expression. 'It's not a tragedy, Harry. I'll settle for trying to be the best in Australia.'

'When did you decide all this?'

'About six weeks ago.'

'Not knowing if I was alive, but afraid I wasn't.'

'Hoping you were. If not, intending to take our bun in the oven home and bring it up there, where it belongs.'

'We must stop calling it "*it*".'

'When we know what it is. We don't want to prejudice things by calling it he or she. So let's call it the bun.'

He laughed, and kissed her. They walked home to the guesthouse with their arms around each other.

'Dearest, wonderful Kate,' he said. 'I've been in love with you since I was thirteen years old.'

'My brother tried to tell me you just stood and stared because you were dopey. But I knew.'

'Did you really?'

'Well, I hoped so.'

Later on he said, 'It must have been terrible – the past months. After Rupert – on your own, just you and the bun. No word, no reply from me.'

'Not the best of times,' she said. 'But it's nice this month.'

The days fled. They planned lots of bus trips to see the sights, promised themselves visits to Corfe Castle and Poole Harbour, but never went. The fishermen rugged up against the winter on the beach became used to seeing them trudging the sand in all weathers; waved to them and wondered about the boy in his army officer's greatcoat, and the girl clumsy and swollen with child, who seemed so private and so happy, in a world apart.

They considered a move to Bournemouth, to treat themselves

to a few days' luxury at the Grand Hotel, but then rejected it. The seaside guesthouse suited them and they couldn't bear the thought of leaving it. It was so completely out of season that there were few other guests. At night they ate early, then went up to their room. They needed no one else, wanted no intrusion. They saw no newspapers, declined invitations to join anyone in the lounge after supper, because inevitably there would be talk about the war. Harry was once asked what it was like 'over there', and replied that he was attached to a catering corps in Hammersmith.

They went back to London the day before his leave ended. It was a miserable journey, the train unheated, the winter landscape misty with drizzle, and the sky pewter grey. They had a compartment to themselves until Basingstoke, where a well-dressed couple with a French poodle got in.

'This'll do, Eleanor,' the man said. 'Ample room in here.'

They sat down. The poodle perched on the woman's lap. All three stared at Kate and Harry, and the poodle barked.

'Be quiet, Jessie, or we'll put you in the guard's van,' the woman called Eleanor said, eyeing Kate, as though challenging her to complain. The dog growled, a high-pitched neurotic sound.

'Ouch,' Kate said suddenly.

'What's the matter?' Harry asked.

'The bun in the oven. Little brute.'

'What's happened?'

She took his hand and placed it on her swollen belly, as if oblivious to the couple exchanging glances.

'Not on the move, is it?' Harry showed alarm. 'Not going to launch itself between here and London?'

'I certainly hope not,' Kate said. 'Have a listen and see what you think.'

Harry leaned down and put his ear to her body. The couple with the poodle openly stared. The dog growled.

'Well? Can you hear anything?'

'Kicking like buggery. Do you think the waters might break?'

The poodle gave a puzzled yap. Kate jumped and clutched her stomach. She seemed finally to notice the couple staring at them.

'We're going to have a baby,' she confided, as if this might not be apparent. 'Probably any second.'

'It's about ten days overdue,' Harry added. 'Probably brought on by the dog barking in my wife's face.'

'Jessie is not barking in anyone's face,' her female owner said. 'She's far too well behaved for that.'

'Jessie has done not much else since you got in. If you can just hang on, darling, I'll get the guard. He can decide what to do about Jessie, and give a hand with the umbilical.'

The woman rose, holding her poodle. 'Charles,' she said, 'we can find better seats than this. And decidedly better company.'

'Yes, dear,' the man said.

'Orstralian,' she pronounced it with scorn, noticing the insignia on the army greatcoat. 'I should have known.'

'Should have known what?' Harry asked.

'Colonials. You're the absolute dregs,' she said.

'Then you should order us all home, Madame. Not allow us to fight for you a day longer.'

'Charles, dear, no need for us to put up with this.' She spoke to the man with her, as though Harry did not exist. 'I'm sure you agree. They're appalling.'

Harry would not let this go unchallenged. 'I'll tell my friends,' he said, in a voice so thick with rage that Kate was alerted to the extent of his anger, 'I'll tell those who are still alive, and visit the graves of the dead. I'll tell them all, we met a poodle called Jessie, whose mummy says we're unfit to die for her.'

'Look, old boy,' Charles said, clearly embarrassed, 'fair do's and all that. No offence meant.'

'Why not do what she says, Charles.' Kate felt she had to intervene. 'Go and find somewhere better to sit. You seem like a reasonable man. Take that bitch – and your dog – and spoil someone else's day.'

'Sorry,' Harry said that night. There was yet another air raid, this time to the east, somewhere over Bromley and the perimeter of Kent. 'It was a stupid thing to do, losing my temper over a cow like her.'

'Forget her.'

'How? Bloody colonials. The dregs. Jesus Christ, Kate, what are we doing here, supposedly fighting for people like that?'

'There are lots of fine English people,' Kate said. 'As you well know.'

'Of course there are.'

'So while we're on the subject, what about the Australians back home, sunbaking at the beaches?'

'What about them?'

'Or the crowds at the vaudeville theatres? David says it's hard to believe there is a war, if you look around Sydney. Shops full of goods, everyone spending, more people than ever at the picture shows, and the pubs and the racecourses are packed.'

'Wonderful,' he said, 'just what I needed to know.'

'What you need to know,' Kate told him, 'is that this is a selfish, futile war. There are no winners.'

'Terrific. What are you trying to tell me?'

'To remember you're going to be a dad. So never mind about being a hero. Promise?'

'I promise. You look after the bun.'

'Agreed.'

'Please don't come to Victoria tomorrow,' he said. 'I can't bear waving you goodbye again on that bloody station.'

'All right,' she said. 'Meet you when it's over.'

'Whenever that is.'

'It must be over soon,' Kate said. 'Please God.'

Chapter 37

The group of men planned it patiently, and bided their time. When it became local knowledge that Elizabeth Muller and her husband had received news of their son's marriage in England, and that friends in the village were giving a big party to celebrate, they knew this was the night they had been waiting for. The neighbours, all certain to be invited, would be absent. It was a little over a week until harvest time, and the perfect opportunity.

They came in the night by trucks. One of the vehicles towed a tractor. They brought spraying equipment and drums of salt and acid. Two of them, both farmer's sons, had scythes as well as home-made fuses and 44-gallon drums of petrol. They had strong lights, and carried rifles in their trucks, in case of trouble.

There were seven of them. Six were from German families. All had sons or fathers interned, and for weeks they had brooded at the injustice of Stefan Muller's early release because of his wife's influence, while their own relatives remained locked away. Two of them had discussed some kind of retaliation. The conversation had been overheard by a man who informed them he might be able to help. Warily, they asked him why, and he said that, just like them, he had his reasons.

Jim Carson went home and discussed it with his wife. She felt it was dangerous, and might mean trouble with the police. He laughed and said his friend Ed Delaney, now their silent partner in many of their recent land acquisitions, was always going on about how his boss Inspector Lucas had been furious ever since Muller's release. Carson had a feeling he would be doing himself a favour, and the police would make routine enquiries and be unable to solve the case. He promised his wife he would not contemplate helping this bunch of vindictive huns, unless he checked with Delaney, and was given the sergeant's nod that it was in order.

He was given a great deal more than that. Equipment arrived one night at the dairy. Rifles, ammunition, floodlights, and most bizarre of all – a new army flame-thrower. They were delivered and the truck driven off without a word exchanged, but it was a clear gesture of assent from Lucas, and encouraged Carson to become fully involved, to ensure that nothing went wrong. On the night chosen by the six Germans, he was the seventh man.

He was also in charge, because he knew the place better than the others, from the days when he and his wife delivered the mail here. The poverty-stricken days, the bitter times when they were dependent upon charity. He was sure that people like the Mullers had despised them. Well, no longer.

He knew where to put the lights and the trucks so that they could not be seen from the road, and the men with the sprayers could begin their work of poisoning the vines.

Bruno Heuzenroader, the blacksmith, had begun these past few months to visit Eva-Maria Lippert, and if she had been able to call herself a widow, he would have asked if he could court her. He was that kind of a man. Simple, and old-fashioned. Built like an oak, gentle as a child.

He would ever after regret the party that was held in his barn, for had it not taken place, he felt he might have been there at the farm, calling on Eva-Maria, and seen the trucks on the adjacent vineyard.

When they first heard the news that Elizabeth had received a cable, and Harry had married his childhood sweetheart, their friends all decided it was the occasion for a real celebration. They needed one. It would be good for Stefan, and they wanted to commemorate the event. Most of them remembered Harry - they had accepted his new name - as a boy who had come back to the valley decreasingly and reluctantly through the years, but that wasn't what this was about. They all wanted to show their affection for his parents. Sigrid felt she and Oscar should give the party, since she had nursed the bridegroom from the time he was a year old, but Bruno said her quarters above the *Apotheke* were not large enough to accommodate all those who would want to attend, whereas if he cleaned out his barn, there would be space for everyone from miles around.

It became a compromise; Oscar and Sigrid insisting they would provide the food, Elizabeth saying she and Stefan must bring the wine, and Bruno removing the blacksmith's forge and decorating his massive barn so that there was a vast space for the musicians and for dancing. Bruno made a speech, startling Oscar who was mentally rehearsing his own, pleasing them all with his charm, saying he hardly knew Harry, and had not met Kate, but it sounded a romantic story, which would be in keeping with the family tradition, because Stefan and Elizabeth's own life was full of romance and tenderness and love.

He said he claimed the first dance with Elizabeth, facing her new challenge of being a mother-in-law; soon perhaps a grandmother, although she was far too young and no one would believe it. Amid laughter and applause, they danced, and then she danced with Stefan, and Bruno spent the rest of his evening close to Eva-Maria. It was almost the first time the town had been festive since the war began.

A light shone on the orderly rows of vines, and the scythes swung in unison, severing the foliage and leaving only exposed and bleeding stems. On the stepped terraces above, the sprays pumped and drenched the bursting grapes with a deadly mixture of arsenic and salt. Another figure drowned the newer plantings with acid. Carson came down from the crest of the hill, satisfied that the neighbourhood was otherwise deserted and it was safe. He told one of the men to start the tractor. It began to tear up the older established grape vines, scattering and shredding them.

In a short space of time it ravaged the work of years.

The lights were moved, guiding the continuing destruction, as other rows of vines were slashed or poisoned. Carson picked up the flame-thrower, and they took turns with it, blackening the leaves, leaving a trail of smoke and flickering fire. Then they wheeled the drums of petrol towards the storage and fermentation sheds. Another hour, if no one interrupted, they would be done with the vines and ready to light the fuses.

Stefan danced several times with Elizabeth, then with Sigrid, and with all the ladies in turn. He even managed to prise Eva-Maria briefly away from Bruno. Smiling and radiating charm, he seemed like his old self.

'Good party,' Dr Hardy said, dancing with Elizabeth. 'Thank you for inviting me.'

'It's a night for friends, Keith, and you've become a friend.'

'It seems to be a night for graceful remarks, and I thank you for yours. I also thought Bruno was splendid.'

'Wasn't he just. Nice speech.'

'I gather he's more than fond of Eva-Maria Lippert.'

'Yes.' She smiled. 'More than fond.'

'How does she feel?'

'Responsive.'

'He's a good man,' Dr Hardy observed.

'So was Gerhardt. That's her problem. Until there's proof he's dead she feels bound. And unless there is, she remains married.'

'Poor Eva-Maria. And poor Bruno,' he added.

'Yes. It's unfair.'

'I wish I could help.'

'No one can. One day we'll learn what really happened. Until the war's over, it's too dangerous to even attempt to find out.'

'Sadly, I'm afraid you're right.'

They danced effortlessly together. She relaxed, and began to hum the music, one of the popular songs from the current favourite: Franz Lehar's *The Merry Widow*.

'How's Stefan?' Hardy asked her. 'Things any better?'

'He enjoyed tonight. Like old times.'

'I saw it. I mean when you're alone? Day to day, at home?'

'Perhaps it's wishful thinking, but I feel it's gradually starting to improve. Not - not everything, but –'

'Less tension?'

'Yes.'

'You talk more?'

'Sometimes. He still has his dark days.'

'That's understandable,' Hardy said.

'He was pleased about Harry.'

'Good. I'd call that promising.'

'It is. For years they never got on. Now Stefan is eager to see him again, and to meet Kate. We all seem to like Kate, although we've never met her,' she said, smiling.

The music ended; the dancers applauded the band and began to leave the floor. She noticed Carl, surrounded by a group of village girls, and was pleased to see him relaxed and enjoying himself. It was good for them all, this night, and she was grateful to Bruno for arranging it.

'Come and have a drink with Stefan,' she said to Keith Hardy, 'and you can cast your expert eye over him. Subtly, of course.'

That was when she looked around the crowded barn, and realised Stefan was missing.

Because moving the tractor was such a slow process, it was first loaded on its trailer, and they waited until the truck towing it drove off, before taking the final step. The driver would be safely back on his farm before any alarm was raised.

The remaining men used crowbars to break the locks on the main storage shed, and shone their lights on the interior. Some of them hesitated when they saw the vats and the oak barrels and thousands of bottles stored there. Vandalising the vineyard had been done in a hasty frenzy, driven by anger, but this was a cold-blooded, callous destruction of vintages that had taken years to harvest. Much of their wrath had been dispelled, and they felt a sense of shame at what they were going to do.

'A bit bloody late for second thoughts,' Carson said, defining their moment of uncertainty, and they knew it had gone too far, and they could not leave until this was done.

They rolled the drums inside the shed, and opened the taps. The liquid flowed out. A wave of benzine fumes overwhelmed the soft aroma of the wine, and stung their throats and made their eyes water. It began to flood the floor as they backed out, stringing lengths of cotton waste soaked in fuel behind them as they went. They lit the fuses, and ran towards their waiting trucks below.

The flames travelled until they reached the swirling petrol, and exploded. Although already some distance off, the men could feel the force of the eruption. Within seconds, the largest storage shed was engulfed by flames. The fire lit up the surrounding countryside, as the group, terrified by their success, climbed into the trucks and drove rapidly away.

At the barn the music wavered, discordant, then stopped when Bruno came in brandishing his arms and yelling for silence, as he raised the alarm. He had gone to collect hams being kept warm in the ovens of the local bakery, and seen the night growing crimson with the distant flames.

'Somewhere out on the Nuriootpa road,' he shouted, and there was a rush for the door, to see for themselves. The sky was kindled with a fiery glow, and the stars almost obscured by smoke.

Elizabeth felt as if her heart might stop.

Stefan was driving leisurely, singing and trying to remember the words to one of the *Merry Widow* songs so favoured by the band. It was such a good night, such a success, that he had made a sudden decision to drive home and get the last few bottles of his finest wine, the 1909 Elizabeth, because what better use could there be for it than to share it with friends in celebration of his son's wedding.

He was less than half a mile from the vineyard when he heard the blast of the explosion. The shock made him stop in the centre of the winding road, as he tried to grasp what had happened, then he saw the surging flames beginning to rise on the far side of the hill, and knew what it must be.

At almost the same moment, two trucks drove past without their lights, and his own headlamps glimpsed the occupants trying to shield their faces. One of them, he thought he recognised, was a farmer from Rowland Flat. He tried to think of the man's name, as he drove the last short stretch towards the bridge over the creek. Turning in, the beam of his lights picked up the outline of another truck driving away in the opposite direction, and without having to memorise the number on the tailgate, he knew it was Carson.

He drove up the track, barely registering the chaos where the vines had been uprooted and nothing remained but stumps. He stopped outside the house, and ran towards the blazing shed. Nearly twenty years of his life was in there, burning, and flames were already reaching for the other buildings. In them was stored the wood and sheathing that made the barrels, the equipment, the vats in which the harvest germinated, bottles and labels, all the records and photographs of past years. If they had burnt the house, it could have been rebuilt. But this – all of it – was irreplaceable.

He tugged open the door of the irrigation shed, to turn on the system. As he did, the fire reached the adjoining building, and the windows burst. He felt the pain of the glass shards in his shoulder, then dimly heard the thud as the fermentation shed exploded.

Bruno was the first to reach there, driving like a madman, with Elizabeth and Carl in the utility truck with him. The blaze was so bright now, it revealed the chaos of the ruined vines, and she cried out at the sight of the destruction. They pulled up alongside the car, and Elizabeth was first out of the truck, running towards the inferno of the burning sheds. She saw Stefan lying on the ground, and tried to get closer to pull him away, but the intensity of the heat drove her back. Carl shouted something behind her – he seemed to be trying to make her stop, then Bruno's voice screamed a frantic warning that was lost in the rapid series of explosions which followed.

Concussion hit her like a hammer blow, and afterwards there was no sound, no fire, nothing but stillness.

Chapter 38

Maria sat in the train, her eyes blurred with tears as the lush highlands countryside passed unnoticed. She wished her grandfather and Hannah were here with her.

They had left just a few short weeks ago on a bright Sydney day, the band playing, gangways removed, and their ship beginning to drift away from the quayside. Tugs, fore and aft guiding it out, as William flung a streamer and Maria, on the wharf, had caught it. She had seen Hannah laughing and clapping, and blown them both a kiss, holding her end of the streamer until it tightened and finally broke. She gave a last wave as the liner moved out of Woolloomooloo Bay, past Garden Island and turned eastward down the harbour.

Ahead of them was a voyage to San Francisco, via Noumea, Samoa and Tahiti, the first stage of a journey around the world.

It had all happened so swiftly. The cable had arrived early one morning several weeks ago. Mrs Forbes had brought it to the terrace where they were breakfasting, clearly nervous about its contents, and seeing what she was carrying, Maria glimpsed her grandfather's face and realised he had a moment of terror. In bad dreams, this was how it happened. An official telegram. *The Department of the Army regrets to inform you . . .*

But it wasn't that at all. When he opened it, he had begun to laugh with joy. He read it aloud to Hannah and Maria, and insisted on calling Mrs Forbes and her husband to listen.

KATE AND I TIED THE KNOT. RIDICULOUSLY HAPPY. YOU CAN EXPECT TO BE A GREAT-GRANDPARENT IN 3 MONTHS. REPEAT – THREE MONTHS. FELT YOU SHOULD KNOW HOW SOON IN ORDER TO PREPARE FOR YOUR NEW PATRIARCHAL AND VENERABLE STATUS. LOVE TO HANNAH. TELL MARIA SHE IS ALMOST AN AUNTIE. DELIRIOUSLY . . . HARRY.

By lunchtime he had completed a series of phone calls, and asked Hannah how she felt about leaving for the United States at the end of the month, and could they, despite the sinking of the American liner *Lusitania* by German U-boats, risk crossing the Atlantic to see Kate and be there to lend support, not to mention wetting the head of their very own first great-grandchild?

In case she liked the idea, he said, he had tentatively booked a stateroom on the next ship to leave Sydney, as well as rooms at the Francis Drake Hotel in San Francisco, a Pullman suite for the journey across America by train to New York, and a week there at the Waldorf Astoria. From New York they would travel on a Cunard liner for Liverpool. With luck, German subs permitting, and the baby not being premature, they should be in London with Kate in time for the birth. What did she think? Hannah thought she should buy a cabin trunk and start packing.

Maria had pinned up a map of the Pacific Ocean on the wall of her room, and each day tried to estimate their progress. After two weeks she knew they were probably leaving Tahiti. By then she had begun her first term at medical school, and discovered that the next five years were going to be a challenge.

Already she had found herself confronted with attitudes that ranged from overt male hostility to furtive flirtation – and if given a choice, would have preferred the former. She was now aware that each time there was a study of human physiology, it would bring smirks and sly glances in her direction. The appearance of the college skeleton had, and doubtless would continue to evoke silly questions about its genitalia, and ribald *double entendres* that seemed hilarious to her fellow students. She was astonished at their immaturity, and juvenile conduct.

Because she had been at school for so short a time in Sydney, she had no close friends in whom to confide. She missed Hannah deeply, even more than her grandfather, for she needed someone of her own sex to laugh about it, and help her deride their witless and vapid behaviour. But they were not here, and it was probably just as well, for in the end it was something she would have to deal with alone. And deal with soon, before the sneers and leers became custom, and the situation was beyond control. She even wondered about a transfer to Adelaide University, but had a feeling she would encounter the same problem.

One thing she knew. No matter how much of an ordeal each day became, she was not giving up medicine. She had come too far, and worked too hard, to let a bunch of overgrown schoolboys discourage her. But each night she fell asleep pondering on how to cope with and deflect the antipathy. For that's what it was.

Masculine acrimony. Resentment.

I'm on their turf, she thought, *and they feel vulnerable.*

It was in the third week, just when she was beginning to feel one or two of the students had begun to tacitly accept her, that the telephone call came from Carl, and her whole world fell to pieces.

Chapter 39

Something was soft, like endless folds of silk. It seemed to be wrapped around her, sedating, enclosing her in a protective cocoon. *My chrysalis*, she thought, and felt akin to the golden pupa of an awakening butterfly. *I'll spread my gossamer wings, and float and fly.*

She tried to tell people this, but no one seemed to hear. When they spoke, it was not to her but to each other, in voices so hushed that she asked them to talk louder, but they did not answer. There was constantly a strange smell, astringent, not unpleasant, but it began to bother her, because she knew it but could not give it a name.

In time she came to remember it was called antiseptic. Later, she realised the chrysalis was a bandage that encased her body. The muted voices became shapes, shadowy figures that smiled frequently at her and made consoling noises. She was able to recognise nurses, and sometimes she felt the chill of a stethoscope against her skin, and saw a man in a white coat who looked like Keith Hardy. Once every day they removed the cocoon, and spread a soothing ointment over her. The pain was intense, but they gave her morphine. She heard fragments of conversation – talk of burns, and how lucky to have shielded her face, or else it would have been dreadfully scarred – the hair had been singed, but it would grow back. She gleaned these facts from the quiet voices, tried to assemble them in her mind, but they made no sense.

She kept asking for Stefan, but could hear no answer.

Once when she woke she saw Carl sitting there. Another time she thought she saw her daughter, Maria, but knew it must be an illusion. Maria was at Sydney University, commencing a degree in medicine. She and Stefan were proud of her; Maria had received one of the State's highest passes in her leaving certificate. She had come home for a brief two-week visit over Christmas and New Year to celebrate her father's release, and by now would have started lectures.

After a time she realised it was not an illusion. Maria *was* there; she began to comprehend that she was at her bedside every day, holding her bandaged hands, often helping to spoonfeed her. Some nights before she fell asleep, she could see them both, Carl and Maria, sitting on either side of her bed. It was nice of them to visit her so often, but somewhere in the recess of her mind it began to disturb her. It seemed as if they were keeping a vigil.

Finally, when it was agreed she was sufficiently recovered from the shock of the concussion, when the burns were stabilised and she was considered well enough to face the news – it was her children who told her that Stefan was dead.

'It'll take years,' Carl said.

There were some days when he could hardly bear to look at the devastation, the burnt and gutted sheds, the slashed vines, the rows of old stock uprooted and rimmed by the marks of tractor tyres, the additional shock as the poisoned vines began to die, their withered foliage making it a scene of such desolation that he felt total despair.

'You've *got* years,' Maria tried to tell him, although the violence and outrage of what had been done made her feel ill. She had grown up here, she and Carl, in neat order and symmetry, each year the vineyard expanding, additional land purchased, new sheds built, but through all of this never losing a sense of harmony, so that every acre purchased, each new building erected, all blended into a balance and serenity that had been her father's great gift. He had created, from the small house and stunted crops she had seen in old photographs, a graceful landmark in this once peaceful valley.

Now he was dead; his life's work vandalised and in ruins.

It had been, everyone said, the largest funeral the district had known. People had come, not just from the Barossa and Adelaide, but from all over the State. Among the mourners she had been surprised and moved to greet Miss Shillington, her former headmistress, and to see Charles Harpur, the solicitor, and a middle-aged Englishman, whose name escaped her, until she remembered it was Mr Barrington of the Gresham Hotel.

There were many friends from her school days in Adelaide, most of them young adults now like herself, who had chosen to come to pay their last respects, whatever their parents might care to say. Maria spent most of the funeral service, and the rest of the endless day, feeling choked with gratitude and emotion for the people who had unexpectedly come to mourn her father. Most astonishing of all, David Brahm had driven halfway across the country from Sydney, to represent his sister, as he put it, since she and Harry could not be present, and to swell the family ranks.

He had read it in the papers – for what would have been an obscure, unreported event had become headlines, with the death of a man freed from imprisonment, and the serious injury of his wife who had fought so long and hard for his release. She had met David just once before, but asked him to stand beside her, with Carl on the other side, as they were the only relatives.

It was a sad irony, at such a massive funeral, that her mother was in hospital, still unconscious, while her grandfather and Hannah were aboard ship on their way to America. She had sent a cable to the Francis Drake Hotel in San Francisco, breaking the news but entreating them not to change their plans and return. Far better that they went to see Kate. There was nothing they could do here.

The funeral was now a memory. Their father was buried in the Lutheran churchyard, his grave still covered with new flowers each day, the chiselled headstone a bleak footnote to his life.

STEFAN MULLER
Born Augsburg, Bavaria, 1873
Died 1918
Loving husband of Elizabeth
Devoted father of Harry, Carl and Maria
Aged 45

After she and Carl had broken the news to their mother, and tried to see her through the worst of the shock, Maria had sent another cable, this time to the Waldorf in New York, to say that Elizabeth was out of danger and recovering. Now she had to resume her own life; return to university, make up for all the lost weeks. She already knew how difficult that was going to be, without losing any more time. But first, she had to somehow help Carl, and encourage him to face the future.

She did at moments wonder, since she was the youngest after all, why the weight of the past weeks seemed to have fallen so heavily on her.

'You've got years,' she repeated. 'Time to remake it all.'

'You think that's easy?'

'Of course it's not easy. What do you want to do, Carl? Leave it a disgusting mess like this? Let Papa down?'

'You and Harry,' he said, 'never cared much about this place. I look around and it breaks my heart.'

'It'll break our mother's,' she said. 'Imagine bringing her home, to see such a ruin.'

'There's no way I can avoid that. Whatever you might say, I can't do anything in so short a time.'

'You can make a start,' Maria told him. 'Hire trucks and labour, remove the stumps and dead vines. Clear the place of debris. And don't tell me people won't work for us because of the war. Things are different now. Everyone's ashamed. You might even get some volunteers.'

'Don't count on it,' he said.

'I'm not. But I *am* counting on you. Once the place is cleared, start to plough and plant. Let Mum's first sight of it make her realise you're going to restore it to how it was. No one else can do that. You're the only one.'

'Do you really think I could?'

He stood waiting for her answer.

In some ways, she thought, *I feel the older of the two of us.*

'I know you can. You'll need money. Lots of it. The more men and trucks you hire, the faster the clean-up. Am I right?'

'You're right,' Carl said. 'But the money's the problem.'

'Why? There must be enough in the bank.'

'There is. But first, probate has to be granted. The bank's not going to give any money to me. It'll all go to Ma eventually – but it takes months.'

'Where's the bank?'

'Tanunda.'

'What's the manager like?'

'A real bastard.'

'My deepest condolences.' The district manager, George Tunstall attempted to sound sincere, but only managed to remind her of the Charles Dickens character Uriah Heep.

'We're sorry you couldn't come to the funeral,' she said.

'Er – yes. I was obliged to be in Adelaide.'

'I mean that the bank failed to even send a representative.'

'A regrettable oversight,' Tunstall said, now taking a more careful look at the girl who sat in his office with her silent brother.

She was smartly dressed. Even the boy – so typically German in manner – wore his best suit. In George Tunstall's world, that meant only one thing. They had come here to borrow money, and would soon be disappointed.

'A tragic business. The loss of wine, apart from the destruction, must be incalculable.'

'Loss of wine? Our concern was the death of our father.'

'Of course,' Tunstall said. 'I daresay the place will be sold.'

'No, Mr Tunstall,' Maria said, 'be assured the place will most certainly not be sold.'

'Then who'll manage it?'

'My brother will.' She noted his sceptical look, but merely said, 'He'll run the vineyard as he has for the past year, while my father was improperly detained by the government.'

'Ah yes - quite,' Tunstall said. 'And what can I do to help?'

'Permit Carl to draw cash or write cheques to the value of - shall we say - five hundred pounds.'

'My dear young lady –'

'You, I expect, are going to tell us it's out of the question. Can't be done. Correct?'

'I'm afraid it can't.'

'Then we'll have to make other arrangements.'

'My dear girl –'

'Mr Tunstall,' she said, 'I am not your dear girl - or your dear young lady. You are a bank manager, who, my brother tells me, is biased against Australians with German names. Names like Muller. You found it difficult to be openly unpleasant to my father because he had a large account - but you made sure you weren't at his funeral.'

'That's a libellous statement,' Tunstall said heatedly.

'It seems like a statement of fact to me.' She studied him long enough to make him uncomfortable. 'So you can't help us, by advancing money from the estate?'

'Certainly not.'

'Even though it means we'll miss the planting season, and lose a year?'

'I'm afraid, Miss Muller, such details are not my concern.'

'They should be, Mr Tunstall. Because you're the manager of a bank in a wine-growing area. You ought to be concerned about vintners, and the future of their crops.'

'I really think we've finished, Madam.' He rose from his chair, but neither Maria nor Carl moved.

'Not quite. I was warned you might behave like this, but didn't believe you'd be so stupid. I'll cable our grandfather, who is abroad but will advance the funds we need to restore the vineyard. When probate is granted, we'll ask Mother to close her account, and change banks. A letter to head office in Melbourne will explain why.'

Tunstall frowned and resumed his seat.

'Let's be sensible, Miss Muller.'

'By all means. Your refusal to help us, your unpleasant and jaundiced attitude means our family cannot possibly leave money in an organisation with which you're associated. We can't trust you. Senator Patterson - my grandfather - banks with your head office in Sydney. You may not be aware, but he's one of their major clients. He'll close all his accounts. You can depend on it - I'll persuade him. He'll write to say precisely why he's doing it to the bank's Chairman, naming you as the reason.'

She stood up and looked at her brother, who also rose.

'Well, *now* I think we've finished, Mr Tunstall.'

'You can't do this,' Tunstall said.

'You watch me,' Maria said, and Carl blinked; she was so exactly like a younger version of their mother.

'All right, Miss Muller. Five hundred pounds, cheques or cash to the value of –'

'Six hundred,' Maria told him.

'But my dear - er, beg your pardon. But Miss Muller –'

'Six hundred.'

'Very well. Six hundred.'

'And you'll make my brother welcome. See to it he's treated

with respect. Remind your staff, in case they've forgotten, that he runs the largest vineyard in this part of the valley. One single complaint, and we switch banks, like that.' She clicked her fingers.

The manager looked shaken. Carl was astonished, impressed.

'Of course, Miss Muller,' Tunstall said.

As they drove out of town, Carl laughed.

'Bloody marvellous. You were wonderful. Walked all over him. Silly old Tunstall didn't know if he was Arthur or Martha.'

'My guess is he might be Martha,' Maria said, and Carl let out a shout of laughter. She was glad she'd been able to deal with the unctuous banker, and this new affinity with her brother made it even more enjoyable.

'You'll start hiring men and trucks?'

'Tomorrow,' Carl said. 'When do you have to go back?'

'Tomorrow, or as soon as there's a train,' Maria said. 'But I promise I'll be back again in the mid-winter vacation.'

'To check up on me.' Carl grinned, and with a sudden sense of surprise she realised he was handsome. She had always felt that of her brothers Harry was the good-looking one; they had so much in common, and Harry had a sense of fun, but today had brought her and Carl close together. It was extraordinary the way things happened: a winning encounter with a disagreeable banker had made them friends.

They drove over the creek by the wooden bridge, and felt the same dismay as they approached the devastated property. The sheer magnitude of the task ahead of Carl made her feel discouraged. He slowed the car as they looked out at the uprooted bushes, and the shrivelled leaves of the poisoned vines on either side.

'Once they're gone, it won't look quite so terrible.'

'If you plant this season, how long before you can harvest?'

'We'll have a few grapes next year. But it'll be at least three years before we can make decent wine.'

Three years!

Reading her thoughts, he reassured her, 'We'll manage. I can fence off some of the river flats, to run cattle. Pity of it is, we had a fortune in stored wine they destroyed.'

'Was it insured?'

'Nothing was insured.'

'Why?'

'Insurance companies all stopped taking our business when the war broke out.'

Near the house there was a loitering figure. Carl stamped on the brakes, and the car came to a halt.

'Who are you?' he called. 'What do you want?'

He was a farm worker, a young man – little more than a boy. He looked nervous and poised to run. Maria noticed there was a suitcase on the ground beside him.

She asked, 'We're looking for people to help. Have you come for a job?'

The young man shook his head. He glanced apprehensively at Carl. A head taller, Carl who had sat silent at the bank was a dominant figure here, suspicious and aggressive.

'Why are you hanging about? Where do you come from?'

'I've been working at my uncle's, over at Rowland Flat.'

'Who is he? What's his name?'

'Doesn't matter. I'm leaving there. I just come to tell you something before I went.'

His fear was palpable. Maria sensed he was terrified of Carl.

'My brother won't hurt you. Tell us, whatever it is you came to say. Please tell us.'

Still he hesitated, eyes flickering from her to Carl.

'Is it about all this?' Carl asked him, indicating the carnage. His voice, as if taking his cue from Maria, was less demanding.

'They said - we'd just mess up the vines. That it was unfair him getting out of Langley Island, while others were left to rot –' He tried to step back, as Carl's hand reached for him. 'Jesus, don't,' he cried.

'You fucking little shit.' Carl held his shirt with one hand, as he bunched his fist and hit him in the mouth. 'You killed my father.'

'Carl!'

Maria shouted in time to prevent the youth being hit again.

'Maria, he was one of them.'

'I said you wouldn't hurt him. Let him go.' When he did so reluctantly, she said to the boy, 'Your lip's cut. I'll bathe it for you.'

'No,' he said. 'I just want to tell you and leave here. Only keep him off me.'

'I'll try. Who's your uncle?'

'He wasn't the ringleader.'

'You tell us his name,' Carl said softly, 'or no matter what my sister promised, I'll take you over there and beat the living Christ out of you. Then I'll put you in the dam and drown you.'

Maria felt a shiver. He *sounded* as if he meant it.

'Tell us,' she asked again. 'Who's your uncle?'

'Wolfgang Mannkopff.'

'I know him,' Carl said. 'Now the others.'

'Please,' the young man said, 'nobody meant to kill anyone. It started out like – we'll show him – mess up his vines – it started like that. Only this man, he wouldn't let us stop. He brought the petrol, and equipment, even a flame-thrower. When we broke into the buildings and saw all the wine, we didn't want to do it. He said it was too late to stop – even then, I swear, nobody knew your father would come back when he did . . .'

'Who was this man?' Carl asked him.

'I don't know his name.'

'You're going to have to do better than that.'

'I swear I don't.'

'Was he German?'

'No. My uncle and the others were. Not this one.'

'You were there, without even knowing who organised it?'

'My uncle said for me to come along – an extra man. I don't even know the names of most of the others – for God's sake believe me.'

'I believe you,' Maria said.

He turned to her gratefully.

'I wish I'd never gone. I feel sick. I had to come to tell you.'

'He had petrol drums and a flame-thrower,' Carl repeated.

'Yes.'

'Was he from the army?'

'I don't think so.'

'Why do you say that?'

'Because there were milk churns in his truck.'

'Milk churns?'

'We mixed the poison for the vines in one.'

'Jesus Christ,' Carl said. 'So that's who it was.'

~

They sat and talked about it, after the youth had made his last frightened apology, and gone. Maria thought it was simple; they would go to the police and give them the evidence.

Carl explained the facts to her. Not the local police; not if it was Jim Carson.

'But he can't have that much influence.'

'Carson and Sergeant Delaney buy land together. Most of it is land that belonged to people who've been interned.'

'Can't that be proved?'

'Around here, nothing can be proved. Carson's the one who does the buying, but we know Delaney's in it. Probably Lucas, too. So tell me – who do you go to for help when the police are corrupt?'

He related their father's conflicts with Inspector Lucas, and the way he and Delaney behaved the night of the arrest. Maria had never known the details. She was shocked at the deceit, and the law that let a man be arrested on such a blatantly fraudulent pretext.

'I bet we'd find,' Carl said, 'that Lucas knew about this. So he'd protect Carson, if we were silly enough to make a complaint.'

'But we can't let them get away with it. We just can't.'

Maria felt a helpless rage. She wanted to galvanise her brother, shake him into some kind of action.

'Calm down,' he said.

'I won't calm down. Do something.'

'I intend to. No police. There are other ways.'

'How?'

'Can you stay a few more days?'

Yes, she decided. Yes. Weeks, if she had to.

That night they went to visit Elizabeth in hospital. Her hair was beginning to grow back where it had been singed, and she said the burns on her body were starting to itch, where new skin was beginning to grow. Doctor Hardy was pleased with her progress, but refused to let her leave the hospital for at least another week. She was not yet able to face Stefan's death. She held their hands, trying not to cry, but the tears ran down her cheeks.

Maria wanted to cry with her.

Instead she gently wiped her mother's face, and started to recount the details of the meeting with Mr Tunstall, making Elizabeth unsure whether to laugh or continue crying, and then Carl began to tell her about the youth, and what they had found out from him, and what he intended to do.

Elizabeth Muller listened. Now she gazed at her two children, and felt a rush of love and pride.

'Can you do it?'

'Carl can do it,' Maria assured her. 'If anyone can, he can.'

The farmer saw them coming. He watched them get out of the sedan and he stopped his tractor. He recognised Carl. The young and pretty girl with him was so like Muller's wife that she had to be the daughter. He wondered, warily, uneasily, why they were here?

'Wolfgang Mannkopff?'

'Yes. Who wants to know?'

'I'm Carl Muller. This is my sister.'

The farmer nodded, tense, then mumbled his condolences.

'Terrible thing. The vineyard . . . your father . . . dreadful.'

Carl appeared not to hear him. He looked at Maria.

'They're running late.'

'Perhaps we're early,' she said.

'What do you want?'

Mannkopff was becoming decidedly more nervous.

'We're meeting people here,' Carl stated, almost casually.

'What people?'

'A reporter from the Adelaide *Herald*. And a photographer.'

'Adelaide *Herald*?' They could feel his slow bewilderment turn to alarm. 'Why? I don't know what you mean.'

'They may be accompanied by a detective, but Mr Boothby, the editor, is trying to organise an interview before you're questioned.'

'Questioned? You're stupid. This is private property. You get out or I'll call –'

'You won't call the police,' Carl said, and the chill in his voice silenced the older man. 'You won't do that, Mr Mannkopff.'

'And there's no point in calling Carson,' Maria added, 'we know about his involvement.'

The farmer stared from one to the other, a line of sweat starting to run down his face.

'You were unwise to use your nephew, Mr Mannkopff. Your nephew Claus. He didn't like it. He's made a statement, about how you and the others, using your tractor, dug up and poisoned our vines. How you poured petrol into the storage shed, and lit a fuse, and burnt all that wine. Destroyed all that work. Years and years of it. And killed our father - and that makes it manslaughter.'

The dusty T-model pulled up alongside their own car, and two men jumped out. One of them carried his camera and a tripod. Carl and Maria tried not to show their relief. James Boothby had promised not to let them down, saying it was strictly against the law not to go first to the police, but in view of his affection for their mother, and the fact that it might be a considerable scoop for his newspaper, he would do his best to overlook the illegality.

The reporter greeted them, and told his photographer to start getting some pictures. Carl took a bulky envelope from his pocket. It was filled with blank pages, but Mannkopff did not know that.

'There's the nephew's statement. Mr Boothby said he'll run it on the front page.'

'If there's room,' the reporter grinned. 'I think this joker himself is going to take up most of pages one and two. What a story!' He turned to the shocked farmer. 'How do you spell your name? First thing we learn as cadet reporters, get the names spelt right.'

'You can't do this,' Wolfgang Mannkopff said.

'Mate, you're already trussed and stuffed,' the reporter said. 'You're a gone goose.'

'Others were involved. Not only me.'

'We know that. But you get first chance. My boss has done some deal with the Commissioner of Police in Adelaide. If you make a full statement, it seems you can plead guilty to a lesser charge.'

'What charge?'

'That's for you and the police to work out. If I get a sworn statement of all the details - and names - particularly Carson and his local cop friends, you may not be accused of helping to kill this girl's father. Though if I had my way, sport, you'd go in for the rest of your lousy life. So what's it to be? Do you give us the story, or do we go to the next name on the list?'

'Stand over there,' the photographer said, and Carl and Maria watched as the dazed farmer walked slowly across to be photographed beside his tractor, which they knew would still have the evidence of vine leaves on its plough blades.

James Boothby sat in the back of his chauffeur-driven car, as he passed through Gawler, saw the Mount Lofty Ranges and then the beginning of the valley, as they approached Lyndoch. It had been a unique few days.

He had taken immense risks on the word of a boy and his eighteen-year-old sister, named names in vivid headlines, received a threatening torrent of abuse from the Commissioner of Police, and then an abject apology, when it turned out the inspector and sergeant concerned were guilty of perjury, corruption, false arrest, conspiracy to pervert the course of justice, and accessory to the manslaughter of Stefan Muller. There was also, it appeared, the death of a naturalised Australian named Gerhardt Lippert, who had been beaten by members of the local militia, and died in police custody. This crime had been concealed by Inspector Lucas, together with a superintendent at police headquarters in Adelaide, and there would be more charges to follow.

Boothby's car stopped outside the cottage hospital. It was a large bungalow with screened verandahs. A uniformed nurse showed him into the room where Elizabeth was the sole occupant. He leaned down and kissed her cheek.

'You received all the newspapers I sent you?'

She nodded, and he sat on a chair beside the bed.

'Carson should get twenty years. And Lucas is finished. He and Delaney will go to gaol. A nest of vipers, Elizabeth. I hope in years to come, people will regret the appalling things that were done under the pretence of patriotism.'

She shrugged, as if she somehow suspected it would all soon be forgotten. He looked at her with deep concern. She seemed so resigned and defeated. He could scarcely believe it. So much vivacity, so much fighting spirit; she appeared to have lost it all. He wished he knew what else to say.

'One thing I'm going to tell you, before I have to go. Those two children of yours – as well as the one overseas – you should be very proud of them.'

'Stefan was proud of them. I just love them,' she said. 'And now the one overseas is making me a grannie. Just imagine it.'

She smiled at last, and he knew then, with profound relief, that she was going to recover.

Chapter 40

'We're going to call him William,' Kate said, and William looked proud and delighted.

Hannah who was more practical said, 'But what if "William" is a girl?'

'Then we'll try again. We plan to have about four of them. But I feel the way the bun kicks and shuffles about, he's William.'

'Shouldn't you be resting?' William asked.

'I rested all last week, when he was expected,' Kate said. 'The stubborn little chap decided he'd wait for your arrival. Not to mention the fact his dad is insulting senior officers, trying to get sent back as a nut case, now that they've refused his application for leave.'

'How could they be so insensitive?' Hannah wondered.

'Easily. Harry says with leaders like ours, we haven't a chance of winning the war. The only hope is if the Germans lose it.'

'Sounds just like Harry.'

'Trouble is, he had a month's leave when we married, then two more weeks when we got the news about his father.'

There was a silence for a moment. William studied her.

'How did he take it?'

'Very badly. He'd wanted so much to go home and make peace with him. And for me to see the vineyard, and meet his dad.'

'It was a terrible shock,' Hannah said. 'We were so worried about Elizabeth.'

'Bloody unfair,' William said. 'After all he'd achieved, and what he'd been through.'

They linked arms with her, as they walked down Primrose Hill. Above the tops of plane trees in Regents Park they could see the graceful line of the Nash Terraces. Everywhere there was spring blossom, new flowers and green leaves that seemed refreshed from the long winter. It was mid-April, and they had been in London only two days. They already loved it, and adored Kate.

Later it grew cooler, and there was a shower of rain. They found shelter in a tea shop near Lords Cricket Ground.

'Convenient,' Kate said. 'The nursing home is just around the corner in St John's Wood.'

She asked them about Elizabeth. What a relief she was out of hospital. She asked about Carl, working to restore the vineyard, and Maria, back at university. She wanted to know everything about them, as they were going to be her family when she and Harry came home.

'You *will* come home?'

'The minute the war ends, and Harry can get us on a ship.'

'How about your music? You won't give up the cello?'

'Not on your life.' Kate smiled. 'But at the moment, nine months and one week pregnant, it's a bit hard to reach the cello.'

William and Hannah were staying at Claridges. They took Kate back there for dinner. Halfway through the entrée, she looked at Hannah with a wry smile, and suggested they might call a taxi.

'The bun is on the move,' she said, and when the maître d' came to enquire if the meal was not to their satisfaction, Kate said they were just off to have a baby – but might be back for the main course.

William David Patterson was born in the early hours of the next morning. Seven pounds ten ounces. As William said in a cable to his daughter: MOTHER AND SON WELL. HANNAH AND I EXHAUSTED.

In Sydney Maria also received a cable, and immediately telephoned David Brahm. A celebration dinner was arranged at the Brahm house for that evening. David suggested he collect her at her front gate after breakfast; they could take the university tram together, which would give them a chance to discuss the arrival of their joint nephew. He said it was a major responsibility, and required regular meetings for forward planning of the infant's future. Did Maria agree? Maria said she would be at the gate, waiting for him. When she hung up, she was smiling.

So much had changed. She had been back at medical school for almost two months. The first day, after missing so many critical weeks, and edgy about the campaign of derision and harassment her male peers might well resume against her, she had walked into the lecture hall. It was to be a lecture on biology, and the professor, whose main teaching methods were ridicule and scorn, had not yet arrived. David was lounging on one of the benches, talking with her fellow students, which was a surprise, since he was in third year, and seniors regarded induction students as a lower species. They were grouped around him, flattered by his presence. When she walked in, braced for the fray, all eyes swivelled towards her. David rose and kissed her cheek.

'You chaps know Maria, of course,' he said casually. 'Maria's my sister-in-law.'

That was their first surprise.

'A bit of a heroine,' he added.

'Heroine?' someone asked, looking blank.

'Don't you read anything except medical books? She helped the South Australian police catch the bastards who killed her father.'

Once again, all eyes turned to her. Then the measured tread of footsteps on the stone cloister outside broke the silence.

'Well, good luck. Here cometh the witchetty grub,' David said, and departed amid laughter as Professor Wilson-Grubb strode past him to the podium, where he surveyed the class, and Maria in particular. She was without a seat, standing clutching her books.

'Biology,' he announced, 'is the science of life. Primitive man would have experimented in human anatomy – and no doubt primitive woman, too.' He stared at Maria. 'Do you wish to remain standing, Miss Muller? If so, perhaps we could use you to discuss Darwin's origin of the species.'

He paused for the expected laughter. There was none.

'Over here, Maria.' It was one of her former tormentors who spoke, making room for her.

'I'll lend Miss Muller my notes, Professor,' another said, 'so she can catch up.'

'And where exactly has Miss Muller been, that she needs to catch up?' The professor was at his most lethal when he was being corrosively polite.

'Don't you read the newspapers, sir?' a third asked.

'Not if I can help it.' He turned back to Maria. 'Miss Muller?'

'Professor?'

'Would it be asking too much to enlighten me where you've been? Taken a job – in a shop? Or decided to train as a nurse, after all? Do, pray, explain your failure to honour us with your presence.'

Maria stood up.

'I've been burying my father, who was killed with the collusion of the local police,' she said quietly, and saw his face change colour as his cheeks flamed. 'Our vineyard was destroyed, and my mother was burnt in an explosion and seriously injured.' She turned to her fellow students. 'I'm glad to say she is now out of danger.'

There was a murmur around the lecture hall, a sound that she interpreted as relief and approval, then a complete silence as they all looked at the professor. The witchetty grub was a brilliant teacher, but regarded as an appalling man, who had never been known to apologise to anyone in his life. He gestured to her to be seated.

'I'm terribly sorry,' he said quietly. 'Do please forgive me. We'll continue with the lecture.'

From that moment on, she was just another student. No hostility or harassment. No innuendoes.

She waved as she saw David coming to collect her. She knew he had been in the lecture room deliberately that day; she had a great deal for which to thank him. She had become fond of him, but she was going to be a doctor, and nothing must prevent that. Besides, it would be too ridiculous, marrying – what on earth would he be? Her sister-in-law Kate's brother? Her own brother Harry's brother-in-law? She started to smile at the complexity of it.

'When you smile,' David said, as he arrived, 'you remind me of your mother. In fact, most of the time you look like her.'

'You only want to ride on the tram with me because I look like Mum. Harry said you were besotted with her.'

'True,' he said. 'I was. Probably still am. But with you there's one small difference.'

'What's that?'

'You're more my age.'

They saw the tram in the distance, and ran to catch it.

Chapter 41

The sniper lay in a cleft on the ridge, outside of Saarburg. His grey uniform was ragged and stripped of all insignia. He was caked with mud, and the barrel of his rifle smeared with it so that he was almost invisible. He had been in the war for only a month, while his German comrades died around him, and his army had been driven out of Belgium and across France; Cambrai abandoned, Lille and Reims lost, Ghent retaken; the Argonne the scene of bloody carnage, and the enemy across the Moselle River.

The sniper was only nineteen years old.

He had been told his commander, Ludendorff, the legendary field-marshall, had resigned, the Kaiser had fled, and the war would come to an end this morning. In a few hours the firing would stop.

He had never killed anyone. Never really been a soldier.

There were only a few hours left, in which to remedy that.

Harry Patterson was there by mistake. Weeks earlier, the last of the Australian brigades had thrust into the village of Montbrehain, and then been pulled back to rest. They had been fighting without respite all year, and were exhausted. Meanwhile, a squadron of American tanks had inadvertently crossed a minefield, and most of them had been blown to pieces. The mines had been laid by the French the previous year, the information lost or filed and forgotten, and had not been made available to General Pershing.

In the ensuing row between allies, some officers were assigned to liaise with the Americans. They were an improvised mix of Belgians, British, Canadians, and a few Australians. Harry, to his dismay, was one of them. And thus he was a few miles outside of Saarburg, on the morning of November 11th, 1918. He was shaving, having decided to wash his uniform and polish his Sam Browne. Anything that might help him jump the queue for a repatriation convoy back to England. He could barely wait to be free of this place. In less than two hours from now, the guns would stop, and the war would be over at last.

He had seen his son once. One glorious week in June, he had finally obtained leave. Two months late for the birth, but the Brigade Major said the approval had gotten lost, then a follow-up application had gone to someone in the wrong unit.

'The usual army fuck-up,' Harry said, and made his way to Boulogne, hitching rides on army trucks and with French farmers, and then by hospital ship where a kind nursing sister turned a blind eye and let him sleep on deck while they made the night crossing to Folkestone.

To his surprise, his grandfather and Hannah were still there, but after a joyful reunion dinner, had tactfully announced they were going to spend the rest of the week touring the West Country, and that Kate and Harry and the baby should occupy their Claridges hotel suite.

Which they did. They savoured the luxury, taking William

at his word – that if he returned and found his account showed they hadn't eaten the most expensive meals, and ordered the best wines, he would be seriously disappointed. It became their main objective – not to seriously disappoint Grandfather, and consequently they had a luxurious and ecstatic week. Harry nursed and marvelled over the tiny baby, and at night they made love.

'At this rate,' Kate gasped, as they lay tousled and expended in the canopied bed, 'we'll have another one in less than a year.'

'You said we'll have four. Don't want them too far apart.'

Carl and I are only a year apart, he thought, and wondered if it had been like this for his father and mother. Not that it could be quite like this; no one, in the entire history of the world, could have found such rapture in each other as they did.

They both got the giggles when they realised the baby was awake and quietly gurgling, and had doubtless gurgled all through their frenzied and passionate coupling.

'Whatever will he think when he grows up?' Harry said, and Kate laughed and he tickled her until she could no longer stand it and pummelled him with her fists, whereupon he secured them, kissed her and wrapped his legs around hers, while he grew erect and hard, and Kate took him gently, and slid him inside her, already moist again as she did so, and she told him to be nice to her, to behave himself, and to spend the night in there.

The days were warm. They took William in his pram, window-shopped in Mayfair, and walked to Green Park, where they bought sandwiches and fed crusts to the ducks, and it brought a moment of nostalgia, not only for the time they fed the pigeons on his leave when they first became lovers, but each remembered doing this as children in Centennial Park. They knew they were homesick.

'I'm more homesick than you are,' she told him. 'I've been away five years. Five years since that awful day when the ship left.'

'I was there, remember? Singing.'

'You said you were crying your eyes out.'

'Singing,' he repeated, 'and crying my eyes out.'

'Will we always be this much in love, Harry?'

'Always,' he said, tenderly. 'As long as we live.'

Harry checked his watch. Ten minutes past ten o'clock. It was damp and cold, and there was a lifeless November sun in the pallid sky. In less than an hour, the armistice would begin. Meanwhile, as if in a last act of defiance, the big guns fired a relentless barrage. Artillery shells screamed overhead, and distantly exploded. *Why don't we just stop,* he thought. *What the hell is the point of prolonging this? Some poor bastard is going to get blown to bits about five minutes before the curtain comes down.*

Across the world, the startling news that a ceasefire had already occurred swept Sydney on the night of Friday the eighth of November. The city celebrated. People formed happy groups and kissed strangers, trams clanged their bells, cars and buses tooted, and out on the dark of the harbour the ferries sounded their sirens. Later that night, it was discovered the festivities were somewhat premature. Twenty-four hours premature, according to all the reliable rumours. So they celebrated again the following night, Saturday the ninth, and when that proved yet another false alarm, people went soberly to church on Sunday, and prayed earnestly there would soon be an end to this carnage.

Early on Monday the eleventh, confirmation came that there

would be a ceasefire at 11 a.m. in France, which meant early evening, Sydney time. By now, many people were unsure if this might be just another rumour. Some rabid hysterics - burning the Kaiser in effigy - expressed the sentiment that the whole thing might be a clever German ploy to lull Australia into a false sense of security, and then invade our shores.

It was ten-forty.

Harry put on his tunic and the officers' smart belt and strap he had hardly ever worn. It gleamed in the thin sunshine. He thought again about that wonderful week in June. Taking out his wallet, he looked at the tiny snapshots it contained of his wife and his son.

Darling Kate, *he thought.* I want us to have such a good life.

He began to be aware that the guns were falling silent. Just a few distant explosions now. No rifle fire. No machine guns. Everyone waiting. No one wanted to be brave, or have the honour of dying in the final minutes of four long bitter years of war.

The sniper had his rifle resting on a rock, so there was no need to raise it. The slightest movement might be visible from over there. He was alone in the cleft. He did not know how the war would end, but he imagined there would be a signal, and everything would stop. Before then, he would find a target and take one of the enemy into eternity.

The silence was so gradual. It developed without their being conscious of it happening; it existed but no one realised that until they heard the startling sound of a blackbird.

'Shit,' one of the Canadians said. 'Was that real?'

Nobody could quite place the moment when the sound of gunfire had ceased. Harry and the others with him, a motley collection of nationalities, had lived with the noise of it for so long, that when it stopped they all felt something was wrong.

They checked their watches. It was within minutes of eleven.

'Put your head up, see if it's over,' a Scots captain suggested.

'Up your Edinburgh arse, my old son,' said a British voice.

'How will we know?' It was one of the Belgians.

'They'll play bagpipes,' said the Scot, grinning. 'And we can all eat haggis, and get pissed on Glenfiddich.'

'Not the haggis,' said the Englishman. 'Please God, not the bloody haggis, today of all days.' They laughed, then stopped, because it was more important to listen.

They waited a few more minutes.

'Can you hear that?' Harry asked.

It sounded like a chorus of cheers in the far distance, but they felt unsure. It's over, *Harry told himself.* Kate and I and the baby are going home, and nobody is going to make me leave Australia again. It was not our war, and we should never have been here.

He remembered having been told so. And of all places, it had happened, ironically, in the very heart of Empire.

On his leave in June, Green Park, near Constitution Hill, had been filled with people. Like many of them, Kate and Harry were drawn in the direction of the gates of Buckingham Palace, and the tall guards with their beaver hats. Kate had a camera, and he thought they should certainly get a photograph of her and the baby in front of the palace – just to show people at home their own little cosy London residence. Harry wore his uniform with the A.I.F. insignias, and his officer's cap. Kate was in a skirt and blouse, pushing the pram. It was a cloudless, perfect midsummer day.

'Australians and their tarts,' a voice said. 'Why don't you clear off where you belong?'

Harry turned towards them. They were a couple in their late middle age, ordinary, innocuous. Quite pleasant looking, really. They could easily have been Mr and Mrs Forbes.

He knew Australians had become unpopular this past year in Britain. In the early days, after Gallipoli, when they went to France and fought on the Somme, when they lost five thousand men in one futile battle in one terrible day, then refused to retreat, and the French brought them flowers and wine, and declared they felt safe - *because the Australians are here* - in those years the digger and his slouch hat was a symbol in England. They were loved and welcomed.

But the mood had changed. Boredom, drunken behaviour, a series of unruly, larrikin incidents had taken their toll. Resentment had replaced respect. Australian soldiers, lonely in cities like London, sought to find girls, and the English girls responded. The Tommies began to dislike them, and this spread to the civilian population. In magazines, Australian troops were often depicted as an uneducated, ill-disciplined rabble. The antagonism was not one-sided. Many of the A.I.F. responded to the antipathy, and what they had been led to think of as 'home' was now a hostile place.

'Yeah, you,' the man said. 'Colonials, come over here takin' our wimmen. Ought to be bloody ashamed.'

'Excuse me,' Kate said loudly, and they turned to leave.

'Forget it,' Harry said, but she followed them, insistently.

'Listen to me,' she said. 'I'm not *"your wimmen"*. I was born in

Australia, the same as my husband. And we're not *"colonials"*. Years ago we became a nation, thanks to people like his grandfather. As for clearing off home, I truly wish he could, because I'm going to have another baby, and the last thing in the world I want is for him to go back to France to fight for people like you.'

'Kate,' he said, holding her arm, while the couple scuttled away in acute embarrassment. 'Kate! It can't be true?'

'I have every confidence it's true.'

'But I've only been back a few days –'

'You only needed that long the first time. You remember the feeling I told you I had, saying goodbye at Victoria Station?'

'Yes.'

'Well, I had it when I woke up this morning. A distinctly intuitive sensation. And it's getting stronger. I was going to tell you tonight, over candlelight and Claridge's best wine.' She suddenly laughed and hugged him. 'Fancy losing my block like that, and telling them first.'

'If I kiss you, in the middle of all these people, do you think they'll cheer or boo?'

'Let's find out,' Kate said.

He sat in the trench, warmed by the memory. No one had cheered or booed, but a couple had smiled as they embraced, and admired young William in his pram, and dinner that night had been a magical evening. Kate had confirmed the pregnancy barely six weeks ago, in September. According to his reckoning, here on November the 11th, their new 'bun' would be born sometime in March, and the children would be almost exactly a year apart.

Thank God it would be over soon – if it wasn't already. The hands of his watch showed a few minutes past eleven. They could go home. Harry realised all the guns were silent. Another bird had begun to sing. One day, he thought, this awful piece of bloodstained and muddy ground might grow grass and flowers again.

The distant sound was definitely a crowd cheering. It was over. He followed the others out of the trench. For the first time since he had been made an officer, his badges shone in the pale sunlight.

The sniper saw the badges, the polished leather belt and cross strap that denoted an officer. He could see the three pips on each of his shoulders. Even better, *he thought, and steadied his rifle. The figure was in his sights. He remembered what his instructor had told him – to hold his breath and gently squeeze the trigger.*

The German officer looked at his watch, and decided it was time to emerge. He thanked God that someone in the High Command had had the sense to make peace with some kind of honour. He had been on the Western Front for three years, and all he could feel was a great sense of relief that it was over. As he appeared from the trench, he saw the sniper. His first instinct was that the rifle should be lowered; instead it was aimed at someone across the mud and wire, someone like himself, emerging to breathe the air, and look at the sky, and say a prayer to their God that it was finished.

He realised he had discarded his pistol. He shouted, but it brought no response. In desperation he picked up a stone and flung it at the sniper. It hit the prone figure a glancing blow, as he squeezed the trigger.

Harry heard the familiar sound of a rifle shot, and instinctively ducked his head, but the bullet – if it was a bullet – must have gone in some other direction. He looked around, warily, but there seemed no danger. Across the wire of no-man's-land, he saw a German soldier with a rifle, and an officer taking it from him. The officer seemed to be shouting, but it was too distant, and Harry could not hear the words. Now the officer raised an arm in a farewell wave, and Harry replied with a similar gesture.

They moved away.

He stood there and thought about the sound.

It had been a rifle, but who it was aimed at, and where it had gone, he did not know. One thing he did know.

If he had his way, it would be the last shot he would ever hear fired in anger.

Epilogue

The children were down by the creek. Elizabeth could hear the young excited voices, like an echo, a memory of their first years here. She could see Harry with Carl, as they walked up the terraced hillside, inspecting the flourishing new vines, and in her mind's eye they were playing together by the chicken coop, while Stefan dug and turned the soil by hand, then Heinrich, as he still was, running down to meet Gerhardt, with Carl tottering behind, the day the letter came about her mother's accident.

Now they were strolling together, talking, Harry enthusing and admiring the way Carl had restored the vineyard. Maria came out to join her, and smiled as she looked up towards the hilltop, and the magnolia tree with its creamy white flowers, where her brothers stood.

Her daughter, soon to be a doctor, Elizabeth thought. Telling her she might marry David Brahm, when she graduated. Perhaps start a medical practice together. Almost incestuous, Elizabeth had laughed, but he's perfect for you.

Her three children, Kate, and the two grandchildren, all here for the long holidays and New Year. Her father and Hannah coming tomorrow. The Pattersons and the Mullers sitting down to Christmas dinner together.

Stefan, she thought, would like to have seen this.

'Let's walk,' Maria said, reading her thoughts, and Elizabeth smiled. They climbed the hill where she had planted roses, and joined her sons. The headstone was beneath the canopy of the magnolia tree, where she had arranged to have the grave moved, to the consternation of the minister and the church elders.

This is where he belongs, she had told them, and preparing to fight had found there was no need. She was no longer alone. Harry and Kate, Carl and Maria had all supported her. It had been done, and Sigrid, Eva-Maria, Bruno and a few close friends had joined her family, to attend the very private ceremony.

She stood in the shade of the tree, and looked down towards the creek. Kate waved. Two tiny figures danced around her. Kate had confided last night she hoped there would be a third.

'Come and see us swim,' shouted two-year-old William.

'Come up here first, to see my favourite view,' she called.

And the children began to run up the hill towards her.

Acknowledgements

To those people in Hahndorf and the Barossa Valley, who assisted my research by allowing me access to private family papers that revealed the hostility their grandparents encountered in the 1914–1918 war, I will be forever grateful. This initial research was done on returning to Australia, after a period spent living and writing in England, and provided me with the stimulus to write this book. Some of the material was first incorporated in a mini-series I wrote for the Australian Broadcasting Corporation, under the title *The Alien Years*.

I am indebted to several published sources for background material, including *The Australian People and The Great War* by Michael McKernan, *Australia's Yesterdays* by Cyril Pearl, the Sydney Morning Herald's *History as it Happened*, edited by L.V. Kepert, and Max Kelly for the photographic book entitled *Plague, Sydney 1900. The Centennial Diary*, edited by Harry Gordon, featured a letter written by Lieutenant John Alexander Raws, who died aged twenty-four at Pozières. It moved me so deeply, and seemed so much in accord with my fictional character Harry Patterson, that I adapted some of his words into one of Harry's letters from France.

Finally, to Robert Sessions, my publisher Ali Watts, my editor Saskia Adams, designer Cameron Midson and all those at Penguin who contributed to the new publication of this book, my very sincere thanks.

Peter Yeldham
pyeldham@bigpond.net.au

Peter Yeldham © Paul Wright